SPY SINKER

SPY SINKER

Len Deighton

A Cornelia & Michael Bessie Book
An Imprint of HarperCollins*Publishers*

FIRST EDITION

Designed by Helene Berinsky

Library of Congress Cataloging-in-publication Data
Deighton, Len, 1929–
    Spy sinker / Len Deighton. —1st ed.
        p.   cm.
    "A Cornelia & Michael Bessie Book."
    ISBN 0-06-039118-9
    I.   Title.
PR6054.E37S69   1990
823'.914—dc20   89-46568

---

90 91 92 93 94 CC/HC 10 9 8 7 6 5 4 3 2 1

Berlin Game, Mexico Set, and *London Match* together cover the period from spring 1983 until spring 1984.

Winter covers 1900 until 1945.

Spy Hook picks up the Bernard Samson story at the beginning of 1987, and *Spy Line* continues it into the summer of that same year.

Spy Sinker starts in September 1977 and ends in summer 1987. The stories can be read in any order, and each one is complete in itself.

—Len Deighton

SPY SINKER

London, England:

September 1977

"BRET RENSSELAER, YOU ARE A RUTHLESS BASTARD." IT was his wife's voice. She spoke softly but with considerable force, as if it was a conclusion arrived at after long and difficult reasoning.

Bret half opened his eyes. He was in that hedonistic drowsy half-sleep that makes awakening so irksome. But Bret Rensselaer was not a hedonist, he was a puritan; he saw himself as a direct descendant of those God-fearing, unyielding nonconformists who had colonized New England. He opened his eyes. "What was that?" He looked at the bedside clock.

It was very early still. The room was flooded with sunlight colored deep yellow by the Holland blinds. He could see his wife sitting up in bed, one hand clutching her knees and the other holding a cigarette. She wasn't looking at him. It was as if she didn't know he was there beside her. Staring into the distance she puffed at the cigarette, not letting it go far from her mouth, holding it ready even as she exhaled. The curls of drifting smoke were yellow like the ceiling, and like his wife's face.

"You're utterly cold-blooded," she said. "You're in the right job." She hadn't looked down to see whether he was awake. She didn't care. She was saying the things she was determined to say, things she'd thought a lot about but never dared say before. Whether her husband heard her or not seemed unimportant.

Without a word of reply, he pushed back the bedclothes and got out of bed. It was not a violent movement. He did it gently so as not to disturb her. She turned her head to watch him go across the carpet. Naked he looked thin, if not to say skinny—that was why he looked so elegant in his carefully cut suits. She wished she were skinny too.

Bret went into the bathroom, drew back the curtains, and opened the window. It was a glorious autumnal morning. The sunlit trees made long shadows across the gold-tipped grass. He'd not seen the flower beds so crowded with blooms. At the end of his garden, where the fidgeting boughs of weeping willows fingered the water, the slow-moving river looked almost blue. Two rowboats tied up at the pier bobbed gently up and down amid a flotilla of dead leaves. He loved this house.

Since the eighteenth century, many wealthy Londoners have favored such upstream Thameside houses. With grounds that reach the water's edge, they are hidden behind anonymous brick walls all the way from Chiswick to Reading. They come in all shapes, sizes, and styles, from palatial mansions in the Venetian manner to modest three-bedroom residences like this one.

Bret Rensselaer breathed deeply ten times, the way he did before doing his exercises. The view of the garden had reassured him. It always did. He had not always been an Anglophile, but once he'd arrived in this bewitching land, he knew there was no escape from the obsessive love he had for everything connected with it. The river that ran at the foot of his garden was not an ordinary little stream, it was the Thames! The Thames with its associations of old London

Bridge, Westminster Palace, the Tower, and of course Shakespeare's Globe. Still, after living here for years, he could hardly believe his good fortune. He wished his American wife could share his pleasure, but she said England was "backward" and could only see the bad side of living here.

He stared at himself in the mirror as he combed his hair. He had the same jutting chin and blond hair as his mother and his brother. The same good health too, and that was a priceless legacy. He put on his red silk dressing gown. Through the bathroom door he heard a movement and a clink of glass and knew it was his wife taking a drink of bottled water. She didn't sleep well. He'd grown used to her chronic insomnia. He was no longer surprised to wake in the night and find her drinking water, smoking a cigarette, or reading a chapter of one of her romantic novels.

When he returned to the bedroom she was still there: sitting cross-legged on the bed, her silk nightdress disarranged to expose her thighs and its lacy shoulder trimming making a ruff behind her head. Her skin was pale—she avoided the sun—her figure full but not overweight, and her hair tousled. She felt him examining her and she raised her eyes to glare at him. In the past such a pose, that fierce look on her face, and a cigarette in her mouth, had aroused him. Perhaps it was a shameless wanton that he had hoped to discover. If so, his hopes had soon been dashed.

He stepped into the alcove that he used as a dressing room and slid open the mirrored wardrobe door to select a suit from the two dozen hanging there, each one in its tissue paper and plastic bag as it had arrived from the cleaners.

"You have no feelings!" she said.

"Don't, Nikki," he said. Her name was Nicola. She didn't like being called Nikki, but it was too late now to tell him so.

"I mean it," she said. "You send men out to die as if you

were sending out junk mail. You're heartless. I never loved you; no one could."

What nonsense she spoke. Bret Rensselaer's position at SIS was Deputy Controller of European Economics. Yet it was a shrewd guess; there were times when he had to give the final okay on dangerous jobs. And when those tough decisions were to be made, Bret did not shy from making them. "You left it a darn long time before telling me," he said reasonably, while hanging a lightweight wool-and-mohair suit near the light of the window and attaching suspenders to the trousers. He screwed up the blue tissue wrapping and tossed it into the wastebasket. Then he selected shirt and underclothes. He was worried. In this quarrelsome mood Nikki might blurt out some melodramatic yarn of that kind to the first stranger she came across. She hadn't done such a thing before, but he'd never known her in this frame of mind before.

"I've been thinking about it lately," she replied. "Thinking about it a lot."

"And did this thought process of yours begin before or after last Wednesday's lunch?"

She looked at him coolly and blew smoke before saying, "Joppi has nothing to do with it. Do you think I would discuss you with Joppi?"

"You have before." The way she referred to that Bavarian four-flusher by his silly diminutive name made him mad. No matter that just about everyone else did the same.

"That was different. That was years ago. You ran out on me."

"Joppi is a jerk," said Bret and was angry with himself for betraying his feelings. He looked at her and knew, not for the first time, murderous anger. He could have strangled her without a remnant of remorse. No matter; he would have the last laugh.

"Joppi is a real live prince," she said provocatively.

"Princes are ten a penny in Bavaria."

"And you are jealous of him," she said, and didn't bother to conceal her pleasure at the idea of it.

"For making a play for my wife?"

"Don't be ridiculous. Joppi has a wife already."

"One a day, from what I hear."

"You can be very childish sometimes, Bret."

He didn't respond except to look at her with fierce resentment. He deplored the way that Americans like his wife revered these two-bit European aristocrats. They'd met Joppi at Ascot the previous June. Joppi had a horse running in the Coronation Stakes and was there with a big party of German friends. Subsequently he'd invited the Rensselaers for a weekend at a house he'd leased near Paris. They had stayed with him there, but Bret had not enjoyed it. He'd watched the unctuous Joppi looking at Nikki in a way that Bret did not like men to look at his wife. And Nikki had not even noticed it, or so she said when Bret complained of it afterward. Now Joppi had invited Nikki to lunch without going through the formality of inviting Bret along. It made Bret sizzle.

"Prince Joppi," said Bret with just enough emphasis upon the first word to show his contempt, "is a two-bit racketeer."

"Have you had him investigated?"

"I ran him through the computer," he said. "He's into all kinds of crooked deals. That's why we're going to stay clear of him."

"I don't work for your goddamned Secret Intelligence Service," she said. "Just in case you forgot, I'm a free citizen, and I choose my own friends and I say anything I want to say to them."

He knew she was trying to provoke him, but still he wondered if he should phone the night duty officer. He'd have a phone contact for Internal Security. But Bret didn't relish the idea of describing the nuances of his married life to some young subordinate who would write it down and put it on file somewhere.

He went and ran the bath: both taps fully on gave him the temperature he preferred. He squirted bath oil into the rushing water and it foamed furiously. While the tub was filling he returned to Nikki. Under the circumstances, reasoning with her seemed the wiser course. "Have I done something?" he asked with studied mildness. He sat down on the bed.

"Oh, no!" said his wife sarcastically. "Not you!" She could hear the water beating against the bathtub with a roar like thunder.

She was tense, her arms clamped around her knees, the cigarette forgotten for a moment. He looked at her, trying to see something in her face that would give him a hint about the origin of her anger. Failing to see anything that enlightened him, he said, "Then what?" And then, more briskly but with a conciliatory tone, "For goodness' sake, Nikki. I have to go to the office."

" 'I have to go to the office.' "

She attempted to mimic the Englishness that he'd acquired since living here. She was not a good mimic, and her twanging accent, that had so intrigued him when they first met, was still strong. How foolish he'd been to hope that eventually she would embrace England and everything English as lovingly as he had.

"That's all that's important to you, isn't it? Never mind me. Never mind if I go stir-crazy in this godforsaken dump." She tossed her head to throw her hair back, but when it fell forward again she raked her fingers through it to get it from her face.

He sat at the end of the bed, smiling at her, and said, "Now, now, Nikki, darling. Just tell me what's wrong."

It was the patronizing "just" that irritated her. There was something invulnerable about his resolute coldness. Her sister had called him "the shy desperado" and giggled when he came around. But Nikki had found it easy to fall in love with Bret Rensselaer. How clearly she remembered it. She'd never had a suitor like him: slim, handsome, soft-spoken, and considerate. And there was his lifestyle too. Bret's suits fitted in the way that only expensive tailoring could contrive, and his cars were waxed shiny in the way that only chauffeur-driven cars were, and his mother's house was cared for by loyal servants. She loved him, of course, but her love had always been mingled with a touch of awe, or perhaps it was fear. Now she didn't care. Just for a moment, she was able to tell him everything she felt. "Look here, Bret," she said confidently. "When I married you I thought you were going to—"

He held up his hand. "Let me turn off the water, darling. We don't want it flooding the study downstairs." He went back into the bathroom; the roar of water stopped. A draft was coming through the window to make steam that tumbled out through the door. He emerged, tightening the knot of his dressing gown: a very tight knot; there was something neurotic in that gesture. He raised his eyes to her and she knew that the moment had passed. She was tongue-tied again; he knew how to make her feel like a child, and he liked that. "What were you saying, dear?"

She bit her lip and tried again, differently this time. "That night, when you first admitted that you were working in secret intelligence, I didn't believe you. I thought it was another of your romantic stories."

"Another?" He was amused enough to smile.

"You were always an ace bullshitter, Bret. I thought you were making it all up as some kind of compensation for your dull job at the bank."

His eyes narrowed; it was the only sign he gave of being angry. He looked down at the carpet. He had been about to do his exercises but she'd hammer at him all the time and he didn't want that. Better to do them at the office.

"You were going to bleed them white. I remember your saying that: bleed them white. You told me one day you'd have a man working in the Kremlin." She wanted to remind him how close they had been. "Remember?" Her mouth was dry so she sipped more water. "You said the Brits could do it because they hadn't grown too big. You said they could do it but they didn't know they could do it. That's where you came in, you said."

Bret stood with his fists in the pockets of the red dressing gown. He wasn't really listening to her; he wanted to get on, to bathe and shave and dress and spend the extra time sitting with a newspaper and toast and coffee in the garden before his driver came to collect him. But he knew that if he turned away, or ended the conversation abruptly, her anger would be reaffirmed. "Maybe they will," he said, and hoped she'd drop it.

He lifted his eyes to the small painting that hung above the bed. He had many fine pictures—all by modern British painters—but this was Bret Rensselaer's proudest possession. Stanley Spencer: buxom English villagers frolicking in an orchard. Bret could study it for hours; he could smell the fresh grass and the apple blossoms. He'd paid far too much for the painting, but he had desperately wanted to possess that English scene forever. Nikki didn't appreciate having a masterpiece enshrined in the bedroom, to love and to cherish. She preferred photographs; she'd admitted as much once, during a savage argument about the bills she'd run up with the dressmaker.

"You said that running an agent into the Kremlin was your greatest ambition."

that he was even more of a romantic dreamer than she was. This craving he had for everything English was ridiculous. He'd even talked of renouncing his U.S. citizenship and was hoping to get one of those knighthoods the British handed out instead of money. An obsession of that kind could bring him only trouble.

There was enough work in the office to keep Bret Rensselaer busy for the first hour or more. It was a wonderful room on the top floor of a modern block. Large by the standards of modern accommodation, his office had been decorated according to his own ideas, as interpreted by one of the best interior designers in London. He sat behind his big glass-topped desk. The color scheme—walls, carpet, and long leather chesterfield—was entirely gray and black except for his white phone. Bret had intended that the room should be in harmony with this prospect of the slate roofs of central London.

He buzzed for his secretary and started work. Halfway through the morning, his tray emptied by the messenger, he decided to switch off his phone and take twenty minutes to catch up with his physical exercises. It was a part of his puritanical nature and upbringing that he would not make a confrontation with his wife an excuse to miss his work or his exercises.

He was in his shirt sleeves, doing his thirty push-ups, when Dicky Cruyer—a contender for the soon-to-become-vacant chair of the German Stations Controller—put his head around the door and said, "Bret, your wife has been trying to get through to you."

Bret continued to do his push-ups slowly and methodically. "And?" he said, trying not to puff.

"She sounded upset," said Dicky. "She said something

"Did I?" He looked at her and blinked, discon
both by the extent of his indiscretion and its naïveté.
kidding you."

"Don't say that, Bret!" She was angry that he sh
airily dismiss the only truly intimate conversation she c
remember having with him. "You were serious. Dammit,
were serious."

"Perhaps you're right." He looked at her and at the b
side table to see what she'd been drinking, but there was
alcohol there, only a liter-size bottle of Malvern water. She
stuck to her rigorous diet—no bread, butter, sugar, potatoe:
pasta, or alcohol—for three weeks. Nikki was amazingly dis
ciplined about her dieting and she had never been much of
a drinker; it went straight to her waistline. When Internal
Security had first vetted her, they'd remarked on her absti-
nence and Bret had been proud.

He got up and went around to her side of the bed to give
her a kiss. She offered her cheek. It was a sort of armistice but
his fury was not allayed, just repressed. "It's a glorious sunny
day again. I'm going to have coffee in the garden. Shall I bring
some up?"

She pulled the bedside clock round to see it. "Jesus
Christ! The help won't be there for an hour yet."

"I'm perfectly capable of fixing my own toast and coffee."

"It's too early for me. I'll call for it when I'm ready."

He looked at her eyes. She was close to tears. As soon as
he left the room she would begin weeping. "Go back to sleep,
Nikki. Do you want an aspirin?"

"No I don't want a goddamned aspirin. Anytime I bug
you, you ask me if I want an aspirin, as if talking out of turn
were some kind of feminine malady."

He had often accused her of being a dreamer, which by
extension was his claim to be a practical realist. The truth was

like, 'Tell him, you get your man in Moscow and I'll go get my man in Paris.' I asked her to tell me again but she rang off." He watched while Bret finished a few more push-ups.

"I'll talk to her later." Bret grunted.

"She was at the airport, getting on the plane. She said to say goodbye. 'Goodbye forever,' she said."

"So you've said it," Bret told him, head twisted, smiling pleasantly from his position full length on the floor. "Message received and understood."

Dicky muttered something about its being a bad phone line, nodded, and withdrew with the feeling that he'd been unwise to bring the ugly news. He'd heard rumors that all was not going well with the Rensselaer marriage, but no matter how much a man might want to leave his wife it does not mean that he wants her to leave him. Dicky had the feeling that Bret Rensselaer wouldn't forget who it was who had brought the news of his wife's desertion; it would leave a residual antipathy that would taint their relationship ever after. In this assumption Dicky was correct. He began to hope that the appointment of the German Stations Controller would not be entirely in Bret's hands.

The door clicked shut. Bret began the push-ups over again. He had inflicted that mortifying rule on himself: if he stopped during exercises he did them all over again.

When his exercises were done, Bret opened the door that concealed a small sink. He washed his face and hands, and as he did so he recalled in detail the conversation he'd had with his wife that morning. He told himself not to waste time pondering the rift between them; what was gone was gone, and good riddance. Bret Rensselaer had always claimed that he never wasted time on recriminations or regrets, but he felt hurt and deeply resentful.

To get his mind on other matters, he began to think about those days long ago when he'd wanted to get into

Operations. He'd drafted some ideas about undermining the East German economy, but no one had taken him seriously. The Director-General's reaction to the big pile of research he'd done was to give him the European Economics Desk. That wasn't really something to complain about; Bret had built the desk into a formidable empire. But the economics desk work had been processing intelligence. He always regretted that they hadn't taken up the more important ideas: the ideas of promoting change in East Germany.

Bret's goal had never been to get an effective agent into the top of the Moscow KGB. He would prefer having a really brilliant agent, with a long-term disruptive and informative role, in East Berlin, the capital of the German Democratic Republic. It would take a long time; it was not something that could be hurried in the way that so many SIS operations were done in a hurry.

The Department probably had dozens of sleepers who'd established themselves, in one capacity or another, as long-time loyal agents of the various communist regimes of Eastern Europe. Now Bret had to find such a person, and it had to be the right one. But the long and meticulous process of selection had to be done with such discretion and finesse that no one would be aware of what he was doing. And when he found this man, he'd have the task of persuading him to risk his neck in a way that sleepers were not normally asked to do. A lot of sleepers assigned to deep cover just took the money and relied on the good chance that they'd never be asked to do anything at all.

It would not be simple. Neither would it be happy. At the beginning there would be little or no cooperation, for the simple reason that no one around him could be told what he was doing. Afterward there would be the clamor for recognition and rewards. The Department was very concerned about such things. It was natural that these men, who labored so secretly, should strive so vigorously and desperately for the admiration and respect of their peers when things went well. And if things did not go well there would be the savage recriminations that accompanied post-mortems.

Lastly there was the effect that an operation like this would have upon the man who went off to do the dirty work. Such men did not come back. Or if they did come back they were never fit to work again. Of the survivors Bret had seen, few returned able to do anything but sit with a rug over their knees, talk to the officially approved departmental shrink, and try vainly to put together ruptured nerves and shattered relationships.

It was easy to see why they couldn't recover. You ask a man to leave all that he holds most dear, to spy in a strange country. Then, years later, you snatch him back again—God willing—to live out his remaining life in peace and contentment. But there is no peace and no contentment either. The poor devil can't remember anyone he hasn't betrayed or abandoned at one time or another. Such people are destroyed as surely as if they'd faced a firing squad.

On the other hand it was necessary to balance the destruction of one man—plus perhaps a few members of his family—with what could be achieved by such a coup. It was a matter of the greater good of the community at large. They were fighting against a system that killed hundreds of thousands in labor camps, used torture as a normal part of its police interrogation, put dissenters into mental asylums. It would be absurd to be squeamish when the stakes were so high.

Bret Rensselaer closed the door that hid his sink and went to the window and looked out. Despite the haze, you could see it all from here: the Gothic spike of the Palace of Westminster, the spire of St. Martin's in the Fields, Nelson balancing gingerly on his column. There was a unity to it.

Even the incongruous Post Office tower would perhaps look all right, given a century or so of weathering. Bret pushed his face close to the glass in order to see Wren's dome of St. Paul's. The Director-General's room had a fine view northward. Bret envied him. One day perhaps he would occupy that room. Nikki had made jokes about it and he'd pretended to laugh at them, but he'd not given up hopes that one day . . .

Then he remembered the notes he'd made about the whole project. A great idea struck him: now that he had more time, and a staff of economists and analysts, he'd have it all updated. Maps, bar charts, pie charts, graphs, and easy figures that even the Director-General would understand could all be done on the computer. Why hadn't he thought of it before? Thank you, Nikki.

And that brought him back to his wife. Once again he told himself to be resolute. She had left him. It was all over. He told himself he'd seen it coming for ages, but in fact he hadn't seen it coming at all. He'd always taken it for granted that Nikki would put up with all the things of which she complained just as he put up with her, in order to have a marriage. He would miss her, there was no getting away from that fact, but he vowed he wouldn't go chasing after her.

It simply wasn't fair. He'd never been unfaithful to her all the time they'd been married. He sighed. Now he would have to start all over again: dating, courting, persuading, cajoling, being the extra man at parties. He'd have to learn how to suffer rejection when he asked younger women out to dinner. Rejection had never been easy for him. It was all too awful to contemplate. Perhaps he'd get his secretary to dine with him one evening next week. She'd told him it was all off with her fiancé.

He sat down at his desk and picked up some papers, but the words floated before his eyes as his mind went back to

Nikki. What had started the breakdown of his marriage? What had gone wrong? What had Nikki called him: a ruthless bastard? She'd been so cool and lucid, that's what had really shaken him. Thinking about it again, he decided that Nikki's cool and lucid manner had all been a sham. Ruthless bastard? He told himself that women were apt to say absurd things when they were incoherently angry. That helped.

2

East Germany:

January 1978

"BRING ME THE MIRROR," SAID MAX BUSBY. HE HADN'T
intended that his voice should come out as a croak. Bernard
Samson went and got the mirror and placed it on the table so
Max could see his arm without twisting inside out. "Now
take the dressing off," said Max.

The sleeve of Max's filthy old shirt had been torn back
as far as the shoulder. Now Bernard unbound the arm, finally
peeling back a pad that was caked with pus and dried blood.
It was a shock. Bernard gave an involuntary hiss and Max saw
the look of horror on his face. "Not too bad," said Bernard,
trying to hide his real feelings.

"I've seen worse," said Busby, looking at it and trying to
sound unruffled. It was a big wound: deep and inflamed and
oozing pus. Bernard had stitched it up with a sewing needle
and fishing line from a survival kit, but some of his stitches
had torn through the soft flesh. The skin around it was mot-
tled every color of the rainbow and so tender that even to
look at it made it hurt more. Bernard was pinching it together
tight so it didn't break right open again. The dressing—an old
handkerchief—had got dirty. The side that had been against
the wound was dark brown and completely saturated with

blood. More blood had crusted in patches all down his arm. "It might have been my gun hand."

Max bent his head until, by the light of the lamp, he could see his pale face in the mirror. He knew about wounds. He knew the way that loss of blood makes the heart pound as it tries to keep supplying oxygen and glucose to the brain. His face had whitened because the blood vessels were contracting as they tried to help the heart do its job. And the heart pumped more furiously as the plasma was lost and the blood thickened. Max tried to take his own pulse. He couldn't manage it but he knew what he would find: irregular pulse and low body temperature. These were all the signs, bad signs.

"Put something on the fire and then bind it up tight with the strip of towel. I'll wrap paper around it before we leave. Don't want to leave a trail of blood spots." He managed a smile. "We'll give them another hour." Max Busby was frightened. They were in a mountain hut, it was winter, and he was no longer young.

A onetime NYPD cop, he'd come to Europe in 1944, wearing the bars of a U.S. Army lieutenant, and he'd never gone back across the Atlantic except for an attempted reconciliation with his ex-wife in Chicago and a couple of visits to his mother in Atlantic City.

After Bernard had replaced the mirror and put something on the fire, Max stood up and Bernard helped him with his coat. Then he watched as Max settled down carefully in his chair. Max was badly hurt. Bernard wondered if they would both make it as far as the border.

Max read his thoughts and smiled. Now neither wife nor mother would have recognized Max in his battered jeans and filthy overcoat with the torn shirt under it. There was a certain mad formality to the way he balanced a greasy trilby hat on his knees. His papers said he was a railway worker but his papers, and a lot of other things he needed, were at the railway station and a Soviet arrest team was there too.

Max Busby was short and squat without being fat. His sparse hair was black and his face was heavily lined. His eyes were reddened by tiredness. He had heavy brows and a large straggly black mustache that was lopsided because of the way he kept tugging at one end of it.

Older, wiser, wounded, and sick, but despite all that, and the change in environment and costume, Max Busby did not feel very different from that green policeman who'd patrolled the dark and dangerous Manhattan streets and alleys. Then, as now, he was his own man; the bad guys didn't all wear black hats. Some of them were to be found spooning their beluga with the police commissioner. It was the same here: no black and white, just shades of gray. Max Busby disdained communism—or "socialism," in the preferred terminology of its practitioners—and all it stood for, with a zeal that was unusual even in the ranks of the men who fought it, but he wasn't a simplistic crusader.

"Two hours," suggested Bernard Samson. Bernard was big and strong, with wavy hair and spectacles. He wore a scuffed leather zip-up jacket and baggy corduroy trousers, held up by a wide leather belt decorated with a collection of metal communist *Parteitag* badges. On his head there was a close-fitting peaked cap of the design forever associated with the ill-fated Afrika Korps. It was a sensible choice of headgear, thought Max, as he looked at it. A man could go to sleep in a cap like that, or fight without losing it. Max looked at his companion: Bernard was still in one piece, and young enough to wait it out without his nerves fraying and his mouth going dry. Perhaps it would be better to let him go on alone. But would Bernard make it alone? Max was not at all sure he would. "They have to get through Schwerin," Bernard reminded him. "They may be delayed by one of the mobile patrols."

Max nodded and wet his lips. The loss of blood had sapped his strength: the idea of his contacts being challenged by a Russian army patrol made his stomach heave. Their papers were not good enough to withstand any scrutiny more careful than a cop's casual flashlight beam. Few false papers are.

He knew that Bernard wouldn't see the nod. The little room was in darkness except for the faint glimmer from an evil-smelling oil lamp, its wick turned as low as possible, and from the stove a rosy glow that gave satin toecaps to their boots, but *Qui tacet, consentire videtur,* silence means consent. Max, like many a New York cop before him, had slaved at night school to study law. Even now he remembered a few basic essentials. More pertinent to his ready consent was the fact that Max knew what it was like to be crossing 150 kilometers of moonlit Saxon countryside when there was a triple-A alert and a Moscow stop-and-detain order that would absolve any trigger-happy cop or soldier from the consequences of shooting strangers on sight.

Bernard tapped the cylindrical iron stove with his heavy boot and was startled when the door flipped open and red-hot cinders fell out on the hearth. For a few moments there was a flare of golden light as the draft fed the fire. He could see the wads of brown-edged newspaper packed into the cracks around the door frame and a chipped enamel washbasin and the rucksacks that had been positioned near the door in case they had to leave in a hurry. And he could see Max as white as a sheet and looking . . . well, looking like any old man would look who'd lost so much blood he should be in an intensive-care ward but was trudging across northern Germany in winter. Then the fire went dull again and the room darkened.

"Two hours, then?" Bernard asked.

"I won't argue." Max was carefully chewing the final mouthful of rye bread. It was delicious but he had to chew carefully and swallow it bit by bit. They grew the best rye in the world in Mecklenburg, and made the finest bread with it. But that was the last of it and both men were hungry.

"That makes a change," said Bernard good-naturedly. They seldom truly argued. Max liked the younger man to feel he had a say in what happened. Especially now.

"I'll not make an enemy of the guy who's going to get the German Desk," said Max very softly, and twisted one end of his mustache. He tried not to think of his pain.

"Is that what you think?"

"Don't kid around, Bernard. Who else is there?"

"Dicky Cruyer."

Max said, "Oh, so that's it. You really resent Dicky, don't you?" Bernard always rose to such bait, and Max liked to tease him.

"He could do it."

"Well, he hasn't got a ghost of a chance. He's too young and too inexperienced. You're in line, and after this one you'll get anything you ask for."

Bernard didn't reply. It was a welcome thought. He was in his middle thirties and, despite his contempt for desk men, he didn't want to end up like poor old Max. Max was neither one thing nor the other. He was too old for shooting matches, climbing into other people's houses, and running away from frontier guards, but there was nothing else he could do. Nothing, that is, that would pay him anything like a living wage. Bernard's attempts to persuade his father to get Max a job in the training school had been met with spiteful derision. He'd made enemies in all the wrong places. Bernard's father never got along with him. Poor Max. Bernard admired him immensely. Bernard had seen Max doing the job as no one else could do it. But heaven only knew how he'd end his days. Yes, a job behind a desk in London would come at exactly the right stage of Bernard's career.

Neither man spoke for a little while after that. For the last few miles Bernard had been carrying everything. They were both exhausted, and like combat soldiers they had learned never to miss an opportunity for rest. They both dozed into a controlled half-sleep. That was all they would allow themselves until they were back across the border and out of danger.

It was about thirty minutes later that the *thump-thump-thump* of a helicopter brought them back to wide-eyed awakening. It was a medium-sized chopper, not transport size, and it was flying slowly and at no more than a thousand feet, judging from the sound it made. It all added up to bad news. The German Democratic Republic was not rich enough to supply such expensive gas-guzzling machines for anything but serious business.

"Shit!" said Max. "The bastards are looking for us." Despite the urgency in his voice he spoke quietly, as if the men in the chopper might hear him.

The two men sat in the dark room neither moving nor speaking; they were listening. The tension was almost unbearable as they concentrated. The helicopter was not flying in a straight line and that was an especially bad sign; it meant it had reached its search area. Its course meandered as if it was pinpointing the neighboring villages. It was looking for movement: any kind of movement. Outside, the snow was deep. When daylight came, nothing could move without leaving a conspicuous trail.

In this part of the world, to go outdoors was enough to excite suspicion. There was nowhere to visit after dark; the local residents were simple people, peasants in fact. They didn't eat the sort of elaborate evening meal that provides an

excuse for dinner parties, and they had no money for restau-
rants. As to hotels, who would want to spend even one night
here when they had the means to move on?

The sound of the helicopter was abruptly muted as it
passed behind the forested hills, and for the time being the
night was silent.

"Let's get out of here," said Max. Such a sudden departure would be going against everything they had planned, but
Max, even more than Bernard, was a creature of impulse. He
had his "hunches." He wrapped folded newspaper around his
arm in case the blood came through the towel. Then he put
string around the arm of the overcoat and Bernard tied it very
tight.

"Okay." Bernard had long ago decided that Max, not-
withstanding his inability to find domestic happiness or turn
his professional skills into anything resembling a success
story, had an uncanny instinct for approaching danger. Without hesitation and without getting up from his chair, Bernard
leaned forward and picked up the big kettle. Opening the
stove ring with the metal lifting tool, he poured water into
the fire. He did it very carefully and gently, but even so there
was a lot of steam.

Max was about to stop him but the kid was right. Better
to do it. At least that lousy chopper was out of sight of the
chimney. When the fire was out, Bernard put some dead
ashes into the stove. It wouldn't help much if they got here.
They'd see the blood on the floorboards, and it would require
many gallons of water to cool the stove, but it might make
it seem as if they'd left earlier and save them if they had to
hide nearby.

"Let's go." Max took out his pistol. It was a Sauer Model
38, a small automatic dating from the Nazi period, when they
were used by high-ranking army officers. It was a lovely gun,
obtained by Bernard from some underworld acquaintance in

London, where Bernard's array of shady friends rivaled those he knew in Berlin.

Bernard watched Max as he tried to move the slide back to inject a round into the chamber. He had to change hands to do it, and his face was contorted with pain. It was distressing to watch him but Bernard said nothing. Once done, Max pressed on the exposed cocking lever to lower the hammer so the gun was ready for instant use but with little risk of accident. Max pushed the gun into his inside breast pocket. "Have you got a gun?" he asked.

"We left it at the house. You said Siggi might need it." Bernard swung the rucksack over his shoulder. It was heavy, containing the contents of both packs. There was a grappling hook and nylon rope as well as a small digging implement and a formidable bolt cutter.

"So I did. Damn. Well, you take the glasses." Bernard took them from around Max's neck, careful not to jar his arm. "Stare them to death, Bernard. You can do it!" A grim little laugh. Silently Bernard took the field glasses—rubber-clad Zeiss 7×40s, like the ones the Grenzpolizei used—and put his head and arm through the strap. It made them uncomfortably tight, but if they had to run for it he didn't want the glasses floating around and banging him in the face.

Max tapped the snuffer that extinguished the flame of the oil lamp. Everything was pitch black until he opened the door and let in a trace of blue starlight and the bitterly cold night air. "Attaboy!"

Max was expecting trouble, and Bernard did not find the prospect cheering. Bernard had never learned to face the occasional violent episodes that his job provided in the way that old-timers like Max accepted them, even when injured. Was it, he wondered, something to do with the army or the war, or both?

The timber cabin was isolated. If only it would snow

again, that would help to cover their tracks, but there was no sign of snow. Once outside Max sniffed the air, anxious to know if the smoke from the stove would carry far enough to alert a search party. Well, at least choosing this remote shelter had proved right. It was a hut the cowherds úsed in summer when the cattle moved to the higher grazing. From this elevated position they could see the valley along which they had come. Here and there, lights indicated a cluster of houses in this dark and lonely landscape. It was good country for moving at night, but when daylight came it would work against them; they'd be too damned conspicuous. Max cursed the bad luck that had dogged the whole movement. By this time they should have all been across the border, skin intact and sound asleep after warm baths and a big meal and lots to drink.

Max looked up. A few stars were sprinkled to the east but most of the sky was dark. If the thick overcast remained there, blotting out the sun, it would help, but it wasn't low enough to inconvenience the helicopters. The chopper would be back.

"We'll keep to the high ground," said Max. "These paths usually make good going. They keep them marked and maintained for summertime walkers." He set off at a good pace to show Bernard he was fit and strong, but after a little while he slowed.

For several kilometers the beech forest blocked off their view of the valley. It was dark walking under the trees, like being in a long tunnel. The undergrowth was dead, and crisp brown fern crunched under their feet. As the trail climbed, the snow was harder. Trees shielded the footpath, and on the hard surfaces they made reasonably good speed. They had walked for about an hour and a half, and were into the evergreens, when Max called a halt. They were higher now, and through a firebreak in the regimented plantations they could see the twist of the next valley ahead of them. Beyond that, through a dip in the hills, a lake shone faintly in the starlight, its water heady with foam, like good German beer. It was difficult to guess how far away it was. There were no houses in sight, no roads, no power lines, nothing to give the landscape a scale. Trees were no help; these fir trees came in all shapes and sizes.

"Five minutes," said Max. He sank down in a way that revealed his true condition and wedged his backside into the roots of a tree. Alongside him there was a bin for feeding the deer: the herds were cosseted for the benefit of the hunters. Resting against the bin, Max's head slumped to one side. His face was shiny with exertion and he looked all in. Blood had seeped through the paper and there was a patch of it on the sleeve of the thick overcoat. Better to press on than try to fix it here.

Bernard took out the field glasses, snapped the protective covers from the lenses, and looked more carefully at the lake. It was the haze on the water that produced the boiling effect and softened its outline.

"How are your feet?" said Max.

"Okay, Max."

"I have spare socks."

"Don't mother me, Max."

"Do you know where we are?"

"Yes, we're in Germany," he said, still staring through the glasses.

"And on the scenic route."

"But that's our lake, Max," Bernard affirmed. "Mouse Lake."

"Or Moulting Lake," suggested Max.

"Or even Turncoat Lake," said Bernard, suggesting a third possible translation.

Max regretted his attempt at levity. "Something like

that," he said. He resolved to stop treating Bernard like a child. It was not so easy: he'd known him so long it was difficult to remember that he was a grown man with a wife and children. And what a wife! Fiona Samson was one of the rising stars of the Department. Some of the more excitable employees were saying that she was likely to wind up as the first woman to hold the Director-General's post. Max found it an unlikely prospect. The higher echelons of the Department were reserved for a certain sort of Englishman, all of whom seemed to have been at school together.

Max Busby often wondered why Fiona had married Bernard. He was no great prize. If he got the German Desk in London it would be largely due to his father's influence, and he'd go no further. Whoever got the German Desk would come under Bret Rensselaer's direction, and Bret wanted a stooge there. Max wondered if Bernard would adapt to a yes-man role.

Max took the offered field glasses to have a closer look at the lake. Holding with only one hand meant resting against the tree. Even holding his arm up made him tremble. He wondered if it was septic. He'd seen wounds go septic very quickly, but he put the thought to the back of his mind and concentrated on what he could see. Yes, that was the Mause See, exactly as he remembered it from the map. Maps had always been a fetish with him; sometimes he sat looking at them for hours on end, as other men read books. They were not only maps of places he knew or places he'd been or places he might have to visit, but maps of every kind. When someone had given him the *Times Atlas of the Moon,* Max took it on vacation. It was his sole reading matter.

"We must come in along the southern shore," said Bernard, "and not too close to the water, or we'll find ourselves in some Central Committee member's country cottage."

"A boat might be the best way," Max suggested, handing the glasses back.

"Let's get closer," said Bernard, who didn't like the idea of a boat. Too risky from every point of view. Bernard was not very skilled with a set of oars, and Max certainly couldn't row. In winter a boat might be missed from its moorings, and even if the water was glassy smooth—which it wouldn't be—he didn't fancy being exposed to view like that. It was an idea typical of Max, who liked such brazen methods and had proved them in the past. Bernard hoped Max would forget that idea by the time they'd covered the intervening countryside. It was a long hike. It looked like rough going, and soon it would be dawn.

Bernard felt like saying something about the two men with whom they had been supposed to rendezvous yesterday afternoon, but he kept silent. There was nothing to be said; they had gone into the bag. Max and Bernard had been lucky to get away. Now the only important thing was for them to get back. If they didn't, the whole operation—"Reisezug"— would have proved useless, more than three months of planning, risks, and hard work wasted. Bernard's father was running the operation, and he would be desolated. To some extent, his father's reputation depended upon him.

Bernard got up and dusted the soil from his trousers. It was sandy and had a strange musty smell.

"It stinks, right?" said Max, somehow reading his thoughts. "The North German Plain. Goddamned hilly for a plain, I'd say."

"German Polish Plain they called it when I was at school," said Bernard.

"Yeah, well, Poland has moved a whole lot closer to here since I did high school geography," said Max, and smiled at his little joke. "My wife, Helma, was born not far from here. Ex-wife, that is. Once she got that little old U.S. passport she went off to live in Chicago with her cousin."

As Bernard helped Max to his feet he saw the animal. It was lying full length in a bare patch of ground behind the tree against which he'd rested. Its fur was caked with mud and it was frozen hard. He peered more closely at it. It was a fully grown hare, its foot tight in a primitive wire snare. The poor creature had died in agony, gnawing its trapped foot down to the bone but lacking either the energy or the desperate determination required for such a sacrifice.

Max came to look too. Neither man spoke. For Max it seemed like a bad omen. Max had always been a great believer in signs. Still without speaking, they both trudged on. They were tired now, and the five-minute break that had helped their lungs had stiffened their muscles. Max found it difficult to hold his arm up, but if he let it hang it throbbed and bled more.

"Why didn't he go back?" said Max as the path widened and Bernard came up alongside him.

"Who?"

"The poacher. Why didn't he go back and look at his snares?"

"You mean we are already in the Sperrzone? There was no fence, no signs."

"Locals know where it is," said Max. "Strangers blunder onward." He unbuttoned his coat and touched the gun. There was no practical reason for doing so except that Max wanted to make it clear to Bernard that he hadn't come all this way in order to turn himself in to the first person who challenged them. Max had shot his way out of trouble before, twice. Some people said those two remarkable instances of good luck had given him a false idea of what could be done when facing capture; Max thought the British with whom he worked were too damned ready to let their people put their hands up.

He stopped for a moment to look at the lake again. It would be so much easier and quicker to be walking in the valley instead of along this high path. But there would be villages and farms and dogs that barked down there. These high paths were less likely to have such dangers, but the ice on the northern aspects meant they were sometimes slower going and the two men didn't have time to spare.

The next hill was higher, and after that the path would descend to cross the Besen valley. Perhaps it would be better to cross it somewhere else. If the local police were alerted they were sure to put a man at the stone bridge where the footpath met the valley road. He looked at the summit of the hill on the far side of the river. They'd never do it. The local people called these hills "mountains," as people do in regions where no mountains exist. Well, he was beginning to understand why. After you walked these hills they became mountains. Everything was relative. The older he got the more mountainous the world became.

"We'll try to get over the Besen at that wide place where the stones are," said Max.

Bernard grunted unenthusiastically. If they'd had more time Max would have made it into more of a discussion. He would have let Bernard feel he'd had a say in the decision, but there was no time for such niceties.

Scrambling down through the dead bracken and the loose stones caused both men to lose their balance now and again. Once Max slid so far he almost fell. He knocked his wounded arm when recovering himself, and the pain was so great that he gave a little whimper. Bernard helped him up. Max said nothing. He didn't say thanks; there was no energy to spare.

Max had chosen this place with care. Everywhere on its east side the Wall occupied a wide band of communist territory. Even to get within five kilometers of the Wall itself required a permit. This well-guarded and constantly patrolled prohibited region, or Sperrzone, was cleared of trees and any shrubs or growth that could conceal a man or child. Any agricultural work permitted in the Sperrzone was done only in daylight and under the constant surveillance of the guards in their watchtowers. Artfully the towers were different in height and design, varying from low observation bunkers to tall modernistic concrete constructions that resembled airport control towers.

But in the Sperrzone of that section of the frontier that NATO code-names "piecemeal," good or bad fortune has called upon the DDR to contend with the lake. It was the presence of a lake at a part of the Wall that was undergoing extensive repair work that caught Max Busby's attention in the so-called Secret Room.

For the regime it was a difficult section: the Elbe and the little river Besen that feeds into it, plus the effect of the Mause See, all contributed to the marshiness of the flatland. The Wall was always giving them problems here no matter what they did about waterproofing the foundations. Now a stretch almost three kilometers long was under repair at seven different places. It must be bad or they would have waited until summer.

Getting through the Sperrzone was only the beginning. The real frontier was marked by a tall fence, too flimsy to climb but rigged with alarms, flares, and automatic guns. After that came the *Schutzstreifen,* the security strip, about five hundred meters deep, where attack-trained dogs on *Hundelaufleine* ran between the minefields. Then came the concrete ditches, followed by an eight-meter strip of dense barbed wire and a variety of devices arranged differently from sector to sector to provide surprises for the newcomer.

To what extent this bizarre playground had been dismantled, for the benefit of the repair gangs, remained to be discovered. It was difficult to forget the helicopter. The whole military region would be alerted now. It wouldn't be hard to guess where the fugitives were heading.

When they reached the lake it was not anything like the obstruction that either of them had anticipated. They'd been soaked to the knees wading across the slow-moving Besen. The necessary excursion into the Mause See—to get around the red buoys, which Max thought might mark underwater obstacles—did no more than repeat the soaking up to the waist. But there was a difference. The hard muscular legs had been brought back to tingling life by brisk walking, but the icy cold water of the lake up to his waist drained from Max some measure of his resolution. His arm hurt, his guts hurt, and the arctic water pierced through his belly like cold steel.

The snow began with just a few flakes spinning down from nowhere and then became a steady fall. "What a beautiful sight," said Bernard, and Max grunted his agreement.

There was a faint tinge of light in the eastern sky as they cut through the first wire fence. "Just go!" said Max, his teeth chattering. "There's no time for all the training school tricks. Screw the alarms, just cut!"

Bernard handled the big bolt cutters quickly and expertly. The only noise they heard for the first few minutes was the clang of the cut wire. But after that the dogs began to bark.

Frank Harrington, the SIS Berlin Resident, would not normally have been at the reception point in the Bundesrepublik waiting, in the most lonely hours of the night, for two agents breaking through the Wall, but this operation was special. And Frank had promised Bernard's father that he would look after him, a promise Frank Harrington interpreted in the most solemn fashion.

He was in a small subterranean room under some four meters of concrete and lit by fluorescent blue lights, but Frank's vigil was not too onerous. Although such forward command bunkers were somewhat austere—it being NATO's assumption that the Warsaw Pact armies would roll over these border defenses in the first hours of any undeclared war—it was warm and dry and he was sitting in a soft seat with a glass of decent whisky in his fist.

This was the commanding officer's private office, or at least it was assigned to that purpose in the event of a war emergency. Among Frank's companions were a corpulent young officer of the Bundesgrenzschutz—a force of West German riot police who guard airports, embassies, and the border—and an elderly Englishman in a curious nautical uniform worn by the British Frontier Service, which acts as guides for all British army patrols on land, air, and river. The German was lolling against a radiator and the Englishman perched on the edge of a desk.

"How long before sunup?" said Frank. He'd kept his tan trenchcoat on over his brown tweed suit. His shirt was khaki, his tie a faded sort of yellow. To the casual eye he might have been an army officer in uniform.

"An hour and eight minutes," said the Englishman after consulting his watch. He didn't trust clocks, not even the synchronized and constantly monitored clocks in the control bunker.

Hunched in a chair in the corner—melton overcoat over his Savile Row worsted—was a fourth man, Bret Rensselaer. It was almost half an hour since he'd spoken. He'd come from London Central on a watching brief and he was taking it literally. Now he checked his watch. Bret had already committed the time of sunrise to memory; he wondered why Frank hadn't bothered to do so.

The two men had worked together for a long time and

their relationship was firmly established. Frank Harrington regarded Bret's patrician deportment and high-handed East Coast bullshit as typical of the CIA top brass he used to know in Washington. Bret saw in Frank a minimally efficient although congenial time-server, of the sort that yeoman farmers had supplied to Britain's Civil Service since the days of Empire. These descriptions, suitably amended, would have been acknowledged by both men, and thus a modus vivendi had been reached.

"Germans who live near the border get a special pass and can go across nine times a year to see friends and relatives," said Frank, suddenly impelled for the sake of good manners to include Bret in the conversation. "One of them came through yesterday evening—they are not permitted to stay overnight—and told us that everything looked normal. The work on the Wall and so on. . . ."

Bret nodded. The hum of the air-conditioning seemed loud in the silence.

"It was a good spot to choose," Frank added.

"There are no good spots," interposed the BGS officer loudly. He looked like a ruffian, thought Frank, with his scarred face and beer belly. Perhaps riot policemen had to be like that. Meeting no response from either of the strange foreigners, the German officer drank what remained of his whisky, wiped his mouth, belched, nodded his leave-taking, and went out.

The phone in the next room rang and they listened while the operator grunted, hung up, and then called loudly, "Dogs barking and some sort of movement over there now."

Bret looked at Frank. Frank winked but otherwise didn't move.

The English guide swallowed the last of his whisky hurriedly and slid off the desk. "I'd better be off too," he said. "I might be needed. I understand two of your freebooters might be going in to try to help."

"Perhaps," said Frank.

"It won't work," said the Englishman. "In effect it's an invasion of their soil."

Frank stared at him and didn't reply. He didn't like people to refer to his men as freebooters, especially not strangers. The guide, forgetting his glass was empty, tried to drink more from it. Then he set it down on the desk where he'd been sitting and departed.

Left to themselves, Bret said, "If young Samson pulls this one off I'm going to recommend him for the German Desk." He was sitting well back in the chair, elbows on its rests, hands together like a tutor delivering a homily to an erring student.

"Yes, so you said."

"Can he do it, Frank?" Although framed as a query, he said it as if he were testing Frank with an exam question rather than asking help with a difficult decision.

"He's not stupid."

"Just headstrong," supplied Bret. "Is that what you mean?"

"Are you sure you wouldn't like a drink?" asked Frank, holding up the bottle of Scotch, which was on the floor near his chair. Bret had bought it in the duty-free shop at London airport but he hadn't touched a drop.

Bret shook his head. "And the wife?" said Bret, adding in a voice that was half joking, half serious, "Is Mrs. Samson going to be the first female Director-General?"

"Too fixed in her viewpoint. All women are. She's not flexible enough to do what the old man does, is she?"

"A lead pipe is flexible," said Bret.

"Resilient, I mean."

"Elastic," said Bret, "is the only word I can think of for the capacity to return to former shape and state."

"Is that the primary requirement for a D-G?" asked Frank coldly. He'd trained with Sir Henry Clevemore back in wartime and been a personal friend ever since. He wasn't keen on discussing his possible successors with Bret.

"Primary requirement for a lot of things," said Bret dismissively. He didn't want to talk, but he added, "Too many people in this business get permanently crippled."

"Only field agents surely?"

"It's sometimes worse for the ones who send them out."

"Is that what you're worried about in the case of Bernard Samson? That too much rough stuff might leave a permanent mark? Is that why you asked me?"

"No. Not at all."

"Bernard would do a good job in London. Give him a chance at it, Bret. I'll support it."

"I might take you up on that, Frank."

"Freebooters!" said Frank. "Confounded nerve of the man. He was talking about my reception team."

From the next room the operator called, "They've put the searchlights on!"

Frank said, "Tell them to put the big radar jammer on. I don't want any arguments: the Piranha!" The army hated using the Piranhas because they jammed the radars on both sides of the line. "Now!" said Frank.

The first searchlight came on, spluttering and hissing, and its beam went sweeping across the carefully smoothed soft earth ahead of them. Now neither Max nor Bernard could hope that they'd get through undetected.

Bernard went flat on the ground but Max was a tough old veteran, and he went running on into the darkness behind the searchlight beam, confident that the region around the beam was darkest to the eyes of the guards.

The Grenzpolizei up in the tower were caught by surprise. They were both young conscripts, sent here from the far side of the country and recommended for this special job after their good service in the Free German Youth. There had been an alert, two in fact. Their sergeant had read the teleprinter message aloud to them to be sure they understood. But alerts were commonplace. None of the Grepos took them too seriously. Since the boys had arrived here six months ago there had been nine emergencies, and every one of them had turned out to be birds or rabbits tripping the wires. No one tried to get through nowadays, no one with any sense.

On the western side of the Wall, Frank's reception team—Tom Cutts and Gabby Green—had come up very close by that time. They weren't directly in Frank's employ, they were specialists. Despite being in their middle thirties, they were, according to their papers, junior officers of the Signal Corps. With them was a genuine soldier, Sergeant Powell, who was a radar technician. His job was to make sure nothing went wrong with their equipment, although, as he'd told them quite frankly, if something did go wrong with it, it was unlikely that he'd be able to repair it there in the slit trench. It would have to go back to the workshop, and then probably to the manufacturer.

These "freebooters" had been dug in a long time, dressed in their camouflage battle dress, faces darkened with paint, brown knitted hats pulled down over the tops of their ears. Helmets were too heavy and, if you dropped them, dangerously noisy. It was a curious fact that they were safer dressed as soldiers than as civilians. Those Grepos over there were cautious about shooting soldiers, and soldiers on both sides of the Wall were garbed almost identically.

They didn't speak very often. Every sound carried a long way at night, and they'd worked together often enough to know what had to be done. They'd manhandled the little

radar set forward and got the antenna into a favorable position ahead of them as soon as darkness came the previous
evening, and then spent all night with the set, watching the
movements of the vehicles and the guards. Both men were
wearing headphones over their knitted hats, and Gabby,
whose taciturn disposition had earned him his nickname, had
his eye to the big Hawklite image-intensifying scope.

"Yes," he said suddenly, the rubber-sided microphone
clamped tight to his mouth. "One! No, two of them. One
running . . . the other on the ground. Jesus!"

The searchlight had come on by that time, but it provided no help for anyone trying to see what was happening.

"And there go the infrared lights too. My, my, they are
getting serious," said Gabby calmly. "Can we jam?" Tom had
already tuned the jammer to the required wavelength, but it
was a low-power machine that would only affect the small
sets. "I'll have to go forward. I can't get it from here."

Tom said nothing. They'd both hoped that it wouldn't
be necessary for either of them to cross into DDR territory.
Over the last year they'd had a couple of close shaves, and
their opposite numbers—the two-man team responsible for
the stretch of Wall to the north—had both been killed after
one of them stepped on a mine that had been "accidentally"
left on the west side of the Wall when DDR repair parties had
finished work.

Tom Cutts's misgivings would have been confirmed had he
had a chance to see into the Russian Electronic Warfare Support Vehicle that was parked out of sight behind the dog
kennels. Inside its darkened interior a senior KGB officer
named Erich Stinnes could just about fit between the collection of electronic equipment. His face was tense and the
lenses of his glasses reflected the screen of a battlefield radar

far more sophisticated than the "man-portable" infantry model that the two "freebooters" had placed into position.

"One of them is moving forward," the Russian army operator told Stinnes. The blip that was Gabby glowed brighter as he scrambled from his trench and exposed more of his body to the radar.

The EW support vehicle provided more than one indication of what was happening in the sector. There was a thermal imager rendering the warmth of human bodies into revealing white blobs, and now that the infrared lights were on, the automatic IR cameras were taking a picture every five seconds. If it came to an inquiry, there would be no chance of proving the DDR was in the wrong.

"Let him come," said Stinnes. "Perhaps the other fellow will come too. Then we'll have both of them."

"If we wait too long, the two spies will escape," said the Grepo officer who'd been assigned to give Stinnes all the help and assistance he required.

"We'll get them all, never fear. I've followed them a long way. I'll not miss them now." They didn't realize how circumscribed he was by the rules and regulations. But without breaking any applicable rules, Stinnes had supervised what can only be described as an exemplary operation. The two agents arrested in Schwerin had yielded the details of their rendezvous after only two hours of interrogation. Furthermore, the methods used to get this "confession" were by KGB standards only moderately severe. They had detected the two "Englishmen" at the log cabin and kept them under observation all the way here. Apart from the misrouting of a helicopter by some imbecilic air traffic controller, it was a textbook operation.

"The second man is coming forward," said the operator.

"Colossal!" said Stinnes. "When he gets to the wire you can shoot." The unrepaired gap in the Wall had enabled them to plan the fields of fire. It was like a shooting gallery: four men trapped inside the enclosure formed by the Wall, the wire, and the building materials.

It was Gabby who shot the searchlight out. Afterward Bernard said it was Max, but that was because Bernard wanted to believe it was Max. The death of Max distressed Bernard in a way that few other losses had ever done. And of course Bernard never shook off the guilt that came from his being the only survivor.

He saw the other three die: Max, Tom, and Gabby. They were cut to pieces by a heavy machine gun, an old reliable 12.7mm Degtyarev. The noise of the machine gun sounded very loud in the night air. Everyone for miles around heard it. That would teach the English a lesson.

"Where's the other one?" said Stinnes, still watching the radar screen.

"He tripped and fell down. Damn! Damn! Damn! They're putting the big jammer on now!" As the two men watched, electronic clutter came swirling up from the bottom of the screen: major interference like a snowstorm.

"Where is he?" Stinnes slapped his hand upon the blinded radar and its useless screen and shouted, "Where?" The men in the bunker with him jumped to their feet and stared straight ahead, standing stiff and upright as good Russian soldiers are taught to stand when a senior officer shouts at them.

Thus it was that Bernard Samson drowned in the clutter and scrambled away unhurt, running like he'd never run before, eventually to fall into the arms of Sergeant Powell.

"Shit!" said Powell. "Where did you come from, laddie?" For one wild moment Sergeant Powell thought he'd captured a prisoner. When he realized it was only an escaper from the East he was disappointed. "They said there'd be two. Where's the other fellow?"

3

Cambridgeshire, England:
February 1978

SIR HENRY CLEVEMORE WAS NOT RENOWNED FOR HIS HOSPI-
tality, and rightly so. As the Director-General of the Secret
Intelligence Service, he carefully chose the people he met and
where he met them. The chosen venue was unlikely to be
his own home, a magnificent old timber-and-stone mansion,
a large part of which dated from the sixteenth century. In any
case Lady Clevemore did not enjoy entertaining; she never
had. If her husband wanted to entertain he could use the
Cavalry Club in Piccadilly. It was more convenient in every
way.

So it was a flattering exception when on a chilly February
evening he invited Bret Rensselaer, a senior departmental
employee, to drive out to Cambridgeshire for dinner.

Sir Henry appeared to have overlooked the fact that
Rensselaer was the sort of American who liked to wear formal
clothes. Bret had agonized about whether to wear a tuxedo
but had finally decided on a charcoal suit, tailored in that
waisted style so beloved of Savile Row craftsmen, lightly
starched white shirt, and gray silk tie. Sir Henry was wearing
a blue lounge suit that had seen better days, a soft-collared
shirt with a missing button, and highly polished scuffed

black brogues that needed new laces.

"For God's sake, why a woman?" said Bret Rensselaer more calmly than his choice of words suggested. "Why ever did you choose a woman?" This was not the way departmental staff usually addressed Sir Henry Clevemore, but Bret Rensselaer had a special relationship with the Director-General. It was a relationship based to some extent on Bret Rensselaer's American birthplace, his influential friends in the State Department, and to some extent on the fact that Bret's income made him financially independent of the Secret Intelligence Service and of most other things.

"Do smoke if you want to. Can I offer you a cigar?"

"No, thank you, Sir Henry."

Sir Henry Clevemore sat back in his armchair and sipped his whisky. They were in the drawing room staring at a blazing log fire, having been served a grilled lobster dinner and the last bottle of a particularly good Montrachet that Sir Henry had been given by the Permanent Under-Secretary.

"It doesn't work like that, Bret," said Sir Henry. He was being very conciliatory. They both knew how the Department worked but the D-G was determined to be charming. Charm was the D-G's style, unless he was in a hurry. "I wasn't looking for a female," said Sir Henry. "Of that you can be quite sure. We have a number of people . . . I know you wouldn't expect to go into details . . . but several. Men and women we have been patiently playing to the Russians for years and years, in the hope that one day we'd be able to do something spectacular with one of them."

"And for her that day has come?" said Bret. He extended an open hand toward the fire to sample its heat. He hadn't been really warm since getting out of his car. That was the trouble with these stately old homes, they could never be efficiently heated. Bret wished he'd taken a chance on what sort of evening it would be and worn warmer, more casual clothes, a tweed jacket perhaps. Sir Henry probably wouldn't have cared or even noticed.

The D-G looked at Bret to see if there was an element of sarcasm there. There wasn't; it was just another example of the American directness of approach that made Bret the best candidate for looking after a really promising double agent. He turned on the charm. "You started this thing rolling, Bret. When, a few weeks back, you floated this idea I didn't think much of it, to tell you the truth. But I began looking at possible candidates, and then other things happened that made it seem more and more possible. Let's just say that the float has twitched, which may be a sign the other side is ready to bite. It may be, that's all."

Bret suppressed a temptation to say that in too many such situations the Russians had devoured the bait so that the Department had reeled in an empty hook. Everything indicated that the Russians knew more about turning agents than their enemies did about running them. "But a woman . . ." said Bret, to remind the D-G of his other reservation.

"An extraordinary woman, a brilliant and beautiful woman," said the D-G.

"Enter Miss X." Bret's feelings were bruised by the D-G's stubborn reluctance to provide more details of this candidate. He'd expected to have a say in the final selection process.

"*Mrs.* X, to be precise."

"All the more reason that the Russkies will not want her over there. It's a male-dominated society, and the KGB is the last place we'll ever see change."

"I'm not sure I agree with you there, Bret." The D-G permitted himself a little grin. "They *are* changing their ways. So are we all, I suppose." He couldn't hide the regret in his voice. "But my feeling is that we'll gain from their old-fashioned entrenched attitudes. They will never suspect that we would try to plant a woman into the Committee."

"No. I guess you're right, Sir Henry." It was Bret's turn to wonder. He liked the way the old man's mind worked. There were people who said the D-G was past it—and the D-G sometimes seemed to go to great lengths to encourage that misreading—but Bret knew from firsthand experience that, for the overall strategy, the old man had an acute mind that was tortuous and sometimes devious. That was why Bret had taken his idea about "getting a man into the Kremlin" to Sir Henry in person.

The old man leaned forward. The polite preliminaries, like the evening itself, were coming to an end. Now they were talking as man and master. "We both know the dangers and difficulties of working with doubles, Bret. The Department is littered with the dead bodies of people who have misread their minds."

"It goes with the job," said Bret. "As the years go by, a double agent finds it more and more difficult to be sure which side he's committed to."

"They forget which side is which," said the D-G feelingly. He reached forward for a chocolate-covered mint and unwrapped it carefully. It was the very devil trying to do without a cigar after dinner. "That's why someone has to hold their hand, and get inside their head, and keep them politically motivated. We learned that from the Russians, Bret, and I'm sure it's right."

"But it was never my idea to become the case officer," said Bret. "I have no experience." He said it casually, without the emphasis that would have been there had he been determined not to take on this new task the D-G was giving him. That softening of attitude was not lost upon the D-G. That was the first hurdle.

"I could give you a million reasons why we don't want an experienced case officer on this job."

"Yes," said Bret. The sight of a known case officer in

regular contact with an agent would ring every alarm bell in the KGB.

But the D-G did not put that argument. He said, "I'm talking about an agent whose position and opportunity may be unique. So this is a job for someone very senior, Bret. Someone who knows the whole picture, someone whose judgment I can trust completely." He put the mint in his mouth and screwed the wrapper up very tight before placing it in the ashtray.

"Well, I don't know if I fit that picture, Sir Henry," said Bret, awkwardly adopting the role that Englishmen are expected to assume when such compliments are paid.

"Yes, Bret. You fit it very well," said the old man. "Tell me, what do you see as our most serious shortcomings?"

"Shortcomings? Of the British? Of the Department?" Bret didn't want to answer any questions of that sort, and his face showed it.

"You're too damned polite to say, of course. But a fellow less inhibited than you, speaking recently of British shortcomings, told me that we British worship amateurism without having intuitive Yankee know-how. Result: disaster."

Bret said nothing.

Sir Henry went on. "Whatever the truth of that assessment, I am determined that this operation is going to be one hundred percent professional, and it's going to have the benefit of that 'can do' improvisation for which your countrymen are noted." He raised his hand in caution. "I will still need to go through the details of your plan. There are a number of points you raise that are somewhat contentious. But you realize that, of course."

"It's a ten-year plan," said Bret. "They're in a bad way over there. A well-planned attack on their economy, and the whole damned communist house of cards will collapse."

"Collapse? What does that mean?"

"I think we could force the East German government into allowing opposition parties and free emigration."

"Do you?" The idea seemed preposterous to the old man, but he was too experienced in the strategies of White-hall to go on record as a disbeliever. "The Wall comes down in 1988? Is that what you are saying?" The old man smiled grimly.

"I don't want to be too specific, but look at it this way. In World War Two, RAF Bomber Command went out at night and dropped bombs on big cities. Subsequent research discov-ered that few of the bombers had found their way to the assigned targets, and the few that did bombed lakes, parks, churches, and wasteland so that only one bomb in ten was likely to hit anything worthwhile."

Sir Henry was fingering the colored cards on which there were graphs and charts showing various statistics, mostly con-cerned with the skilled and unskilled working population of the German Democratic Republic. "Go on, Bret."

"When Carl Spaatz and Jimmy Doolittle took the U.S. Eighth Air Force into the bombing campaign, they went in daylight with the Norden bombsight. Precision bombing. And they had a plan. They bombed only synthetic-oil plants and aircraft factories. No wasted effort and the effect was mortal."

"Weren't they called panacea targets?"

"Only by the ones who were proved wrong," said Bret sharply.

"I seem to remember some other aspects of the strategic bombing campaign," mused the old man, who hadn't missed the point that the RAF got it wrong and the Americans got it right. Neither did he miss the implication that the efforts of the SIS had up till now been ninety percent futile.

"I wouldn't want to labor the comparison," said Bret, who belatedly saw that this example of the RAF's wartime

inferiority to U.S. bombing performance might be less com-
pelling to an English audience. He tried another approach.
"That 'Health and Hospitalization' chart you're holding
shows how many physicians between the ages of twenty-five
and thirty-five are holding the East German health scheme
together. I estimate that the loss of twenty-five percent of that
labor force—that's the red sector on the chart—would make
the regime start closing hospitals, or hospital departments, at
a rate that would be politically unacceptable. Or take civil
engineering. Look at the chart I see on the table there. . . ."

"I've looked at the charts," said Sir Henry, who had
never liked visual presentations.

"We must target the highly skilled labor force. It will put
acute strain on the communist society because the regime
tells its people that they endure low wages and a drab life to
get job security and good social services: health care, urban
transportation, and so on. A brain drain is something they
can't counter. It takes seven years to train a physician, an
engineer, or a chemist; even then you need a bright kid to
start with."

"You mentioned political opposition," said the D-G. He
put Bret's charts aside.

Bret said, "Yes. We also have to change our disdainful
attitude toward these small East German opposition groups.
We must show a little sympathy, advise the church groups
and political reformers, help them get together. Did you see
my figures for church denominations? The encouraging thing
the figures demonstrate is that we can forget the rural areas;
Protestants in the large cities will give us enough of the sort
of people we want, and we can reach townspeople more easily."

"Strategic bombing. Ummm," said the D-G. Even the
Cabinet Secretary might see the logic of that approach when

he was being told about all the extra money that would be needed.

"And the people we want are the people in demand in the West. We don't have to invent any fancy high-paid jobs for the people we entice away. The jobs are here already." Bret pulled out another sheet. "And see how the birthrate figures help us?" Bret held up the graph and pointed to the curving years of the early eighties.

"How do we get them here?"

Bret grabbed another chart. "These are people leaving East Germany for vacations abroad. I've broken them down according to the country they vacation in. Under the West German constitution, every one of those East Germans is entitled to a West German passport on demand."

The D-G stopped Bret's flow with a gesture of his hand. "You are proposing to offer a crowd of East German holiday-makers getting off a bus in Morocco a chance to swap their passports? What will the Moroccan immigration authorities say about that?"

Bret gave a fixed smile. It was typical of the old man that he should take a country at random and then start nit-picking. "At this stage it would be better not to get bogged down in detail," he replied. "There are many ways for East German citizens to get permission to travel, and the numbers have been going up each year. The West German government press for a little more freedom every time it forks out donations to that lousy regime over there. And remember, we're after the middle classes—respectable family men and college-educated working wives—not blue-denim, long-haired hippy Wall-jumpers. And this is exactly why we need Mrs. X over there, looking at the secret police files and telling us where the effective opposition is: who to see, where to go, and how to apply the pressure."

"Tell me again. She's to . . . ?"

"She must get access to the KGB files on opposition groups, who they are and how they operate: church groups, democrats, liberals, fascists, even communist reformers. That's the best way we can evaluate whom we should team up with and prepare them for real opposition. And we need to know how the Russian army would react to widespread political dissent."

"You're the right man for Mrs. X," said Sir Henry. He remembered the PM saying that every Russian is at heart a chess player, and every American is at heart a public-relations man. Well, Bret Rensselaer's zeal did nothing to disprove that one. The sheer audacity of the scheme, plus Bret's enthusiasm, was enough to persuade him that it was worth a try.

Bret nodded to acknowledge the compliment. He knew there were other things that had influenced the old man's decision. Bret was American. And if Sir Henry was persuaded by Bret's projections for the East German economy, then Bret must be the prime choice to run the agent too. He had a roomful of experts in statistics, banking, economics, and even an expert in "group and permutation theory" he'd raided from the cryptanalysts. Bret's economic analysis department was a success story. It would make perfect deep cover for a case officer. And since a woman was involved there was another advantage. Now that he was separated from his wife, Bret could be seen in the company of a "brilliant and beautiful woman" without anyone thinking they were discussing their work.

"I take it that Mrs. X has managed without a case officer for a long time," said Bret.

"Yes, because Silas Gaunt was involved. You know what Gaunt is like. He squeezed a promise from me that nothing would be on paper and that he would be the only contact."

"Literally the only contact?" said Bret, without dreaming for a moment that the answer would be in the affirmative.

"Literally."

"Good God! So why . . . ?"

"Bring someone else in now? Well, I'll tell you. Gaunt only comes up to town once a month, and I'm not sure that even that isn't too much for him."

And of course Silas Gaunt was a dedicated exponent of the sort of public school amateurism that the D-G apparently had rejected. "Has something happened?"

Bret's reaction confirmed the D-G's belief that this was the right man for the job. Bret had instinct. "Yes, Bret. Something has happened. Some wretched Russian wants to defect."

"And?"

The D-G sipped some whisky before saying, "And he's made the approach to Mrs. X. He took her aside at one of those unacknowledged meetings those Foreign Office fellows like to arrange with our Russian friends. I have never known anything good to come from them yet."

"A KGB man wants to defect." Bret laughed.

"Yes, it's a good joke," said the D-G bitterly. "I wish I were in a position to join in the merriment."

"I'm sorry, sir," said Bret. "Was this a high-grade Russian?"

"Pretty good," said the D-G guardedly. "His name is Blum, described as third secretary, working in the service attaché's office: almost certainly KGB. The contact was made in watertight circumstances," he added.

"She'll have to tell them," said Bret without hesitation. "Watertight or not, she'll have to turn him in."

"Ummm." Bret Rensselaer was completely cold-blooded, thought the D-G. It wasn't an attractive characteristic, but for this job it was just the ticket.

"Unless you want to throw away all those years of good work."

"You haven't heard all the circumstances, Bret."

"I don't have to hear all the circumstances," said Bret. "If you don't turn in that Russkie, you will erode the confidence of your agent."

"This particular Mrs. X—"

"Never mind the psychologist's report," said Bret. "She'll know that you measured the risk, that you put her in the scales, with this Russian defector in the other pan."

"I don't see it that way."

"Never mind how *you* see it. In fact, never mind the way it really is. We are sitting here talking about an agent whom you call 'unique.' Right?"

"Whose position and opportunity may be unique."

"May be unique. Okay. Well I'm telling you that if you compromise her, in even the slightest degree, in order to play footsie with a Russian agent, Mrs. X will never deliver one hundred percent."

"It might go the other way. Perhaps she'll feel distressed that we sacrificed this Blum fellow," said the D-G gently. "Already she's expressed her concern. Remember, it's a woman."

"I'm remembering that. She must contact them right away and reveal Blum's approach to her. If you show any hesitation in telling her that, she'll deeply resent your inaction for ever after. A woman may express her concern, but she doesn't want to be neglected in favor of a rival. In hindsight it will infuriate her. Yes, I'm remembering it's a woman, Sir Henry."

"This fellow Blum might be bringing us something very good," said the D-G.

"Never mind if he's bringing an inside line to the Politburo. You'll have to choose one or the other: not both." The two men looked at each other. Bret said, "I take it that Mrs. X is separated from her husband?"

The D-G didn't answer the question. He sat back and

sniffed. After a moment's thought he said, "You're probably right, Bret."

"On this one, I am, sir. Never mind that I don't know Mrs. X; I know that much about women."

"Oh, but you do."

"Do?"

"You *do* know Mrs. X. You know her very well."

The two men looked at each other, both knowing that the old man would only divulge the name if Bret Rensselaer agreed to take on the job of running her.

"If you think I'm the right person for the job," said Bret, yielding to the inevitable. They'd both known he'd have to say yes right from the very beginning. This wasn't the sort of job you posted on the bulletin board.

"Capital!" said the D-G in the firm bass tone that was the nearest he ever got to expressing his enthusiasm. He looked at his watch. "My goodness, it's been such a splendid evening that the time has flown."

Bret was still waiting to hear the name, but he responded to his cue. He got to his feet and said, "Yes, I must be going."

"I believe your driver is in the kitchen, Bret."

"Eating? That's very civil of you, Sir Henry."

"There's nowhere round here for a chap to get a meal." Sir Henry pulled the silk cord, and a bell jangled somewhere in a distant part of the house. "We're in the wilds here. Even the village shop has closed down. I don't know how on earth we'll manage in future," he said, without any sign that the problem was causing him great stress.

"It's a magnificent old house."

"You must come in summer," said Sir Henry. "The garden is splendid."

"I would like that," Bret responded.

"Come in August. We have an open day for the local church."

"That sounds most enjoyable." Bret's enthusiasm dampened as he realized that the D-G was inviting him to be marshaled around the garden with a crowd of gawking tourists.

"Do you fish?" said the D-G, shepherding him toward the hall.

"I never seem to have enough time," said Bret. He heard his driver at the door. In a moment the servants would be in earshot and it would be too late. "Who is it, sir? Who is Mrs. X?"

The D-G looked at him, relishing those last few moments and anticipating Bret's astonishment. "Mrs. Samson is the person in question."

The door opened. "Mr. Rensselaer's car is here, sir." Sir Henry's butler saw the look of dismay on Bret's face and wondered if he was not well. Perhaps it was something about the food or the wine. He'd wondered about that Montrachet; in the same case he'd come upon a couple of corked bottles.

"I see," said Bret Rensselaer, who didn't see at all and was even more surprised than Sir Henry thought he would be. All sorts of thoughts and consequences were whirling around in his mind. Mrs. Bernard Samson. My God! Mrs. Samson had a husband and young children. How the hell could it be Mrs. Samson?

"Good night, Bret. Look at all those stars. . . . It will freeze hard tonight unless we get the rain those idiots on the TV keep forecasting."

Bret almost got back out of the car. He felt like insisting that he needed another half an hour to discuss it all. Instead he dutifully said, "Yes, I'm afraid so. Look here, sir, we can't possibly give Bernard Samson the German Desk in view of what you've told me."

"You think not? Samson was the only one to get across alive the other night, wasn't he?"

"Yes, that's right."

"What bad luck. It was the other one—Busby—we

needed to talk to. Yes, that's right: Samson. No proper school-
ing, of course, but he has flair and deserves a shot at the
German Desk."

"I was going to make it official tomorrow."

"Whatever you say, old chap."

"It's unthinkable with this other business on the cards.
From every point of view . . . unthinkable. We'd better give
the desk to Cruyer."

"Can he cope?"

"With Samson as an assistant he'll manage." Bret shifted
position on the car seat. He began to think that the D-G had
planned all this, knowing Bernard Samson was about to be
promoted. He'd invited Bret out here to dinner just to prevent
his appointing Samson and thus threatening the prospect of
the big one: putting Mrs. Samson into "the Kremlin." The
cunning old bastard.

"I'll leave it with you," said the D-G.

"Very well, sir. Thank you. Good night, Sir Henry."

The D-G leaned into the car. "Oh, yes. On that matter
we discussed: not a word to Silas Gaunt. For the time being
it's better he doesn't know you're a party to it."

"Is that wise, sir?" said Bret, piqued that the D-G had
obviously passed it off as his own idea when talking to
"Uncle" Silas.

The D-G knew what was going through Bret's mind. He
touched the side of his nose. "You can't dance at two weddings with one bottle of wine. Ever hear that little proverb?"

"No, sir."

"Hungarian."

"Yes, sir."

"Or Romanian, or Croatian. One of those damned countries where they dance at weddings. Get started, old chap.
You've got a long journey and I'm getting cold."

Sir Henry slammed the door and tapped the roof of the
car. The car moved away, its tires making loud crunching

noises on the gravel roadway. He didn't go back into the house; he watched the car until it disappeared around the bend of the long drive.

Sir Henry rubbed his hands together briskly as he turned back and went indoors. All had gone well. It would need a lot of tough talking to get it all approved, but Sir Henry had always been good at tough talking. Bret Rensselaer could do it if anyone could do it. The projections were convincing; this was the way to tackle the German Democratic Republic. And it was Bret's idea, Bret's baby. Bret had the right disposition for it: secretive, obsessional, patriotic, resourceful, and quick-witted. He'd cottoned on to the fact that we couldn't have Samson running the German Desk while his wife was defecting; that would be a bit too much. Yes, Bret would do it.

So why did the Director-General still have these odd reservations about what he'd set in motion? It was because Bret Rensselaer was too damned efficient. Given an order, Bret would carry it out at all costs. The D-G had seen that determination before in rich men's sons, overcompensation or guilt or something. They never knew where to stop. The D-G shivered. It was cold tonight.

As the car turned onto the main road, Bret Rensselaer sank back into the soft leather and closed his eyes to think more clearly. So Mrs. Bernard Samson had been playing out the role of double agent for God knows how many years and no one had got even a sniff of it. Could it be true? It was absolutely incredible, but he believed it. As far as Mrs. Samson was concerned, Bret would believe anything. Fiona Samson was the most radiant and wonderful woman in the whole world. He had been secretly in love with her ever since the day he first met her.

4

Kent, England:
March 1978

"WE LIVE IN A SOCIETY FULL OF PREVENTABLE DISORDERS, preventable diseases, and preventable pain, of harshness and stupid, unpremeditated cruelties." His accent was Welsh. He paused; Fiona said nothing. "They are not my words, they are the words of Mr. H. G. Wells."

He sat by the window. A caged canary above his head seemed to be asleep. It was almost April; the daylight was fading fast. The children playing in the garden next door were being called in to bed; only the most restless of the birds were still fidgeting in the trees. The sea, out of sight behind the rise, could be faintly heard. The man named Martin Euan Pryce-Hughes was a profile against the cheap net curtains. His almost completely white hair, long and inclined to waviness at the ends, framed his head like a helmet. Only when he drew on his curly pipe was his old, tightly lined face lit up.

"I thought I recognized the words," said Fiona Samson.

"The Fabian movement, fine people. Wells the theorist, the great George Bernard! . . . The Webbs, God bless their memory. Laski and Tawney. My father knew them all. I remember many of them coming to the house. Dreamers, of course. They thought the world could be changed by writers and poets and printed pamphlets." Without looking at her he smiled at the idea, and she could hear his disdain in the way he said it. His voice was low and attractive with the sonorous call of the Welsh valleys. It was the same accent she'd heard in the voice of his niece, Dilwys, with whom she'd shared rooms at Oxford. The Department had instructed her to encourage that friendship, and through Dilwys she'd met Martin.

On the bookshelf there was a photo of Martin's father. She could see why so many women had thrown themselves at him. Perhaps free love was a part of the Fabian philosophy he'd so vigorously embraced when young. Like father, like son? Within Martin too there was a violent and ruthless determination. And when he tried he could provide a fair imitation of his father's famous charm. It was a combination that made both men irresistible to a certain sort of young woman. And it was a combination that brought Martin to the attention of the Russian spy apparatus even before it was called the KGB.

"Some people are able to do something," said Fiona, giving the sort of answer that seemed to be expected of her. "Others talk and write. The world has always been like that. The dreamers are no less valuable, Martin."

"Yes, I knew you'd say that," he said. The way he said it scared her. There often seemed to be a double meaning—a warning—in the things he said. It could have meant that he'd known she'd say it because it was the right kind of banality, the sort of thing a class enemy would say. She infinitely preferred to deal with the Russians. She could understand the Russians—they were tough professionals—but this embittered idealist who was prepared to do their dirty work for them was beyond her comprehension. And yet she didn't hate him.

"You know everything, Martin," she said.

"What I don't know," he admitted, "is why you married that husband of yours."

"Bernard is a wonderful man, Martin. He is brave and determined and clever."

He puffed his pipe before replying. "Brave, perhaps. Determined, undoubtedly. But not even his most foolish friends could possibly call him clever, Fiona."

She sighed. They had been through such exchanges before. Even though he was twice her age he felt he must compete for her. At first he'd made sexual advances, but that was a long time ago; he seemed to have given up on that score. But he had to establish his own superiority. He'd even shown a bitter sort of jealousy toward her father when she'd mentioned the amazing fur coat he'd given her. Any fool can make money, Martin had growled. And she'd agreed, in order to soothe his ego and pacify him.

Only lately had she come to understand that she was as important to him as he was to her. When the KGB man from the Trade Delegation appointed Martin to be her father figure, factotum, and cutout, he'd never in his wildest dreams hoped that she would wind up employed by the British Secret Intelligence Service. This amazing development had proceeded with Martin monitoring and advising her on each and every step. Now that she was senior staff in London Central, Martin could look back on the previous ten years with great satisfaction. From being no more than a dogsbody for the Russians, he'd become the trustee of their most precious investment. There was talk of giving him some award or KGB rank. He affected to be uninterested in such things but the thought of it gave him a warm glow of pleasure, and it might prove an advantage when dealing with the people at the London end. The Russians respected such distinctions.

She looked at her watch. How much longer before the courier came? He was already ten minutes late. That was unusual. In her rare dealings with KGB contacts they'd always been on time. She hoped there wasn't trouble.

Fiona was a double agent, but she never felt frightened. True, Moscow Centre had arranged the execution of several men over the previous eighteen months—one of them on the top deck of a bus in Fulham, killed with a poison dart—but they had all been native Russians. Should her duplicity be detected, the chances of their killing her were not great, but they would get her to tell them all she knew, and the prospect of a KGB interrogation was terrifying. But for a woman of Fiona's motivation it was even worse to contemplate the ruin of years and years of hard work. Years of preparation, years of establishing her bona fides. Years of deceiving her husband, her children, and her friends. And years of enduring the poisonous darts that came from the minds of men like Martin Euan Pryce-Hughes.

"No," Martin repeated as if relishing the words. "Not even his best friends could call Mr. Bernard Samson clever. We are lucky you married him, darling girl. A really clever man would have realized what you are up to."

"A suspicious husband, yes. Bernard trusts me. He loves me."

Martin grunted. It was not an answer that pleased him. "I see him, you know," he said.

"Bernard? You see Bernard?"

"It's necessary. For your sake, Fiona. Checking. We make contact now and again. Not only me but other people too."

The self-important old bastard. She hadn't reckoned on that, but of course the KGB would be checking up on her, and Bernard would be one of the people they'd be watching. Thank God she'd never confided anything to him. It wasn't that Bernard couldn't keep a secret. His head buzzed with them. But this was too close to home. It was something she had to do herself without Bernard's help.

"I suppose you know they have given me a direct emergency link with a Moscow case officer?" She said it in a soft and suggestive voice that would have well suited the beginning of a fairy story told to a wide-eyed and attentive audience of five-year-olds.

"I do," he said. He turned and gave her a patronizing smile, the sort of smile he gave all women who aspired to be his comrades. "And it's a fine idea."

"Yes, it is. And I shall use that contact. If you or Chesty or any of those other blundering incompetents in the Trade Delegation contact any of the people round me with a view to checking, or any other stupid tricks, they'll have their balls ripped off. Do you understand that, Martin?"

She almost laughed to see him: mouth open, pipe in hand, eyes popping. He'd not seen much of that side of her; for him she usually played the docile housewife.

"Do you?" she said, and this time her voice was hard and spiteful. She was determined that he'd answer, for that would remove any last idea that she might have been joking.

"Yes, Fiona," he said meekly. He must have been instructed not to upset her. Or perhaps he knew what the Centre would do to him if Fiona complained. Lose her, and he'd lose everything he cherished.

"And I do mean stay away from Bernard. You're amateurs; you're not in Bernard's league. He's been in the real agent-running business from the time he was a child. He'd eat people like you and Chesty for breakfast. We'll be lucky if he's not alerted already."

"I'll stay away from him."

"Bernard likes people to take him for a fool. It's the way he leads them on. If Bernard ever suspected . . . I'd be done for. He'd take me to pieces." She paused. "And the Centre would ask why."

"Perhaps you're right." Pretending indifference, the man

got to his feet, sighed loudly, and looked out the window over the net curtain as if trying to see the road down which the messenger would come.

It was possible to feel sorry for the old man. Brilliant son of a father who had been able effortlessly to reconcile his loudly espoused socialist beliefs with a lifetime of high living and political honors, Martin had never reconciled himself to the fact that his father was an unscrupulous and entertaining rogue blessed with unnatural luck. Martin was doggedly sincere in his political beliefs, diligent but uninspired in his studies, and humorless and demanding in his friendships. When his father died, in a luxury hotel in Cannes in bed with a wealthy socialite lady who ran back to her husband, he'd left Martin, his only child, a small legacy. Martin immediately gave up his job in a public library to stay at home and study political history and economics. It was difficult to eke out his tiny private income. It would have been even more difficult except that, at a political meeting, he encountered a Swedish scholar who persuaded him that helping the USSR was in the best interests of the proletariat, international socialism, and world peace.

Perhaps the cruelest jest that fate had played on him was that after seeing his father thrive in the upper middle-class circles into which he'd shoved his way, Martin—educated regardless of expense—had to find a way of living with those working classes from which his father had emerged. His rebellion had been a quiet one. The Russians gave him a chance to work unobserved for the destruction of a society for which he felt nothing. It was this secret knowledge that provided for him the strength to endure his austere life. The secret Russians and, of course, the secret women. It was all part of the same desire really, for unless there was a husband or lover to be deceived the affairs gave him little satisfaction, sexual or otherwise.

From the household next door there came the sudden sound of a piano. These were tiny cottages built a century ago for agricultural workers in the Kent fields, and the walls were thin. At first there came the sort of grandiose strumming that pub pianists affect as an overture for their recitals, and then the melody resolved into a First World War song, "The Roses of Picardy." The relaxed jangle of the piano completed the curious sensation Fiona already had of going back in time, waiting, trapped in the past. This was the long, peaceful, and promising Edwardian springtime that everyone thought would never turn cold. There was nothing anywhere in sight to suggest they were not sitting in this parlor sometime at the century's beginning, perhaps 1904, when Europe was still young and innocent, London's buses were horse-drawn, HMS *Dreadnought* unbuilt, and Russia's permanent October still to come.

"They're never late," she said, looking at her watch and trying to decide on an explanation that would satisfy her husband if he arrived home before her.

"You seldom deal with them," he said. "You deal with me, and I'm never late."

She didn't contradict him. He was right. She very seldom saw the Russians; they were all too likely to be tailed by MI5 people.

"And when you do contact them, this is the sort of thing that happens." He was pleased to show how important he was in the contact with the Russians.

She couldn't help worrying about this Russian who'd tried to defect. He'd seen she was alone and had approached her in what seemed to be an impulsive decision. Had it all been a KGB plot? She'd seen him only that once, but he'd seemed such a genuine decent man. "It must be difficult for someone like Blum," she said.

"Difficult in what way?"

"Working in a foreign country. Young, missing his wife, lonely. Perhaps shunned because he is Jewish."

"I doubt that very much," he said. "He was a third secretary in the attaché's office; he was trusted and well paid. The little swine was determined to prove how important he was."

"A Russian Jew with a German name," said Fiona. "I wonder what motivated him."

"He won't try that stunt again," said Martin. "And the attaché's office will get a rocket from Moscow." He smiled with satisfaction at the idea. "Everything will go through me, as it was always done before Blum."

"Could it have been a trick?"

"To see if you are loyal to them? To see if you are really a double, working for your SIS masters?"

"Yes," she said. "As a test for me." She watched Martin carefully. Bret Rensselaer, her new case officer, who was now masterminding this double life of hers, said he was certain that Blum was acting on orders from Moscow. Even if he wasn't, Rensselaer had explained, it's better we lose this chance of a highly placed agent than endanger you. Sometimes she wished she could look at life with the same cold-blooded detachment that Bret Rensselaer displayed. In any case, there was no way she could defy him, and she wasn't sure she wanted to. But what would happen now?

Martin gave a cunning smile as he reflected upon this possibility. "Well if it was a test, you came through with flying colors," he said proudly.

She realized then, for the first time, what a stalwart supporter she had in him. Martin was committed to her. She was his investment, and he'd do anything rather than face the idea that his protégée was not the most influential Soviet agent of modern history.

"It's getting late."

"There, there. We'll get you to the train on time. Bernard's coming back from Berlin today, isn't he?"

She didn't answer. Martin had no business asking such things, even in a friendly conversational way.

Martin said, "I'm watching the time. Don't fret."

She smiled. She regretted now the way she had snapped at him. The Russians had decided that the two of them were joined by a strong bond of affection, that Martin's avuncular manner, as well as his unwavering political belief, was an essential part of her dedication. She didn't want to give them any reason to reexamine their theory.

She looked around the tiny room and wondered if Martin lived here all the time or whether it was just a safe house used for other meetings of this sort. It seemed lived in: food in the kitchen, coal by the fireplace, opened mail stuffed behind the clock that ticked away on the mantelpiece, a well-fed cat prowling through a well-kept garden, a clipper ship in full sail on the wall behind spotless glass. There were lots of books here. Lenin and Marx and even Trotsky stared down from the shelves, along with his revered Fabians, an encyclopedia of socialism, and Rousseau and John Stuart Mill. Even the tedious works of his father. It was an artful touch. Even a trained security man was unlikely to recognize a KGB agent who was so openly familiar with the philosophies of the dissidents, revisionists, and traitors. That was Martin's cover: a cranky, old-fashioned, and essentially British left-wing theorist, out of touch with modern international political events.

"It's my son, Billy. His throat was swollen this morning," said Fiona and looked at her watch again. "Nanny should be taking him to see the doctor about now. Nanny is a sensible girl."

"Of course she is." He didn't approve of nannies and other domestic slaves. It took him back to his own childhood and the muddled emotions about his father that he found so difficult to think about. "He'll be all right."

"I do hope it's not mumps."

"I'm watching the time," he said again.

"Good reliable Martin," she said.

He smiled and puffed his pipe. It was what he wanted to hear.

It was a long-haired youth who arrived on a bicycle. He propped it against the fence and came down the garden to go *rat-a-tat* on the front door. The canary awoke and jumped from perch to perch so that the cage danced on its spring. Martin answered the door and came back with a piece of paper he'd taken from a sealed envelope. He gave it to her. It was the printed invoice of a local florist. Written across it in felt-tip pen it said, *The wreath you ordered has been sent as requested.* It bore the mark of a large oval red rubber stamp: PAID.

"I don't understand," she said.

"Blum is dead!" he announced softly.

"My God!" said Fiona.

He looked at her. Her face had gone completely white. "Don't worry," he said soothingly. "You've come out of it as pure as the driven snow." Then he realized it was the news of Blum's death that had shocked her. In a desperate attempt to comfort her he said, "Our comrades are inclined to somewhat operatic gestures. They have probably just sent him home to Moscow."

"Then why . . . ?"

"To reassure you. To make you feel important." He took a cloth from the shelf and wrapped it carefully around the bird cage to provide darkness.

She looked at him, trying to see what he really believed, but she couldn't be sure.

"Believe me," he added. "I know them."

She decided to believe him. Perhaps it was a feminine response, but she couldn't shoulder the burden of Blum's death. She wasn't brave about the sufferings that were inflicted upon others, and yet that was what this job was all about.

She got home after half-past eight, and it was only about ten minutes later that Bret Rensselaer phoned with a laconic, "All okay?"

"Yes, all okay," she said.

"What's wrong?"

Bret had heard something in her voice. He was so tuned to her emotions that it frightened her. Bernard would never have guessed she was upset. "Nothing's wrong," she said carefully, keeping her voice under control. "Nothing we can speak about."

"Are you alone?"

"Yes."

"Usual time, usual place."

"Bernard's not here yet. He was due back."

"I arranged something . . . delayed his baggage at the airport. I wanted to be sure you were home and it was all okay."

"Yes. Good night, Bret." She hung up. Bret was doing it for her sake, but she knew he enjoyed showing her how easy it was for him to control her husband in that way. He was another of those men who felt bound to demonstrate some aspect of their power to her. There was also an underlying sexual implication that she didn't like.

5

Somerset, England:
Summer 1978

THE DIRECTOR-GENERAL WAS AN ENIGMATIC FIGURE WHO was the subject of much discussion among the staff. Take, for instance, that Christmas when a neat panel bearing the poker-work motto ONLY IGNORANCE IS INVINCIBLE was hung in a prominent position on the wall beside his desk. The questions arising from that item were not stilled by the news that it was a Christmas present from his wife.

His office was a scene of incomparable chaos into which the cleaning ladies made only tentative forays. Books were piled everywhere. Most of them were garlanded with colored slips of paper indicating rich veins of research that had never been pursued beyond the initial claims staked out for him by his long-suffering assistant.

Sir Henry Clevemore provided a fruitful source for Bret Rensselaer's long-term anthropological study of the English race. Bret had categorized the D-G as a typical member of the upper classes. This tall shambling figure, whose expensive suits looked like baggy overalls, was entirely different from anyone Bret knew in the United States. Apart from his other eccentricities, the D-G encouraged his staff to believe that he was frail, deaf, and absentminded. This contrived role certainly seemed to provide for him a warm loyalty that many a tougher leader would have envied.

One of the disagreeable aspects of working in close cooperation with Sir Henry was the way he moved about the country in such a disorganized and unplanned style that Bret found himself chasing after him to rendezvous after rendezvous in places both remote and uncomfortable. Today they were in Somerset. In the interests of privacy the D-G had taken him to a small wooden hut. It overlooked the sports field of a minor public school of which the D-G was a conscientious governor. The D-G had made a speech to the whole school and had lunch with the headmaster. Bret at short notice had had to be driven down at breakneck speed. There had been no time for lunch. No matter; on a hot day like this Bret could miss lunch without feeling deprived.

The school's surroundings provided a wonderful view of mighty trees, rolling hills, and farmland. This was the English countryside that had inspired her great landscape painters; it was brooding and mysterious despite the bright colors. The newly cut grass left a pungent smell on the air. Although not normally prone to hay fever, Bret found his sinuses affected. Of course, it was an affliction aggravated by stress and it would be unwise to conclude that the prospect of this meeting with the Director-General had played no part in bringing on the attack.

Through the cobwebbed window two teams of white-clad teenagers could be seen going through the arcane gymnastics that constitute a cricket match. Entering into the spirit of this event, the D-G had changed into white trousers, a linen jacket that had yellowed with age, and a panama hat. He had seated himself in a chair through which he could see the game. The D-G had wiped his piece of window clear but Bret saw the scene through the grimy glass. Bret was standing, having declined to sit on the cushioned oil drum that the D-G had indicated. Bret kept half an eye on the game, for the D-G referred to it at intervals, seeking Bret's opinions about the way it was being played.

"Tell the husband," said the D-G, shaking his head sadly, "and it's no longer a secret."

Bret didn't answer immediately. He watched the left-handed batsman thumping his bat into the ground and waiting for the ball to come. The fielders were well spread out, anticipating some heavy swings. Bret turned to the D-G. He'd already made it clear that in his opinion Fiona Samson's husband would have to be told everything: that she was a double agent and was being briefed to go over there. "I'll see her later today," Bret said. He'd hoped to get the D-G's okay, and then he would brief Bernard Samson too. By tonight it would all have been done.

"What are you doing with her at present?" the D-G asked.

Bret walked away a couple of paces and then turned. From that characteristic movement the D-G knew that unless he nipped it in the bud he was going to get one of Bret's renowned lectures. He settled back in his chair and waited for an opportunity to interrupt. Bret had no one else he could explain things to. The D-G knew that providing Bret with a sounding board at frequent intervals was something he could not delegate. "If we are going to place her in the sort of role where she will pull off the sort of coup we're both hoping for, we can't just leave things to chance."

"Bravo!" said the D-G, reacting to a stroke that sent the ball to the far boundary. He turned to Bret and smiled. "We haven't got too much time, Bret."

"We need ten years, Director, maybe twelve."

"Is that your considered opinion?"

Bret looked at the old man. They both knew what he was thinking. He wanted Fiona Samson in place before he came up for retirement. Forget the modest, self-effacing manner that was his modus operandi; he wanted glory. "It is, Sir Henry."

"I was hoping for something earlier than that."

"Sir Henry, Fiona Samson is nothing more than an agent-in-place as far as Moscow is concerned. She has never done anything. She has never delivered."

"What do you have in mind?"

"She should be posted to Berlin. I want them to have a closer look at her."

"That would speed things up. They would start thinking of getting her over there quickly."

"No, they want her in London where the big stuff is hidden." Bret got out his handkerchief and self-consciously blew his nose, making as little noise as possible. "Forgive me, Sir Henry. I think the newly cut grass . . ."

"Then why Berlin?"

"She will have to do something for them."

The D-G looked at him and pulled a face. He didn't like these stunts, which required that the KGB were given things. They were always given good things, convincing things, and that meant things the Department should keep to itself. "What?"

"I haven't got as far as that, Director, but we'll have to do it, and do it before the end of the year."

"Would you acquaint me with a little of your thinking? Wait one moment, this fellow is their fast bowler."

Bret waited. It was a hot day. The grass was bright green and the boys in their cricket clothes made it the sort of English spectacle that under other circumstances Bret might have relished. The ball came very fast but bounced and went wide. Bret said, "Mrs. Samson goes to Berlin. During her time there she gives them something substantial . . ."—Bret paused while the D-G winced at the thought—" . . . so that we have a big inquiry from which she emerges safe. Preferably with their help.''

''You mean they arrange that one of their agents takes the blame?''

''Well, yes. That, of course, would be ideal,'' said Bret.

The D-G was still watching the match. ''I like it,'' he said, without turning around.

Bret smiled grimly. It was an uphill struggle, but that was something of an accolade coming from Sir Henry Clevemore, although it could of course have been prompted by some cricketing accomplishment that Bret failed to understand. He said, ''Mrs. Samson comes back here to London and they tell her to keep still and quiet.''

''That's one year,'' the D-G reminded him.

Bret said, ''Look, sir. We can deliver Mrs. Samson to them right away; of course we can. She's like a box of nuts and bolts: an all-purpose agent they can use anywhere. But that's not good enough.''

''No,'' said the D-G, watching the cricketers and wondering what was coming.

''We must take this woman and clear her mind of everything she knows.''

''Classified material?''

''I'm already making sure she sees nothing that would affect the Department.''

''How did she take that?''

''We have to make our plans as if she will be interrogated . . . interrogated in the cellars at Normannenstrasse.'' In the silence that followed, a big fly buzzed angrily against the window glass.

''It's a nasty thought.''

''The stakes are high, Sir Henry. But we're playing to win.'' He looked around the hut. It was insufferably hot and the air was perfumed with linseed oil and weedkillers for the lawn. Bret opened the door to let a little air in.

The D-G looked at Bret and said, "A good thunderstorm would clear the air," as if this were something he could arrange. Then he added, "You're making me wonder whether a woman is right after all."

"It's too late to change the plan now."

"Surely not?" Even the D-G was feeling the heat. He mopped his brow with a red silk handkerchief that had been protruding from his top pocket.

"Mrs. Samson knows what we intend. If we change to another agent, our plan is known to her. I have shown her the figures and the graphs. She knows that the skilled and professional labor force is our target. She knows that we want to bleed their essential people, and she knows the sort of opposition groups we intend to support over there."

"Wasn't that a little premature, Bret?"

"It will all depend upon her once she's there. She must understand our strategy so well that she can improvise her responses."

"I suppose you're right. I wish it were you explaining it all to the Cabinet Secretary next week, all your charts and mumbo-jumbo. . . . You see, Bret, if we don't persuade him to go along with the fundamental idea . . . do you have an operational name yet?"

"I thought it was better not to ask the Department for an operational name."

"No, no, no, of course not. We'll think of one. Something that suggests the weakening of the economy without prejudicing the security of our operation. Any ideas?"

"I thought Operation Hemorrhage? Or Operation Bleeder?"

"Blood, casualties. No. And bleeder is an English expletive. What else?"

"Leaker?"

"Vulgarism with connotations of urinating. But Sinker might do."

"Sinker then. Yes, of course, Sir Henry."

"Oh, my God, this fellow is useless. Left-handed, and look at the way he's holding the bat." He turned to Bret. "You understand what I mean about persuading him to the basic idea?"

Bret understood exactly. If the Cabinet Secretary didn't go for the economic target, they'd start having second thoughts about using Bret. Mrs. Samson would be provided with a different case officer.

The D-G said, "There still remains the problem of the Soviets engaging her for operational service over there. We can't leave that to chance."

"Agent X has to be created from scratch," said Bret, having decided that naming Mrs. Samson might be creating doubts in the D-G's mind. "I must deliver to them an agent who is so knowledgeable and experienced in one specific field of activity that they will have to put her in the place we want."

"You've lost me now," said the D-G, without taking his eyes from the cricket.

"I shall spend this year studying the Russian links with the East German security police, particularly the KGB–Stasi operational command in Berlin. I'll come to you with a complete picture of their strengths and weaknesses."

"Can you do that?"

"I spent most of last week reading operational briefs. Give me a closer look at the command structure over there, and my analysts could build a detailed picture. It will take time, but we'll get what we need."

"Their security is good," said the D-G.

"We will be trying to discover what they need . . . the things they *don't* know. I have good people in my section.

They're used to sifting through figures and building a picture of what is going on."

"For economics, yes. It's possible to do that with statistics of banking, exports, imports, and credit and so on because you're dealing with hard facts. But this is far more complex."

"With respect, Sir Henry, I think you're wrong," said Bret Rensselaer, with a slight rasp to his voice that betrayed his tension.

The D-G forgot the cricket and looked at him. Bret's eyes were wide, his smile fixed, and a wavy lock of his blond hair had fallen out of place. Until this very moment he hadn't realized to what extent Bret Rensselaer had become consumed by his new task.

For the first time the D-G began to feel that this mad scheme might actually work. What a staggering coup it would be if Bret really did it: planting Mrs. Samson into the East Berlin command structure where she could use their own secret records on protest groups, dissidents, and other anti-communists to guide the Department as they planned the economic destruction of the communist regime! "Time will tell, Bret."

"Yes indeed, sir."

The D-G nodded to Bret. Was it the prospect of moving from the vitally important, but somewhat wearisome, world of committees into the more dashing excitement of operations that had so animated him? Or had the departure of his wife, now seemingly a permanent separation, provided him with more time? Or had the loss of his spouse to another man made it necessary for Bret to prove himself? Perhaps all of those. And yet the D-G had not allowed for Mrs. Fiona Samson and the influence her participation had had upon Bret Rensselaer's strength and determination.

"Give me a free hand, sir."

"But ten years . . ."

"Perhaps I shouldn't have given a time frame." His sinuses hurt. He felt an overwhelming need to blow his nose again and did so.

The D-G watched him with interest. He didn't know Bret had sinus problems. "Let's see how it goes. What about finance?" He turned back to the cricket. The left-handed batsman had hit a superb catch—up, up, up it went and curved down like a mortar bomb—but luckily for him there was no fielder able to reach it. One fellow ran in for it but was unable to judge where it would land. The ball hit the ground, and there was a concerted groan.

"I'll need money, and it must not be routed through Central Funding."

"There are many ways."

"I have a company."

"Do it any way you like, Bret. I know you won't waste it. What are we talking about? Roughly?"

"A million sterling in the first year. Double that in the second and all subsequent years, adjusted for inflation and the exchange rate. No vouchers, no receipts, no accounts."

"Very well. We'll have to concoct a route for the money." The D-G shielded his eyes with a folded newspaper. The sun had come around to shine through the window. "Have I forgotten anything?"

"No, sir."

"I'll not keep you then. I'm sure you have things to do. Look at this. The captain has put another fast bowler on. And he's rather good. What do you think, Bret?"

"Very good indeed, sir. Very fast. A problem will arise when we send Mrs. Samson to work in Berlin. Will they continue to use this Welsh socialist as the contact? If not, we'll have to be very careful setting up the new one. Berlin is quite different from London: everyone knows everyone."

"And everyone hates everyone," said the D-G. "You'd

better have her float the possibility before them and see what reaction she gets."

"The Welshman is very supportive," said Bret. "He's determined to believe that she's the KGB superspy. She's his protégée. She could make a terrible blunder and he'd still hold on to his trust in her. But when she goes to Berlin they'll be more suspicious. You know how it is when someone's treasure is scrutinized by a rival. The KGB will turn her over."

The D-G frowned. "Is this some narrative form of second thinking?" he said tartly.

"No, sir. I am sure the Berlin tour is an essential part of the plan. I'm simply saying that she will be under a lot of stress."

"Out with it then." The D-G stood tall and bent his head to see Bret over his glasses.

"We're asking her to give up her husband and children. Her colleagues will despise her. . . ."

"When did she say all this to you?"

"She hasn't said it."

"She hasn't expressed doubts at all?"

"Not to me. She's a patriot; she has a wonderful sense of purpose."

The D-G sniffed. "We've seen patriots change their minds, haven't we, Bret?"

"She won't," said Bret firmly and certainly.

"Then what is it?"

"The husband. He should be told. He will be able to give her the sort of help and encouragement she'll need. She'd go east knowing that her husband will be keeping her family intact. It would be something for her to hang on to."

"Oh, don't let's go through that again, Bret." The D-G turned away.

"You said I'd have a free hand."

He swung around, and when he spoke there was a hard note in his voice. "I don't remember saying any such thing. You asked for a free hand; almost everyone in the Department asks for a free hand at some time or another. It makes me wonder what they think I am paid to do. I will of course give you as much freedom as possible. I'll guard you from the slings and arrows of outrageous officialdom. I'll give you non-voucher funds and I'll listen to any crackpot idea you bring me. But a secret is a secret, Bret. The only chance she has of coming out of this in one piece is to have her husband overwhelmed and horrified when she goes over there. That will be the ace card that saves her. Never mind help and encouragement, I want Bernard Samson to become demented with rage." He used the newspaper to slam at the buzzing fly and after a couple of swipes the fly fell to the floor. "Demented with rage!"

"Very well, sir. I'm sure you know best." Bret's tone did nothing to make the D-G think he'd changed his opinion.

"Yes, I do, Bret. I do know best." They both watched as the batsman swung and then seemed to leap backward, blundering into the wicket so that the stumps were knocked asunder. A fast ball had hit him in the belly. He went down clutching his stomach and rolled about in agony. "Left-handed," pronounced the D-G without emotion. The other cricketers gathered around the fallen boy but no one did anything; they just looked down at him.

"Yes, sir," said Bret. "Well, I'll be off."

"She might waver, Bret. Agents do when the time gets close. If she does you'd better make sure she toes the line. There is too much at stake now for a last-minute change of cast."

Bret stood there in case the D-G had more to say. But the D-G flicked his fingers to dismiss him.

Once outside Bret blew his nose again. Damn this grass;

he'd keep away from cricket matches on freshly mowed grass in future. Well, the old man could still provide a surprise or two, thought Bret. What a tough old bastard he was. Bernard must not be told under any circumstances. So that was what ONLY IGNORANCE IS INVINCIBLE meant. By the time he got to his car Bret's sinus problem was entirely gone. It was the stress that brought it on.

6

London:

August 1978

FIONA SAMSON, A THIRTY-ONE-YEAR-OLD CAREERIST, WAS a woman of many secrets and always had been. At first that had made her relish her demanding job in London Central— the most secret of all the government's secret departments— but as her role as a double agent developed and became more complex she found there were times when it all became too much for her. It has always been said that double agents eventually lose their own sense of direction and fail to distinguish which side they really work for, but for Fiona it was different. Fiona could not envisage ever becoming a supporter of communist regimes; her patriotism was a deeply rooted aspect of her upper-middle-class upbringing. Fiona's torment came not from political doubts. She worried that she would not be able to cope with the overwhelming task she'd been given. Bernard would have been perfect for such a double-agent role; like most men he could compartmentalize his brain and keep his family concerns quite separate from his work. Fiona could not. She knew that her task would become so demanding that she would have to neglect her husband and children more and more and finally, with no possible warning, leave them to fend for themselves. She would be branded a traitor and they would be spattered with the dirt. The thought of that distressed her.

Had she been able to discuss it with Bernard it might have been different, but authority had decreed that her husband should not know the plan. In any case she was not good at talking with Bernard. No less spirited than her extrovert sister, Tessa, Fiona's fires were damped down and seldom showed a flicker. Sometimes, or even often, Fiona would have enjoyed being like Tessa. She would have got great and immediate relief and satisfaction from the sort of public performance—displays of anger or exhilarated madness—for which her sister was famous, but there was no choice for her.

Fiona was beautiful in a way that had sometimes separated her from other women. Fiona's beauty was a cold, perfect radiance of the sort that is to be seen in the unapproachable models posing with such assurance in glossy magazines. Her brain was cold and perfect too; her mind had been bent by pedantic university teachers to think in terms of male priorities, and she had sacrificed many of the unbridled joys of femininity in order to become a successful surrogate male. Fiona's miseries, her tensions, and her times of great happiness were shared only reluctantly—sometimes grudgingly— with those around her. Emotion of any sort was always to be hidden; her father had taught her that. Her father was an insensitive and opinionated man who had wanted sons, something he explained to his two children—both daughters—at every opportunity, and told them that boys didn't cry.

Fiona's marriage to Bernard Samson had changed her life forever. It was love at first sight. She'd never met anyone like Bernard before. A big bearlike man, Bernard was the most masculine person she'd ever met. At least he had the qualities that she thought of as being masculine. Bernard was practical. He could fix any sort of machine and deal with any sort of people. He was of course a male chauvinist, categorical and opinionated. He never thought of helping in the house and couldn't even boil an egg successfully. On the other hand he was constantly cheerful, almost never moody, and quite without malevolence. Inclined to be untidy, he gave no thought to his clothes or his appearance, never put on airs or graces, and while enjoying art and classical music he was in no way "intellectual" or "artistic" in the way that so many of her male acquaintances were determined to be.

Fiona's husband was the only person she'd ever met who completely disregarded other people's evaluation of him. Bernard was a devoted father, more devoted to the children than Fiona, if the truth was faced. And yet he was not the unmotivated drifter that her father had warned her about. Bernard was driven by some force or thought or belief in the way that great artists are said to be, and woe betide anyone who got in his way. Bernard was not an easy man to live with. He'd been brought up in postwar Berlin—his father a senior intelligence officer—in an atmosphere of violence and betrayal. He was by nature tough and undemonstrative. Bernard had killed men in the course of duty and done it without qualms. He was well adjusted and enjoyed a self-confidence that Fiona could only wonder at and envy.

The burden of their marriage came from the fact that Bernard was far too much like Fiona. Neither of them found it easy to say the things that wives and husbands have to say to keep a marriage going. Even "I love you" did not come easily from Bernard's lips. Bernard really needed as a wife some noisy extrovert like Fiona's sister, Tessa. She might have found a way of getting him out of his shell. If only Bernard could be foolish and trivial now and again. . . . If only he could express doubts or fears and come to her for comfort. Fiona didn't need a strong silent man; she was strong and silent herself. It was difficult for such a man to be really sympathetic to a woman's point of view. Bernard would never understand the way that women would cry for "nothing."

Lately, there had been many occasions when the complex tangle of Fiona's working life became too much for her. She was using tranquilizers and sleeping tablets with a regularity that she'd never needed before. Bernard had found her crying several times when he'd come into the house unexpectedly. She had told him she was under treatment from her gynecologist; embarrassed, dear old Bernard had not pursued it further.

When she found herself weighed down by her thoughts, and the worries would not go away, Fiona would find an excuse to leave the office and walk to the Waterloo mainline railway station. She'd come to like it. Its size suggested permanence, while its austere design and girder construction gave it anonymity: a vast waiting room made from a construction kit. Coming through the dirty glass of its roof the daylight was gray, dusty, and mysterious. Today, despite the rain, she had benefited from the walk from the office. Now she sat on a bench near number-one platform and quietly cried her heart out. No one seemed to notice these emotional outbursts, except once when a lady from the Salvation Army offered her a chance for prayer at an address in Lambeth. Sobbing was not so unusual on Waterloo Station platforms. Separations were common here, and nowadays it was a place where the homeless and hungry were apt to congregate. London airport was probably just as good a place to go for the purpose of weeping, but that provided too great a chance of seeing someone she knew. Or, more exactly, of someone she knew seeing her. And Waterloo Station was near the office, and there was tea and newspapers, taxicabs, and metered parking available. So she went to number-one platform and cried.

It was the prospect of leaving Bernard and the children, of course. They would end up hating her. Even if she did everything that was expected of her and returned a heroine, they would hate her for leaving them. Her father would hate her too. And her sister, Tessa. And what would happen to the children? She had asked Bret that, but he had dismissed her fears. The children would be cared for in the manner that her sacrifice and heroism deserved, he'd said in that theatrical style that Bret could get away with because he was so damn certain. But how sincere was he? That worried her sometimes. Sincere or not, she couldn't help thinking that her children would be forgotten once she was working in the East. Billy would survive boarding school—and perhaps even flourish there—but Sally would find such an environment unendurable. Fiona had resolved not to put her children through the sort of childhood that she had hated so much.

Bret told her that the only thing that frightened her more than the prospect of finding that her husband and children wouldn't be able to manage without her was the prospect of finding that they could. Bastard! But perhaps there was a glimmer of truth there. Perhaps that was the permanent crippling dilemma that motherhood brought.

She had never been a very good mother, and that knowledge plagued her. She'd never wanted motherhood in the way Tessa so desperately did. Fiona had never liked babies: her friends' babies had appalled her with their endless demands and the way they completely upset the household. Babies cried very loudly; babies vomited very frequently and dirtied their diapers very stenchfully. Even when hugging her own babies she had always been uneasy in case her dress was soiled. The children's nurse had seen that right from the start. Fiona still remembered the accusing look in her eyes. That look said, I am their real mother; you are not fit to look after them.

Fiona was useless with children, but she didn't want to be barren either. She wanted to tick motherhood off the list.

She worried about them always, and wanted them to be clever at school, and most of all she looked forward to sharing their lives with them when they grew up. But it was now that they needed her so much. Perhaps it was not too late. Perhaps she should walk out of London Central and apply herself to the children as she had applied herself to her studies and her work.

Never a day went past but she told herself that she should go to Bret and tell him she had changed her mind. But each time she spoke to him—long before she could bring the conversation to the point she wanted—he persuaded her that her first duty was to her country and the Department. Even the Director-General had spoken with unusual gravity about this scheme to get her into position as a field agent, a field agent of prime importance. It would, of course, show that a woman could bring off an intelligence coup as well as any man. That, more than anything else, had helped her keep going when her spirits were low.

Since the beginning of the year her tiffs and differences with Bernard had multiplied. It wasn't all Bernard's fault; things had been difficult for him too. Operation "Reisezug" had been something of a disaster; three of their own people killed, or so the rumor said. Max Busby was carrying a lot of the material in his memory, and Max never came back. Bernard didn't talk about it, but anyone who knew him could see how shaken he was.

Bernard was now officially "rested" from field work and, in what might have been an effort to comfort her, Bret Rensselaer had let slip the fact that the Department had decided that Bernard should spend the rest of his life behind a desk. Not the German Desk. Dicky Cruyer, a vain and shallow man, had got the German Desk. Bernard was in line for it and would have done it with more skill and intelligence, but Dicky had the administrative experience as well as the per-

sonality and background that the Department favored for top
jobs. Bernard said that all Dicky had was the right old-school
tie, but Bernard could be a bit touchy about such things.
She'd wondered if Bret had decided against Bernard's promo-
tion because of her assignment, but Bret insisted that it was
a decision made at the top.

She was sure that her painful domestic life could be
transformed if Bret would let her confide in her husband. As
it was, she couldn't always account for her movements. It had
been bad enough when she'd only had to have the odd meeting with Martin Euan Pryce-Hughes. Now there were countless covert briefings by Bret and a lot of studying to do. And
the studying was of material that she mustn't let Bernard
catch sight of. Bernard was smart and quick. She wouldn't
have to make many mistakes for him to guess what was happening, and the D-G had taken it upon himself to tell her that
if Bernard discovered what was planned the whole thing was
off.

Poor Bernard, poor Billy, poor Sally. She sat on the bench
at Waterloo and thought about them all. She felt drained and
ill. Crying released the tension within her but did nothing to
alleviate the pain. She cried some more, in the constrained,
unobtrusive, and dignified way she'd learned to cry at boarding school, and stared across the concourse where people were
hurrying for their commuter trains or saying their farewells.
She told herself that their troubles might be worse than hers
but that did nothing to help; in fact it made her feel even
more dejected.

The weather did nothing to cheer her. It was one of those
miserably cold and rainy days that so often punctuate an
English summer. Everyone was bundled into coats and
scarves, and the cold damp air contributed to Fiona's chilly
gloom. Trains arrived; trains departed. A young woman asked
her for the time, and an elderly couple walked past arguing

vociferously. Pigeons and sparrows came gliding down from the girders of the roof, encouraged by a bearded man on a bench nearby who threw crumbs to them. She sat there watching the birds for what seemed a long time.

"Pardon me, madam." Fiona looked up to see two men, a uniformed railway policeman and a man in civilian clothes. "You were talking to a young woman a few minutes back?" It was the policeman who spoke.

At first she thought they were going to tell her to move on, or arrest her for soliciting, or make some other sort of fuss, but then she realized that the man in civilian clothes was not a policeman. "Yes?"

"In a dark blue coat, with a red silk scarf? Dark hair. Pretty girl." It was the man in the camel-hair coat speaking. He'd taken his hat off in a courteous gesture that surprised her, and she noticed the way he gripped it in his suntanned hand. He seemed nervous.

"She just asked me the time. She caught the train for Southampton," said Fiona. A train announcement, resonant and unintelligible, interrupted her and she waited for it to finish. "At least, that's what she said she was going to do."

"She had a big green plastic bag with a shoulder strap," said the man.

It was, she decided, a question. "She had a bag," said Fiona. "I didn't notice anything about it."

"Are you all right, madam?" said the policeman. He'd noticed her reddened, tear-filled eyes.

"I'm quite all right," she said firmly. She looked at her watch and got to her feet to show that she was about to leave.

The policeman nodded. He wanted to believe her; he wasn't looking for more trouble. "It's the gentleman's daughter," explained the policeman.

"My name's Lindner. Adam Lindner. Yeah, she's only sixteen," said the man. "She ran away from home. She looks older." He had a soft transatlantic accent that she couldn't place.

"We'll phone Southampton," said the policeman briskly. "They'll pick her up when the train gets there."

"Was there anyone with her?" asked the father authoritatively.

Fiona looked at him. He was tall and athletic; in his late thirties perhaps. His mustache was full but carefully trimmed. He had doleful eyebrows and a somewhat squashed nose in a weather-beaten face. He was handsome in a seemingly uncontrived way, like the tough-guy film stars whose photos she'd pinned above her bed at school. His clothes were expensive and too perfect, the style that foreigners selected when they wanted to look English: a magnificent camel-hair overcoat, a paisley-patterned tie, its knot supported by a gold pin through the shirt collar, and shiny Oxford shoes. "Yes," she said, "there was a man with her."

"A black man?"

"Perhaps. I didn't notice. Yes, I believe so."

"It makes it easier from our point of view," said the policeman.

A gust of wind lifted discarded newspapers and other litter, enough to scare the birds. Conversation faltered, as English conversations do when minds turn to the delicate and devious rituals of leave-taking.

"We have your phone number, Mr. Lindner," said the policeman. "As soon as we hear from Southampton, the desk sergeant will phone." It ended there. The policeman had other work to do.

"If that's all?" said Fiona moving away. "I have to get a taxi."

"I'm going to Maida Vale," the man said to Fiona. "Can I drop you off anywhere?" She still couldn't recognize the accent. She decided he was a merchant seaman or oil worker, paid off after a long contract and enjoying a spending spree.

"It's all right," she said.

"No, please. It's pouring rain again and I would appreciate company."

Both men were looking at her quizzically. She resented the way that men expected women to explain themselves, as if they were second-class citizens. But she invented an explanation. "I was seeing someone off. I live in Marylebone. I'll get a cab."

"Marylebone? I go right through it." And then, "Thank you, constable, you've been most helpful."

"Children do funny things," said the policeman as he took his leave. "It will be all right. You'll see."

"It was bad luck," said the man. "Another fifteen minutes and we would have stopped her." Fiona walked toward the cab rank and he fell into step alongside her. "Will you look at that rain! You'd better ride with me." There were about fifty people standing in line for taxis and no taxis in sight.

"Very well. Thank you."

They walked to his car, talking about the treacherous English weather. His manner now was ultra-considerate and his voice was different in some way she could not define. She smiled at him. He opened the door for her and helped her into the seat. It was a Jaguar XJS convertible: gray, shiny, and very new. "I suppose Mrs. Lindner is worried," said Fiona. As the engine started with a throaty roar the stereo played a bar or two of a Strauss waltz before he switched it off, twisted his neck, and carefully backed out of the parking place.

"There is no Mrs. Lindner," he said while craning to see behind the car. "I was divorced five years back. And anyway this girl is not my daughter; she's my niece."

"I see."

Down the ramp and through the cars and buses he went

with no hesitation; he didn't drive like a man unaccustomed
to London traffic. "Yeah, well, I didn't want to say it was my
niece. The cops would immediately think it was some bimbo
I was shacked up with."

"Would they?"

"Sure they would. Cops think like that. And anyway I'm
a Canadian and I'm here without a work permit." He bit his
lip. "I can't get tangled up with cops."

"Did you give them a false name?"

He looked around at her and grinned admiringly. "As a
matter of fact, I did."

She nodded.

"Oh, boy! Now you're going to turn out to be a cop from
the Immigration Department. That would be just my sort of
lousy luck."

"Would it?"

"Yeah. It would." A pause. "You're not a cop. I mean,
you're not going to turn me in, are you?"

"Are you serious?"

"You're damn right, I'm serious. I was working in Syd-
ney, Australia, and the hall porter turned me in. Two heavies
from Immigration were waiting in my suite when I got back
that night. They'd gone through my mail and even cut the
lining out of my suits. Those Aussies are rough. Mind you,
in Uruguay in the old days it was worse. They'd shake you
down for everything you had."

"It sounds as if you make a study of illegal immigration."
She smiled.

"Hey, that's better! I thought maybe you'd given up
smiling for Lent. Immigration? Yes, well, my cousin buys and
sells airplanes. Now and again I take time off to deliver one
of them. Then maybe I get tempted to take on a few local
charters to make a little extra money."

"Is that what you're doing in London?"

My real name is Harry Kennedy. Good to know you, Mrs. Samson. Yeah, the girl will maybe come out okay. I've seen cases like this before. No call to worry her folks. It's not drugs. At least I hope to God it's not drugs. She doesn't get along very well at school. She's not the academic sort of kid. She likes parties and music and dancing; she's always been like that, from the time she was tiny. She doesn't like reading. Me, I couldn't live without books."

"Me too."

"You weren't seeing anyone off, were you?" he said suddenly without looking away from the road.

"No."

"Why were you at the station then?"

"Does it matter?"

"I'm being very nosy. But it was my good fortune that Patsy spoke with you. I couldn't help wondering about you."

"I wanted to think."

"Sad thoughts?"

"Everything is relative. I have a good life. No complaints."

"You need a drink."

She laughed. "Perhaps I do," she said.

He drove right through Marylebone. The traffic was light. She should have said something, made him take her directly home, but she said nothing. She watched the traffic and the rain, the grim-faced drivers, and the endless crowds of drenched people. He pulled into the parking lot behind a well-kept block of flats in Maida Vale. "Come up and have a drink," he said.

"I don't think so," she said and didn't move.

"There's no need to be afraid. Like I told you, my name is Harry Kennedy. I have an allergic reaction to work permits, but other than that I'm quite harmless. I work in the psychiatric department of the St. Basil Clinic in Fulham. Eventually

"Airplanes? No, that's just my playtime. I learned t
in the air force and kept it up. In real life I'm a psychiatr.

"This niece of yours . . . was she another inventio
asked Fiona.

"No, I'm not completely off my trolley. She's the daug
ter of my cousin Greg, and I was supposed to be looking aft
her in London. I guess I'll have to phone Winnipeg and te
Greg she's jumped ship."

"Will he be angry?"

"Sure, he'll be angry, but he won't be surprised. He
knows she can be a pretty wild little girl."

"How come you . . . ?"

"Greg was in the air force with me, and he owns a big
slice of the airplane brokerage outfit."

"I see."

"Because I'm a psychiatrist, he thinks I can straighten
her out. Her local quack's treatment was just to keep doping
her with amitryptiline and junk like that."

"But you can't straighten her out either?"

"Girls who . . ." The flippant answer he was about to give
died on his lips. "You really want to know? It could be she
has a schizophrenic reaction to puberty, but it will need
someone with a whole lot more specialized experience to
diagnose that one."

"Does her father know you think that?"

"I don't know what made me tell you. . . . No, it's too
early to tell Greg. It's a heavy one to lay on parents. I want
to talk to someone about her. I was trying to arrange for a
specialist to look at her without letting her catch on." He
stole another glance at Fiona. "Now it's my turn to guess
about you. I'll bet you're a student of philosophy. Am I right,
Miss . . . ?" he said with a big grin.

"Mrs. Samson. I'm married and I have two children."

"No fooling. Two children? They must be very young.

they will get me a work permit, and I will live happily ever after."

"Or perhaps move on to pastures new?"

"Could be."

"And you really are a psychiatrist?"

"It's not something I'd invent, is it?"

"Why not?"

"It's the ultimate deterrent to all social relationships. Look at the effect it's already having on you."

"One drink."

"And then home to husband and children," he promised.

"Yes," she said, although the children were being looked after by a competent nanny and Bernard was in Berlin for a job that would take three days.

Kennedy's flat was on the second floor. She followed him up the stairs. This block had been built in the nineteen thirties and, apart from a few chunks of granite chiseled from the façade by bomb fragments, it had survived the war intact.

"I'm renting this place from a rich ear, nose, and throat man at the clinic. He's in New York at Bellevue until next April. If they renew his contract he'll want to sell it." The apartment was big; in the thirties architects knew the difference between a bedroom and a cupboard. He took her damp raincoat and hung it on a bentwood rack in the hall. Then he removed his own coat and tossed his hat on a pile of unopened mail that had been placed alongside a bowl of artificial flowers on the hall stand. "I keep meaning to forward all that mail to him, but it's mostly opportunities to purchase vacations and encyclopedias from the credit card companies."

His three-piece suit—a chalk stripe, dark gray worsted—was cut in a boxy American style that made him look slimmer than he really was. On his vest there was a gold watch chain with some tiny gold ornament suspended from it.

He ushered her into the drawing room. It was spacious enough to take a baby grand piano, a couple of sofas, and a coffee table without seeming cramped. "Come right in. Welcome to Disneyland. Take a seat. Gin, whisky, vodka, vermouth . . . a martini? Name it." She looked around at the furnishings. Someone had gone to a lot of trouble to keep everything in sympathy with the art deco that had been in style when the block was built.

"A martini. Do you play the piano?"

He went into the kitchen and she heard him open the refrigerator. He returned with two frosted martini glasses, chilled gin, and chilled vermouth. Under his arm there was a box of snacks. He poured two drinks carefully. "I'm fresh out of olives," he said as he carried the drinks across to her. "The help eats them as fast as I buy them. She's Spanish. Yeah, I play a little."

"A quick drink and then I must go."

"Have no fear. I'll drive you home."

"It's an attractive room." She took the glass by its stem and held it against her face, enjoying the feel of its icy coldness.

"You like this art deco junk?" He drank some of his martini and then put the glass down, carefully placing it on a coaster. "The E.N.T. man inherited it. His parents were refugees from Vienna. Doctors. They got out early and brought their furniture with them. I had to take an oath about not leaving Coca-Cola glasses on the polished tables and not smoking."

"It's lovely."

"He's a sentimental kind of guy. It's okay, I guess, but I prefer something I can relate to. Have one of these." He indicated the snacks, tiny cheesy mouthfuls, in a freshly opened red box bearing a picture of an antique steamship on the Rhine.

"I'm not hungry."

"Would it help to talk about it?"

"No, I don't think so."

"You're a beautiful woman, Mrs. Samson. Your husband is a lucky man." He said it artlessly and was not self-conscious: no Englishman she'd met could deliver such compliments without bluster and embarrassment.

"I'm lucky too," she said quietly. She wished he wouldn't look at her. Her hair was a mess and her eyes were red.

"I'm sure you are. Is your drink all right? Too much gin?"

"No, it's just the way I like it." She drank some to show him that it was true. She was uneasy. After a few minutes of small talk—Kennedy had been discovering the pleasures of the opera—she said, "Perhaps you could ring for a taxi? They sometimes take ages to come at this time."

"I'll drive you."

"You must wait for the phone call from the police."

"You're right. But must you go so soon?"

"Yes, I must."

"Could I see you again?"

"That would be less wise."

"I'm delivering a Cessna to Nice next week—Friday, maybe Saturday—and collecting a Learjet. It's a sweet job; not many like that come along. There's a really good restaurant twenty minutes along the highway from Nice airport. I'll have you back in central London by six P.M. Now don't say no right away. Maybe you'd like to bring your husband or your children? It's a four-seater."

"I don't think so."

"Think it over. It could make just the sort of break that would do you good."

"Is that a medical opinion?"

"It sure is."

"It's better not."

"Let me give you my phone number," said Kennedy. Without waiting to hear what she decided, he gave her a printed card. "This lousy weather keeps up, maybe you'll feel like a spot of Riviera sunshine." She looked at the card: Dr. H. R. Kennedy and the Maida Vale address and phone number. "I had them done last month at one of these fast print shops. I was going to see patients here, but I decided not to."

"I see."

"It was against the terms of the lease, and I could see there would be arguments if my patients started using the parking spaces." He went to the phone and asked for a taxi. "They're usually very prompt," he said. "I have an account with them." Then he added thoughtfully, "And seeing patients here might have set the immigration guys on my tail."

"I hope your niece returns soon."

"She'll be okay."

"Do you know the man she's with?"

Kennedy paused. "He's a patient. At the clinic. He met her when she was waiting for me one afternoon."

"Oh."

"He can be violent. That's why the police were so good about it."

"I see."

"You helped me, Mrs. Samson. And I appreciate your keeping me company, I really do." The phone rang to say the cab was waiting outside. He helped her on with her coat, carefully making sure that her long hair was not trapped under the collar. "I would like to help you," he said. In bidding her a decorous goodbye, his hand held hers.

"I don't need help."

"You go to railway stations to hide your unhappiness. Don't you think a marriage in which a wife is frightened to be unhappy in the presence of her husband might leave something to be desired?"

Fiona found his apparent simplicity and honesty disarming. She had no great faith in psychiatry and in general she distrusted its practitioners, but she felt attracted to this amusing and unusual man. He was obviously attracted to her, but that had not made him fawn. And she appreciated the way that Kennedy so readily confided his fears of the Immigration Department and the trust he'd shown in her. It made her feel like a partner in his lawless activities. "Is that the sort of dilemma patients like me bring along to you?"

"Believe me, I have no patients who in any way resemble you, Mrs. Samson, and I never have had."

She gently pulled her hand away from his and went through the door. He didn't follow her, but when she glanced up, before getting into the taxi, she could see his face at the window.

She looked at her watch. It was late. Bernard tried to phone about this time each evening.

"Hello, sweetheart." To her astonishment she arrived home to find Bernard, Nanny, and the two children sitting around the little kitchen table. The scene was printed upon her memory for ever after. They were all laughing and talking and eating. The table displayed the chaos she had seen at Bernard's mother's house: tea in cups without saucers, teapot standing on a chipped plate, tinfoil frozen food containers on the tablecloth, sugar in its packet, a slab of cake sitting on the bag in which it was sold. The laughter stopped when she came in.

"We wondered where you'd got to," said Bernard. He was wearing corduroy trousers and an old blue turtleneck sweater she had twice thrown away.

"Mr. Samson said the children could eat down here," said the nanny nervously.

"It's all right, Nanny," said Fiona and went and kissed the children. They were newly bathed and smelled of talcum powder.

"You've got a cold nose," said Billy accusingly and then chuckled. He looked so like Bernard.

"You're rude," his little sister told him. She had been raised to the level of the table by sitting on a blue silk cushion from the drawing room sofa. Fiona noticed that a dollop of tomato sauce had fallen upon it but kept smiling as she gave her daughter a kiss and a hug. She had a special love for little Sally, who sometimes seemed to need Fiona in a way no one else had ever done.

Fiona embraced Bernard. "What a wonderful surprise. I didn't expect you until the weekend."

"I slipped away." Bernard put an arm around her, but there was a reluctance to his embrace. For some other wives such a hesitation might have been a danger signal. Fiona knew it was a sign that something had gone wrong in Berlin. A shooting? A killing? She looked at him to make sure he was not injured. She wouldn't ask him what had happened, they didn't talk about departmental matters unless they concerned the both of them, but she knew it would take a little time before Bernard would be capable of physical contact with her.

"You're all right?"

"Of course I'm all right." A smile did not hide the hint of irritation. He did not like her to show her concern.

"Will you have to go back?" The children were watching them both with great interest.

"We'll see." He contrived a cheerfulness. "Nothing will happen for a few days. They think I'm chasing around Bavaria."

She gave him another decorous kiss. She wished Bernard would not be so intractable. Deliberately disobeying instructions in order to come home early was flattering, but it was the sort of behavior that the Department found inexcusable. This was not the time to say that. "It's a lovely surprise," she said.

"Eat some dinner, Mummy," said Sally. "There's plenty."

"Mummy doesn't eat frozen meals, do you, Mummy?" said her brother.

Nanny, who had no doubt purchased the Delicious Ready-to-eat Country Farmhouse Dinner, looked embarrassed. Fiona said, "It depends."

"It's not meaty," said Billy, as if that were a recommendation. "It's all sauce and pasta." He pushed a spoon into the remains to show her.

"It's very salty," said Sally. "I don't like it."

The nanny took the spoon away from Billy and then went to get a cup and saucer for Fiona to have tea with them.

Fiona took off her coat and hat. Then she moistened a paper towel to see what could be done to remove the sauce from the silk cushion. She knew that in doing so she would be spoiling the *gemütlich* atmosphere into which she had intruded, but she simply could not sit down and laugh and talk and forget it. She couldn't. Perhaps that was what was wrong with her and with her marriage.

Before she could get started, Nanny poured tea for her and began clearing the table. Bernard leaned over and said to the children, "Now who's my first passenger on the slow train to Dreamland?"

"Me, Daddy, me!" They both yelled together.

Soon Fiona was left alone, dabbing at the stain on the cushion. From somewhere above she could hear the excited calls of the children as Bernard carried them up to bed. *"Choo-choo! Choo-choo!"*

Darling, darling Bernard. How she wished he could be a wonderful father without making her feel like an inadequate mother.

7

London:

September 1978

SYLVESTER BERNSTEIN WAS A FIFTY-YEAR-OLD AMERICAN.
Together with his wife he lived in a Victorian red-brick terrace
house in Battersea, one small room on each of three floors
with a kitchen and bathroom that had been added at the back
by a previous owner in the early seventies. Now that this
south side of the river had been invaded by affluent young
couples who'd discovered how close it was to central London,
the whole street was undergoing a transformation. There
were yellow-colored front doors, and even pink ones with
brass knockers, and nowadays more and more of the cars
parked nose to tail along the street were without rust. The
local "planning department" regulations prohibited the use
of these houses as offices, but Bernstein was confident that no
one would complain about the way he'd fixed up his garret
room with a typewriter, a couple of desks, two phone lines,
and a telex machine. Private investigators didn't spend much
time in offices, at least Sylvester Bernstein didn't.

Bernstein had been a CIA man for twenty-one years. He
took retirement after the wounds in his leg refused to heal.
He'd married a girl he'd met in Saigon, an English nurse
working for Christian Aid, and she suddenly decided that

they must live in England. At that time the dollar was high against sterling, so his retirement pay gave him enough to live well in London. When the dollar weakened, Bernstein was forced to go back to work. His contacts in Grosvenor Square helped him to get that elusive work permit, and he set up in business as Sylvester Bernstein, private investigator. But truth to tell, most of his clients came to him because of his long career as a CIA man. Some of those clients were still in the twilight world of "security"; people who wanted a job done while they remained at arm's length from it. The work Bernstein was doing for Bret Rensselaer was typical, and because he'd known Bret a long time, and because Bret was a demanding client, Bernstein did not have one of his subcontractors do the job for him. He did most of it personally.

They were sitting in the downstairs room. On the walls hung cheap Victorian prints of scenes from Walter Scott novels. The elaborate fireplace was complete with lily-patterned tiles and polished brass fender and all the fire irons. The iron grate, however, held not coal but an arrangement of dried flowers. Virtually everything, even the furniture, had come with the house. Only his wife's china collection, the beige wall-to-wall carpet, the American-style bathroom, and such things as the large-screen TV on a smart stand were new. It was a diminutive room, but paneled wooden connecting doors were open to reveal an even smaller dining room, and through its window a view of the tiny back garden. Bret lounged on the sofa, the papers Bernstein had prepared for him fanned out so that he could refer to them.

"Is Martin Euan Pryce-Hughes his real name?" asked Bret, who was unfamiliar with Welsh names. He had to look down at the papers to remember it.

"His old man was Hugh Pryce-Hughes." Bernstein was a short pot-bellied man wearing a gray three-piece suit that he'd been heard to describe as "native costume." It was more or

less like the suit Bret Rensselaer wore—and which gave him
the urbanity one expected of a diplomat or surgeon—but the
suit looked wrong on Bernstein, for his features, complexion,
and demeanor suggested a manual laborer, or maybe an infan-
tryman. He was not now, however, in the right physical shape
to be either; his face was red, the sort of complexion that
comes with high blood pressure, and he had a wheeze that
smoking aggravated. Enough gray hair remained to see that it
had once been brown and curly, and his hands were strong,
with short thick fingers, on one of which he wore a fraternity
ring and on another a flashy diamond. With ramrod spine, he
sat splayfooted on a little bentwood chair. One black sock had
sagged to reveal a section of bare leg. He was aware of his stiff
unnatural pose, but it reconciled his legs with the fragments
of Vietnamese metal embedded in them. His voice was low
and firm, unmistakably American but not stridently so. "The
famous Pryce-Hughes."

Bret looked down and furrowed his brow.

"The writer," said Bernstein. "Internationally famous
. . . the one who wrote those books about the Fabian Society.
His memoirs created all the fuss about Wells and Shaw. You
must have heard of him." Bernstein was a great reader. The
bookcase held Dreiser, Stendhal, Joyce, Conrad, and Zola—
he was not too fond of the Russian novels—and he'd read
them all not once but several times. He was proud to be a
graduate of Princeton but he was also aware that Bret, and
others like him, regarded Bernstein as reassuring proof that an
Ivy League education did not guarantee success in what Bret
called "the real world."

"No, Sylvy, I've never heard of him," said Bret. "For
these Brits, internationally famous means known in England,
Scotland, Ireland, and Wales. How many books?"

Bernstein smiled briefly. "Maybe half a dozen."

"You'd better get them for me."

"His father's books? What for? You're not going to read them?"

"Of course I am." Bret was thorough. He wanted Bernstein to be reminded of that.

"As long as you don't ask *me* to read them," said Bernstein.

"No," said Bret. "There's no call for *you* to read them, Sylvy."

"You haven't suddenly turned against smoking, have you?" When Bret shook his head, Bernstein took out a pack of Lucky Strikes and shook one loose.

Bret said, "Could you initiate a file for me?"

Bernstein flicked open a well-worn Zippo lighter with an inscription that read *Rung Sat Special Zone,* a souvenir of an unhealthy trip into a mangrove swamp southeast of Saigon during the Vietnam war. He kept it to remind himself, and anyone else who had to be reminded, that he'd had another sort of life not so long ago. He took his time lighting a cigarette and then said, "What's on your mind?"

"A secret file, recording meetings, reports, and payments and so on. A file of stuff coming in from one of our own people."

"We don't work like that. No one works like that. No one keeps all the information from one agent in the same file. The Coordination people take it and distribute it. They make damn sure no name, and no clue to the source, is on it."

"I didn't ask you how we work," said Bret.

Bernstein blew smoke while looking at Bret. Bret stared back. "Oh, I see what you mean. A bogus file." Bret nodded. "A file to prove that someone *was* one of our people when actually he *wasn't* one of our people."

"Don't let's get too deeply into existentialism," said Bret.

"A file with real names?"

"A few real names."

"You want to frame Martin Pryce-Hughes? You want to make someone think he's reporting to us?"

"That's what I want."

Sylvy blew more smoke. "Sure. It can be done; anything can be done. How far back would you want to go?"

"Ten years?"

"That would take us back to the days of mechanical typewriters."

"Maybe."

"You're not thinking of something they could take back to Moscow and put under the microscope?"

"No. Something to show someone briefly."

" 'Cause real good forgeries cost. We'd need real letter-heads and authentic department names."

"Not that ambitious."

"And I get it back?"

"What for?"

"To feed it into the shredder."

"Oh, sure," said Bret.

"Why don't I throw something together then? I'll sort out some photocopies and provide a sequence of material the way it would be if we filed it that way. It will give us something to look at and talk about. When we get it the way you want it, I'll find someone good to do the forgeries."

"Great," said Bret. He wished Bernstein wouldn't use words such as forgeries; it made him feel uneasy. "Keep it very circumstantial. We're not trying to produce Exhibit A for Perry Mason."

"A subtle, tasteful kind of frame-up. Sure, why not? But I'd need to know more."

"You take it and show it to this creep and lean on him."

"How's that?"

"Lean on him. Say you're from a newspaper. Say you're

from the CIA, say anything, but scare the shit out of him.''

''Why?''

''I want to see which way he jumps.''

''I don't see your purpose. He'll know it's a fake.''

''Do it.''

Bernstein looked at him. He knew Bret because he knew other men like him. Bret didn't have any operational purpose for frightening the old man; he just felt vindictive. ''It would be cheaper just to beat him up,'' said Bernstein.

Bret scowled. He knew exactly what Bernstein was thinking. ''Just do it, Sylvy. Don't second-guess me.''

''Whatever you say, doc.''

Bret smiled politely. ''Anything more on the woman?''

''No. She hasn't seen the boyfriend for a week. Maybe they had a fight.''

''Boyfriend? Is that it?'' said Bret as casually as he could.

''Oh, sure. She doesn't go along to his fancy apartment in Maida Vale to play chess.''

''He's a psychiatrist,'' said Bret.

''I'll bet he is.''

Bret found that offensive. He didn't want that kind of wisecrack; this was strictly business. ''Just four beats to the bar, Sylvy,'' he said. It was the nearest he got to a reprimand.

Bernstein smoked and didn't reply. So this wasn't just a job, there was more to it. Was this guy Kennedy a relative of Bret Rensselaer or what? ''If she wanted to consult him, why wouldn't she go and consult him at the hospital?''

''She would have to report any kind of medical treatment, especially a visit to a psychiatrist,'' said Bret. ''Remember the way it goes?''

''So this might be a way of seeing a shrink in secret? Is that what you mean?''

''She's under a lot of strain.''

Bernstein took a quick drag at his cigarette. ''Yeah, well,

I'm not asking you too many questions about this one, Bret, because you told me it's touchy, but . . .''

"But what?"

"Kennedy isn't that kind of shrink. Not any more he's not. At the clinic he's doing work on crowd hysteria and hallucination. He doesn't see patients; he analyzes figures, gives lectures, and writes dissertations on the herd instinct and that kind of junk. The clinic is paid by some big U.S. foundation, and the work they publish is studied by various police departments.''

"So tell me your theory,'' said Bret.

"What can I tell you? He's a good-looking guy. An airplane freak. Canadian. Soft-spoken, well-heeled, smartly dressed, very, very bright, and *muy simpatico*. You get the picture? This Samson lady . . . she's a very attractive woman.'' He stopped. A conversation with Bret, when he was in a touchy mood like this, was like a stroll through a minefield. He smoked his cigarette as if trying to decide what to say next. "Maybe that kind of soft shoulder, and the Canadian charm this guy Kennedy peddles, is just what she's short of.''

"A good-looker, is he?''

"You saw the photos, Bret.''

"Looked like he was assembled from a plastic kit.''

"He's a natty dresser, I said that. But even people who don't like him admit he's brilliant. Good flyer, good doctor, and good lover too, maybe. He's one of those people who always come out on top in exams: fluent, adaptable, and sophisticated.''

"And on the down side?''

"My guess is neurotic, restless, and unhappy. He can't settle down anywhere. But lots of women go for guys like that; they figure they can help them. And look at her husband. I've met him a few times. He's a really rough diamond, isn't he?''

"You said . . ."

"That I liked him. And I do up to a point. He's dead straight; I wouldn't like to cross him." It was quite an accolade, coming from Bernstein. "He's a man's man: not the sort you'd expect to find hitched to a twin-set-and-pearls lady like that."

Bret bit his lip and was silent for a moment before saying, "Sometimes things are not—"

"Oh, I know what you're going to say. But I've been doing this kind of work for a long time now. Two people like that. . . . She goes to his apartment alone, never with her husband. . . . He never goes to her place. And you only have to see them together to know he's crazy about her." He flicked ash into an ancient ceramic ashtray, around the rim of which the words LONG MAY THEY REIGN: CORONATION 1937 were faintly visible. It was part of his wife's collection of commemorative chinaware. He moved it, so there was no danger of its being knocked and broken, and waited for Rensselaer to react.

"It's improbable," pronounced Bret.

"You say it's improbable. Okay, you're the boss. But do *my* job for a little while, and maybe you'd start thinking you can't use that word improbable, because when boys and girls get together, *nothing* is improbable."

Bret smiled but he felt sick at heart. In his own futile way he loved and cherished Fiona Samson and didn't want to believe she was having a casual affair. "Okay, Sylvy. You usually get it right."

"There's always a first time. Maybe they just drink tea, look at pictures of his airplanes, and talk about the meaning of life. But really I don't think so, Bret."

Bret Rensselaer got up, overcome with anger. He looked around angrily, as if an escape from the room would bring with it escape from the facts he didn't want to face. He couldn't get out of his mind the wonderful relationship that he believed had developed between him and Fiona Samson over the weeks and months since he'd started preparing her for what would undoubtedly be the intelligence coup of the century. Fiona was the perfect pupil. "Pupil" perhaps wasn't the right word and it certainly wasn't a word he would use to her about their relationship. Protégée, perhaps, although that wasn't the right word either. In a grimmer truth the relationship was more like the one a prizefighter has with a trainer, a manager, or a promoter.

She needed his support nowadays. The strain was beginning to tell on her, but that was only to be expected. He liked to help her, and of course Bret would not have denied that there was a certain frisson to the way they had to meet covertly, in such a way that her husband wouldn't start suspecting. For by now Bret had reluctantly come round to the D-G's idea that advantages could be obtained from Bernard Samson's dismay at his wife's defection.

"How could she?" It was only when he stole a glance at Bernstein that Bret realized that he'd asked the question aloud. He turned away and went across to the dining table to lean upon it with both arms outstretched. He had to think.

Bret and Fiona. They had become so close that lately he'd dared to start believing she was becoming fond of him. He'd arranged fresh flowers whenever she came, and she'd remarked on it. Her rare but wonderful smiles, the curiously fastidious way she poured drinks for both of them, and the silly little presents she sometimes brought for him, like the automatic corkscrew that replaced the one he'd broken. There was the birthday card too; it came in a bright green envelope and said *With all my love, Fiona.* Bad security, as he told her at their next meeting, but he'd placed it by his bedside clock. It was the first thing he saw when he woke up each morning. Bret closed his eyes.

Bernstein watched him twisting and turning but said nothing. Bernstein waited. He wasn't puzzled; he didn't puzzle about things he wasn't paid to puzzle about. He'd discovered over the years how mysterious could be the ways of men and women, and Bret Rensselaer's wild pacing and unrestrained mutterings didn't alarm him or even surprise him.

Bret hammered a fist into his palm. It was inconceivable that Fiona was having an affair with this man Kennedy. There must be some other explanation. Bret had come to terms with the fact that, when she said goodbye to him, Fiona Samson went home to her husband and children. That was right and proper. Bret liked Bernard. But who the hell was Kennedy? Did Fiona smile and make jokes with Kennedy? Even more awful to think about, did she go to bed with this man?

It was at that point that Bret Rensselaer steadied himself on the mantelpiece, drew back his foot, and kicked the brass fender as hard as he could. The matching fire irons crashed against the fireplace with such force that the grate sang like a tuning fork, and one of the tiles of the hearth was hit hard enough to crack.

"Take it easy, Bret!" said Bernstein in a voice that, for the first time, betrayed his alarm. He found himself standing up, holding, for safety, the two Queen Victoria Diamond Jubilee plates that were his wife's most treasured items.

This displacement activity seemed to release some of Bret's anger, for the desperate nature of his movements subsided, and he stepped more carefully about the room and pretended to look at the books and then out the window to where his car was parked. It was not often that Bret was lost for words, but he simply could not get his thoughts in order. Jesus Christ! he said to himself, and resolved to get Fiona Samson assigned to Berlin right away, perhaps by the weekend.

When Bret sat down again, both men remained silent for

a while and listened to the dustmen collecting the garbage; they banged the bins and yelled to each other and the truck gave a plaintive little hooting noise whenever it backed up.

"Give me a butt, Sylvy."

Bernstein let him take one and flicked the Zippo open. He noticed that Bret was trembling, but the cigarette seemed to calm him down.

Bret said, "What would you say to a regular job?"

"With your people?"

"I just might be able to fix it."

"Are you getting teed off with paying me out of your own pocket?"

"Is that what I'm doing?" said Bret calmly.

"You never ask for vouchers."

"Well, what do you say?"

"I wouldn't fit into a British setup."

"Sure you would."

"The truth is, Bret, I wouldn't trust the British to look after me."

"Look after you how?"

"If I was in trouble. I'm a Yank. If I was in a jam, they'd feed me to the sharks." He stubbed out his cigarette very hard.

"Why do you say that?" Bret asked.

"I know I'm stepping out of line, Bret, but I think you're crazy to trust them. If they have to choose between you and one of their own, what do you think they're going to do?"

"Well, let me know if you change your mind, Sylvy."

"I won't change my mind, Bret."

"I didn't know you disliked the Brits so much, Sylvy. Why do you live here?"

"I don't dislike them; I said I don't trust them. London is a real nice place to live. But I don't like their self-righteous attitude and their total disregard for other people's feelings and for other people's property. Do you know something, Bret? There isn't an Englishman living who hasn't at some time or other boasted of stealing something: at school or in the army, at college or on a drunken spree. All of them, at some time or other, steal things and then tell about it, as if it were the biggest joke you ever heard."

Bret stood up. Bernstein could be sanctimonious at times, he thought. "I'll leave all this material. I've read it all through. I don't want it in the office."

"Anything you say, Bret."

Bret brought out his wallet and counted out twenty fifty-pound notes. Bernstein wrote *one thousand pounds sterling* on a slip of paper without adding date or signature or even the word "received." It was the way they did business.

Bret noticed the freshly cut leather on the toe of his shoe and touched it, as if hoping it would heal of its own accord. He sighed, got up, and put on his hat and coat and began thinking of Fiona Samson again. He would have to face her with it; there was no alternative. But he wouldn't do it today, or even tomorrow. Much better to get her off to Berlin.

"This guy Pryce-Hughes," said Bret very casually as he stood near the door. "What do you make of him, Sylvy?"

Bernstein was not sure what Bret wanted to hear. "He's very old," he said finally.

Bret nodded.

8

West Berlin:

September 1978

THE AFTERNOON WAS YELLOWING LIKE ANCIENT NEWSPA-
per, and on the heavy air there came the pervasive smell of the
lime trees. Berlin's streets were crowded with visitors, column
upon column, equipped with maps, cameras, and heavy rucksacks, less hurried now as the long day's parading took its toll.
The summer was stretching into autumn, and still there were
Westies here, some of them fond parents using their vacations to visit draft-dodging sons.

Her day's work done, Fiona sighed with relief to be back
in their new "home." There was a bunch of flowers, still
wrapped in paper and cellophane, on the hall table. It was
typical of Bernard that he'd not bothered to put them in
water, but she didn't touch them. She took off her hat and
coat, checked to be sure there was no mail in the cage behind
the letter box or on the hall table, and then examined herself
in the mirror for long enough to decide that her makeup was
satisfactory. She had aged, and even the makeup could not
completely hide the darkened eyes and lines around her
mouth. She flicked her fingers through her hair, which had
been crushed under the close-fitting hat, then took a breath

and put on a cheerful smile before going into the drawing room of her rented apartment.

Bernard was already home. He'd taken off his jacket and loosened his tie. Shirt wrinkled, red suspenders visible, he was lolling on the sofa with a big drink in his hand. "What a mess you look, darling. A bit early for boozing, isn't it?" She said it loudly and cheerfully before seeing that Bernard's father was sitting opposite him, also drinking.

Despite her flippant tone, Mr. Brian Samson, still technically her superior in the office, frowned. He came forward and gave her a kiss on the cheek. "Hello, Fiona," he said. "I was just telling Bernard all about it." If it did anything, the kiss confirmed her father-in-law's feelings about upper-class wives who came home and reprimanded their husbands for making themselves comfortable in their own homes.

"All about it?" she said, going to one of the display shelves above the TV, where by common consent the mail was placed until both of them had read it. There was only a bill from the wine shop and an elaborate engraved invitation to her sister's birthday party. She'd seen both pieces of mail but examined them again before turning around and smiling. Since neither man offered to get her a drink, she said, "I think I'll make some tea. Would anyone like tea?" She noticed some spilled liquor and took a paper napkin to mop it up and then tidied the tray before she said, "All about what, Brian?"

It was Bernard who answered. "The Baader-Meinhof panic, as they are now calling it."

"Oh, that. How boring. You were lucky to miss it, darling."

"Boring?" said her father-in-law, his voice rising slightly.

"Much ado about nothing," said Fiona.

"I don't know," said her father-in-law. "If the Baader-Meinhof people had hijacked the airliner and flown it to Prague . . ." Ominously he left the rest unsaid.

"Well, that would have been impossible, Father-in-law,"

she said cheerfully. "The signal that came back from Bonn said that Andreas Baader committed suicide in Stammheim maximum security prison a year ago, and the rest of them are in other prisons in the Bundesrepublik."

"I know that," said the elder Samson with exaggerated clarity, "but terrorists come in many shapes, sizes, and colors, and not all of them are behind bars. It was an emergency. My God, Fiona, have you been to Bonn lately? They have barbed wire and armed guards on the government buildings. The streets are patrolled by armored cars. It's not boring, Fiona, whatever else it may be."

Fiona made no concession to her father-in-law. "So you don't want tea?" she said.

"The world is going mad," said Samson senior. "One poor devil was murdered when his own godchild led the killers into the house carrying red roses. Every politician and industrialist in the country is guarded night and day."

"And complaining because they can't visit their mistresses, or so it said on the confidential report," said Fiona. "Did you read that?"

"What I can't understand," said her father-in-law, ignoring her question and holding Fiona personally responsible for any delinquency attributed to the younger generation, "is the way in which we have people demonstrating in favor of the terrorists! Bombs in German car showrooms in Turin, Leghorn, and Bologna. Street demonstrations in London, Vienna, and Athens. *In favor of the terrorists.* Are these people mad?"

Fiona shrugged and picked up the tray.

Bernard watched but said nothing. Throughout the world 1977 had seen an upsurge in the terrorist activities of religious fanatics and assorted crooks and maniacs. People everywhere were expressing their bewilderment. The older generation was blaming everything on their children, while younger people saw the mindless violence as a legacy they had inherited. Bernard's wife and his father provided a typical example of this. Any conversation was likely to degenerate into an exchange in which they both assumed archetypal roles. Bernard's father thought Fiona had too many airs and graces: too rich, too educated, and too damned opinionated, he'd told Bernard once after a difference of opinion with her.

As Fiona went to the kitchen she delivered a Parthian shot. "In any case, hardly a suitable cue for panic, Father-in-law."

Bernard wished she wouldn't say "father-in-law" in that tripping way. It irritated his father, but of course Fiona knew that only too well. Bernard tried to intercede. "Dad says it was the Russian message ordering the Czechs to keep their airfield open all night that did it. We put two and two together and made five."

Fiona was amused. "At this time of the year hundreds of East Bloc military airfields are working round the clock. This, darling, is the time of their combined exercises. Or hasn't that military secret filtered back to London Central yet?"

She wasn't in view, but they could hear her pouring hot water into the teapot and putting cups and saucers on a tray. Neither man spoke. The animated discussion they'd been having before Fiona's arrival had been killed stone dead. Brian looked at his son and smiled. Bernard smiled back.

Fiona came in and set the tray down on the table where Bernard had been resting his feet. Then she knelt on the carpet to pour the tea. "Are you both sure . . . ?" she said. She had arranged cups and saucers for all three of them, and a sugar bowl because her father-in-law took sugar in his tea.

"No thank you, darling," said Bernard.

She looked at Bernard. She loved him very much. The hurried assignment to Berlin had not been wonderful for either of them, but it had given her a chance to break away from the foolish relationship with Kennedy. These brushes with Samson senior were upsetting, but he was old, and in fact she'd found that the more she disliked the old man, the more she came to appreciate Bernard. He was always the peacemaker but never showed weakness either to her or to his father. Bernard, what a wonderful man she'd found! Now she'd had a chance to see things in perspective, she knew he was the only man for her. The perilous relationship with Harry Kennedy was behind her. She still didn't comprehend how that frenzied affair could have happened, except that it disclosed some alarming sexual vulnerability of which she'd never been aware.

Even so, she couldn't help but wonder why he hadn't sent the postcard. One was forwarded here every week: a colored advertising card from a "hair and beauty salon" off Sloane Street. Some friend of his owned it: a woman friend, no doubt.

"No mail?" she asked as she measured milk into her tea and stirred it to see the color of it.

"Only that Sloane Street crimpers," said Bernard.

"Where did you put it?"

"You didn't want it, did you?"

"If I take the card they said I could get a price reduction," said Fiona.

"It's in the waste bin. Sorry."

She could see it now. From where she knelt on the floor she could almost have reached it. It was in the basket together with an empty Schweppes tonic bottle and a crumpled Players cigarette packet that must have been Brian's. The postcard was torn into small pieces, almost as if Bernard had sensed the danger it held. Fiona resolved not to touch it, although her first impulse was to go and get it and piece it together.

"Anyway," added Bernard, "you won't be in London for a bit, will you?"

"No, that's right." She sat back on her heels and sipped her tea as if unconcerned. "I was forgetting that."

"I told Dad that you're going out tonight. He wants me to go to some little farewell party at the club and have dinner with him afterward. Is that okay?"

She could have laughed. After all the trouble she'd gone to to arrange the secret meeting with Bret Rensselaer this evening, she now found that her husband was completely uninterested in her movements. She told him anyway. "I'm at a familiarization briefing. Someone is coming from London."

Bernard was hardly listening to her. To his father he said, "If Frank will be there, I'll return some books I borrowed from him."

"Frank will be there," said his father. "Frank loves parties."

"Too bad you're not free, darling," Bernard told his wife.

"Farewell parties are usually more fun without wives," said Fiona knowingly.

"Another drink, Dad?" said Bernard and got to his feet. His father shook his head.

"Where will you have dinner?" she asked.

"Tante Lisl's," announced Bernard with great pleasure. "She's cooking venison specially for us." Tante Lisl owned a hotel that had once been her home. Brian Samson and his family had been billeted upon her when the war ended. It had become a sort of second home for Bernard, and old Tante Lisl was a surrogate mother. Bernard's undisguised delight in the old house sometimes gave Fiona a feeling of insecurity. She felt that now.

Bernard came over and gave her a kiss on the top of her head. "Goodbye, love. I might be late." As he went out with his father he said, as if to himself, "I mustn't forget to take those flowers for Lisl. She loves flowers."

As she heard the front door close behind the two men, Fiona closed her eyes and rested her head back in the armchair. Of course the flowers were not for her, how could she have imagined they were? The flowers were for that dreadful old woman against whom Bernard would hear no word said.

Bernard could sometimes be the archetypal selfish male. He took her for granted. He was delighted at the prospect of spending an evening with his father and his cronies, drinking and telling their stories. Stories of secret agents and daring deeds, exaggerated in the course of time and in the course of the evening's drinking.

It said a great deal about their relationship that Bernard would have been uncomfortable with her at such a gathering. Bernard respected her, but if he really loved her he would have wanted her with him whatever the company he was in. Secretly she lived for the day when he would be forced to see her for what she was, someone who could play the agent game as well as he could play it. Perhaps then he would treat her as she wanted to be treated—as an equal. And if meantime she used the same sort of secrecy to steal a little happiness for herself, could she be blamed? No one had been hurt.

She looked around the room at the mess Bernard had left for her to tidy up. Was it any wonder that she had found such happiness in the short and foolish love affair with Harry Kennedy? He had given her a new lease of life at a time when she was almost in despair. During the time she'd been with Harry she had stopped the pills and felt like a different person. Harry treated her with care and consideration and yet he was so wonderfully outgoing. He wasn't frightened to tell her how much he adored her. For him she was a complex and interesting human being whose opinions counted, and with him she found herself exchanging personal feelings that she had never shared with Bernard. When it came down to hard facts, she loved Bernard and put up with him, but Harry loved her desperately and made her feel deeply feminine in a way she'd never experienced before.

Now it was all over and finished with, she told herself. She could look back soberly and see the affair with Harry for what it was, the most glorious luxury, a release in a time of stress, a course of treatment.

She looked at the time. She must have a bath and change her clothes. Thank heavens she'd brought with her some really good clothes. For this evening's meeting she would need to look her best as well as have her wits about her.

Fiona Samson's appointment was in Kessler's, a family restaurant in Gatower Strasse, Berlin-Spandau. Its premises occupied the whole house, so that there were dining rooms on every floor. Downstairs old Klaus Kessler liked to supervise his dining room waiters in person. He stood there in his long apron amid dark green paintwork, red checked gingham tablecloths, and the menu written on small slates. Kessler described it as a "typical French bistro," but in fact its decor, and the menu too, showed little change from the Berlin *Weinstube* where the family had been serving good simple food since his grandfather's time.

Up the narrow creaking stairs there was a second dining room, and above that three upper rooms were more elaborately furnished, with better cutlery and glass, linen cloths, and handwritten menus without prices. These were booked for small and very discreet dinners. It was in one of them that Fiona had dinner with Bret Rensselaer that evening.

"You got away all right?" Bret said politely. She offered her cheek and he gave her a perfunctory kiss. There was champagne in an ice bucket; Bret was already drinking some.

The waiter took her coat, poured her a glass of champagne, and put a menu into her hands.

"There was no problem," said Fiona. "Bernard is at a party with his father."

"I hear the venison is good," said Bret, looking at the menu.

"I don't like venison," said Fiona, more forcefully than she intended. She sipped her champagne. "In fact I'm not very hungry."

"Kessler says he'll do a cheese soufflé for us."

"That sounds delicious."

"And a little Westphalian ham to start?" Anticipating her approval, he put down the menu and whipped off the stylish glasses that he wore when reading. He was vain enough to hate them, but his attempts to wear contact lenses had not worked out well.

"Perfect." Neither of them was interested enough in the food to read the menu all through. It was a relief, thought Fiona. Bernard could never sit down in a restaurant without cross-examining the waiter about the cooking in its most minute details. What was worse, he was always trying to persuade Fiona to try such things as smoked eel, tongue, or—what was that other dish he liked so much?—*Marinierter Hering.*

"How are you enjoying Berlin?" Bret asked.

"Having Bernard with me makes a difference."

"Of course. His mother went to England to look after the children?"

"It was sweet of her, but I miss them awfully," she said. A platter of ham arrived garnished with tomatoes and pickles, and there was a lot of fussing about as the waiter offered them a selection of bread rolls and three different types of mustard. When the waiter had departed, she said, "I suppose at heart I'm a housewife." She spread butter on her black bread, but she watched Bret's reaction. Exactly a week ago she'd decided that she would not be able to go through with this mad project of defecting to the KGB as some sort of superspy.

Fiona's life had become too complex for her. The clandestine meetings with Martin Euan Pryce-Hughes had not been too stressful. She was a sleeper; they met rarely. Her assignment had provided her with a smug feeling of serving her country and the Department, while demanding little or nothing from her. Then had come the bombshell from Bret Rensselaer that the Prime Minister had asked the D-G for a long-term commitment to getting someone into the top echelons of the enemy intelligence service. Of course she hadn't entirely dismissed the thought that Bret had exaggerated the way it had happened, especially now that she saw the gain in prestige—and self-esteem, too—that her planned mission brought to Bret.

Perhaps she could have handled the secret meetings with Martin and Bret, especially since at first Bret had been so understanding and sensitive about the strain on her. But that totally unexpected *coup de foudre* that had smitten her after the chance meeting with Harry Kennedy was the last straw. And while the meetings with Martin and with Bret could be kept to a minimum, canceled at short notice with no questions asked and no recriminations, the meetings with Harry were something quite different. She sometimes ached to see him. On the days when they were to meet, she became so consumed by the prospect that she could think of nothing else. It was amazing that no one—not Bernard, not Bret, not Tessa—had seen the turbulence within her. Well, it all had to stop. No more Martin, no more Bret, and no more Harry. She was even considering resigning from the Department. If Bret put up any sort of resistance to letting her go free, she would do exactly that. She had enough money from her father to tell them all to go to hell. Bret would argue, whine, and maybe yell, but she only had one life and what she did with it was going to be her decision.

When a woman reaches her thirties, she starts to ask herself some demanding questions. What was she doing with her life that was more important than having a real home and looking after her husband and her children? How could she contemplate prolonged separation from them? Let them send some other agent to the East. There must be dozens who wanted to make their name by such an operation. But not she.

She ate some ham and a piece of the warm bread roll. Since Bret had not spoken, she said it again. "I suppose at heart I'm a housewife."

If Bret guessed what was in store he gave no immediate sign of it. "We're changing the name of my department. Instead of the European Economics Desk it's officially to be the Economics Intelligence Section, and I am named Department Head. Rather grand, isn't it?" It came as no surprise to either of them. When Bret had told her about his master plan—"Sinker"—for bringing down the German Democratic Republic by targeting the respectable middle class, she knew it was right. Anyone who'd read a history book could see that Hitler gained power by wooing the German middle classes while the communists disdained them.

"So congratulations are in order?" she asked.

"They surely are," he said and they raised their glasses and drank. She smiled; how proud Bret was of his new appointment. She would never really understand him; she wondered if anyone did. He was so perfect and yet so contrived, right down to that perfect suntan. His navy blue cashmere jacket and gray slacks were probably chosen to show her how informal he could be but, together with the silk bow tie and starched shirt complete with cuffs long enough to reveal onyx links, he looked like a fashion plate. He was highly intelligent, charming, and, although no longer young, handsome, and yet he remained completely devoid of any sort of sexual attraction.

"Have you seen Frank?" she asked.

"About the big panic? Yes, I spent this afternoon with him."

"Is there going to be a row?"

"Maybe but I don't think so. For us, in fact, it provides a perfect opportunity."

"To fire Frank?" It was a mischievous and provocative question that she knew Bret would let pass.

Impassively Bret asked, "Were you there when the intercept came in?" She nodded. "Tell me about it."

"It was in the small hours of the morning—I can look it up in the log if you want it timed exactly. The duty cipher clerk brought it; they'd deciphered it very quickly. It came through the Russian Army transmitter at Karlshorst with the authorization of the commanding general's office. It was an order that some military airfield in southwest Czecho be kept on a twenty-four-hour operational status."

"Did Frank see it?"

"It was handed to him. Frank pooh-poohed it at first and then did his usual sitting-on-the-fence routine."

"Who was in charge of communications room security?"

"You must have got all this from Frank," said Fiona.

"Who was in charge?"

"Werner Volkmann."

"Bernard's German buddy?" asked Bret.

"Yes, that's him."

"Good. It will all work nicely."

"What will?"

"You're going to take a copy of that intercept and give it to Pryce-Hughes."

"Give it to Martin?"

"That's what I said. Be precise. I've written down exactly what I want you to say."

She drank some champagne. "You know what will happen?"

"Tell me what will happen, Fiona."

"Moscow will tell Karlshorst immediately. They're very touchy about military signals. No matter what I stipulate about secrecy, they'll send an intercepted traffic warning to the commanding general's office and change everything."

"Yes, they'll change the codes and ciphers. We can live with that," said Bret.

"I'm not an expert on signals," said Fiona. "But surely they change the codes and ciphers three or four times a week anyway? For a penetration like this they will change the system."

"Whoever gave approval must know what they'll do," said Bret, without concern for anything but his own plans.

"What is this all about?"

"I'm going to make you a star," said Bret. "I'm going to get the Soviets to sprinkle you with stardust and start thinking of you as a potential big shot."

"I don't like it, Bret."

She was expecting him to ask why, but he dismissed her reservations with a wave of his hand. "I had to get the D-G's authority for this one, Fiona. It's a big concession, and it shows that the old man is really convinced."

"Won't NATO make a fuss? Moscow will change everything. Everything!"

"There is no question of confiding our secrets to NATO," said Bret. "You know what we decided."

"Yes, I know." She was about to tell him of her decision to pull out when there was the sound of heavy footsteps on the stairs and Kessler himself came with the soufflé. It was magnificent, a great yellow dome of beaten egg, with flecks of browned cheese making a pattern all over it.

Fiona made the appreciative ohhs and ahhs that old

Kessler expected, and Bret added his compliments in hesitant German. Kessler served the soufflé and the side salad and offered rolls and butter and topped up their glasses until Fiona wanted to scream.

Once the old man had gone she tried again. "I've been thinking of the whole operation, thinking hard and very carefully."

"And now you want out?" He looked at her and nodded before probing into the soufflé on his plate. "It's exactly right. Look at that, soft in the middle but not raw."

She didn't know how to react. "Yes, I do, Bret. How did you guess?"

"I know you well, Fiona. Sometimes I think I understand you even better than your husband does."

She drank, nodded nervously, but didn't answer. That had always been Bret's angle. He understood her; it was the style any sensible case officer adopted with the agent he ran. She'd seen it all from the other side, so she knew the way it was done. She needed a drink and emptied her glass of champagne greedily.

Bret took her glass to refill it. He brought the bottle from its ice bucket, holding it fastidiously as the water dripped from it. Then he poured carefully so that it didn't foam too much. "Yes, I understand," he said, without looking up from the glass.

"I'm serious, Bret."

"Of course you are. It's a strain, I know that. I worry about you. You surely must know I worry."

"I can't do it, Bret. For all sorts of reasons. . . . If you want me to explain . . ." She was angry at herself. She had decided before coming here that she wouldn't put herself in the position of a supplicant. She had nothing to apologize for. Circumstances had changed. She simply couldn't continue with it.

"There is nothing to explain, Fiona. I know what you're going through."

"I won't change my mind, Bret."

He looked up at her and nodded with an affectionate, paternal indifference.

"Bret! I won't change my mind. I can't go."

"It's the buildup," he said. "That's what makes it so stressful, this long time of preparation."

"Look, Bret. Don't think you can just let it go and that I'll reconsider and eventually it will all be on again."

"Ummm." He looked at her and nodded. "Maybe a big glass of champagne is what I need too." He poured more for himself. It gave him something to do while she fretted. "Every agent goes through this crisis, Fiona. It's not any failure of nerve; everyone gets the jitters sometime or other." He reached across and touched the back of her hand. His fingers were icy cold from holding the champagne bottle, and she shivered as he touched her. "Just hang on; it will be all right, I promise you. It will be all right."

It was anger that restored to her the calm she required to answer him. "Don't patronize me, Bret. I'm not frightened. I am not on the verge of a nervous breakdown, neither am I suffering from premenstrual tension or any other weakness you may believe that women are prey to." She stopped.

"Get mad! Better you blow a valve than a gasket," said Bret, smiling in that condescending way he had. "Let me have it. Say what you have to say."

"I've worked in the Department a long time, Bret. I know the score. The reason I'm not going ahead with the plan—your plan, I suppose I should say—is that I no longer feel ready to sacrifice my husband and my children in order to make a name for myself."

"I never, for one moment, thought you might be motivated by the prospect of making a name for yourself, Fiona."

The way he maintained his gentle and conciliatory tone moderated her anger. "I suppose not," she said.

"I knew it to be a matter of patriotism," he said.

"No."

"No? Is this the same woman who told me,

> *'There is but one task for all—*
> *One life for each to give.*
> *Who stands if Freedom fall?*
> *Who dies if England live?'* "

She wet her lips. A favorite quote from Kipling was not going to divert her from what she had to say. "You talk of a year or two. My children are very young. I love them; I need them and they need me. You are asking too much. How long will I be away? What will happen to the children? What will happen to Bernard? And my marriage? Use someone without a family. It's madness for me to go."

She had kept her voice low but the expression on his face, as he feigned interest and sympathy, made her want to scream at him. Who stands if Freedom fall? Yes, Bret's words had scored a point with her. She was shaken by being suddenly brought face-to-face with the resolute young woman she'd been not so long ago. Was it marriage and motherhood that had made her so damnably bovine?

"It *is* madness," he said. "And that is exactly what will make you so secure. Bernard will be distraught and the Soviets will give you their trust."

"I simply can't cope, Bret. I need a rest."

"Or you could look at it another way," said Bret amiably. "A couple of years over there might be just the sort of challenge you need."

"The last thing I need right now is another challenge," she said feelingly.

"Sometimes relationships come to an end and there is nothing to be done but formally recognize what has happened."

"What do you mean?"

"That's the way it was with me and Nikki," he said, his voice low and sincere. "She said she needed to find herself again. Looking back on it, our marriage had diminished to a point where it was nothing but a sham."

"My marriage isn't a sham."

"Maybe not, but sometimes you have to look closely in order to see. That's the way it was for me."

"I love Bernard and he loves me. And we have two adorable children. We are a happy family."

"Maybe you think it's none of my business," said Bret, "but this sudden instability—this ring-down-the-curtain-and-send-the-orchestra-home I-can't-go-on nonsense—hasn't resulted from your work but from your personal life. So you need to take a look at your personal affairs to find the answer."

Bret's words acted upon her like an emetic. She closed her eyes in case the sight of the plate of food caused her to vomit. When finally she opened her eyes she looked at Bret, seeking in his face an indication of what he was thinking. Failing to find anything there but his contrived warmth, she said, "My personal affairs are personal, Bret."

"Not when I find you in an emotional state and you tell me to abandon the most important operation the Department has ever contemplated."

"Can you never see anything except from your own viewpoint?"

Bret touched his shirt cuff, fingering the cuff link as if to be sure it was still there. But Fiona recognized in the gesture, and in the set of his shoulders and the tilt of his head, something more. It was that preparation for something special, seen in the nervous circular movement of the pen before a vital document is signed, or the quick limbering-up movements of an athlete before the start of a record-breaking contest. "You are not in a position to accuse anyone of selfishness, Fiona."

She bit her lip. It was a direct challenge; to let it go without responding would be to admit guilt. And yet to react might bring down upon her the grim avalanche that loomed over her in nightmares. "Am I selfish?" she asked, as timorously as possible, and hoped he'd laugh it off.

"Fiona, you've got to keep to the arrangements. There's a hell of a lot riding on this operation. You'll do something for your country the equal of which few men or women ever get a chance at. In just a year or two over there, you could provide London Central with something that in historical terms might be compared with a military victory, a mighty victory."

"A mighty victory?" she said mechanically.

"I've told you before: the economic projections suggest that we could make them knock the Wall down, Fiona. A revolution without bloodshed. That would go into the history books. Literally, into the history books. Our personal affairs count for nothing against that."

He knew everything she wanted to hide; she could see it in his eyes. "Are you blackmailing me, Bret?"

"You're not yourself tonight, Fiona." He feigned concern but without putting his heart into it.

"Are you?"

"I can't think what you mean. What is there to blackmail you about?"

"I don't respond to threats; I never have."

"Are you going to tell me what I'm supposed to be threatening you about? Or do I have to start guessing?" Fiona could see he was loving it; what a sadist he was. She hated him, and

yet for the first time ever she saw within him some resolute
determination that in other circumstances might make a
woman love him. He would fight like this on her behalf too;
there was no doubt about that. It was his nature.

"Answer one question, Bret. Are you having me followed?"

He put down his fork, leaned back in his chair, clasped
his hands with interlocked fingers, and stared at her. "We are
all subject to surveillance, Fiona. It's part of the job."

He smiled. She took her glass of champagne and tossed
it full into his face.

"Jesus Christ!" He leaped to his feet, spluttering and
fluttering and dancing about to dab his face and shirtfront
with the napkin. "Have you gone mad?"

She looked at him in horror. He went across the room to
get more napkins from a side table. He dabbed his suit and
the chair, and as his anger subsided he sat down again.

She hadn't moved. She hated to lose control of herself,
and rather than look at him she picked up her fork and used
it to follow a blob of soufflé across her plate. "But Bernard
doesn't know?" She said, without looking up. She didn't eat
the piece of soufflé; the idea of eating was repugnant now.

He ran a finger around inside his collar. The champagne
had made it stick to the skin. "Such housekeeping is done
outside the Department. It would be bad security to use our
own people."

"Promise me that Bernard won't know."

"I could promise that he won't be told by me. But Bernard is a shrewd and resourceful man. . . . I don't have to tell
you that." He looked at his watch. He wanted to go and
change.

"It's all finished anyway."

"I'm glad." He looked at her and—despite the wet stains

on his shirt and the disarranged hair—gave her his most charming smile.

"You know what I'm talking about?" she asked.

"Of course not," he said, and kept smiling.

"It's clearly understood that I'm over there for only a year and then I must be pulled out?"

"A year. Yes, that was always the plan," said Bret. "Have you got a purse? I'll give you the details of the intercept. Phone the contact number for Pryce-Hughes first thing tomorrow. It's his morning for being at the office number he gave you." Even being doused with champagne had not unnerved him.

"You're a cold-blooded bastard," she told him.

"It never was a job suited to hot-blooded people," said Bret.

9

London:

April 1983

FOR BRET RENSSELAER THAT LONG-AGO DINNER IN BER-
lin was a hiccup in the lengthy preparation that Fiona Samson
had undergone for her task. Looking back, he saw it as just
a chance for him to provide some of the comfort and reassurance that become necessary to agents when traumatic indeci-
sion attacks them. It had been, he told the D-G, in one of the
reviews Bret liked to provide, an inevitable stage in the briefing and preparation period of any long-term agent placement.
"It was a role change for her. Some would call it the 'schizo-
thymic period,' for we had to inflict upon a normal personality the task of becoming two separate ones."

The D-G was about to challenge both the terminology
and the scientific basis of what sounded like a distorted over-
simplification, but just in time he remembered a previous
discussion in which Bret—who had been psychoanalyzed—
buried him under a barrage of psychological doctrine that had
included extensive notes, statistics, and references to "the
fundamentally important work of James and Lange." So the
D-G nodded.

Bret reminded him that in this case the agent was a
woman, a highly intelligent woman with young children.

Thus the attack had been more acute than usual. On the other hand, the factors that made her vulnerable to doubts and worries were the same elements that would make her less suspect when she went to bat for them. Fiona Samson was a stable personality, and Bret's subtle conditioning had reinforced her behavior, so that by the time she was "put into play" Bret was confident that the "transference" would be complete. Since that awful champagne-throwing scene, an emotional dependence upon Bret—and thus upon the decisions made in London Central—had provided her with the necessary motivation and internal strength of mind.

"You know far more about these things than I do," declared the D-G with a genial conviction that did not reflect his true feeling. "But my understanding was that in a scientific context 'transference' sometimes means the unconscious shifting of hatred, rather than love and respect."

"Entirely true!" said Bret. Jolted, not for the first time, by the old man's sharpness, he recovered quickly enough to add, "And that's an aspect of the work that I have already taken into account."

"Well, I'm sure you have everything under control," said the D-G, looking at his watch.

"I do, Director. Depend upon it."

Bret Rensselaer was not basing these conclusions on his personal experiences with field agents; he'd had little personal contact with those strange animals in the course of his career (although of course the day-to-day decisions he'd made had had an effect on the whole service). The Director-General was well aware of Bret's purely administrative background. He'd chosen him largely because he had no taint of Operations on him—and no one had guessed that a dedicated desk man like Bret could function as a case officer—and thus Fiona's role of double agent would be even more secure.

But Bret Rensselaer and Fiona Samson were not the only

ones coping with the problems of the role change. For if Fiona
had never been an agent before, and Bret had never been a
case officer, it was also true that the D-G had never before
faced the harrowing experience of sending into enemy territory someone he knew as well as he knew Fiona Samson.
However, it was too late now to change his mind. The D-G
allowed himself to be comforted by Bret's optimistic reassur-
ances because he could think of no possible course of action
if he became anxious.

If that long-ago dinner at Kessler's was remembered by
Bret as no more than a temporary failure of Fiona's resolution,
it was burned into her memory as a program is burned into
a microchip. She remembered that horrifying evening in
every last humiliating detail. The condescension with which
Bret Rensselaer had treated her desire to pull out of the operation, and the insolent way he had so smoothly blackmailed
her into continuing. The contempt he'd shown for her when
she'd thrown the champagne, humoring her as one might the
infant daughter of a respected friend. And, most shaming of
all, the way in which she had done exactly what he told her
to do. For, like so many humiliations, hers was measured by
the success of the opposing party, and Bret's dominance by
the end of that dinner had been absolute.

From that dire confrontation onward, she had never
again expressed any desire to withdraw from the task ahead.
After those first few agonizing weeks, during which she desperately hoped that Bret Rensselaer would leave the Department, be transferred, or suffer a fatal accident, no idea of
being released from her contract entered her head. It was
inevitable.

Like most women—and here Fiona thought of women
customs and immigration officers, women police officers, and
the secretaries in her own office—she was more conscientious
and painstaking than her male peers. Her detached contempt

for Bret, and other men like him, was best demonstrated by doing her job with more care and skill than he did his. She would become this damned "superspy" they wanted her to be. She would show them how well it could be done.

Fiona's meetings with Martin Euan Pryce-Hughes continued as before, except that Bret made sure that the little tidbits she was able to throw to him, and the responses to his requests for specific information, were better than the *Spielmaterial* he'd been given before. Pryce-Hughes was pleased. Reacting to a broad hint from him, Fiona asked for more money: not much more but enough to assert her worth. Moscow responded promptly and generously, and this pleased Bret and pleased Pryce-Hughes too. And yet, as month after month became a year, and time went on and on, she began to hope that the Department's long-term plan to place her in the enemy camp would be abandoned. Bret continued with their regular briefing sessions, and her duties were arranged to that purpose. Her use of the computers was strictly defined, and she never handled very sensitive papers. But the D-G appeared to have forgotten about her, and forgotten about Bret Rensselaer too. Once or twice she came near to asking the D-G outright but decided to let things continue. Bernard said the D-G was becoming eccentric to the point of disability, but Bernard always inclined to overstatement.

Typically it was Tessa who made the whole thing erupt again. "Darling Fi! You are always there when I need you."

"You have such good champagne," said Fiona, in an effort to reduce the tension that was evident in her sister's face, and in the way she constantly twisted the rings on her fingers.

"It's my diet: caviar, champagne, and oysters. You can't get fat on it."

"No. Only poor," said Fiona.

"That's more or less what Daddy said. He disapproves."

As if in contravention Tessa picked up her glass, looked at the bubbles, and then drank some champagne.

Tessa had always shown a constitutional spirit that bent toward trouble. The relationship between Fiona and her younger sister provided a typical example of sibling rivalry—it was a psychological phenomenon to which Bret referred many times during their sessions together. Their father, a single-minded man, had his favorite motto—*What I want are results, not excuses*—embroidered on a cushion displayed on the visitor's chair in his office. He believed that any form of forgiveness was likely to undermine his daughters' strength and his own.

Tessa had discovered how undemanding and convenient it was to play the established role of younger child and let Fiona fulfill, or sometimes fail to fulfill, her father's expectations. Tessa was always the one of whom little was expected. Fiona went to Oxford and read Modern Greats; Tessa stayed at home and read Harold Robbins. Temperamental, imaginative, and affectionate, Tessa could turn anything into a joke; it was her way of avoiding matters that were demanding. Her own boundless generosity made her vulnerable to a world in which people were so cold, loveless, and judgmental. In such a world did it matter much if she indulged in so many frivolous little love affairs? She always went back to her husband and gave him her prodigious love. And what if, one casual night in bed with this silly drunken lover, he should confide to her that he was spying for the Russians? It was probably only a joke.

"Describe him again," said Fiona.

"You know him," said Tessa. "At least he knows all about you."

"Miles Brent?"

"Giles Trent, darling. Giles Trent."

"If you'd stop eating those damned nuts I might be able

to understand what you're saying," she said irritably. "Yes, Giles Trent. Of course I remember him."

"Handsome brute: tall, handsome, gray wavy hair."

"But he's as old as Methuselah, Tessa. I always thought he was queer."

"Oh, no. Not queer," said Tessa and giggled. She'd had a lot of champagne.

Fiona sighed. She was sitting in Tessa Kosinski's elaborately furnished apartment in Hampstead, London's leafy northwestern suburb, watching the blood-red sun drip gore into the ruddy clouds. When, long ago, London's wealthy merchants and minor aristocracy went to take the waters at regal and fashionable Bath, the less wealthy sipped their spa water in this hilly region that was now the habitat of successful advertising men and rich publishers.

Tessa's husband was in property and motorcars and a diversity of other precarious enterprises. But George Kosinski had an unfailing talent for commercial success. When George bought an ailing company, it immediately recovered its strength. Should he wager a little money on an unwanted stock, his investment flourished. Even when he obliged a local antiques dealer by taking off his hands a painting that no one else wanted, the picture—dull, dark, and allegorical—was spotted by one of George's guests as the work of a pupil of Ingres. Although many nonentities can be so described, Ingres's pupils included the men who taught Seurat and Degas. This, the coarse canvas, and the use of white paint so typical of the Ingres technique, was what persuaded the trustees of an American museum to offer George a remarkable price for it. He shipped it the next day. George loved to do business.

"And you told Daddy all this, Trent saying he was a Russian spy and so on?"

"Daddy said I was just to forget it." Idly Tessa picked up

a glossy magazine from the table in front of her. It fell open at a pageful of wide-eyed people cavorting at some social function of the sort that the Kosinskis frequently attended.

"Daddy can be very stupid at times," said Fiona with unmistakable contempt. Tessa looked at her with great respect. Fiona really meant it, while Tessa—who also called her father stupid, and worse, from time to time—had never completely shed the bonds of childhood.

"Perhaps Giles was just making a joke," said Tessa, who now felt guilty at the concern her elder sister was showing.

"You said it *wasn't* a joke," snapped Fiona.

"Yes," said Tessa.

"Yes or no?"

Tessa looked at her, surprised by the emotions she had stirred up. "It wasn't a joke. I told you; I went all through it with him . . . about the Russians and so on."

"Exactly," said Fiona. "How could it have been a joke?"

"What will happen to him?" Tessa tossed the magazine onto a pile of other such periodicals.

"I can't say." Fiona's mind processed and reprocessed the complications this would bring into her life. She looked at her younger sister, sitting there on the yellow silk sofa in an emerald-green Givenchy sheath dress that Fiona—although the same size—could never have got away with, and wondered whether to tell her that she might be in physical danger. If Trent told his Soviet contact about this perilous indiscretion, it was possible that Moscow would have her killed. She opened her mouth as she tried to think of some way to put it but, when Tessa looked at her expectantly, only said, "It's a gorgeous dress."

Tessa smiled. "You were always so different from me, Fi."

"Not very different."

"The Chanel type."

"Use the one in the bedroom if you want privacy."

Fiona went into the bedroom. Upon the big four-poster, an antique lace bedspread was spread over a dark red cover to show it off. The bedside table held a smart new phone and an assortment of expensive perfumes, pill bottles, and paperback books. An aspirin bottle had been left open and tablets were scattered about. Fiona picked up the phone but hesitated before dialing.

Despite Bret Rensselaer's sanguine theories, Fiona Samson was not a person who readily turned to other people—male or female—for advice or instruction. She was self-sufficient, and self-critical too, in a way that an eldest child so often can be. But now she felt the need of a second opinion. She looked at her watch. Having carefully rehearsed the story in her mind, she dialed Bret's number. His phone rang for a long time but there was no reply. She tried again, it was always possible that she had misdialed, but again the ringing was unanswered. This frustration put her off balance, and it was then she was suddenly struck with the idea of phoning Uncle Silas.

Silas Gaunt's career was little short of a legend in the unwritten story of the Department. Uncle Silas could not be compared to other men; he was virtually unique. Every now and again, the British establishment decorously embraces a rogue, if not to say a rogue elephant, a man who breaks every rule and delights in doing so, one who recognizes no master and few equals. Gaunt's career was marked by controversy. He began his time as Berlin Resident by having a vociferous argument with the Director-General. It was an indication of both his diplomacy and his ruthlessness when he emerged with no enemies in high places.

Gaunt, a distant relative of Fiona's mother, was the man who had so energetically protected Brian Samson, and then his son Bernard, against well-placed people who believed that the senior ranks of the Secret Intelligence Service were the exclusive province of a certain sort of upper-class Englishman quite unlike Samson and his son. The Samsons survived; the opposition didn't reckon on Gaunt's ingenuity, devious games, or rage. But when Gaunt finally retired, the collective sighs of relief were heard throughout the service. Gaunt, however, was not out of the game. The Director-General knew and respected him, and his regard could be measured by the way Sir Henry handled the Fiona Samson operation. Only Bret Rensselaer, who'd come to him with the idea, Silas Gaunt, and himself were party to the secret.

Now, on impulse, Fiona dialed the number of the White-lands farm in the Cotswolds. Finding it was Silas himself who answered, Fiona didn't hesitate or waste time with pleasant-ries; she didn't even give her name. Relying upon him to recognize her voice, she said, "Silas, I must see you. I must. It's urgent."

There was a long silence. "Where are you? Can you talk?"

"At my sister's flat. No, I can't."

"Next weekend soon enough?"

"Perfect," she said.

Another long silence. "Leave it to me, darling. Bernard will be invited, plus you and the children."

"Thank you, Silas."

"Think nothing of it. It's a pleasure."

She replaced the phone. When she looked down to see what was crunching underfoot she found she'd crushed aspi-rins and other pills into the gold-colored carpet. She looked at the mess; she worried about Tessa. To what extent had she made her sister into the sort of woman she'd become? Fiona had always been the "eldest son," with effortless top marks and a relationship with her father that Tessa never knew.

Despite being her father's favorite she was never taken

into his confidence, for he kept his financial affairs secret to the extent of employing several different accountants and lawyers, so that no one would know the full picture of his investments and interests. But Fiona was taken to his office to meet the staff, and there seemed to be a tacit agreement that eventually Fiona would replace her father.

It never happened, of course. Fiona went to university and flourished. She enjoyed being in a man's world, and while there she was recruited into the most masculine preserve of all, that mystic and exclusive British brotherhood that enjoys a duality of name and a profoundly secret purpose. The obsessional secrecy that her father had maintained prepared her for the Secret Intelligence Service, but nothing her father showed her of his business world could compete with it.

And when, within this brotherhood, she found a man unlike any other she had ever met, she wanted him and got him. Bernard Samson had grown up in this secret world of physical hardship and brutality. A kill-or-be-killed world. Many of her father's friends had seen service in the war—some had been decorated as heroes—but Bernard Samson was fundamentally different from any of them; his war was a dark, dirty, private war. Here at last was a man her father could not fathom and heartily detested. But if, as Chandler said, "Down these mean streets a man must go who is not himself mean, who is neither tarnished nor afraid. . . . Complete man, common man, and yet an unusual man," Bernard Samson was such a man. The day she first saw him she knew it would be unendurable to lose him to another.

Fiona married. Tessa, neglected and insecure, floated away, a victim of Fiona's career-making and her father's indifference. Poor Tessa, what might she have been if Fiona had guarded her and advised her and given to her according to need?

"Are you all right?" Tessa called from the next room.

"I'm coming, Tessa. It will all be all right. I promise you, I'll sort it out."

Tessa came to her. "I knew you would." She threw her arms around Fiona's neck and kissed her. "Dearest, darling, wonderful Fi, I knew you would."

Such displays of affection embarrassed Fiona, but she stood stiff and still and put up with it.

Had the invitation to see Silas come in other circumstances, Fiona Samson would have enjoyed every minute of the week-end she spent with her husband and children at Whitelands, the farming estate to which Silas Gaunt had retired. His six hundred acres of the Cotswolds provided superlative walks and breath-taking views across the mighty limestone plateau that borders the shining River Severn.

But in this context everything was fraught with worries and dangers. Dicky Cruyer, the enterprising German Desk controller, and his arty wife, Daphne, were there. Bret Rensselaer had brought a young blond girl. Diffident in the company of so many strangers, she clung tight to him; so tight in fact that they'd arranged to have the only two bedrooms with a connecting door. Fiona guessed that Bret had requested those two rooms when she asked Silas if she could have the two children next to her, and Silas had replied that there were other needs greater than hers, and laughed.

Silas was a pirate, or at least he looked the part: a huge pot-bellied ruffian with a jowly face surmounted by a huge forehead and bald head. His baggy clothes were of high quality but he preferred old garments—as he preferred old wine and old friends—and he displayed the faded patches and neat darns that were the work of his faithful housekeeper, Mrs. Porter, as an old warrior his medals.

The house itself was made of local stone, a lovely tan color, and the furnishings—like the family portraits obscured behind murky coach varnish and the superb early eighteenth-century dresser—were in appropriate style. Silas Gaunt liked the dining room, especially when it was crowded, as it was this Saturday lunchtime. Gaunt stood at the head of the lovely Georgian mahogany table, carving an impressive beef sirloin for his professional cronies—the Samsons, Tessa, the Cruyers, Bret Rensselaer—and dominating them by the force of his personality.

Fiona Samson watched it all with a feeling of detachment. Even when Billy spilled gravy down his shirt, she only smiled contentedly, as if it were an incident depicted in an old home movie.

She watched the Cruyers with interest. Fiona had been at Oxford at the same time as Dicky. She remembered seeing him being cheered to victory at the debating society, and his making a pass at her that day when he was celebrating his cricket blue. One of the brightest of the bright boys at Balliol, he'd got the German Desk for which Bernard had been short-listed, and there was talk he'd get the Europe job when the time came. Now she wondered if Silas Gaunt was going to propose that he be made a party to her secret. She hoped not; already enough people knew, and if Dicky was to be told while Bernard was kept in ignorance she would find it intolerable. Dicky noticed her looking at him, and he smiled at her in that shy manner he'd found so effective with the Oxford girls.

She looked too at Tessa. Her husband, George Kosinski, was away. It was typical of Silas, and his luck and intuition, to guess that Tessa was connected with the phone call and to go to the trouble of inviting her in case he needed to know more.

When, after lunch, Silas took the men into the billiards

room with a trayful of cigars and brandy, Fiona took Billy and Sally upstairs to do their homework.

"In leap year, Mummy, do ladies ask men to marry them?" said Sally.

"I don't think so," said Fiona.

"My teacher said they do," said Sally, and Fiona realized she had walked into the sort of trap Sally was fond of setting for her.

"Then teacher is no doubt right," she said.

"It was Miss Jenkins," said Sally. "Daddy said she's a fool."

"Perhaps you misheard Daddy."

"I was there," said Billy, joining in the conversation. "He said that Miss Jenkins was a *bloody* fool. It was when she told him not to leave our car in the headmaster's car space."

"It was a Saturday," said Sally in defense of her father.

"That's quite enough," said Fiona sharply. "Let's start the math homework."

There was a knock, and then Tessa looked around the door. "Yes?" said Fiona.

"I wondered if the children would like to go to the stables."

"They must do their homework."

"There's a foal, born last week . . . just for half an hour, Fi."

"They have a test on Monday," said Fiona.

"Leave them with me, Fi. I'll see they do their home-work. Go for that long walk to Ringstone; you are always saying you enjoy that." Tessa was keen to be rid of her; she loved to be with the children and they seemed to respond to her. Tessa was a born rebel, and they sensed it and were intrigued.

Fiona looked at them. "Very well. Thirty minutes and

then you must do your homework." She turned. "I'm relying on you, Tess."

There was a happy chorus as they declared their intention to work hard under their aunt's direction. Sally came around and squeezed her mother's hand as if asserting her love. Billy wasted no time before getting into raincoat and scarf. As Tessa took the children off, Fiona heard Billy telling her, "If the Russians restore the monarch, he will have to be a commie-tsar." It was his favorite joke since Silas had laughed at it.

Tessa was right, Fiona needed a little time to herself. There was so much to think about. She found an old raincoat and a man's hat in the hall and, wearing the walking shoes she kept in the back of her beloved red Porsche, she slipped away. Alone, striding through the misty rain, she made for the summit of Ringstone Hill above Singlebury. It was about six miles, and she walked with the brisk determination with which she did so many other things.

She knew the way; she had done it many times, sometimes with the family and sometimes just with Bernard. She was gratified by the sight of accustomed gates, streams, and hedgerows, as familiar as the faces of old friends, varying sometimes with fresh patches of soft mud, a shiny new brass padlock, or the rusting frame of an abandoned bike. The boundary of Whitelands was marked by six fallen firs, casualties of the winter gales. Shallow-rooted trees, like their human counterparts, were always the first to go. She looked at one. From its rotting bark came primroses uncurling their canary heads. She counted their petals as she had when a child: five petals, six petals, some with eight petals. All different, like people. She'd grown up believing that four-petaled primroses were lucky, no four-petaled ones in sight today. It was Bernard who explained that four-petaled primroses were a necessity of cross-fertilization. She wished he'd not told her. She strode on and waded through a vast rippling lake of bluebells before starting to climb again. No surprises, just the expectation before each grand view.

The light changed constantly. The wet fields became ever more radiant under the drizzling dark-gray sky, and the bright yellow gorse left its scent on the air. She scrambled up to the bare hilltop—for the stone is a stone in name only— and stopped to catch her breath. She'd not been aware of the wind, but now it sent the light rain to sting her face and crooned gently through the wire fence. She turned slowly to survey the whole horizon. Her kingdom: three hundred and sixty degrees and not a person or even a house in sight, just the distant clamor of a rookery settling down for the night. To the north the sky was buttressed by black columns of heavy rain. The exertion of the climb had driven from her mind all thoughts of what disturbing conclusions tomorrow's dialogue with Silas Gaunt might bring. But now her mind raced forward again.

She was not an explorer or an experimenter; Fiona's brain was at its best when evaluating material and planning its use. It was a capacity that provided her with an excellent chance to judge her own potential as a field agent. Secrecy she had in abundance, but she didn't have many of the qualities she saw in Bernard. She didn't have his street-wise skill at fast thinking and fast moving. Fiona could be mean, stubborn, and coldhearted, but these for her were long-term emotions; Bernard had that mysterious masculine ability to switch on cold-blooded hostility at a moment's notice and switch it off a split second later. She pulled the hat down over her ears. The sky blackened and the rain was getting worse. She must get back in time to bathe and change for dinner. Saturday-night dinners were dress-up affairs when you stayed with Uncle Silas. She would have to do something with her hair and borrow the iron to smooth her dress. Tessa and the other women would have been preparing themselves all afternoon. She looked at her watch and at the route back. Even the friendly rolling Cotswolds could become hostile when darkness fell.

"You looked very glamorous last night, my dear," said Uncle Silas.

"Thank you, Silas. But to tell you the truth I can't keep up with the smart chatter these days."

"And why should you want to? I like you when you're serious; it suits you."

"Does it?"

"All beautiful women look their best when sad. It's different for men. Handsome men can be a little merry, but jolly women look like hockey captains. Could any man fall in love with a female comic?"

"You talk such rubbish, Silas."

"Was it that dreadful architect's prattle that pissed you off?"

"No. It was a wonderful evening."

"Swimming pools and kitchens; I don't think he can talk about anything else. I had to invite him though; he's the only blighter who knows how to repair my boiler."

He laughed. It was some complicated joke that only he appreciated. He'd grown accustomed to his own company, and remarks like this were solely for his own satisfaction. They were sitting in the "music room," a tiny study where Silas Gaunt had installed his hi-fi and his collection of opera recordings. A log fire was burning, and Silas was smoking a large Havana cigar. He was dressed in a magnificent knitted cardigan. It had an intricate Fair Isle pattern and was coming unraveled faster than Mrs. Porter could repair it, so that woolen threads trailed from his elbows and cuffs.

"Now tell me what's troubling you, Fiona." From the next room there was the measured and intricate sound of a piano; it was Bret playing "Night and Day."

Fiona told Silas about Tessa's exchanges with Giles Trent, and when she had finished he went and looked out the window. The gravel drive made a loop around the front lawn where three majestic elms framed the house. Tessa's racing-green Rolls-Royce was parked outside the window. "I don't know how your sister manages that car," he said. "Does her husband know she uses it when he's away?"

"Don't be such a pig. Of course he does."

He looked at her. "Then it sounds as if we've got an orange file on our hands, Fiona."

"Yes, it does." An orange file meant an official inquiry.

"Giles Trent. The treacherous swine. Why do these people do it?" She didn't answer. "What would you have done if Tessa had put this to you but without the special situation you are in?"

Without hesitation Fiona said, "I'd have taken it to Internal Security. The Command Rules spell it out."

"Of course you would." He scratched his head. "Well we can't have the IS people in on this one, can we?" Another pause. "You wouldn't have mentioned it to your husband first?"

"No."

"You seem very sure of that, Fiona."

"It would be the same for him, wouldn't it?"

"I'm not sure it would."

"Uncle Silas! Why?"

He turned and looked at her. "How can I put it to you. . . . You and I belong to a social class obsessed by the notion of conduct. At our best public schools, we have always taught young men that 'service' is the highest calling, and I'm proud that it should be so. Service to God, service to our sovereign, service to our country."

"You're not saying that because Bernard wasn't at public school—"

He held up a hand to stop her. "Hear me out, Fiona. We all respect your husband. Me more than anyone, you know that. I cherish him. He's the only one out there who knows what it's like to be in the firing line. I'm simply saying that Bernard's background, the boys he grew up with and his family, have another priority. For them—and who is to say they are in error?—loyalty to the family comes before everything. I really do mean before *everything*. I know, I've spent my life commanding men. If you don't understand that aspect of your husband's psyche you might get into a lot of trouble, my dear."

"Working-class boys, you mean?"

"Yes. I'm not frightened to say working-class. I'm too old to care about taboos of that sort."

"Are you saying that if Tessa had taken her problem to Bernard he would have hushed it up?"

"Why don't we put it to the test? Sit your husband down next week and have Tessa tell him her story."

"And what do you think he'll do?"

"More to the point, what do *you* think he'll do?" said Silas.

"I can't see that any benefit could come of such speculation," said Fiona. Silas laughed at the evasion. Fiona was irritated and said, "You're the one making the allegations, Silas."

"Now, now, Fiona, you know I'm doing nothing of the kind. Put it to Bernard, and he'll find some ingenious solution that will keep you and Tessa out of it." He smiled artfully. The word "ingenious" implied Bernard's flagrant disregard, if not to say contempt, for the rule book—and that was something Silas shared with him.

"Bernard has a lot on his mind right now," said Fiona.

"Make sure you ask him to keep Tessa out of it." He found a loose thread, tugged it off, and dropped it carefully into the fire.

"How?" said Fiona.

"I don't know how. Ask him." He smoked his cigar. "A far more important thing for the moment is that Giles Trent has obviously been used to monitor everything you've been telling them." He blew smoke, making sure it went toward the fire. Whenever Mrs. Porter smelled cigar smoke she nagged him; the doctor had told him not to smoke. "You must have thought about that. Any worries there?"

"Nothing I can think of."

"No, I think not. We've kept you very very secret and given them only strictly kosher material. Whatever Trent has been reporting to them, his reports will have only increased your status with Moscow."

"I hope so."

"Cheer up, Fiona. Everything is going beautifully. This will suit our book. In fact I'll get permission for you to visit the Data Centre again. That should make your masters prick their ears, what?"

"Will you tell Bret about Tessa?" She didn't want to face Bret with it herself; it would become an interrogation.

"Let's tell him now." Having hidden his cigar in the fireplace he pressed a bell push. Seeing the look of alarm on Fiona's face he said, "Trust your Uncle Silas."

"Night and Day" continued in the next room.

When Mrs. Porter put her head around the door, he said, "Ask Mr. Rensselaer if he can spare a moment. I think I heard him playing the piano "

"Yes, sir. I'll tell him right away."

When Bret came—eyebrows raised at seeing Fiona with Silas in what was obviously some kind of discourse—Silas said, "It's good to hear the piano again, Bret. I keep it tuned, but nowadays no one plays." Bret nodded without replying. Silas said, "Bret, we seem to be having another problem with our playmates."

Bret looked from one to the other of them and got the idea instantly. "This is getting to be a habit, Fiona," he said. Bret was huffed that she'd taken her story to Silas Gaunt and didn't disguise his feelings.

"We are all targeted," said Silas. "They focus on London Central. It's natural that they should."

"We are talking KGB?"

"Yes," said Silas, tapping ash into the fire. "This wretched Pryce-Hughes fellow has been rather indiscreet. He's let drop the word to Fiona that they have someone else working in London Central."

"Jesus H. Christ!" said Bret.

"From the context Fiona inclines to the view that it's a fellow called Giles Trent." Silas took a poker and stabbed at the burning log, which bled gray smoke. He carefully rolled it to the very back of the hearth.

"Training," said Bret, after racking his brains to remember who Trent was.

"Yes. He was shunted off to the training school two years ago, but that doesn't make him any less dangerous."

"Does anyone else know?" asked Bret.

"The three of us," said Silas, still brandishing the poker. "Fiona wasn't sure how to handle it. She was going directly to Internal Security. It was, of course, better than she brought it to me, off the record."

Bret's hurt feelings were somewhat soothed by this explanation. "We don't want Internal Security involved," he said.

"No. Better like this," said Silas. "Off duty, off the record, all unofficial."

"What next?" Bret asked.

"Leave it with me," said Silas. "I've worked out a way of doing it. No need for you to know, Bret. What the eye doesn't see. . . . Are you all right?"

"This year my sinuses are playing merry hell with me."

"It's that damned log fire, is it? Let me open the window a fraction."

"If there's nothing else, I'll just go out in the garden for a moment."

"Of course, Bret, of course. Are you sure you'll be all right?"

Bret stumbled out of the room holding a handkerchief to his face.

"Poor Bret," said Silas.

"I won't tell Bernard that I've spoken with you," said Fiona, still unsure of exactly what was expected of her.

"That's right. Now stop worrying. Can you persuade Tessa to tell her story to your husband?"

"Probably."

"Do that."

"Suppose Bernard goes to Internal Security?"

"It's a risk we'll have to take," said Silas. "But I want you kept out of it. If push comes to shove, you'll just have to deny Tessa ever told you. I'll see you are protected."

"That smoke is affecting me now," said Fiona.

"Get back to the others, or they'll start thinking we have a love affair or something."

"You won't want to talk to Tessa?"

"Stop playing the elder sister. If I want to talk to her I'll fix it."

"She gets very nervous, Silas."

"Go and walk about in the garden and get the smoke out of your eyes," he said.

When she'd gone he sank down onto his favorite armchair and let out a groan. He leaned close to the fire and prodded it again. "Why do these things happen to me?" he complained to the log. As if in response, the smoking log burst into a flicker of flame.

If Fiona had seen him now she would have been less confident of Silas Gaunt's ability to make her troubles disappear. "We'll have to put you into the bag neatly and quickly, Mr. Giles Trent," he muttered, and tried to visualize the reactions of Trent's controller when he found his man was uncovered. Would they try to pull him out and save him? Or would Moscow perceive another spy trial, in the very heart of London Central, as a triumph worth sacrificing a piece for? This might be one of those cases where both Moscow and London would agree that a favorable outcome was a permanently silent Trent. If it came to that, Silas had better make sure there was someone available to do the deed. He called to mind a tough old German war veteran who'd once worked as a barman at Lisl's hotel and, while there, had done all sorts of nasty jobs for Silas. He'd gone over to live in the East: perfect! Who'd link such a man with London Central? What was the fellow's name? Oh, yes, Rolf Mauser, a wonderful ruffian. Just the man for a job like this. He wouldn't contact him directly, of course; it would be imperative to keep it at arm's length.

10

Maida Vale, London:
_____

April 1983

"HAVE YOU GONE TO SLEEP, HONEY?"

Fiona buried her head in the pillow and didn't answer. The mattress heaved as he slid out of bed and went into the bathroom. It was a sunny spring day. Being in bed in broad daylight, behind closed curtains, made her feel guilty. What had happened to her? At least a thousand times, over the years, she had vowed never again to see Harry Kennedy, but he was so charming and amusing that he intrigued her. And then she would find herself thinking of him, or a bunch of flowers would arrive, or card from the "hair and beauty salon," and her resolution invariably weakened and she came back to him.

Sometimes it was no more than a quick drink at some pub near the clinic or a few words over the phone, but there were times when she needed him. Now and again it was a meeting like this, and she relished every moment of it.

She watched him walk naked across the room and open the wardrobe. He was muscular and tanned except for the buttocks left pale by his shorts. Lately he'd done three delivery trips to Saudi Arabia. Across his shoulders, like a bandolier, there were livid scars from a forced landing in Mexico ten years ago. He felt her looking at him and leered at her.

This illicit relationship had transformed Fiona. It had thrown a bombshell into the routine of her married life. Being with Harry was exciting; he made her feel glamorous and desirable in a way Bernard had never been able to do. Sex had come to play an important part in it, but it was something even more fundamental than that. She couldn't explain it. All she knew was that the pressure on her in her working life would have been unendurable without the prospect of seeing him, if only for a brief moment. Just to hear his voice on the telephone was both disturbing and invigorating. She was now understanding something she'd never known, the kind of teenage love she'd only heard other girls talk about, the kind they sang about in the pop tunes she couldn't stand. Of course she felt guilty about deceiving Bernard, but she needed Harry. Sometimes she thought she might be able to eliminate some of the guilt that plagued her if they could continue their friendship on a different—platonic—basis. But as soon as she was with him any such resolve quickly faded.

"Ah, so you *are* awake. How about a champagne cocktail? I've got everything right here."

She laughed.

"Is that funny?" he said. He put on his checkered silk dressing gown while looking at himself in the mirror and smoothing it and adjusting the knot in the belt.

"Yes, darling, very funny. Tea would be even better."

"Tea? You got it."

After Harry went out she reached over to the bedside table and picked up the lunchtime edition of the evening paper. There on the front page a headline proclaimed the CHELSEA BATHROOM SHOOTING. An intruder had broken into Giles Trent's house and shot him in the shower. The killer had used the plastic shower curtain to avoid being splashed with blood and washed his hands before leaving. A conveniently unnamed Scotland Yard spokesman called it "very professional indeed," and one of those experts who are always ready to speak to newspapers said it had "all the signs of a typical New York Mafia execution." The reporter seemed to imply that narcotics were involved. There was a blurred photo, one column wide, of a very young Giles Trent in bathing trunks and broad smile, arms akimbo. On an inside page there was a large photo of the house in Chelsea with a policeman on duty outside it.

Thank God Bernard had kept Tessa and Fiona out of the whole business. Uncle Silas had been entirely right about Bernard. It was disconcerting that certain of his male friends understood him in a way she had never been able to. He was so secretive. Without any discussion or explanation to her, he'd got Giles Trent to confess—and confess without mentioning Tessa. Now Trent was dead, and however ugly his death she couldn't help but feel a measure of relief.

There were other portentous signs. Bret had asked her to copy out a long secret document about Bank of England support for sterling. It was all in her handwriting and she never handed it over to Martin. As far as Fiona could see that meant only one thing. Bret was going to pass that to the KGB through some other agent. Why her handwriting? Only a complete fool would produce a document so incriminating unless this was going to be concrete evidence of her personal work for the other side. There was something ominous about the way Bret brushed her questions aside.

Another forewarning came from the amount of material she'd handed over to Martin in recent weeks. Bret said none of it was of vital importance, but there was such a lot of it. London Central wouldn't want to keep passing it through at this rate, and yet what excuse would she be able to provide for lessening the flow? It all added up to one thing. They intended that she should go East, and go soon. She dreaded it, but in some ways the waiting was even worse.

Every day now she looked at her husband and the children with love and longing. Each time she saw her sister she wanted to warn her that they would soon be separated, but any sort of hint or preparation was out of the question. To make it more painful, Fiona had become convinced that she'd never return. There was no logical reason, no evidence to support her failure of confidence. The premonition was purely instinctive and purely feminine. It was a calm fatalism that a matriarch might feel, surrounded by her family, on her deathbed.

If only it could be possible to settle some of the vital things that would now be decided without her. She kept worrying about Billy and his school. She'd always hoped that eventually Bernard would come to see the advantages that little Billy would enjoy from going to a good public school. She could get him in; her father had promised her that. But with her absent, there was no chance at all that Bernard would do anything about it. Bernard had a phobia about public schools—"beating, buggery, and bad manners"—and about those who'd ever attended one, or so it seemed.

Harry came in with a tray of tea. "You've read that newspaper story at least three times, darling. Does it have some special significance?" He leaned over and kissed her.

"The eternal psychologist," she said and, throwing the paper aside as casually as she could manage, she took the tray onto her knees. A tiny vase contained what must have been the very last violets of the year. How delicate they looked. Lovely transparent china, silver teaspoons, and two slices of the rich English fruitcake she adored. He must have had it all prepared. "How splendid!" She held the tray steady as he climbed back into bed alongside her. "Harry, what do you know about the English public school system?"

"You don't take milk with Earl Grey tea, do you, honey-child?"

"No. I drink it plain."

"Public schools? What oddball things go around in that brain of yours. Most of the guys at the clinic seemed to have survived them without visible damage. But then how can I tell? And mind you, there are not many of them I'd want to be in the shower with if the lights went out. What's on your mind?"

"I have close friends. . . . Her husband is being sent abroad by his company. They're thinking of putting the boy into a boarding school."

"And you're asking me if that's a good idea." He set the cups on their saucers. "My opinion as a psychiatrist, is that it? How can I tell you without seeing the kid? And the husband and wife too."

"I suppose you're right."

"If the husband doesn't want it done that way, the wife would be dumb to defy him, wouldn't she?" He poured some tea. "Is that strong enough?"

"He hates all public schools. Yes, it's perfect."

"Why's that?"

"Snobbery, bullying, privilege: the instilling into certain sorts of children that they are an elite. He thinks it contributes to British class hatreds."

"Yeah, and he's probably right, but you could say the same about shopping in Knightsbridge."

"Bullying too?" She laughed.

"You bet. You mean you never tackled those determined old ladies with their sharpened umbrellas?"

"Were you at boarding school?" She drank some tea and, before he answered, said, "We don't really know each other, do we?"

"That's why we should get married," he said.

"I wish you would stop saying that."

"I mean it."

"It upsets me."

"Listen, I'm crazy about you. I'm free, white, and over twenty-one. I'm in good shape at the gym and in pretty good shape at the bank. I now have a twenty-year lease on this place, and you chose most of the new furniture. I love you more than I knew I could love anyone. I think of you day and night; I only come alive when we are together."

"Stop it. You know nothing about me."

"Then tell me about yourself."

"Harry, we both know that this relationship is stupid and selfish. The only way we preserve it is by keeping our other lives to ourselves."

"Non-sense!" he always said it in two even syllables. "I don't want to keep anything from you."

"I don't know anything about you: your politics, your parents, your wife . . . or wives. I don't even know how many you've had."

He held up the teaspoon. "My parents are dead. I have no politics, and I no longer have any wife. My divorce is final. No children. My ex-wife is French-Canadian and lives in Montreal. She was always dunning me for money. That's why I skedaddled and had to keep moving. Now she has remarried and I'm really free." He drank tea. "Like I told you, my niece Patsy is back with her father in Winnipeg, and the guy she ran away with is in jail for shoplifting. That's all ancient history. What else would you like to know?"

"Nothing. I'm saying it's better that we don't know too much about each other."

"Or?"

"Or we'll start discussing our problems."

"Would that be so awful? What problems do you have, honey?"

Poor Harry. The probability was that she'd soon be moving away to the East. When that happened the SIS would stage a full-scale inquiry just for the look of the thing. It would be foolish to rule out the possibility that Special Branch would find out about her relationship with Harry. Should they come to talk to him, it was vital that everyone was left with the idea that she was a long-term Marxist. Anything else could spell danger. "Only silly things, I suppose."

"For instance?" He leaned over and kissed her on the cheek.

"Perhaps you'd no longer love me if you knew," she said, and ruffled his hair in what she hoped was the appropriate patronizing gesture of a Marxist spy.

"I'll tell you something," he said impulsively. "I'm thinking of giving up the shrink business."

"You're always saying that."

"But this time for real, baby! For a hundred thousand dollars my cousin Greg will sell me a quarter share in his airplane brokerage. If I worked with him full-time we could let one of the pilots go. He needs the extra hundred thousand to buy a new lease on the Winnipeg hangar and buildings."

"You said it was a risky business," said Fiona.

"And it is. But no more risk than I can handle. And I've had about as much psychiatry as I can stomach." He stopped, but she said nothing. "It's all office politics at the clinic: who gets this and who gets that."

"But you have a work permit now. You could go anywhere and get a job."

"No, I couldn't. It's not that sort of permit. And what kind of job could I get? I only went into the crowd hysteria research at the clinic to get away from neurotic housewives going into menopause. I've got to get away, Fiona. I've got to."

"I didn't realize you were so unhappy." At moments like this she loved him more than she could say.

"Having you is all that keeps me going. There is nothing more important to me than you are." Growing more serious, he added, "No matter how long you live, I want you always to remember this moment. I want you to remember that my life is yours."

"Darling Harry." She kissed him.

"I don't ask you to say the same. Your circumstances are different. I make no demands of you. I love you with everything I've got."

She laughed again. The hours she spent with Harry were the only times she was able to forget what was in store for her.

11

London:

May 1983

"MY GOD, BRET, I WISH YOU WOULDN'T SUDDENLY AP-
pear unannounced, like an emissary from the underworld." It
was a silly expression from her schooldays, hardly an appropriate way to greet Bret Rensselaer even if he *had* walked into
her home unannounced. Yet, as she said it, Fiona realized
that nowadays she *was* beginning to think of him as some
svelte messenger from another, darker world.

The idea amused Bret. He was standing in the kitchen
with his hat in his hand, smiling. A spring shower glittered
like sequins all over his black raincoat. He said, "Is that how
you rate me, Fiona, a go-between for Old Nick? And what
form does he assume when he's not the Director-General?"

Fiona was in her apron, her hair a complete mess, empty-
ing the dishwasher. Silverware in hand, she smiled, a nervous
twitch of the lips, and said, "I'm sorry, Brett." She picked up
a cloth and wiped a knife blade. "The cutlery never comes
out without marks," she said. "Sometimes I think it would
be quicker to wash everything in the sink." She spoke mechanically as her mind rushed on to Bernard.

"Your lovely au pair let me in; she seemed to be in a
hurry." Bret unbuttoned his black raincoat to reveal black

suit and black tie. "I *am* looking a bit somber, I'm afraid. I've been to the service for Giles Trent."

She didn't offer to take his coat or ask him to sit down. "You startled me. I was waiting for a phone call from Bernard."

"That might be a long wait, Fiona. Bernard went over there to sort out the Brahms Four fiasco. No one knows where he's got to."

Over there, those awful words. She went cold. "What was the last contact?"

"Relax, Fiona. Relax." She was standing as if frozen, ashen-faced, with a handful of knives and forks in one hand and a cloth in the other. "There is absolutely no reason to think he's run into trouble."

"He should never have gone; they know him too well. I pleaded with him. When did he make contact?"

"You know how Bernard likes to operate: no documents, no preparations, no emergency link, no local backup, nothing! He insists it be done that way. I was there when he said it."

"Yes, I know."

"Bernard likes to play the technocrat, but when he hits the road he's strictly horse-and-buggy." Bret touched her arm for a moment to comfort her. "And his track record says he's right."

She said nothing. He watched her. Mechanically, with quick movements of the cloth, she polished the cutlery and continued to put it into the drawer, knives, forks, and spoons each in their separate compartments. When the last one was done, she took the damp cloth and carefully draped it along the edge of the table to dry. Then she sat down and closed her eyes.

Bret hadn't reckoned on her being so jumpy, but he had to tell her; it was the reason he'd come. So after what seemed an appropriate time, he said, "Everything points to the notion that they will take you over there some time over the next seventy-two hours."

"Me?"

"If they're smart, they will. They think you're blown. You'd better be ready."

"But if they arrest Bernard . . ."

"Forget Bernard! He went because he's the most experienced Berlin agent we have. He'll be all right. Start thinking of yourself."

"But if he's arrested?"

Bret stayed calm. In a measured voice he said, "If Bernard is held, you can do more for him over there than you can sitting here waiting for the phone."

"You're right, of course."

"Don't try playing it by ear yourself. Leave that to Bernard. Sit down right now and make sure you have everything committed to memory: out-of-contact devices, the 'commentary,' and your own goodbye codes in case things go wrong. We'll get you home, Fiona, don't worry about that." A cat strolled in and, standing on the doormat, looked first at Bret and then at Fiona. With her foot Fiona pushed the plastic bowl of food nearer to the door, but after sniffing it very closely the cat walked out again.

"I've learned it all and destroyed my notes."

"Once there, you won't be contacted for several weeks. They'll be watching you at first."

"I know, Bret."

She sounded listless, and he tried to snap her out of it. "They'll try to trick you. You must be ready for them."

"I'm not frightened."

He looked at her with admiration. "I know you're not, and I think you're an extraordinary woman."

The compliment surprised her. It was delivered with

warmth. "Thank you, Bret." Perhaps somewhere under that smooth silky exterior there was a heart beating after all.

"Is there anything we've forgotten, Fiona? I keep going over it again and again. Try to imagine that you *really* are the agent they think you are. . . ." He snapped his fingers. "Money! Wouldn't you want to leave some money—maybe money for the children—and instructions of some kind? A final letter?"

"My father arranged a trust fund for the children. Letter? No, that's too complicated. Bernard would find some way of reading between the lines."

"My God!" said Bret in real alarm. "You think he could?"

"I've lived with Bernard many years, Bret. We know each other. Quite honestly, I don't know how we've been able to keep everything secret from him for so long."

"I know it's been rugged at times," said Bret, "but you came through." He looked at his watch. "I'll leave you now. I know you well enough to know you'll want a little time alone, to think. Take time out to rest and get ready. We'll monitor your journey right up to the time we can't stay with you."

She looked at him, wondering what would happen at the point he wouldn't be able to stay with her, but didn't ask. "Shall I let you know if Bernard phones?"

"No need. I have someone tapping into your phone." He looked at his watch. "As of an hour ago. If you want me I'll be at home." He buttoned his raincoat. "If my guess is right, this is where it all begins."

She smiled ruefully.

"Good luck, Fiona. And see you soon." He was going to kiss her but she didn't look as if she wanted to be embraced, so he winked and she responded with a smile.

"Goodbye, Bret."

* * *

"Suppose it's all a KGB caper? Suppose the Russkies grab her and keep her husband too? Suppose they then ask you to do a deal?" Sylvester Bernstein was wearing a raincoat with a wool lining, the sort of garment a man buys soon after he starts surveillance duties.

"We'll worry about that when it happens," said Bret. He shivered. He wasn't expecting it to be so cold, even in Scotland at night.

"You'd sure be behind the eight ball, old buddy. Two agents down the tube."

"We have others."

"Is that official policy?"

"Once deposited, an agent is dead," said Bret. "There are no second chances or retirement plans."

"Does Mrs. Samson know that?" said Bernstein.

"Of course she does, unless she's stupid. We can't count on getting her back in one piece. Even if we do, she won't be in good shape. Even getting her set up for this task has taken a lot out of her. She used to be sweet, gentle, and trusting; now she's learned to be tough and cynical."

"Nice going, Bret," said Bernstein. So Bret was taking it badly. This kind of nonsense was Bret's way of dealing with his worries about Fiona Samson. Sylvy had seen other case officers in similar circumstances. They often formed an emotional attachment to the agent they were running.

Bret didn't reply. He huddled closer to the wall of the ruined building in which the two men had found shelter from the cold rainy wind off the sea. It was a wild night, a Götterdämmerung that you had to be on this lonely piece of coastline to appreciate. The sea was black, but a can opener, inexpertly used, had torn open the horizon to reveal a raging tumult of reds and mauves lit with the livid flashes of an

electrical storm. What a night to bid goodbye to your home-
land. What a night to be out of doors.

"This is some desolate place," said Bernstein, who had
known many desolate places in his life.

"Once it was a submarine base," said Bret. "The last time
I was here that anchorage was full of ships of the Home Fleet.
Some big battle wagons too."

Bernstein grunted and pulled up the collar of his coat
and leaned into it to light a cigarette.

Bret said, "The Royal Navy called this place HMS Pea-
fowl, the sailors called it HMS Piss-up. That jetty went all the
way out in those days. And there were so many depot ships
and subs you could have walked on them right across the
bay."

"How long ago was that?" said Bernstein. He blew smoke
and spat a shred of tobacco that had stuck to his lip.

"The end of the war. There were subs everywhere you
looked. The flat piece of tarmac was the drill field that the
Limeys called 'the quarterdeck.' The British are obsessed with
marching and drilling and saluting. They do it to celebrate,
they do it for punishment, they do it to pray, they do it for
chow. They do it in the rain, in the sunshine, and in the
snow, morning and afternoon, even on Sunday. This—where
we are now—was the movie theater. Those concrete blocks
along the roads are the foundations for Quonset huts, row
upon row of them."

"And stoves maybe?" said Bernstein. He clamped the
cigarette between his lips while he used his night glasses to
study the water of the bay.

"I can hardly believe it's all gone. When the war was on,
there must have been eight thousand servicemen stationed
here, counting the engineering facilities on the other side of
the bay."

"I never had you figured for a sailor, Bret."

"I was only a sailor for twenty-five minutes," said Bret. He was always self-conscious about being invalided out of the service. Angry at having to divert and land him, his submarine captain told him he was a Jonah. Bret, who had falsified his age to volunteer, never forgot that Jonah label and never entirely freed himself from it.

"Twenty-five minutes. Yes, like me with Buddhism. Maybe it was long enough."

"I didn't lose faith," said Bret.

"You were in the U.S. Navy?" said Bernstein, wondering if Bret had been with the British so long ago.

"No, I was in U-boats," said Bret sourly. "I won the Iron Cross, first class."

"Pig boats, eh?" said Bernstein, feigning interest in an attempt to pacify the older man.

"Submarines. Not pig boats, submarines."

"Well, now you've got yourself another submarine, and it belongs to the Russkies," said Bernstein. He looked at his watch. It was an antiquated design with green luminescent hands; another item acquired when he began surveillance work.

To the unspoken question, Bret said, "They're late but they'll turn up. This is the way they always do it."

"Here? Always here?"

"It's not so easy to find a place where you can bring a sub in close to the shore, somewhere some landlubber can launch an inflatable boat without getting swamped. Somewhere away from shipping lanes and people."

"They sure are late. What kind of car are they in?" Bernstein asked with the glasses still to his eyes. "A Lada? One of those two-stroke jobs maybe?"

"Deep water, too," explained Bret. "And sand and fine gravel; it's got to have a sea bed that won't rip the belly out of you. Yes, they'll come here. It's one of the few landing spots the Soviets would dare risk a sub at night."

"Take the glasses. I think I saw a movement on the water." He offered them. "Beyond the end of the jetty."

"Forget it! You won't see anything. They won't surface until they get a signal, and they won't get a signal until their passengers are here."

"Don't the Brits track them on the ASW . . . the sonar or radar or whatever they got?"

"No way. It can be done but there's the chance that the Russkie countermeasures will reveal they're being tracked. Better they don't know we're on to them."

"I suppose."

"I could have asked the navy to track them with a warship, but that might have scared them away. Don't fret, they'll come."

"Why not a plane, Bret? Submarines! Jesus that's *Riddle of the Sands* stuff."

"Planes? This is not 'Nam. Planes are noisy and conspicuous and too risky for anything this important."

"And where do they go from here?"

"Somewhere close, East Germany; Sassnitz has submarine facilities. From there the train ferry could take her to Stockholm. Plane to Berlin."

"A long way round. Why not take a train from Sassnitz to Berlin?"

"They're devious folk. They like to route their people via the West. It looks better that way," said Bret. "I'm going back to the car to phone. There was a car following them right from the time they left London."

Bernstein pulled a face. His confidence in the British security and intelligence organizations, right down to their ability to follow a car, was very limited.

Bret Rensselaer walked back along the road and climbed the broken steps to where they'd left the car. It was out of sight behind the last remaining wall of the sick bay where, in 1945, Bret had been ignominiously deposited by his submarine captain after falling down a ladder during an Atlantic patrol.

Before getting into the car he took a look at the bay. The water was like black syrup, and the horizon was getting brighter as the storm headed their way. He sighed, shut the door, and phoned the other car. "Johnson?"

It was answered immediately. "Johnson here."

"Boswell. Where the hell have you got to?"

"A spot of trouble, Boswell. Our friends had a little collision with another car."

"Anyone hurt?"

"No, but a lot of arguments about who was drunk. They've sent for the police."

"How far away are you?"

"About an hour's drive."

"Get them back on the road, Johnson. I don't care how you do it. You've got a police officer with you?"

"Yes, he's here."

"Get him to sort it out. And do it quick."

"Will do, Boswell."

"And phone me when they're on their way. I'll stay in the car."

"Will do."

The phone gave the disengaged tone and Bret put it back in its slot. He looked up to find Bernstein standing by the car. "Get inside and warm up," said Bret. "Another hour. At least another hour."

Bernstein got into the car and settled back. "Is it all okay? It's beginning to rain."

Bret said, "I figured I might sometimes be wiping the backsides of the Brits, but I didn't figure I'd be doing it for the Russkies too."

"You're really masterminding this one, Bret. I hope you know what you're doing."

"If I do," said Bret, "I'm the only one who does." He started the engine and switched on the heater.

"Who owns this spread nowadays?" said Bernstein, looking down on the abandoned brick buildings that had once been the administration block.

"The British Admiralty hangs on to it."

"Some chutzpah, those Russkies." He reached into his pocket.

"It suits us," said Bret. "We know where to find them." He raised his hand in warning. "Don't smoke, please, Sylvy. It affects my sinuses."

Bernstein sat fidgeting with his hands as he tried to decide whether it was better to smoke outside in the freezing cold or sit desperately deprived in the warm. Bret watched him clasping his hands together and after five minutes or more of stillness and silence said, "Are you all right?"

Bernstein said, "I was meditating."

"I'm sorry."

"It's okay."

Bret said, "Did you really get into Buddhism?"

"Yeah. In 'Nam. Zen Buddhism. I was living with a beautiful Cambodian girl who taught me about meditation. I was really taken with it."

"You're a Jew."

"The beliefs are not mutually exclusive," said Bernstein. "Meditation helped me when I was captured."

"Captured by the Viet Cong?"

"Only for about twelve hours. They questioned me." He was silent for a moment, as if just saying it caused him pain. "It was dark when I came to, and I got loose and escaped crawling away into the jungle."

"I didn't know that, Sylvy."

"So who wants to know about 'Nam? The guys who fought there were shafted by everyone, from the White House down to the liberal newspapers, and that's pretty damn low. That's why I came and lived in Europe."

"Look at that lightning. It's going to be rough out there. How would you like to be putting out to sea tonight?"

"She was still seeing that guy Kennedy, right up to the end."

Bret swung his head around with an abrupt movement that betrayed his surprise. "She swore it was all over."

"How many husbands send their wife a dozen dark red long-stem roses with a note inviting them to come for tea?"

"You're sure?"

"Florists are a must."

"What do you mean?"

"Bret, for a spell, when times were tough, I took divorce jobs. I can probably get the bill for the roses if you want to see it."

"We'll have to turn Kennedy over," said Bret.

"We found nothing last time. We checked his medical qualifications and his military service. The clinic where he works says he's hard-working and reliable. Anyway, it's a bit late now, isn't it?" said Bernstein. "She's on her way."

Bret looked at him. He'd told him only as much as he had to be told, but Sylvy Bernstein had spent a lifetime in the intelligence world. He knew what was happening. "We still need to know," said Bret.

"It was kind of fortuitous, the way Kennedy picked her up at Waterloo Station, wasn't it?" Bernstein rubbed his chin. He had a tough beard and he needed a shave. "Serendipitous is the word. I read it in a book."

"She's a very attractive woman," said Bret, repeating what Bernstein had said many times, and dismissed the idea of its being an enticement.

"And he's a real smooth shrink. But is he the kind of guy who picks up ladies in railroad stations?"

Bret still couldn't face it. "It was a special situation, Sylvy. Kennedy's daughter ran away. You talked to the railway cop. You said—"

"Okay, okay. It was really his cousin's daughter, and Kennedy is a Canadian. It won't be easy to do a complete vetting job on him. And a guy who gives a false name to a cop is likely to have given a few false names to a lot of other people. But why should I talk myself out of an assignment? I need the money."

"We'd better turn him right over, Sylvy," said Bret, as if saying it for the first time. The preliminary check on Kennedy had turned up nothing incriminating, but foreign nationals—especially those who moved around a lot—were sometimes difficult to investigate. Perhaps he should have been more thorough right from the start, but he'd been so shocked at the idea of Fiona being unfaithful to her husband that he'd not given proper consideration to a full investigation of the man. And yet what could be more obvious? If the KGB was going to use her in a top job, it would be standard procedure to place someone close to her, very close to her. A lover! That was the way the minds of the KGB always worked. Bret said, "Do a complete vetting job: birth record, the Canadian police computer, Washington too. Check his medical school and military service. Have someone talk to his neighbors, colleagues, friends, and family—the full procedure. Your way of doing things is faster than if I do it through official channels."

"What am I looking for?"

"Jesus, Sylvy! Suppose this guy Kennedy turns out to be a KGB fink?"

"Okay. I'll work as fast as I can, but you can't hurry

these things without showing your hand, and I know you want the lid kept on it."

"A dozen red roses," said Bret. "Well, maybe we'll find they were from her sister or her father."

"I think I'll stretch my legs," said Bernstein. He felt as if he'd expire unless he smoked a cigarette.

12

London:

May 1983

FIONA'S DEFECTION—DESPITE THE WAY IN WHICH THE DE-partment made sure no word of it leaked to press or TV—caused a sensation among her immediate circle.

Of those working in the Department that day, Bret Rensselaer was the only person who knew the whole story of Fiona Samson's going. Temporarily assigned to him as a secretary was a nineteen-year-old blond "executive officer" called Gloria Kent. Bret had contrived to have this strikingly attractive trainee working with him, and her presence helped to straighten an ego bent after his wife's departure. Alone in Bret's office, it was Gloria who was the first to hear that Bernard Samson had been arrested in East Berlin. She was appalled.

Gloria Kent had had a schoolgirl crush on Bernard Samson ever since she had first seen him in the office. Perhaps her feelings showed on her face when she brought the bad news to Bret Rensselaer, for after a muttered curse he told her, "Mr. Samson will be all right."

"Who will tell his wife?" said Gloria.

"Sit down," said Bret. Gloria sat. Bret said, "According to our latest information, Mrs. Samson is also in East Germany."

"His car is on a meter and covered in parking tickets."

Bret disregarded this complication. "I don't want this to go all around the office, Miss Kent. I'm telling you because I will need you to work with me to allay fears and stop silly rumors." He looked at her; she nodded. "We will have to assume that Mrs. Samson has defected, but I have no reason to believe that her husband was a party to her activities."

"What will happen to her children?"

Bret nodded. Miss Kent was quick; that was one of the problems on Bret's mind. "There's a nanny with them. I have been trying to phone Mrs. Samson's sister, Tessa Kosinski— but there is no reply."

"Do you want me to go and knock on the door?"

"No, we have people to do that kind of thing. Here's the phone number. Keep trying it. And the office number for her husband is in my leather notebook under Kosinski International Holdings. See if he knows where his wife might be. Don't tell him anything other than that both Samsons are delayed on duty overseas. I'm going to the Samsons' house. Ring me there and tell me what's happening. And tell the duty armorer I'm coming down to collect a gun."

"Yes, sir." She went back to the office and started phoning. The idea of Fiona Samson defecting to the communists was too overwhelming for her to properly consider the consequences. Everyone in the Department had watched the steady rise of Fiona Samson. She was a paragon, one of those amazingly lucky people who never put a foot wrong. It was impossible not to envy her: a beautiful woman from a rich family who had left her mark on Oxford, Cordon Bleu cook, charming hostess, with two children and a wonderfully unconventional husband whom Gloria secretly coveted.

"Yes?" came a slurred and sleepy voice. "Ahhhh. What's the time? Who's there?"

It was Tessa, who liked to sleep until eleven o'clock,

awakened by the phone. Gloria told her that Mr. and Mrs. Samson had been unavoidably detained abroad. Would it be possible for Mrs. Kosinski to go to the Samsons' house and take charge of the children? She tried to sound very casual.

It took a few moments to allay Tessa's fears that her sister had been hurt in an accident, but Gloria's charm was well up to the situation and Tessa soon decided that the best way to find out more was to go to the Samson house and ask Bret Rensselaer.

In record time Tessa bathed, put on her makeup, found the Chanel beret with camellia that she always wore when her hair was a mess, and threw a plaid car coat around her shoulders. She looked into the study where her husband was studying share prices on his computer and told him what little she knew.

"Both of them? What's it all about?" he said.

"Neither of them said anything about going anywhere," said Tessa.

"They don't tell you everything." George had grown used to the secretiveness of his wife's family.

"I don't like the sound of it," said Tessa. "I thought there was something odd going on when Fiona asked me to look after her fur coat."

"Is there anything for lunch?" asked George.

"There's a homemade chicken stew in the freezer."

"Is that still all right? It's dated 1981."

"I spent hours on that stew," said Tessa, aggrieved that such rare forays into domesticity were not appreciated.

By the time Tessa arrived at the Samson house, two heavily built men who answered to Bret were rolling up the overalls they had worn to probe between the floorboards and investigate every inch of the dusty attic. Bret Rensselaer was standing before the fireplace wearing a black trenchcoat. He finished the coffee he was drinking.

He'd recently seen Tessa at Whitelands and said, without preliminaries, "Mrs. Samson has taken a trip to the East." He put his cup on the mantelpiece. "For the time being the children need someone to reassure them. . . . The nanny seems to be taking it very calmly, but your presence could make all the difference." Bret had insisted that Fiona engage a reliable girl who could survive a proper security vetting. The present nanny was the daughter of a police inspector. Fiona had complained that she was not a very good nanny, but now Bret's caution was paying off.

"Of course," said Tessa. "I'll do anything I can."

"We're very much in the dark at present," Bret told her, "but whatever the truth of it there will be no official comment. If you get any calls from the press, or any other kind of oddball, say you're the housekeeper, take their number, and call my office." He didn't tell Tessa that every call to this phone was being monitored and two armed men were watching the house to make sure that Moscow didn't try to kidnap the children.

Billy came from the kitchen where Nanny was frying eggs and sausages for lunch. "Hello, Auntie Tess. Mummy is on holiday."

"Yes, isn't that fun?" said Tessa, leaning down to kiss him. "And we're going to have a wonderful time together too."

Billy stood there looking at Bret for a moment and then summed up the courage to say, "Can I look at your gun?"

"What's that?" said Bret, uncharacteristically flustered.

"Nanny says you have a gun in your pocket. She says that's why you won't take your raincoat off."

Bret wet his lips nervously, but long before he could think of any reply, seven-year-old Sally appeared and grabbed

Billy by the arm. "Nanny says you are to come to the kitchen and have your lunch."

"Come along, children," said Tessa. "We'll all have lunch together. Then I'll take you somewhere lovely for tea." She smiled at Bret, and Bret nodded his approval and appreciation.

"I'll slip away soon," said Bret. He'd heard somewhere that Tessa Kosinski had been using hard drugs, but she seemed quite normal today, thank heavens.

In the dining room, Nanny was dishing up the food. She had set the big polished table for four, as if guessing that Tessa would eat with them.

After the two technicians had packed away their detection apparatus and left, Bret took a quick look around on his own account. Upstairs on Fiona's side of the double bed a nightdress was folded neatly and placed on the pillow ready for her. On the bedside table he saw a book from the Department's library. He picked it up and looked at it: a postcard advertising a "hair and beauty salon" off Sloane Street was being used as a bookmark. He stood there for a moment, relishing the intimacy of being in her bedroom. From a security point of view there was nothing to worry him anywhere. The Samsons had worked for the Department a long time; they were careful people.

As he let himself out of the front door, Bret heard Billy insisting, "Well, I'll bet he's shot lots of people."

Bernard Samson had been arrested in a *Biergarten* near Müggelheimer Damm. It was a forest that stretched down to the water of the Müggelsee. A thousand or so inebriated men celebrating Himmelfahrt—Ascension Day—had provided the congestion and confusion in which Bernard, and his closest friend Werner Volkmann, had helped two elderly refugees to escape westward. It was not a simple act of philanthropy. One of the escapees was an agent of the Department.

Werner and the others had got away when Bernard created a diversion. It was a brave thing to do, but Bernard had had ample time to regret his rash gesture. They had locked him in an office room on the top floor of the State Security Ministry's huge office block on Frankfurter Allee.

This office was not like the cells in the basement—from which some prisoners never emerged—but its heavy door and barred window, plus the difficulty of moving from floor to floor in a building where every corridor was surveyed by both cameras and armed guards, was enough to hold anyone but a maniac.

Bernard had been interrogated by an amiable KGB officer named Erich Stinnes. He spoke the same sort of Berlin German that Bernard had grown up with, and in many things the two men saw eye to eye. "Who gets the promotions and the big wages? Desk-bound Party bastards," said Stinnes bitterly. "How lucky you are not having the Party system working against you all the time."

"We have got it," said Bernard. "It's called Eton and Oxbridge."

"What kind of workers' state is that?" said Stinnes as if he'd not heard.

"Are you recording this conversation?" asked Bernard.

"So they can put me in prison with you? Do you think I'm crazy?"

It was the sort of soft treatment that was usually followed up by browbeating from a ferocious tough-guy partner, but Stinnes was waiting for a "KGB colonel from Moscow"— who turned out to be Fiona Samson from London.

By that time Bernard Samson had begun to suspect what was about to happen. Some of the clues Bret Rensselaer had so artfully supplied to the other side had become evident to the ever more worried Bernard.

The desperate realization that his wife was a KGB colonel was a betrayal of such magnitude that Bernard felt physically ill. But the effect on him—and the agony of it—was not greater than many men have suffered when discovering that their wife has been unfaithful to them with another man. For each individual there is a threshold beyond which pain does not increase.

For Fiona the pain was made worse by the guilt of inflicting it upon a man who loved her. She was very tired—and the journey had left her with a splitting headache—that morning when they brought Bernard in to face her. It was a test—perhaps the toughest one she would face—of her ability, her conviction, and her resolution to pursue her role even in the face of Bernard's contempt and hatred.

Brought in by a guard, he was dirty and unshaven. His eyes stared at her in a way she had never seen before. It was a horrible, hateful exchange, but she played her part determined that Bernard would see no glimmer of hope. Only his despair would protect her.

There was a tray with coffeepot and cups on the desk, but Bernard didn't want any. "Is there anything to drink in this office?" he demanded.

She found a bottle of vodka and gave it to him. He poured some into a cup and drank a large measure in one gulp. Poor Bernard; she suddenly became afraid that this would be the beginning of a long drunken bout. "You should cut down on the drinking," she said.

"You don't make it easy to do," he said. He smiled grimly and poured more for himself.

"The D-G will send for you, of course," she said, more calmly than she felt. "You can tell him the official policy at this end will be one of no publicity about my defection. I imagine that will suit him all right, after all the scandals the service has suffered in the past year."

"I'll tell him."

She watched him; he'd turned green. "You never could handle spirits on an empty stomach," said Fiona. "Are you all right? Do you need a doctor?"

"It's you I'm sick of," he said.

It was as much as she could bear. She pressed the floor button and the guard came to take her husband away. Against her training, and her better judgment, she blurted out, "Goodbye then, darling. Do I get one final kiss?"

But Bernard thought she was gloating. He turned away.

As soon as Bernard had been taken through Checkpoint Charlie and released, Fiona pleaded tiredness and went back to the hotel suite they had provided as temporary accommodation. She took a long hot bath, two sleeping pills, and went to bed. She slept the clock around. When she finally awoke there was a moment in which she believed that it was all a terrible dream, that she was at home in London with no complications to her life. She pulled the bedclothes over her head and stayed there unmoving while she slowly came to terms with the bizarre world in which she found herself.

After that terrible encounter with her husband, Fiona's arrival and installation in East Berlin was more endurable. The debriefing seemed to go on forever, but Bret Rensselaer had thought of just about everything, and her prepared answers seemed to satisfy the men who asked the questions.

The KGB personnel chief had gone to a lot of trouble to make her as comfortable as possible, and the minuscule apartment with its hard bed and outdated kitchen had to be compared with the crowded rooms and shared kitchens and bathrooms that were a normal part of living in the capital of the DDR.

Her office in the KGB–Stasi operational command building was light, and it had a new sheepskin rug and a pinewood
desk, imported from Finland. These were considered status
symbols. More important, they'd assigned to her a fifty-year-
old male secretary named Hubert Renn who spoke fluent
Russian, some French, a little English and could take short-
hand. Renn was a hard-line communist of a kind which only
Berlin produced, and which was now almost extinct. He was
the son of a stonemason, and together with his fifteen brothers and sisters had grown up in a dark three-room tenement
in a cobbled alley in Wedding. During the nineteen twenties
das rote Wedding was so solidly communist that the block
was run on communal lines by appointed Party officials.
Renn's mother had been a member of the ISK—Internationaler Sozialistischer Kampfbund—a political sect so strict that
its members rejected alcohol, tobacco, and meat. She left the
ISK upon marriage, since only full-time workers were permitted membership.

Short, agile, undernourished, and eternally combative in
spirit, Renn was also efficient. It was typical of his frugality
and practicality that when he turned back the lapel of his
jacket he revealed a selection of straight pins, safety pins, and
even a needle.

When Fiona first came face-to-face with her newly appointed secretary she thought they'd met before. This mistaken familiarity came from her memories of people depicted
in old photos of Berlin streets. Despite this feeling, she was
to discover that Renn was like no other person she'd ever met.
With his thick neck, ruddy face, neglected teeth, and short
hair that responded to neither brush nor comb, here was a
character straight out of Brecht.

Little Hubert Renn had been exposed to Leninism and
Marxism while in the dented tin bath that doubled as his
cradle. Essentially militant, the ISK rejected Marx's theory

about the inevitable collapse of capitalism. The necessity of violent struggle was something he had heard his mother and father endlessly debating. After such an upbringing no one could teach Renn anything about the phraseology of left-wing politics. Even Pavel Moskvin, a "Moscow-backed bully" with whom Fiona had that morning crossed swords, could not best him in political argument. But Renn didn't mince words about "the German road to socialism" or spend much time discussing why, at the vital *Parteitag* in April 1946, the party's declared aspirations had been based on Marx and Engels and not Lenin and Stalin. Renn—who had been present at that historic congress—preferred to ask, somewhat archly, why it had taken place in the Admiralspalast theater, noted otherwise for "top comedy routines."

"My father was an anarchist," he told Fiona once when they were discussing some of the heresies, and that was the key to Renn's character, for Renn too was an anarchist in his soul. Fiona wondered if he realized it; perhaps he simply didn't give a damn any more. Some who'd waited too long for the millennium became like that. Renn's description of Pavel Moskvin as a "Moscow-backed bully" was freely offered to Fiona that morning before she'd met the man. And Renn was just as ready to be outspoken about everyone else in the building.

For the first couple of weeks Fiona had suspected that this outlandish old fellow had been put into her office as some sort of agent provocateur, or because no one else in the building would put up with such an oddball, but it didn't take her long to understand that in the DDR the bureaucratic process didn't work like that. It wasn't so easy for even the most senior staff to arrange to get the secretary they wanted, and old Renn would not be an agent provocateur easy to run. The truth was that staff members were assigned according to a fixed order of rotation in the personnel office. Her grade was eligible for a clerk of Renn's seniority, and his previous boss had retired the week before she arrived.

Fiona and her secretary had spent all of Wednesday in a small conference center in Köpenick Altstadt, in the wooded outskirts of Berlin. She had witnessed lengthy and sometimes acrimonious exchanges among her colleagues. There had been senior security men from Poland, Czechoslovakia, and Hungary meeting to discuss the still somewhat muddled and disorganized political reform groups and religious groups in the East Bloc. Agreeing on a concerted policy of dealing with them was not so easy. Fiona was pleased at the material she was gathering. It was exactly the sort of intelligence that Bret Rensselaer was so keen on, and the anxiety the communist security men had revealed at this meeting in every way supported Bret's projections. When contact was eventually established with London, she would have a policy formulated.

She was going through the meeting in her mind while they waited for the car that would take them back to the Mitte. The others had been collected by a bus from the transport pool, but Fiona was entitled to her own car. Cars, more than any other perquisite or privilege, were a sign of status, and establishing status was all-important in the DDR. So they waited.

Fiona walked down to the river, admiring the cobbled streets and the crooked old buildings. Surrounded with trees, Köpenick's church and *Rathaus* huddled on a tiny island at a place where the River Spree divided. On the adjacent island—the *Schlossinsel*—there was a richly decorated seventeenth-century palace. In its magnificent *Wappensaal*, Frederick the Great had stood trial for desertion. From where they were standing it was possible to raise a loud cheer for the dilatory rate at which East Berlin was being rebuilt. From this view it was easy to visualize Köpenick on the day that renowned bogus captain marched in to discover how devoutly the Germans revere a military uniform, no matter who wears it.

She had hoped the fresh air would help rid her of her headache: she'd been having too many of these racking headaches lately. It was stress, of course, but that didn't make the pain any easier to endure.

"Herr Renn," said Fiona; she never called him by his first name.

Renn had been looking at the traffic crossing the bridge. Soon the East would be clogged with cars just as the West already was. He looked at her. "Did I forget something, Frau Direktor?"

"No. You never forget anything. You are the most efficient clerk in the building."

He nodded. What she said was right, and he acknowledged the truth of it.

"Do you trust me, Herr Renn?" It was a deliberate way of shocking him.

"I don't understand, Frau Direktor." He glanced around but there was no one else standing along the riverfront, just workers and shoppers going home.

"I never get the minutes of the morning meetings until late in the afternoon of the following day. Is there a reason for that?"

"Everyone receives the minutes by the same delivery." He gave a sly smile. "We are slow; that is the only reason." A large air-conditioned bus came crawling over the bridge. Pale Japanese faces pressed against its gray smoked glass. From inside came the shrill commentary of the tour guide, of which only the words *"Hauptmann von Köpenick"* could be easily distinguished. The bus moved slowly on and was lost behind the trees. "They never go and see the Schloss or the Art Museum," said Renn sadly. "They just want to see the town hall. The tour guide will tell them about the bootmaker who bought an army captain's uniform from a pawnshop, assumed command of some off-duty grenadiers, and arrested the mayor and the city treasurer. Then they will all laugh and say what fools we Germans are."

"Yes," said Fiona. Despite the Schloss and the dark green woodland and the clear blue lakes and the rivers, the only thing anyone ever remembered about Köpenick was its captain.

"The sad thing is," said Renn, "that poor old Wilhelm Voigt, the bootmaker, didn't want the city funds; he wanted a residence permit, and Köpenick had no department authorized to issue one. He wasn't a Berliner, you see, and his escapade was a fiasco."

"I am not a Berliner, nor even a German by birth—" She did not finish.

"But you speak the most beautiful German," said Renn, interrupting her. "Everyone remarks upon it, wonderful *Hochdeutsch.* When I hear it, I feel self-conscious about my miserable accent." He looked at her. "Do you have a headache?"

She shook her head. "Do you not sometimes wonder if I am a class enemy, Herr Renn?"

Renn pursed his lips. "Vladimir Ilyich Lenin was born into a bourgeois family," he said, in what was a typically ambivalent reply.

"Leaving the birth of Comrade Lenin aside for the moment," said Fiona. "If there was an attempt to have me removed from this job, what would be your attitude?"

His already contorted face became agitated as he wet his lips and frowned to indicate deep thought. "I would have to consider the facts," he said finally.

"Consider the facts?"

"I have a wife and family," said Renn. "It is them I have to consider." He turned to see the river, slow and unctuous now; once it had been fast, clear, and fresh. Not so long ago anglers had landed big fish here, but there was no sign of any now. He stared down into the water and hoped the Frau Direktor would be satisfied.

"Are you saying you would throw me to the wolves?" said Fiona.

"Wolves? No!" He turned to her. "I am not a thrower, Frau Direktor. I am one of the people who are thrown." The church clock struck six. His working day was over and done. He opened his overcoat in order to reach into his back pocket for a flask. "About this time I sometimes take a small glass of schnapps . . . if the Frau Direktor would permit."

"Go ahead," said Fiona. She was surprised. She didn't know the old man was such a dedicated drinker, but it explained a lot of things.

He unscrewed the top, to use it as a cup, and poured a sizable measure. He offered it to her. "Would the Frau Direktor . . . ?"

"No, thank you, Herr Renn."

He brought it up toward his mouth carefully, so as not to spill it, bending his head to meet it. He drank half of it in one gulp, looked at her as it warmed his veins, and said, "I'm too old to get into vendettas." A pause. "But that doesn't mean I have no guts for it." A streetcar went past, its wheels screaming protest on the rails as it turned the corner. "Is the Frau Direktor quite sure . . . ?"

"Quite sure, thank you, Herr Renn."

He held the drink and stared across the river as if she weren't there, and when he spoke it was as if he were talking to himself. "Most of the people on our floor are Germans, time-serving officials like me. None of them are looking for a battle; they are waiting for their pension. The eight 'friends' are another matter." He drank the rest of the vodka from the metal cup.

Fiona nodded. Since 1945 Russians were always called "friends," even when some German war veteran found himself recounting the way in which such "friends" had jumped into his trench and bayoneted his comrades. "Perhaps I will have a drink," said Fiona.

Renn wiped the rim of the cup with his fingers and poured one for her. "Six of those friends are in other departments and would not be promoted whatever happened to you."

Fiona took a tiny sip of vodka. It was damned strong stuff; she nearly choked on it. No wonder the old man had a red-veined face. "I see what you mean," she said. It left the two Russians, both German specialists, Pavel Moskvin and the one who affected the operating name of Stinnes (as Lenin and Stalin had assumed theirs). These were the two men she had clashed with during the conference that afternoon, tough professionals who had let her know that working for a woman was not a relationship to which they would gladly accede. The argument had come about because of a proposed operational journey to Mexico City. She suspected that the whole thing was chosen simply as a way of showing her how formidable their combined strengths could be against her.

Renn said, "The big man, Moskvin, is the dangerous one. He has considerable influence within the Party machine. At present he is in disgrace with Moscow—some black-market scandal that was never made public—and such men will go to absurd lengths to prove their worth. He is emotional and violent; and well-adjusted people fall victim to action that is sudden and unpremeditated. The other man, Erich Stinnes, with his convincing Berlin German complete with all the slang and expletives, is an intellectual, icy cold and calculating. He will always think in the long term. For someone as clever as you, he will prove easier to deal with."

"I hope so," said Fiona.

"We must drive a wedge between them," said Renn.

"How?"

"We will find a way. Moskvin is a skillful administrator, but Stinnes has been a field agent. Field agents never really settle down to the self-discipline and cooperation that our work demands."

"That's true," said Fiona, and for a moment thought of her husband and his endless difficulties at the London office.

"Don't allow your authority to be undermined. Moscow has put you here because they want to see changes. If there is resistance, Moscow will support change and whoever is making the changes. Therefore you must be sure you are the one making the changes."

"You are something of a philosopher, Herr Renn."

"No, Frau Direktor, I am an apparatchik."

"Whatever you are, I am grateful to you." She looked in her handbag, found some aspirins, and swallowed two of them without water.

"It is nothing," said the old man as he watched her gulp the pills, although of course they both knew he'd stuck his neck out. Even more important, he'd indicated to her that under other circumstances he'd probably yield more. Fiona wondered whether he was already calculating what she could do for him in return. She dismissed the idea; better to wait and see. Meanwhile he might prove an invaluable ally.

"Nothing to you, perhaps, but a friendly word goes a long way in a new job."

Renn, who'd been watching the bridge, touched his hat as if in salutation but in fact he eased the hat because the band was too tight. "From each according to ability; to each according to need," the old man quoted, stuffing the flask back into his pocket. "And here comes our Volvo." Not car, she noted, but Volvo. He was proud that she rated an imported car. He smiled at her.

In a year or so she would scuttle off back to the West and Hubert Renn would be left to face the music; Stasi interrogations were not gentle. They would be bound to suspect that he was in league with her. She hated the thought of what she was doing to him. It made her feel like a Judas, but that of course is exactly what she was. Bret had warned her that these conflicting loyalties were stressful, but that didn't make them any easier to bear.

When she got home, to one of the coveted apartments in the wedding-cake blocks that line Frankfurter Allee, she sat down and thought about the conversation for a long time. Finally she began to understand something of Renn's motivation. Just as the Russians could not fathom the way in which some Europeans could be staunch capitalists but rabidly anti-American, Fiona had not understood the deeply felt anti-Russian feelings that were a part of Hubert Renn's psyche. Renn, she was later to discover, had seen his mother raped by Russian soldiers and his father beaten unconscious during those memorable days of 1945 when the commander's Order of the Day told the Red Army, "Berlin is yours." And later she was to hear Hubert Renn refer to his Russian "friends" by the archaic and less friendly word *"Panje."*

She washed a lettuce and cut thin slices from a *Bockwurst.* It was fresh fruit she missed so much; she still couldn't understand why such things were so scarce. She had found a privately owned bakery near the office and the bread was good. She'd have to be careful not to put on weight; everything plentiful was fattening.

It was an austere little room well suited to reflection and work. The walls were painted light gray, and there were only three pictures: an engraving of a Roman emperor, a sepia photo of fashionable ladies circa 1910, and a colored print of Kirchner's *Pariser Platz.* The frames, their neglected condition, as well as the subject matter, suggested they had been selected at random from some government storage depot. She was grateful for that human touch just the same. Her bedroom was no more than an alcove with a hinged screen. The old tubular-frame bed was painted cream and reminiscent of the one she'd slept in at her boarding school. There were many aspects of life in the DDR—from the endless petty restrictions to the dull diet—that reminded her of boarding school. But she told herself over and over that she had survived boarding school and so she would survive this.

When she went to bed that night she was unable to sleep. She hadn't had one night of sound natural sleep since coming over here. That terrible encounter with Bernard had been a ghastly way to start her new life. Now every night she found herself thinking about him and the children. She found herself asking why she'd been born lacking a certain kind of maternal urge. Why had she never delighted in the babies and wanted to hug them night and day as so many mothers do? And was she now being acutely tortured by their absence because of the way she had squandered those early years with them? She would have given anything for a chance to go back and see them as babies again, to cuddle them and feed them and read to them and play with them the nonsense games that Bernard's mother was so good at.

Sometimes, during the daytime, the chronic ache of being separated from her family was slightly subdued as she tried to cope with the overwhelming demands made upon her. The intellectual demands—the lies and false loyalties—she could cope with, but she hadn't realized how vulnerable she would be to the emotional stress. She remembered some little joke that Bret had made about women adapting to a double life more easily than a man. Every woman, he said, was expected to be hooker or matron, companion, mother, servant, or friend at a moment's notice. Being two people was a simple task for any woman. It was typical Rensselaer bull-shit. She switched on the light and reached for the sleeping pills. In fact she knew she would never return to being that person she'd been such a short time ago. She had already been stretched beyond the point of return.

Whitelands, England:
June 1983

"No, Dicky, I can hear you perfectly," said Bret Rensselaer as he pressed the phone to his ear and shrugged at Silas Gaunt, who was standing opposite him with the extension earpiece. Dicky Cruyer, German Stations Controller, was phoning from Mexico City and the connection was not good. "You've made it all perfectly clear. I can't see any point in going through it again. . . . Yes, I'll talk to the Director-General and tell him what you said. . . . Yes. . . . Yes, good to talk to *you*, Dicky. I'll see what I can do. Goodbye." He replaced the handset and sighed deeply.

Silas Gaunt put the earpiece in the slot and said, "Dicky Cruyer tracked you down."

"Yes, he did," said Bret Rensselaer, although there had been little difficulty about it. The Director-General had told Bret to visit Silas and "put him in the picture." Bret had left the Whitelands telephone number as his contact, and Mrs. Porter—Gaunt's housekeeper—had put the call from Mexico through to the farm manager's office.

Having thanked the greenhouse boy who'd run to get them, Silas, wearing an old anorak, muddy boots, and corduroy trousers tied with string at the ankles, led the way out to the cobbled yard, ducking under the low door. Bret was being shown around the farm.

"I don't encourage hunting guns any more," said Silas. "Too damned hearty. Those gigantic early breakfasts and mud all through the house. It became too much for Mrs. Porter and, to tell you the truth, too much for me too. Anglers are not so much trouble: quieter, and they're gone all day with a packet of cheese sandwiches."

Silas swung open the yard gate and fastened it again after Bret. The fields stretched away into the distance. The harvest would be gathered early. The field behind the barn would be the first one cut, and flocks of sparrows, warned by the sound of the nearby machinery that the banquet would not be there forever, were having a feed that made their flight uncertain as they swooped and fluttered among the pale ears.

It was a lovely day: silky cirrus torn and trailed carelessly across the deep blue sky. The sun was as high as it could get, and, like a ball thrown into the air, it paused and the world stood still, waiting for the afternoon to begin.

As they walked along they kept close to the hedge so that Silas could be sure it had been properly trimmed and weeded. He grabbed ears of unripe wheat and, with the careless insolence of the nomad, crushed them in his hand, scattering chaff, husk, and seed through his splayed fingers. Bret, who had no interest in farms or farming, plodded awkwardly behind in the rubber boots that Silas had found for him, with a stained old windbreaker to protect his elegant dark-blue suit. They went through a door set in the tall walls that surrounded the kitchen garden. It was a wonderful wall, light and dark bricks making big diamond patterns that were just visible under the espaliered fruit trees.

"I am not convinced that it was a wise move to send both Dicky Cruyer and Bernard Samson to Mexico City," said Bret, to resume the conversation. "It leaves us somewhat depleted, and those two seem to fight all the time.''

Silas pointed to various vegetables and said he was going to start a little rose garden next year and reduce the ground given to swedes, turnips, and beetroots. Then he said, ''How is Bernard taking it?''

''His wife's defection? Not too well. I was thinking of making him take a physical, but in his present paranoid state he'd resent it. I guess he'll pull out of it. Meanwhile, I'll keep an eye on him.''

''I have no real experience as an agent in the field,'' said Silas. ''Neither have you. I can think of very few people in your building who know what's involved. In that respect, we are like First World War generals, sitting back in our château, sipping our brandy, and subjecting the troops to nastiness that we don't comprehend.''

Bret, not knowing exactly what was coming and never ready to state his views without time to think, made a sound that indicated measured agreement.

''But I have seen a lot of them,'' said Silas, ''and I know something of what makes such people tick. Fiona Samson will not wind down slowly like a neglected clock. She'll keep going at full power until she has nothing more to give. Then, like a light bulb, she'll glow extra bright before going out.''

It sounded too melodramatic to Bret. He looked at Silas, wondering if this same little speech, with other names, had been used many times before, like next-of-kin letters when the unthinkable happened. He couldn't decide. He nodded. ''When the question of her going over there was first discussed, I was in favor of taking the husband into our confidence.''

''I know you were. But his ignorance has proved a great asset to us, and to his wife. It's given her a good start. Now it's up to her.'' Silas looked around him in a proprietorial manner and crushed a clod of earth with the toe of his heavy boot. It was good fertile soil, dark and rich with leaf mold.

Bret undid his borrowed windbreaker and fingered a bundle of computer printouts to be sure he hadn't dropped it during his walk.

It was hot in the garden, everything silent and still, protected by the high garden walls. This was the culmination of the gardener's year. There was billowing greenery everywhere, but all too soon the summer would be over, the leaves withered, the earth cold and hard. "Look at these main-crop carrots," said Silas. He bent over to grab the feathery leaves. For a moment he seemed on the point of uprooting one but then he changed his mind and let go. "Carrots are tricky," said Silas. "They grow to maturity and you have to decide whether to lift them and store them or leave them in the earth."

Bret nodded.

"Leave them in the earth and you get a sweeter-tasting carrot, but if there is a really severe frost, you lose them." He found a carrot and pulled it up. It was small and thin but of a beautiful color. "On the other hand, if you lift them, you can be sure they haven't been got at by the worms and slugs. See what I mean, Bret?"

"So how do you decide when to pull them?"

"I consult," said Silas. "I talk to the experts."

Bret decided to ignore the wider implications of Silas's agricultural nostrums and return to the subject of Bernard Samson. "But once that decision was taken, it might have been wiser to move Bernard Samson out of Operations. He's too damned curious about what exactly happened."

"That's natural enough," said Silas.

"He pries and asks questions. On that account, and a few others too, Samson was not the man to send to talk to a potential KGB defector in Mexico City, or anywhere else."

"Why?" asked Silas sardonically. "Because he hasn't been to university?"

"This KGB fellow, Stinnes—whatever his motives or intentions—will be expecting an Oxbridge man. Sending a blue-collar type like Samson will make him think he doesn't rate."

"You're a dedicated Anglophile, Bret. No disrespect, I'm delighted that you should be. But it sometimes leads you into an exaggerated regard for our old British institutions."

Bret stiffened. "I have always supported Samson, even when he was at his most intractable. But Oxford and Cambridge attract the most competitive students and will always be the Department's finest source of recruits. I'd hate to see the day come when that policy changed."

Silas ran his hand lovingly over the outdoor tomatoes. One of them, full size and deep red, he picked and weighed in his hand. "Oxford and Cambridge provide an excellent opportunity to learn, although not better than any well-motivated student can find in a first-class library. But an Oxbridge education can make graduates feel that they are members of some privileged elite, destined to lead and make decisions that will be inflicted upon lesser beings. Such elitism must of necessity be based on expectations that are often unfulfilled. Thus Oxbridge has not only provided Britain with its most notable politicians and civil servants but its most embittered traitors too." Silas smiled sadly, as if the traitors had played a long-forgiven and half-forgotten prank upon him.

"Elite?" said Bret. "You'd search a long way to find someone more arrogant than Bernard Samson."

"Bernard's arrogance comes from something inside him, some vitality, force, and a seemingly inexhaustible fund of courage. Our great universities will never be able to furnish inner strength; no one can. What teachers provide is always superimposed on the person that already exists. Education is a carapace, a cloak laid on the soul, a protection, a coloration or something to hide inside.''

To get the conversation back on a more practical plane, Bret said, ''And Samson drinks too much.''

''That's rather judgmental,'' said Silas. ''Few of us would be absolved from that one, truth be told.'' Silas took a clasp knife and cut the tomato in half to study it before biting a piece out of it.

''You're right, of course,'' said Bret deferentially, and added, ''Remember, I recommended Samson for the German Desk.''

Silas swallowed the piece of tomato but some of the juice dribbled down his chin. He wiped his mouth with the back of his hand and said, ''Indeed you did. But you didn't do it with enough vigor and follow-through to get it for him.''

''I plead the Fifth, Silas.'' Bret decided not to explain that his decision was deliberate and reasoned; it would take too long. ''But let's not argue. Samson and Cruyer are both in Mexico. We have a lot riding on this one; a careless move now could set us back severely.''

''Yes, we must move with great caution,'' said Silas. ''We have the woman installed in the East, and now we must hope that all continues to go well for her. No contact yet?'' He offered the remaining half of tomato to Bret, but Bret shook his head. Silas threw the tomato onto the rubbish heap.

''No, Silas, no contact. I'm leaving her alone for as long as possible. It's not primarily an intelligence-gathering operation at this stage of the game. I think you and the D-G both agreed that it shouldn't be. We said that right at the start.''

''Yes, Bret, we did. She has enough problems, I'm sure.''

''For the time being, let her masters digest the material she's providing them with.'' Bret had been moving restlessly, looking around to be sure they were not observed or overheard. Now he fixed his eyes on Silas. ''But before too long we must provide the Soviets with some really solid affirmation of Mrs. Samson's creed. It's going well, but we must exploit and reinforce success." These final words were spoken with fervor.

Silas looked blankly at Bret. The words Bret had emphasized were the sort of axiom to be found in the works of Sun-tzu, Vegetius, Napoleon, or some wretch of that ilk. Silas did not believe that such teachings embodied truths of any relevance to the craft of espionage, but decided that this was not the right time to take that up with Bret.

Thinking Silas might not have heard, Bret said it again. "We must exploit and reinforce success."

Silas looked at him and nodded. Despite that glacial personality there was a certain boyish enthusiasm in Bret, a quality not unusual in Americans of any class. Bret combined it with another American characteristic, the self-righteous passion of the crusader. Silas had always thought of him as warrior prince, hand-woven silk under the heavy armor, marching through the desert behind the True Cross. Austere and calculating, Bret would have made an invincible Richard the Lionheart but an equally convincing Saladin.

Silas said, "I hope you're not thinking of anything costly, Bret. The other evening I calculated that the code and cipher changes and so on that the D-G ordered after Mrs. Samson went over there must have cost the Department nearly a million sterling. Add in the costs we don't shoulder, I'd say there was a worldwide bill for three million. And that's without the incalculable loss of face we suffered at losing her."

"I'm watching the bottom line, Silas."

"Good. And what did you conclude about this fellow in Mexico City, Bret, animal, vegetable, or mineral?" Silas bent over and fingered the spinach like a child dabbling a hand in the water.

"That's what I want to talk about. He's real enough, a forty-year-old KGB major of considerable experience." Bret put on the speed-cop-style glasses he used when reading, and, reaching inside the stained waterproof that Silas had loaned him, he produced a concertina of computer printout. "No need to tell you that our records don't normally extend down to KGB majors, but this fellow has a high profile so we know something of his background." Bret looked down and read from the paperwork. "Sadoff. Uses the name Stinnes. Born 1943. Regular officer as father. Raised in Berlin. Assigned to KGB, Section Forty-four, the Religious Affairs Bureau. With Security Police in Cuba—"

"For God's sake, Bret, I can read all that piffle for myself. I'm asking you who he *is.*"

"And whether he really wants to come over to us. Yes, of course you're asking that, but it's too early yet." He passed the computer printout to Silas, who held it without looking at it.

"What does Cruyer say about him?"

"I'm not sure Cruyer has actually seen him yet."

"Then what the devil are those two idiots doing out there?"

"You'll be pleased to hear that it was Samson who saw Stinnes."

"And?"

"This one is worth having, Silas. We could get a lot out of him if he's properly handled. But we must go very slowly. For safety's sake we must assume he is approaching us under orders from Moscow."

Silas sniffed and handed the printout back unread. A corpulent pirate, scruffy in that self-assured manner that is often the style of such establishment figures, he shuffled along the line of tall stakes up which the broad beans had grown. Long since shunned by the kitchen, there were, among the leaves, a few beans that had grown huge and pale. He plucked one and broke the pod open to get the seeds inside. He ate one. When he turned around to Bret he said, "So. Two possibilities. Either he will go back to Moscow and tell them what he discovered, or he is genuine and will do as we say."

"Yes, Silas."

"Then why don't we play the same game? Let's welcome the fellow. Give him money and show him our secrets. What?"

"I'm not sure I follow you, Silas."

"Abduct the bastard. Moscow screams in anger. We offer Stinnes a chance to go back and work for us. He goes back there."

"And they execute him," said Bret.

"Not if we abduct him. He is blameless."

"Moscow might not see it that way."

"Don't break my heart; this is a little KGB shit."

"I suppose so, yes."

"Romance him, turn him around, and send him back to Moscow. Who cares if he betrays us or betrays them. . . . You don't see it?"

"I'm not sure I do," said Bret.

"Dammit, Bret. He finds us in total disarray after the loss of Mrs. Samson. We're distraught. We give him a briefing designed to limit the damage we've suffered from her defection. He goes back believing that. Who cares which side he thinks he's working for? Even if they execute him, they'll squeeze him first. Come to think of it, that would suit us best."

"It's brilliant, Silas."

"Well, don't sound so bloody woeful."

"It will require a lot of preparation." Bret was beginning to discover that a secret operation shared only between himself, the Director, and Silas Gaunt meant that he himself did virtually all the hard work. "It will be a very time-consuming and difficult job."

"Look at it as a wonderful opportunity," said Silas. "The one thing we must be sure about is that this KGB fellow doesn't cotton to Sinker. I don't want him to even get a hint that our strategy is now directed toward the economy."

"Is that what it's directed at?"

"Don't be bitter, Bret. You've got just about everything you've asked for. We can't go one hundred percent manpower and economy; the military and political considerations are still valid."

"It's a matter of definition, Silas. Rearmament can be described in economic terms or political ones without bending the figures."

Silas took another bean from its pod and examined it. "We'll huff and we'll puff and we'll blow their Wall down." He offered Bret a bean. Bret didn't want one.

"I'm not the big bad wolf," said Bret.

14

East Berlin:

September 1983

F$_{IONA}$ S$_{AMSON}$ $_{WAS}$ $_{SURPRISED}$ $_{WHEN}$ $_{HER}$ $_{SECRETARY}$, Hubert Renn, invited her to his birthday party. She spent an hour or so thinking about it. She knew that Germans liked to celebrate birthdays, but now that she had got to know him better she had found him to be a pugnaciously independent personality, so set in his ways it was hard to imagine him going to the trouble of arranging a birthday party, let alone one to which his superior was to be invited.

Fiona had come to terms with him, but she knew that Renn did not easily adapt to taking orders from a young person or from a woman, let alone a young foreign woman. But Renn was German and he did not make his feelings evident in any way that would affect his work.

And there were the problems of what present to give him and what to wear. The first was quickly solved by a visit to the *valuta* shop where Fiona, as a privilege that went with her job, was permitted to spend a proportion of her salary on goods of Western manufacture. She bought a Black & Decker electric drill, always one of the most sought-after imports in a country where repairs and construction were constant problems. She wrapped it carefully and added a fancy bow.

What to wear was not so easily decided. She wondered what sort of event it was to be. Would it be a small informal dinner, or a big family gathering, or a smart affair with dancing to live music? She rummaged through the clothes she'd brought with her—all of them selected for banality of design and somber colors—and decided on a short afternoon dress she'd bought long ago at Liberty in Regent Street, narrow stripes of black and crimson with pleated skirt and high buttoned collar. She had bought it for a holiday with Bernard and the children. They had stayed at a farm in western Scotland and it had rained almost every day. She had brought the dress home again still unworn. She looked at herself in the mirror and decided that, now she had at last discovered a reasonably good hairdresser, it would do.

The dinner party, for such it turned out to be, was given in a private room in an elaborate sports club complex near Grünau. Although she could have asked for the use of a car, Fiona went on the S-Bahn to Grünau Station and then caught a streetcar.

Here in this attractive suburb southeast of the city, the River Spree has become the Dahme and there is extensive forest on both banks. The club's main entrance, around which the new premises had been built, dated from the 1936 Olympics. Along this 2,000 meters of swastika-bedecked Berlin river, thirty thousand spectators had seen the amazing triumphs of physically perfect German youth using radically new designs of lightweight sculls and shells. Hitler's Olympics were transmitted on the world's first public TV service, and Leni Riefenstahl made her world-acclaimed film *Olympiad.* The golden successes resulting from selection, dedicated training, and German technology—and the way in which the propaganda machine used them—provided the Third Reich with a political triumph. The 1936 Olympics afforded a glimpse of the Nazi war machine in mufti. It had been, in all its aspects, a taste of things to come.

Fiona was in the lobby looking at the Tenth Olympiad photos and some of the old awards, displayed in a big glass case, when Hubert Renn saw her. She offered him her best wishes and he bowed. "Are you interested in sport, Frau Direktor?"

"At college I was on the swimming team. And you, Herr Renn?"

"No. Apart from hockey I was never able to do very much. I was not tall enough." Renn was dressed in a suit she hadn't seen before, with a red bow tie and matching kerchief in his top pocket. "I am so glad you were able to honor us with your presence, Frau Direktor. It will be only a small gathering and it won't go on too late. We are simple people."

The day of the celebration was not his saint's day, of course; Renn's father, a dedicated atheist, could never have sanctioned a baptism. But there were candles in abundance. In Germany, where the pre-Christian heritage is evident in every old festival and custom, no revelry is complete without the flame of the candle.

It was a small gathering, held in the Gisela Mauermayer room, named in honor of Germany's 1936 world discus champion. Her portrait was painted on the wall, a beautiful sad-eyed girl with long blond hair worn in a bun. The table was laid with wines and water already to hand. At the head of the table a few small presents had been placed next to Hubert's plate. Renn's wife, Gretel, was wearing a wonderful dress. When Fiona admired it she admitted it had belonged to her grandmother and she hadn't had a chance to wear it for over eight years. Gretel was a shy slim woman, aged about fifty, with graying hair that had obviously been specially tinted and waved for this evening.

The meal was excellent. Some hunter friend of the Renns always provided venison as a birthday gift. Marinated in wine, spices, and herbs, it made a delicious pot roast at this time of the year when the Berlin evenings were becoming chilly.

It was a curious party, marked by a certain stiffness that was in no way accounted for by any shortcoming in Fiona's grasp of the language. Yet the birthday rituals seemed rehearsed, and even when the drink had been consumed, Fiona noticed no substantial relaxation among the guests. It was as if they were all on their best behavior for her.

Among those seated around the table there was Renn's daughter Käthe, noticeably pregnant, and her dutiful husband, who worked in one of the lignite-burning power stations that polluted the Berlin air. Hubert Renn's bearded brother Felix was a retired airline pilot, seventy years old and a veteran of Spain's civil war. There were also a man and his wife who worked as clerks in the same building as Fiona and Renn and, seated next to Fiona, a cordial Englishwoman named Miranda. She was, like Fiona, in her middle thirties and spoke with the brisk accent affected by smart Londoners and those who wish to be mistaken for them.

"It's an unusual name," said Fiona. "Is that a tedious thing to say?"

"I chose it. I was an actress before I married. It was my stage name. I discovered it when I was in *The Tempest* at school. I was a terrible little snob. It stuck."

"It's a lovely name."

"No one over here thinks it's very unusual of course, and I've got used to it."

"Were you an actress in England?"

"Yes. I was quite good. I should have kept to it, but I was getting on for thirty years old and I'd never had a decent West End part. My agent had decided to retire. A man fell in love with me and I married him. You know how it happens."

"And he was German?"

"Very German . . . young and sexy and masterful, just

what I needed at the time, I suppose. He was on holiday in England and staying with people I knew."

"And he brought you to Berlin?"

"I'd been a member of the party since I was eighteen so I couldn't yield to the capitalist lures of Hollywood, right? And my Mister Right had friends at the Babelsberg film studios. Babelsberg, I thought, the UFA studios: Josef von Sternberg, Emil Jannings, Greta Garbo, Marlene Dietrich. Wow! And this *Wunderkind* guaranteed that there would be plenty of acting work over here."

"And was there?"

"I don't know. I promptly became pregnant, so after a few one-day jobs playing Englishwomen and American women for TV, I looked for other work. I did ghastly little jobs translating for various government departments, travel adverts and that sort of garbage. And then my husband died."

"Oh, I'm sorry. What did your husband do?"

"He got fall-down drunk."

"Oh," said Fiona.

"Little Klaus was born. I managed. I had the apartment, and there was a decent pension. I suppose the DDR is the best place to be if you have to find yourself a widow with a baby."

"I suppose it is."

"You're married?"

"I left my husband to come here," said Fiona. It had become her standard reply to such questions, but it still hurt her to say it. Into her mind there immediately came the picture of Bernard and the two children sitting around the table eating a frozen dinner the night she first met Harry Kennedy. How she yearned for them now.

"Yes, Hubert told me that you'd given up everything for your beliefs. That was a wonderful thing to do. Your perfume is heavenly. Sometimes I think good makeup and perfume are the only things I miss. What is it . . . if you don't mind me asking?''

"No, of course not. Arpège. I haven't graduated to any of the new ones. Was your husband related to the Renns?''

"Arpège, yes, of course it is. Hubert is the godfather to my little Klaus.''

"I see.''

"Not really a godfather, of course; this ersatz arrangement they have over here.''

"*Namengebung,*'' said Fiona. It was the secular ceremony permitted by the communist regime.

"Your German is fantastic,'' said Miranda. "Fancy your knowing that. I wish my German were half as good. When I hear you gabbing away, I envy you.''

"Your German sounded excellent to me,'' said Fiona.

"Yes, it's very fluent, but I don't know what I'm saying half the time.'' She laughed. "I suppose that's how I got myself into trouble in the first place.''

It was then that Hubert's brother Felix stood up to propose a toast. The *Sekt* was poured, and the cake was cut. Cakes are to German-speaking people what soufflés, spaghetti, and smoked salmon are to their European neighbors. Hubert Renn's birthday cake in no way challenged this doctrine. The beautifully decorated multilayered cake was so big that even one thin slice proved too much for Fiona.

Felix, a tall, bony old fellow with a closely trimmed beard, proved to be a good speaker and he kept the company amused for five minutes before toasting the Renns.

When the celebration ended they went outside to find a brilliant moon. A light wind moved the trees and there was no sound other than a distant plane. Felix Renn said it was the late flight heading out of Berlin for Warsaw.

Declining offers of a car ride, Fiona walked back to Grünau Station. She had discovered walking to be one of the few compensations of her life here. A woman could walk in these empty streets without fear of being attacked or accosted, and even this urban neighborhood, so near the center of town, was green and rural.

Living alone in a strange town had not been good for Fiona. She kept telling herself that it provided her with a chance to collect her thoughts in a way she could never do before. In fact the loneliness had slowly given way to periods of deep depression, black and morbid moods, not that state of low spirits that is called depression by those who have never known the real thing. Fiona had the black bouts of despair and self-disgust from which recovery comes slowly. And like most psychological illness her fears were rooted in actuality. It was crippling to be without Bernard and the children—and painful to think how much they must hate her. Only with great difficulty was she able to endure her miseries.

Work was the medicine she took. When she wearied of the work provided by her job, she read German history and improved her spoken and written German; she still got the cases wrong sometimes. She never thought about how long she might be here. Like a committed combat soldier, she adjusted her mind to the idea of being dead. Fortunately, Renn and the others had not known her in her normal frame of mind and assumed that this moody woman with her unexplained silences and flashes of bad temper was the person she had always been.

As she walked along the road under the trees, the moonlight bright enough to throw her shadow onto the grass shoulder, she speculated about Renn's birthday party, and his choice of guests and could not help wondering if there was to be another birthday party that would better reflect the relatives, friends, and neighbors that he clearly had in abundance. Were the people present the ones closest to him and his wife after a lifetime spent here in the city? If not, why not?

And if such an elegant little dinner—extravagant by the standards of life in the DDR—was a normal event in the life of the Renns, why had his wife, Gretel, not worn that dress for eight years?

What of the forthright Miranda? In this puzzling town, with all its half-truths and double meanings, there was nothing more enigmatic than candor. She still hadn't worked it out by the time she reached Grünau. The grandiose nineteenth-century Stadtbahn station was bleak and neglected, a puddle of rain under the arch, cracked paving, its shiny brickwork and enamel signs stained with dribbles of rust. And yet the platforms were swept and tidy and the trash bins emptied. To Fiona a lot of the East sector of the city was like this, like the dilapidated mansion of some impoverished duchess who will not admit defeat. The other people waiting for the train were quietly spoken and respectably dressed. Even the mandatory drunk was sitting on a cart humming softly to himself.

The train came in and the guard, in a smart uniform, watched the drunk stumble safely aboard before giving the go-ahead.

As the train rattled along, elevated above the city on its elaborate iron support, Fiona thought again about the guests. Felix, Hubert's eloquent brother—she wondered which side he'd fought for in the civil war in Spain. If for the communists, how did he survive the Nazi years, and if for Franco how did he endure the ones following? And yet it was the presence of Miranda that puzzled Fiona most. She wondered why Hubert Renn had never mentioned that the mother of his "godchild" was a Londoner born and bred, and why he'd not told Fiona that another Englishwoman was to be with them tonight. Had it been the birthday party of some other person, none of these things might have merited comment, but Fiona knew Renn by now and she knew this birthday dinner was not the sort of function he enjoyed.

Fiona's curiosity would have been satisfied by the scene in the same Gisela Mauermayer room at ten-thirty the next morning. Miranda was there with two Russians and a black girl. She had described the previous evening in great detail.

Fiona's bellicose colleague Pavel Moskvin was also there. He was about fifty years old and weighed over two hundred pounds. He had the build of an American football player. His hair was closely cropped and his eyes set a little too close to the squashed nose, which made his large head look as if it had been bowled along the ground until its protuberances broke off and then stuck on his shoulders without a neck.

Sitting calmly in a corner, occasionally reading a book, was Erich Stinnes, a wiry man with a pointed face and hair thinning enough to show his scalp. His metal-rim spectacles, of the most utilitarian design, brown corduroy suit, and heavy boots made up an ensemble that well-paid communists sometimes found irresistible.

Opposite Stinnes sat a tall, lively Jamaican woman in her late twenties. Her fake leopard-skin coat was thrown across a chair, and she was dressed in a tight white sweater and red pants. She sat toying with a red apple, rolling it across the table from hand to hand. Miranda looked at the black girl. Quite apart from her clothes and makeup, there was something about her manner that had immediately identified her as being from the West.

Staring at Miranda, Moskvin, restless with the contained anger that boiled continually within him, said, "Tell me about her." His voice was hoarse, like that of a man who shouts too much.

"I've told you," said Miranda softly. She stood at the

other end of the table. She refused to sit down and was determined not to be intimidated by him. She'd seen his type of Russian before, many times.

"Tell me again, damn you." He went and studied the painting of the discus thrower with unseeing eyes.

Miranda spoke to his back. "Frau Samson is an inch or so taller than I am. She has longer legs."

Without turning around he said, "That doesn't matter."

"You know nothing," said Miranda, contemptuous now that she was on the firm ground of her own expertise. "If I am to imitate her walk, it will make a difference."

The black girl took a noisy bite out of the apple. Moskvin glared at her. She smiled. They all disliked him; Moskvin knew that. He'd grown up amid such hostility. It was not something that had ever troubled him.

"We'll arrange it so you won't have to imitate the walk," said Moskvin, still looking at the black girl. Then he turned and fixed those eyes on Miranda. "Can you do her voice?"

"Her voice is easy," said Miranda.

The black girl took another bite of the apple. "Keep quiet," said Moskvin.

"I gotta eat, buddy," said the black girl.

Moskvin went to the table and switched on the tape recorder. Fiona's voice came from it, saying, "It's a lovely name." *(pause)* "Were you an actress in England?" *(pause)* "And he brought you to Berlin?" *(pause)* "Oh, I'm sorry. What did your husband do?"

Moskvin switched off the machine. "Now you," he said.

Miranda hesitated only a moment, and then, stiff and formal and holding her hands together as if about to sing lieder, she recited the same words. "It's a lovely name." She took a breath. "Were you an actress in England?" She wet her lips and, completely relaxed now, delivered the last three without pausing. "And he brought you to Berlin? Oh, I'm sorry. What did your husband do?'' Then she smiled. It was an amazing performance and she knew it. She'd always had this ability to mimic voices. Sometimes she found herself copying the voices of people she was speaking with, which could cause annoyance.

"Good," said Moskvin.

"Remarkable," said Stinnes. The black girl clapped her hands very softly. Miranda still couldn't decide whether the girl was hostile to all of them or only to Moskvin.

"But will you be able to do it without the recording to prompt you?" said Moskvin.

"I'd need to see her again."

"That will be arranged, and we'll have lots and lots of recordings for you."

"The recordings are a help, but I must see her speak, too. I have to watch her mouth. So much depends on the tongue if I am to make conversation. And I need to hear more of her vocabulary."

"You will be told exactly what to say. There is no need for you to be sidetracked into any conversation other than the words we want spoken. It's simply a matter of making the voice sound natural and imitating it accurately."

"Good," said Miranda.

"The element of surprise will be on your side," said Moskvin. "You will have spoken to the husband and to the sister before they recover from their amazement."

"The phone is easy, but—"

"I have solved the other problem," said Moskvin. "Her husband will be in a car, the driver's seat, and he'll be prevented from turning around. That will be Harmony's job and she's an expert, aren't you, Harmony?"

"You bet your ass I am, boss," said Harmony, in a tone of self-mockery that Moskvin seemed not to register.

Still looking at Miranda, Moskvin said, "You'll get into

the back seat. You'll be close but he won't see you."

"Good. I'll use the Arpège perfume she likes. He'll recognize the scent."

"He'll smell you but he won't see you," said Moskvin.

"I could never make myself look like her," said Miranda. "Just one glimpse of me and he'd—"

"I have thought of that too," said Moskvin. "No need to make you look anything like her. On the contrary we'll give you a black wig, dark glasses, and heavy makeup. They will not be surprised that she would disguise herself to visit England. For them it will make better sense that way."

"That's a load off my mind. I could never pass myself off as her. She's very beautiful." She looked at the two Russians. "In fact, I like her."

"We all do," said Stinnes. "We are doing this to help her."

"I didn't know that," said Miranda doubtfully.

"But she mustn't know," added Stinnes.

"Under no circumstances must she guess," said Moskvin, and he slammed his hand down on the table. "Or you'll wish you'd never been born."

"Okay," said Miranda more calmly than she felt. She hated to admit it but Moskvin did frighten her, and she was not a person easy to frighten.

"She gets the message," said Harmony. "Can I eat my apple now, boss man?"

Bosham, Sussex, England:
October 1983

FEW ACTIONS WITHIN THE LAW CAN PROVIDE MORE JOY than the dispassionate evaluation of a colleague's failure. And so it happened that the field operation Pavel Moskvin planned against London Central became celebrated in speech and writing, and perhaps in song too, for long after Moskvin was dead and buried.

Some blamed the failure entirely upon Moskvin. He was a desk man, without the practical experience that service in the field provides (it was field agents in particular who inclined to this view). Moskvin was, undeniably, a bully, he was always in a hurry, and he failed to understand the English. But then, many of his peers were bullies, very few of them were not in a hurry, and even in England it was difficult to find anyone who claimed to understand the English.

A more convincing explanation of the fiasco came from less passionate observers, who located the flaw in the duality of the leadership: Pavel Moskvin, a career KGB officer too dependent on his influence in Moscow, in partnership with Erich Stinnes, experienced field agent, who, although senior to Moskvin, had no reason to expect benefit from the operation's success.

216

Others looked at the two women in the team, the black Jamaican woman who had never responded to KGB discipline in all the years of her service, and the Englishwoman who had been bullied into a vital part in the operation simply because she could imitate voices. Some said the women were truculent, others that their English mother tongue bonded the two women and created a potential rebellion. Others, all of them men, believed that no women were suited to such jobs.

"First prize for booboos, shitface," said Harmony Jones to Moskvin. They were in a small cottage in Bosham, near the south coast of England, where Moskvin was laying his trap for Bernard Samson. "London to Berlin, then back to London again. This is the dumbest operation I was ever on, honey."

Moskvin was not used to such defiance. He controlled his terrible anger and said, "It is all part of the plan."

Erich Stinnes looked up from his guidebook, *Chichester and the South Downs,* and watched them dispassionately. It was not his operation, and even if the British caught him he'd already put out feelers to them about defection. He'd told Moscow that the first approaches came from the other side and got permission to continue his contacts, so he would survive come what may.

Pavel Moskvin had reasoned along lines of equal infallibility. This operation was going to make his name, so it had to be dramatic. He was going to entice Bernard Samson into a trap, interrogate him to the point of death, and then leave his mutilated body in an SIS safe house in England! If Samson's interrogation revealed something to question or destroy the reputation of his new superior, Fiona Samson, so much the better. Even the safe house had been chosen because Fiona Samson had revealed its existence during one of her initial debriefing sessions. Should the location prove compromised it would be Fiona Samson's treachery, not his failure.

Miranda looked at her three colleagues and shivered. She

had never expected it to be like this. She had played her part exactly as briefed.

Miranda had been standing on the grass shoulder of a section of road near Terminal 3 at London Airport when she saw Bernard Samson driving a car with Harmony sitting in the seat next to him. The car stopped very near her, and she had climbed into the back seat and mimicked the voice of Fiona Samson.

There had been a moment, when she got into the car behind this man Bernard Samson, when she thought she was going to faint. But it was just like being on the stage; at that final moment her professionalism took over and it all went smoothly.

"It's me, darling. I hope I didn't terrify you." That sweet and careful upper-class voice with just a hint of taunting in it.

"Fiona, are you mad?" said Samson. He didn't look around, and in any case the driving mirror had been twisted away from him. It went just as Harmony said it would. Bernard Samson, Harmony told her, was a professional; pros don't do and die, they reason why.

Samson was convinced. It was the most successful performance of Miranda's career; what a pity there were only two people in the audience. But an allowance had to be made for the fact that fifty percent of the audience was startled out of his senses and being threatened by a very nasty-looking hypodermic syringe held close against his thigh.

Miranda continued, "To come here? There is no warrant for my arrest. I have changed my appearance and my name . . . no, don't look round. I don't want you unconscious." She had rehearsed every syllable of it so many times that it was automatic. The poor devil was completely fooled. Miranda felt sorry for him. Of course he would try to follow Harmony afterward, what husband wouldn't?

When Miranda returned to this fisherman's cottage from her performance at London Heathrow, Moskvin had given no word of appreciation. Miranda hated him.

"Suppose Bernard Samson *doesn't* track Harmony's movements?" said Miranda. "Suppose he *doesn't* come? Suppose he tells the police?"

"He'll come," said Moskvin. "He doesn't get paid to send for the police; it's his job to find people. He'll trace Harmony's movements. He'll think his wife is here, and he'll come."

"Then what?" said Miranda. She was still wearing the expensive wig and makeup that Moskvin had chosen for her. She hoped to keep the wig.

Harmony smiled sourly. She had been the one who had laid the trail for Samson, asking the way three times before buying the tickets, doing the stupid things that mere common sense would have avoided. Moskvin's final obvious vulgarity had been to choose a beautiful black girl, just in case anyone might miss her. What kind of jerk wouldn't be suspicious, following that brass-band parade? And her brief confrontation with Bernard Samson gave her reason to suspect he wasn't a jerk. She didn't want to be here when he arrived.

"Who cares?" said Harmony. "Us girls are getting out of here. Miranda, baby! Go upstairs and scrub that damned makeup off your face, and then we'll scram. A day in Rome is what we both need after three long days with this fat fart." She got to her feet.

"Give me thirty minutes," said Miranda.

Moskvin was annoyed at the way Harmony Jones had sweet-talked him into routing the two women through Rome. She'd given him persuasive operational reasons at the time, but now it was clear that she just wanted to enjoy a side trip.

"I might need you," said Moskvin, but his former ability to terrify the two women had gone, largely because of the insolence with which the black woman treated every order he gave her.

"What you need, boss man . . ." she began but then decided not to provoke him further. She took Miranda's makeup box and went to the stairs. Miranda followed.

"And don't call me shitface," said Moskvin solemnly as the two women went through the low door that led to the stairs.

Harmony made an obscene gesture but did it out of Moskvin's sight. As they went upstairs Miranda began to giggle.

It was a wonderful old house: the crude staircase, confined between white-painted plank walls, echoed with the footsteps of the two women. At the top, the narrow latched door had a corner lopped off to accommodate the pitch of the roof. Its essential Englishness produced in Miranda a sudden but not entirely unexpected yearning to live in England again.

As the sound of the footsteps overhead revealed the movements of the women, Erich Stinnes looked up from his guidebook. "Did you know that Bosham village is depicted on the Bayeux Tapestry?" he asked. "This is where King Canute ordered the incoming tide to go back."

Moskvin knew that Stinnes was only trying to provoke him into a fit of anger, so he didn't reply. He got up and went to the window. Bosham is on a tiny peninsula between two tidal creeks. From here he could see the water and the boats, motorboats and sailboats of all shapes and sizes. When Samson was dead and finished with, they would leave by boat. Stinnes was a skillful yachtsman. Under cover of darkness they would slip away as if they had never been here. The perfect conclusion to a perfect operation.

"I wouldn't stand too near the window," said Stinnes

helpfully. "It's an elementary principle on this sort of operation."

Moskvin moved away. Stinnes was right, of course. He hated Stinnes.

"The backup team should be here by now."

Stinnes looked at him and displayed surprise. "They arrived half an hour ago."

"Then where are they?"

"You didn't expect them to come and knock on the door, did you? They have a mattress; they'll sleep in the van until they're needed. It's parked near the pub."

"How do you know all this?"

"I arranged it, didn't I? Why do you think I've been visiting the bathroom? Did you think I had diarrhea? From upstairs you can see the pub car park."

"Do you have a gun?"

Stinnes shook his head.

"I brought a gun," said Moskvin. He put it on the table. It was a Smith and Wesson .44 magnum, a truly enormous pistol that Moskvin had gone to great trouble to have waiting here for him.

Stinnes looked at the colossal pistol and at Moskvin. "That should be enough gun for both of us," he said.

"Then there is nothing to do but wait," said Moskvin.

Stinnes put a marker into a page of his guidebook and closed it. "Remember, this place—Bosham—is where King Canute ordered the tide to go back."

"What happened?" said Moskvin, who had never heard of King Canute.

"The tide kept coming in." Stinnes picked up his shoulder bag. "I'll be in the way here. I'd better go down and check that the boat is gassed up and ready to sail. You know the phone number."

"Yes, I know it," said Moskvin. He'd been counting on

help from Stinnes, but he was determined not to ask for it.

Upstairs, Miranda was wiping the makeup off her face, using lots of cold cream and peering closely at herself in the mirror.

Harmony, who was packing her case, said, "That bastard. I cleared everything out of the car, just the way I've been trained to do, and he yells at me for being late. Most of the trash belonged to Moskvin anyway. He's an untidy swine." She produced a clear plastic sandwich bag into which she had carefully put everything from the rented car. There were two maps of southern England, bits of scrap paper, a broken ballpoint pen, an old lipstick, three pennies, and a watch crystal. "Any of this junk yours, honey?" she asked Miranda.

"No," said Miranda.

"These rental companies never clean out the cars right; a quick wipe of the ashtray and that's it." She emptied the contents of the bag, to use it for her makeup.

"I'm almost ready," said Miranda. "I think I'll have a day or two in England. I'll join you in Rome the day after tomorrow. Would that be all right?"

"Suit yourself, baby," said Harmony Jones. "I have a lot of catching up to do in Rome."

Stinnes slept on the boat that night. There were three double cabins, and he made himself comfortable in one of them. He had the generator going and stayed up late reading *The White Company.* He was a dedicated Sherlock Holmes fan and was persevering with his favorite author's excursion into medievalism. The weather was good, and Stinnes enjoyed the sounds and motion of the anchored boat and the smells of wet timber and salt water.

It was five o'clock the next morning when Moskvin called him on the phone. "Come immediately," said Moskvin. Stinnes hurried out into the brittle pinkness of early morning and reached the cottage within eight minutes.

"What's happening?" asked Stinnes.

"He's here," said Moskvin. "Bernard Samson arrived about midnight. The backup team in the van spotted him. We brought him inside as easily as anything."

"Where is he now?"

"Upstairs. Don't worry, he's tied up. I let the backup team go. Maybe that was a mistake."

"What do you want me for?" asked Stinnes.

"I'm not getting anywhere with my questions," admitted Moskvin. "I think it's time he faced another interrogator."

"What have you asked him?"

Moskvin smashed his fist against his open hand in frustration. "I *know* that Samson woman is a British spy. I know it, and I'll squeeze it out of her husband if it's the last thing I do."

"Oh, so that's the line of questioning," said Stinnes. To him it seemed the stupid obsession of a man who had repeatedly told him how much he objected to taking orders from a woman.

There was no way that Moskvin could miss the ridicule in his colleague's voice, but he'd become used to the superior attitude that Stinnes always showed toward him. "Go up and talk to him. Play mister nice guy."

When Stinnes went upstairs, Moskvin followed him. Moskvin was not able to sit still downstairs and wait for results; he had to see what was happening. He stood in the doorway behind Stinnes.

The front upstairs room was very small, and much of the space was taken up by a small bed. It was pushed against the wall and there were cushions on it so it could be used as a sofa. In the corner there was a dressing table with a large mirror in which the captive was reflected.

"I'm going to undo this gag, and I want you to—" Stinnes started and then stopped abruptly. He looked around at Moskvin and back to the captive. "This is not Bernard Samson," he told Moskvin.

The man tied to the chair was named Julian MacKenzie. He was a probationer who worked for the Department. Bernard Samson had told him to trace the movements of the black girl, and he'd done so all too efficiently. MacKenzie was fully conscious. His eyes showed his fear as Moskvin waved the pistol in the air.

"What do you mean?" said Moskvin angrily. He grabbed Stinnes's arm in his huge hand and dragged him back into the narrow corridor. Then he closed the door. It was dark. The only glimmer of light was that escaping from the room downstairs.

"I mean it's not Bernard Samson," said Stinnes quietly.

"Who is it?" said Moskvin, shaking him roughly.

"How the hell would I know who it is?"

"Are you positive?"

"Of course I am. Samson is about fifteen years older than this kid. I've seen Samson close to. I know him well. Of course I'm positive."

"Wait downstairs. I'll find out who this one is."

As Stinnes went downstairs he heard Moskvin shouting, and there were replies from the young man that were too quiet to hear properly. Stinnes sat down in the armchair and took *The White Company* from his pocket but found he just kept reading the same paragraph over and over. Suddenly there was the loud bang of the .44 Magnum. A scream. More shots. Stinnes leaped to his feet, worried that the noise would wake up the whole neighborhood. His first instinct was simply to clear out, but he was enough of a professional to wait for the other man.

Moskvin came down the stairs so slowly that Stinnes was beginning to wonder if he'd shot himself or been injured by a ricochet. Then Moskvin lurched into the room. His face was absolutely white; even his lips were bloodless. He dumped his pistol on the dresser and put out a hand to steady himself on the edge of the kitchen table. Then he leaned over and vomited into the sink.

Stinnes watched him but kept well back. Moskvin pushed the gun aside and retched again and again. Finally, slowly and carefully, he wiped his face on a towel and then ran the water into the sink. "That's done," said Moskvin, trying to put on a show of bravado.

"Are you sure he's dead?" said Stinnes. Taking his time, he looked out of both windows. There was no sign that the noise of the shot had attracted any interest from the neighboring cottages.

"I'm sure."

"Then let's get out of here," said Stinnes. "Can you make it to the boat?"

"Damn your stupid smiling face," said Moskvin. "I'll have the last laugh; you just wait."

But Stinnes wasn't smiling, he was wondering how much longer he could endure the stupid antics of this brutal peasant.

In Berlin that evening, Fiona went to the State Opera. The indispensable Hubert Renn could always produce an opera or concert ticket for her at short notice, and this afternoon she'd suddenly noticed that it would be the last chance to catch the much-discussed avant-garde production of *Der Freischütz.*

She sat entranced. It was one of her favorite operas. This extraordinary selection of simple folk melodies and complex romanticism gave her a respite from work. For a brief moment it even enabled her to forget her worries and loneliness.

The intermission came. Still engrossed with the music, she couldn't endure the scrum around the bar and there were a lot of West Berliners here tonight, easily distinguished by their jewelry and flamboyant clothes. She turned away to wander through the lobby and look at the exhibition—ELECTRICITY FOR TOMORROW—atmospheric photos of power-generating stations in the German Democratic Republic. She was looking at the color print of a large concrete building reflected in a lake when someone behind her said, "There you go, sweetheart! How about a glass of white wine?"

She turned and was astounded to see Harry Kennedy standing there with two glasses of wine in his hands and a satisfied smile on his face. "The show really starts in the intermission, doesn't it?"

Her first reaction was not pleasure. She had been dreading an encounter with some old friend, colleague, or acquaintance on the street who would recognize her. Now it had happened. She felt as if she was going to faint. Rooted to the spot, her heart beat furiously. She felt the blood rush to her face and looked down so he wouldn't see the flush of her cheeks.

He saw the effect he'd had. "Are you all right? I'm sorry. . . . I should have—"

"It's all right," she said. She was quite likely to be under surveillance. If so, her reaction to this meeting would be noted and recorded.

Harry spoke hurriedly to save her from speaking. "I knew you wouldn't miss *Der Freischütz*, I just knew it. Oh, boy, what a production: the pits, isn't it? And those trees! But what a great voice he has."

"What are you doing here, Harry?" she said carefully and calmly.

"Looking for you, honey-child." He handed the wine to

her and she took it. "I'm sorry to leap on you this way."

"I don't understand you. . . ."

"I live here," he said.

"In the East?" She drank some wine without tasting it. She hardly knew what she was doing. She didn't know whether to keep talking or cut him dead and walk away.

"I'm here for a year. A professor from the Charité Hospital was in London and came to see the work we were doing at the clinic. They invited me to spend a year working here. They're not paying me, but I finagled a little grant . . . enough to keep me going for the year. I was glad to escape from those jerks in London, and I suspect the clinic was glad to get rid of me."

"Here in East Berlin?" She drank more wine. She needed a drink, and it gave her a chance to study him. He looked even younger than she remembered him, his wavy hair more wavy, and the battered face looking even more battered as he worried how she would react.

"Yeah. At the Charité. And I knew you wouldn't miss *Der Freischütz.* I've been here every performance . . . I love you, Fiona, sweetheart. I had to find you." Again he stopped.

"You came for every performance?"

"You once said it was your favorite opera."

"I suppose it is," she said. She was no longer sure; she was no longer sure about anything.

"Are you mad at me?" he asked. He looked like a West Berliner in his black suit and bow tie. Here was a different Harry Kennedy from the one she'd last seen in London: cautious and diffident. But superimposed upon this diffidence, and almost prevailing over it, was his pride and pleasure in finding her again.

"No, of course not," she said.

Her distant manner made him suddenly anxious. "Is there someone else?"

"Only my husband in London."

It was as if a load was lifted from his shoulders. "When I realized you'd left him, I knew I had to find you. You're the only woman I've ever loved, Fiona. You know that." It wasn't a communication, it was a declaration.

"It's not like London," she said awkwardly, trying to adjust to the idea of his being here.

"Say you love me." He'd taken so much trouble; he was expecting more of her.

"Don't. It's not as easy as that, Harry. I work for the government here."

"Who cares who you work for?"

Why wouldn't he understand? "I defected, Harry."

"I don't care what you did! We're together again; that's all that matters to me."

"Please try and understand what is involved."

Now, for the first time, he calmed down enough to look at her and say, "What are you trying to tell me, baby?"

"If you see me on a regular basis, your career will be ruined. You won't be able to go back to London and take up your life at the place you left it."

"I don't care, as long as I have you."

"Harry. You haven't got me."

"I love you . . . I'll do *anything*, I'll live anywhere, I'll wait forever. I'm a desperate man."

She looked at him and smiled, but she knew it was an unconvincing smile. She felt one of her bad headaches coming on and she wanted to scream. "I can't be responsible, Harry. Everything has changed, and I've changed too."

"You said you loved me," he said, in that reproachful way that only lovers do.

If only he would go away. "Perhaps I did. Perhaps I still do. I don't know." She spoke slowly. "All I'm sure about is that right now I can't take on all the complications of a relationship."

"Then promise nothing. I ask nothing. I'll wait. But don't ask me to stop telling you I love you. That would be unbearable."

The opera bell started to ring. With German orderliness the crowd immediately began to move back toward the auditorium. "I can't go back to the performance," she said. "My head is whirling. I need to think."

"So let's go to the Palast and eat dinner."

"You'll miss the opera."

"I've seen it nine times," he said grimly.

She smiled and looked at her watch. "Will they serve dinner as late as this?" she said. "Things finish so early on this side of the city."

"The ever-practical Fiona. Yes, they will serve as late as this. I was there two nights ago. Give me the ticket, and I'll collect your coat."

It is not far from the State Opera on Unter den Linden to the Palast Hotel, and despite Berlin's ever-present smell of brown coal the walk was good for her. By the time they were seated in the hotel dining room she was restored to something approaching her normal calm. It wasn't like her to be so shattered, even by surprises. But meeting Harry at the opera house had not simply been a surprise; it had shown her what a fragile hold she had upon herself. She had been physically affected by the encounter. Her heart was still beating fast.

She watched him as he read the menu. Was she in love with him? Was that the explanation of the shock? Or was it more fundamental? Was she becoming unbalanced?

Any feeling she had for Harry was not like the stable and enduring love she had for her home, her children, and her husband. Harry's absence from her life had not caused her the heartrending agony that separation from her family had brought, an agony from which she never escaped. That old love for Harry was something quite different, separate and not in conflict with it. But she could not help recalling that the love she once had for Harry was electrifying. It had been illicit and more physical than anything she'd known with Bernard. Sitting here across the table from Harry made her remember vividly the way that not so long ago even a glance from him could be arousing. "I beg your pardon?" she said absently as she realized he was expecting an answer from her.

"I had it the other night," he said. "It was rather good."

"I'm sorry. My mind was wandering."

"The *Kabinett* is always the driest, at least I've learned that in the time I've been here."

"Wonderful," she said vaguely and was relieved when he waved to the waiter and ordered a bottle of some wine he'd discovered and liked. His German was adequate, and even his accent was not too grating upon her ear. She looked around the restaurant to be sure there was no one there she recognized. It was crowded with foreigners, the only ones who had access to the sort of foreign money with which the bill had to be paid.

"My money comes in Western currency. I eat here all the time," he told her.

Could he, by any chance, be an emissary from London Central? No. This was not a man whom Bret or Sir Henry would regard as right for the tricky job of intermediary. And yet a paramour would make the perfect cover for a London contact. If that was his role, he'd reveal it soon; that was how such things were done. She'd wait and see what happened. Meanwhile, she would be the perfect communist. "So what do you suggest we eat?" she asked.

He looked up and smiled. He was so happy that his elation affected her. "Steak, trout, or schnitzel is all I ever order."

"Trout then; nothing to start." And then another

thought struck her like a bombshell. Could he be Moscow's man? Very very unlikely. At that first encounter in London he'd admitted to having no work permit. Had she phoned Immigration they would have pounced on him. . . . Wait a minute, think about it! It was his vulnerability to officialdom that had made her decide not to have him officially investigated. That and the fact that Bernard might have started asking questions about him. She lived again through that first encounter on the railway station, step by step, word for word. His "niece" talked to Fiona and then ran away. It could have been a setup. There was nothing in that meeting that could not have been previously arranged.

"Fiona," he said.

"Yes, Harry?"

"I love you desperately." He did love her. No one could feign adoration in the way she saw it in his eyes. But, said the neurotic, suspicious, and logical side of her, being in love did not mean he couldn't have been sent by Moscow. "I know everything about you," he said suddenly, and she was alarmed again. "Except why you like *Der Freischütz.* I know every mini-quaver of it by now. I can take Schoenberg and Hindemith, but can you find me ten minutes of real melody in that whole darn opera?"

"Germans like it because it is about a completely unified Germany."

"Is that what you want, a unified Germany?" he asked.

Red lights flashed. What was the official line on unification? "Only on the right terms," she said guardedly. "What about you?"

"Who was it who said that he liked Germany so much he preferred there to be two of them?"

"I'm not sure."

He leaned forward and said confidentially, "Forget what I said. I'm just crazy about *Der Freischütz;* every little demi-semi-quaver."

16

London:

October 1983

I<small>T WAS TWO O'CLOCK IN THE MORNING</small>. B<small>RET WAS IN HIS</small> Thameside house, sitting up in bed reading the final few pages of Zola's *Nana.* Influenced by Sylvester Bernstein, Bret had discovered the joy of reading novels. First Sylvy had lent him *Germinal,* and now Bret—always subject to deep and sudden passions—had decided to read every volume of Zola's twenty-volume cycle. The phone rang. He let it ring for a long time, but when the caller persisted he reached for it. "Hello?" Bret always said hello; he didn't believe in identifying himself.

"Bret, my dear fellow. I do hope I didn't wake you."

"I'm reading a superb and moving book, Sir Henry."

"As long as you're not in the middle of anything important," said the D-G imperturbably. "I know you are something of a night owl. Anyway, this won't wait, I'm afraid."

"I understand." Bret put the book aside and closed it regretfully.

"Special Branch liaison came through to me at home a few minutes ago. Apparently a young woman, English by all accounts, walked into the police station in Chichester and said she wanted to talk to someone in our line of business."

"Oh, yes, sir," said Bret.

"You're yawning already, of course. Yes, we've seen a lot of those in our time, haven't we? But this lady says she wants to tell us something about one of our people in London. She's mentioned a man whose wife recently left him. Furthermore, she met that wife recently in Berlin. You're still with me, are you, Bret?"

"Very much with you, Sir Henry. Met her? By name? Mentioned her by name?"

"Apparently, but things usually become a bit vague by the time reports come word of mouth all the way to me. Very very urgent, she said it was. Someone was about to be killed, that kind of thing. But yes, the name was given. Special Branch thought they should check to see if the name rang a bell with us. The night duty officer decided it was important enough to wake me up. I think he was right."

"Yes, indeed, sir."

"A Special Branch inspector is bringing this lady up to London. She gave her name as Mrs. Miranda Keller, née Dobbs. No joy there, of course, the German telephone books are full of Kellers. I wonder if you would be so kind as to talk to her? See what it's all about."

"Yes, sir."

"Special Branch have that estate agent's office in Kensington. The house behind the Sainsbury supermarket. You know it, I'm sure."

"Yes, sir."

"They will be there in under the hour."

"I'll get going immediately, sir."

"Would you really, Bret. I'd be so grateful. I'll be in the office tomorrow. We can talk about it then."

"Yes, sir."

"Of course it may be nothing at all. Nothing at all."

"Well, I'd better hurry."

"Or it could be our old pals getting up to naughty tricks.

Don't take any chances, Bret.''

"I won't, sir. I'd better get started.''

"Yes, of course. Good night, old chap. Although for you I suppose it would be good morning.'' The D-G chuckled and rang off. It was all right for him; he was going back to sleep.

Mrs. Miranda Keller was thirty-six years old, and the wig she was wearing did not make her look younger. It was almost four o'clock in the morning, and she'd endured a long car ride through the pouring rain to this grand old house in Kensington, a shabby residential part of central London. Miranda let her head rest back upon the frayed moquette of the armchair. Under the pitiless blue glare of the overhead lighting—which buzzed constantly—she did not look her best.

"As I told you, we have no one of that name working for us,'' said Bret. He was behind a desk drinking stale black coffee from the delicate sort of chinaware that is de rigueur in the offices of earnest young men who sell real estate. With it on the antique tray there was a bowl of sugar and a pierced can of Carnation milk.

"S-A-M-S-O-N.'' She spelled it out.

"Yes, I know what you said. No one of that name,'' said Bret.

"They are going to kill him,'' said Miranda doggedly. "Have you sent someone to the house in Bosham?''

"That's not something I'm permitted to discuss,'' said Bret. "Even if I knew,'' he added.

"Well, these men will kill him if he goes there. I know the sort of men they are.'' Wind rattled the windows.

"Russians, you say?''

"You wrote their names down,'' she said. She picked up her cup, looked at the coffee, and set it aside.

"Of course I did. And you said there was another woman there too."

"I don't know anything about her."

"Ah, yes. That's what you said," murmured Bret, looking down at his notes. "My writing is not very elegant, Mrs. Keller, but I think it is clear enough. I want you to read through the notes I've made. Start here, the conversation you had in the car at London airport, when you were imitating the voice of this woman you met in Berlin-Grünau." He passed his notes to her.

She read the sheet quickly, nodded, and offered it back. The wind made a roaring noise in the chimney and the electric fire rattled on its mounting. On the window there was the constant hammering of heavy rain.

Bret didn't take the papers from her. "Take your time, Mrs. Keller. Maybe read it twice."

She looked at his notes again. "What's wrong? Don't you believe me?"

"It sounds like a mighty banal conversation, Mrs. Keller. Was it worth having you go to all that trouble, when in the final analysis you simply say things about the children and about laying off this fellow Stinnes?"

"It was just to jolt him, so that he would follow the black girl to find his wife again."

"Yes," said Bret Rensselaer doubtfully. He took the sheets of notes and tapped them on the desktop to get them tidy. Outside a car door slammed and an engine was started. A man yelled good night and a woman screamed "Good riddance!" It was that kind of neighborhood.

"And I've asked for nothing."

"I was wondering about that," said Bret.

"There's no need to be sarcastic."

"Forgive me. I didn't intend to be."

"Could you switch off some of these lights? The glare is giving me a headache."

"Of course. I hate fluorescent lighting, but this place is used as an office. They're all on the same switch."

"I want nothing for what I've told you. Nothing at all."

"But?"

"But if you want me to go back there, it's only fair that I get something in return."

"What do you have in mind?"

"A passport for my five-year-old son."

"Ahhh!" said Bret, in what was unmistakably a groan of agony as he envisaged the arguments that he would have to endure to get a passport for someone not entitled to one. Those professional obstructionists he dealt with in Whitehall would work overtime producing excuses to say no to that one.

"It will cost you nothing," said Miranda.

"I know," said Bret in a soft warm voice. "It's a modest enough request, Mrs. Keller. I'll probably be able to do it."

"If I don't go to Rome tomorrow, or next day at the latest, I'll have a lot of explaining to do."

"You're British. I would have thought your son could claim British nationality."

"I was born in Austria. My father was on a five-year contract there. My son was born in Berlin; I can't pass my citizenship on to him."

"That's a lousy break," said Bret. "I'll do what I can." He brightened as a sudden solution came to mind. Maybe a counterfeit passport would do; he wouldn't say it was counterfeit, of course. "I suppose any Western passport would serve to get him out of there—Irish Republic, Brazil, Guatemala, Belize, or Paraguay."

The woman looked at him suspiciously. "Providing I got

a certificated right to reside in Great Britain. But I don't want some Mickey Mouse passport that I have to renew every two or three years and bribe some embassy official every time I do it."

Bret nodded assent. "Do you have suitable photos of your son?"

"Yes." From her handbag she took three passport pictures and passed them to him together with a piece of paper on which she had written the necessary description.

"So you had this planned before you left Berlin?"

"Those Russian pigs are intolerable," said Miranda. "I always carry passport pictures."

How enterprising, thought Bret. "That's about all we can do right now," he said. "Leave it all with me. How can I contact you in East Berlin?"

"I'll need the passport," said Miranda. "Until I have the passport in my hand I'll do nothing for you."

Bret looked at her. She was an intelligent woman. She must have realized that if she went back to the East she was delivering herself into his hands. But she gave no sign of that; she was one of those people who expected everyone to act fairly. It was good to know that such people still existed. Bret would not disabuse her at this stage. "Would you accept a small payment?"

"I just want the passport for my son."

"Okay, Mrs. Keller. I'll do everything I can to get it for you."

"I'm sure you will," she said.

"One last and vitally important thing, Mrs. Keller. The woman you met in Berlin, Mrs. Fiona Samson, is a KGB officer. She is a very smart woman. Don't underestimate her."

"Are you saying she works for Russian intelligence?"

"Very much so. I should have said, a mean and danger-

ous woman. Under no circumstances should you confide anything to her.''

"No, I won't.''

"So it wasn't a complete waste of time, Bret?'' The D-G was
making one of his rare visits to Bret Rensselaer's magnificent
monochrome office. He sat on the black leather chesterfield,
picking at the buttons and determined not to smoke.

There were times when the D-G's distant joviality reminded Bret of Sassoon's poem of the World War One general: '' *'He's a cheery old card,' grunted Harry to Jack . . . But
he did for them both with his plan of attack.''*

"No, sir. Very instructive,'' said Bret, who was sitting
behind his glass-topped desk wearing a white shirt and spotted bow tie.

"It was a plan to kill Bernard Samson?''

"That is her story.''

"And this other young man was killed instead?''

"Yes, but she doesn't know that. And of course I didn't
tell her.''

"Did Samson report being approached by this black
girl?''

"No, sir, he did not.'' Bret tidied the papers on his desk,
although they didn't need tidying.

"And what else did the house in Bosham reveal? Have
your chaps reported back to you?''

"I have done nothing about the house in Bosham, and
I intend to do nothing.''

After a deliberately audible intake of breath, the Director-General stared at him, thought about it, and finally said,
"Very prudent, Bret.''

"I'm glad you approve, Sir Henry.''

"Where is Samson?''

"Samson is alive and well."

"You didn't warn him?"

"No, sir. I sent him away on a job."

"Yes, that was wise." He sniffed. "So they acted on Mrs. Samson's information about the Bosham safe house. They were quick off the mark on that one. Ummm."

"We come out of it very well, sir."

"I wish you wouldn't keep saying that, Bret. We're not out of it yet. I don't like the fact that Samson didn't report that approach. Do you think he believed it was his wife in the back of that car?"

"Yes, probably. But Samson thinks before he acts. All these ex-field people become ultra-cautious: that's why we have to retire them."

"You'd better make sure Mrs. Samson knows about this impersonation." He sniffed. "So Bernard Samson didn't report any of it? I don't like that, Bret."

"No, sir, but there is no reason to think that Samson is in any way disloyal. Or contemplating disloyalty."

"This Mrs. Keller, is she a potential agent for us?"

"No, sir. Out of the question."

"But we can use her?"

"I don't see how. Not at present anyway."

"Did you get photos of her?"

"Yes, the Kensington office is good from that point of view. Lots of good clear pictures."

The D-G tapped his fingers on the leather arm of the chesterfield. "On the matter of safe houses, Bret. When we agreed that Mrs. Samson should reveal the existence of the Bosham safe house, I understood it was to be kept under surveillance."

Bret pursed his lips, feeling that he was being admonished for something outside his frame of reference. He said, "At present my hands are tied . . . but when it becomes safe to do so, disciplinary action will be taken.''

''I do hope so, Bret. But the scheme is to just wait until the housekeeping people go into the Bosham safe house on a routine checkup and find the body?''

''That's right, sir.''

''Good.'' He produced an encouraging smile, albeit humorless. ''And now this KGB fellow Stinnes. Silas is pestering me about him. He says we mustn't let his approach grow cold.''

''I thought that might be what you wanted to talk about, sir,'' said Bret, diving down into document case. From it he brought a red cardboard file which he opened to display a concertina of that gray angular computer printout that the D-G found difficult to read. And then he found four eight-by-ten-inch shiny photos of Stinnes. Reaching across, he placed them on the glass-topped desk where the D-G could see them. But the D-G didn't crane his neck to look closely.

The photos were arranged side by side with finicky care. It was so typical of Bret Rensselaer, with his boundless faith in charts, graphs, graphics, and projections, that he should bring photos of this damned Russian out at this meeting as if that would help them toward a sound decision. ''Has he provided any evidence of good faith?'' asked the D-G.

''He told Samson that Moscow has broken the new diplomatic code. That's why we did everything 'by hand of messenger.' ''

The D-G extended a finger and touched one of the photos as though it might have been impregnated with some contagious disease. ''You believe him?''

''You probably spoke with Silas Gaunt,'' said Bret, who wanted to know the lie of the land before committing himself to an opinion.

''Silas has got a bee in his bonnet about this one. I was looking for a more sober assessment.''

Bret did not want to say something that would afterward be quoted against him. Slowly he said, "If Stinnes's offer to defect is a Moscow stunt . . ."

The D-G finished the sentence for him. "The way we have reacted will make those chaps in Moscow feel very good, eh, Bret?"

"I try to disregard any personal feelings of triumph or disaster when making decisions of that sort, Sir Henry."

"And quite right too."

"If Stinnes is doing this on Moscow's orders, he'd be more likely to bring us some secret document that we'd be tempted to transmit verbatim, or at least in sequence."

"So that they could compare it and break our code? Yes, I suppose so. So you think he's genuine?"

"Silas thinks it doesn't matter; Silas thinks we should work on him and send him back believing what we want them to believe over there." Bret waited for the reaction and was still ready to jump either way. But he could tell that the D-G was attracted to this idea.

After a moment's pause for thought, the D-G said, "I don't want you to discuss this with Silas for the time being."

"Very well, Sir Henry."

"And in course of time, separate Stinnes from Cruyer and Samson and everyone else. This is for you to do alone, Bret. One to one, you and Stinnes. We have to have one person who understands the whole game and all its minutiae and ramifications. One person is enough, and that person must be you."

Bret put the photos and the printout back into his case. The D-G made agitated movements that indicated he was about to terminate the meeting. "Before I go, Bret, one aspect of this. . . ."

"Yes?"

"Would you say that Bernard Samson has ever killed a man?"

Bret was surprised, and for a moment he allowed it to show. "I imagine he has, sir. In fact . . . well, I know. . . . Yes, many times."

"Exactly, Bret. And now we are subjecting him to a considerable burden of anxiety, aren't we?"

Bret nodded.

"A man like Samson might not have the resilience that you would be able to show in such circumstances. He might take things into his own hands."

"I suppose he might." Bret was doubtful.

"I saw Samson the other day. He's taking it badly."

"Do you want me to give him sick leave or a vacation?"

"Certainly not. That would be the worst thing you could do for the poor fellow. It would give him time to sit and think. I don't want him to sit and think, Bret."

"Would you give me some idea of what . . . ?"

"Suppose he came to the conclusion that his wife had betrayed him and betrayed his country. That she'd abandoned his children and made a fool of him. Might he not then decide to do to her what he's done to so many others?"

"Kill her? But wait a minute, Sir Henry. In fact she hasn't done that, has she?"

"And that leads us on to another aspect of the horrible position that Samson now finds himself in." The D-G heaved himself up out of the low seat. Bret got to his feet and watched but decided against offering him assistance. The D-G said, "Samson is asking a lot of questions. Suppose he discovers the truth? Might it not seem to him that we have played a cruel prank on him? And done it with callous indifference? He discovers that we have not confided in him. He feels rejected and humiliated. He is a man trained to respond violently to his opponents. Might he not decide to wreak vengeance upon us?"

"I don't think so, Sir Henry. Samson is a civilized man." Bret went across the office and held the door open for him.

"Is he?" said the D-G in that cheery way he could summon so readily. "Then he hasn't been properly trained."

17

East Berlin:

November 1983

T O   T H E   F A Ç A D E   O F   T H E   B U I L D I N G   I N   K A R L   L I E B-
knecht Strasse a dozen workmen were affixing a huge red
banner, LONG LIVE OUR SOCIALIST FATHERLAND. The previous one
that had promised both prosperity and peace was faded to
light pink by the sun.

From the window of Fiona Samson's office there were
only the tassels to be glimpsed, but part of the framework for
the new banner cut across the window and reduced the daylight. "I've always wanted to go to America," admitted Hubert Renn as he picked up the papers from her desk.

"Have you, Herr Renn? Why?" She drank her tea. She
must not leave it for it was real Indian tea, not the tasteless
USSR stuff from the Georgian crop. She wondered where
Renn had found it but she didn't ask.

"Curiosity, Frau Direktor. It is a land of contradictions."

"It is a repressive society," said Fiona, dutiful to the line
she always took. "A land where workers are enslaved."

"But they are such an enigmatic people," said Renn. He
replaced the cap on his fountain pen and put it in his pocket.
"Do you know, Frau Direktor, when, during the war against
Hitler, the Americans began to drop secret agents into Ger-

many, the very first of those parachutists were members of the ISK?''

"The Internationaler Sozialistischer Kampfbund?'' She had never heard of that organization until Renn had mentioned that his mother had been a member, and then she'd looked it up in the reference library.

"Yes, ISK, the most radical of all the parties. Why would the Americans select such people? It was as if our friends in Moscow had sent to us, as Stalin's emissaries, White Russian nobility.''

She laughed. Renn gave a skimpy self-conscious grin. There had been a time when such remarks by Renn would have suggested to her that he might be sympathetic to Americans, but now she knew better. If there was anything of his attitude to be deduced from his remarks, it was a criticism of Russia rather than praise for the United States. Renn was a dedicated disciple of Marx and his theories. As Renn saw it, Karl Marx the incomparable prophet and source of all true enlightenment was a German sage. Any small inconsistencies and imperfections that might be encountered in the practice of socialism—and Renn had never admitted to there being any—were caused by the essentially Russian failures of Lenin and Stalin.

But Fiona had learned to live with Hubert Renn's blind devotion to Marxist socialism, and there was no doubt that daily contact with him had opened up to her a world she had never truly perceived.

There were for instance the regular letters that arrived from Renn's twenty-two-year-old daughter Lisa, her father's great pride. Lisa had taken learning the Russian language in her stride and gone on to postgraduate work in marine biology—one of the postgraduate courses the regime permitted to female students—in the university at Irkutsk, near Lake Baikal. The deepest lake in the world, it contains more fresh water than all the North American lakes put together. This region supports flora and fauna not found anywhere else. And yet until Renn had showed her the letter from his daughter she'd not even known where Lake Baikal was! How much more was there to know?

"I will confide a secret," Renn announced when she gave him back the chatty letter he'd just received from his daughter.

"What is it, Herr Renn?"

"You are to get an award, Frau Direktor."

"An award? I've heard nothing of it."

"The nature of the award has still to be decided, but your heroic years in England working for the revolution will be marked by an award. Moscow has said yes, and now there might be a medal from the DDR too."

"I am overwhelmed, Herr Renn."

"It is overdue, Frau Direktor Samson."

Renn had been surprised at the way in which Fiona had settled in to her Berlin job. He didn't realize to what extent Fiona's English background had prepared her for the communist regime. Her boarding school had very quickly taught her to hide every human feeling: triumph, disappointment, glee, love, or shame. Her authoritarian father had demonstrated the art of temporizing and the value of the soft reply. Her English middle-class background—with its cruel double meanings, oblique questions, and humiliating indifference—had provided the final graduation that amply fitted her for East Berlin's dangers. And of course Renn had no inkling of Fiona's bouts of depression, her ache for her children, and the hours of suicidal despair and loneliness.

Hair drawn back in a style that was severe and yet not unbecoming, her face scrubbed and with very little makeup, Fiona, with the slight Berlin accent that she now applied to her everyday speech, had become accepted as a regular mem-

ber of the KGB–Stasi team. Her office was not in the main
building in Normannenstrasse, Berlin-Lichtenberg. As Renn
had pointed out, to be one of the horde coming out of that
big Stasi building at the end of the day's work, to fight your
way down into the Magdalenenstrasse U-Bahn and wait for
a train, was not something to yearn for.

There were many advantages to being in Karl Liebknecht
Strasse. It was in the Mitte, only a stone's throw from the
shops, bars, and theaters, and Unter den Linden ran right into
it. What the cunning old Hubert Renn really meant of course
was that it was near the other government offices to which he
had to go on foot and convenient to the Alexanderplatz
S-Bahn, which took him home.

"I ordered a car for fourteen-thirty," said Renn. He
stopped to admire the fur-lined coat that Fiona had just
bought. Not wanting to attract too much speculation about
her finances, Fiona had debated about what sort of winter
coat she should wear. Hubert Renn had solved the problem
by getting permission for her to buy, with DDR currency, one
of the fancy coats normally only on sale to foreign visitors.
"You have a meeting at the clinic for nervous diseases at
fifteen hundred," said Renn. "I'll make sure the driver knows
where to go. Pankow, near where the Autobahn ends. It's a
maze of little streets. Easy to get lost."

"Thank you, Herr Renn. Do we have an agenda?"

Renn looked at her with an expression she didn't recognize. "No agenda, Frau Direktor. Familiarization visit. You
are meeting with Doktor Wieczorek."

"Can't the doctor come here?"

Renn busied himself with some papers that were on the
filing cabinet. "It is usual to go there," he said stiffly, without
turning to look at her.

She was about to say it all sounded very mysterious and
make a joke of it, but she had learned that jokes of that sort

did not go down well in the East. So she said, "Do I need to take papers or files with me?"

"Only a notebook, Frau Direktor."

"Will you not be there to take notes?" She was surprised by this development.

"I am not permitted to attend the meetings with Doktor Wieczorek."

She looked at him, but he didn't turn around to meet her eyes. "In that case," she said, "perhaps I'll take an early lunch. By the way, Herr Renn."

"Yes, Frau Direktor?"

"There is a doctor, Henry Kennedy. . . . Here, I'll write that down for you." She passed him the slip of paper, and he read it carefully as if he might discover some hidden meaning in the name. "He is from London, working at the Charité on a year's contract."

"Yes, Frau Direktor?"

"For a year's residence he would have been screened, wouldn't he?"

"Yes, Frau Direktor."

She wanted the next bit to sound as casual as possible. "Could you let me see the file?"

"It wouldn't be kept in this building, Frau Direktor." She looked at him. "But I could look it up."

"I don't really need the file or even a copy."

"You just need to know that there are no complications," offered Renn.

"Exactly, Herr Renn. He is someone I know socially. I will have to see him from time to time."

"All is clear, Frau Direktor."

Pankow has long been one of the most desirable residential districts of the central part of Berlin. This was where smartly dressed East Germans arrived to dinner parties in imported cars. And here, Fiona had discovered to her great surprise, there were households that boasted live-in domestic help.

But the clinic was not in the most salubrious part of Berlin-Pankow. It was a three-story building in imitation marble. Its bleak neo-Renaissance style, monumental proportions, and the pockmarks of wartime artillery damage suggested that it was a surviving example of Berlin's Third Reich architecture.

She was glad to have her beautiful fur-lined coat. It was snowing, large flakes that came spinning down like disks and made loud crunching noises underfoot. The temperature had dropped with a suddenness that caught even the residents off guard, and the streets were quiet.

The driver found the clinic without any trouble. There was a wall around the building and a tall gate that opened for her car. The ornamental entrance doors surmounted a wide flight of stone steps with a relief, suggesting columns, on each side of it.

The lobby was lit by soft gray light that came from clerestory windows, set deep into the wall above the entrance. Its floor was an intricate mosaic, depicting Roman maidens broadcasting flowers, and the doors on every side were closed. Dr. Wieczorek's name was painted on a wooden plaque and inserted, together with those of other senior medical staff on duty that day, into a large board on the wall behind the reception desk.

"Yes?" The receptionist was a young man with black hair upon which he'd used a generous amount of hair cream. He wore a washable gray linen jacket, white shirt, and black tie. It was a kind of uniform. He was writing something in a ledger and didn't look up.

"Doktor Samson," said Fiona. The profound trust that Germans showed for doctorates of any sort had persuaded her to start using her academic qualification.

"Your business?" The young man still didn't look up.

"Stand up when you talk to me!" said Fiona. She didn't raise her voice, but the tone was enough to remind the young man that a visitor from the Stasi was expected this afternoon.

He leaped to his feet as if scalded and clicked his heels. "Ja, Frau Doktor."

"Take me to Herr Doktor Wieczorek."

"Doktor Wieczorek . . . Herr Dok Dok Dok . . ." said the young man, stuttering and red-faced.

"Immediately. I am on State business," said Fiona.

"Immediately, Frau Doktor. Yes, immediately."

Dr. Wieczorek was an elegant forty-year-old specialist who had spent time in the Serbsky Institute of Forensic Psychiatry in Moscow and at the well-known mental hospital which was a part of the Chernyakhovsk prison. He had wavy hair that was beginning to gray at the temples and a manner that suggested consummate medical expertise. Under his white jacket he wore a smart shirt and silk tie. His firm voice and avuncular manner relaxed her immediately, and so did his readiness to make little jokes about the bureaucracy that he constantly faced and so seldom defeated. "Coffee?"

"No, thank you," said Fiona. There had been an attempt to make the austere little office look homey with the addition of an oriental carpet and an antique clock that chimed the hours.

"Tea? Tea with milk?" He smiled. "That was the only thing I could remember about the British when I was a child, the way they poured cold milk into their tea and ruined it. No? Well, we'll get on with this familiarization visit. There is not a great deal to see in the building. At present we have twenty-three patients, one of whom I expect to be able to send home in a month or two. Some, I'm afraid, will never go home, but in the matter of clinical psychiatry I am always reluctant to say there is no hope." He smiled at her. "Do you know what we do here?"

"No," she said.

He turned far enough to get from the shelf a large glass jar inside which a brain was to be seen in murky formalin. "Look at that," he said, putting it on the desk. "That's the brain of 'Der Grosse Gustaf,' who was a music hall performer of the nineteen thirties. Anyone in the audience could ask him such questions as who fought Max Schmeling in 1933. He'd immediately tell them it was Max Baer, who won on a technical knockout in the tenth round in New York City."

"That's impressive," said Fiona.

"I'm interested in boxing," explained Wieczorek. He tapped the jar. "But 'The Great Gustaf' could answer any sort of question. He had a brain like an encyclopedia."

"Why is it here?"

"There remains in the Soviet Union a small but influential group of medical men who think that slicing up the human brain will reveal some of nature's secrets. Lenin's brain was sliced up and studied under the microscope. So was Stalin's. So were a lot of lesser brains before and since."

"What did they find?"

"That seems to be a state secret."

"They discovered nothing, you mean?"

"I didn't say that, did I?" He tapped the jar again. "But I saved Gustaf from such indignity. Gustaf has his brain intact."

"Where did you get such a thing?"

"It came from the Charité Hospital at the end of the war. All hospitals have a roomful of such stuff. When the Red Army infantry got into the Charité during the fighting in 1945, they found generals and other high-ups, who'd been hanged for trying unsuccessfully to assassinate Hitler in 1944. Their bodies were still preserved in the post-mortem room refrigerators there. The cadavers had been sent from the Plötzensee prison, and no one had been told what to do with them. And there was the medical museum over there too, with all sorts of other stuff, but the Red Army high command disapproved and the exhibits were sent to other institutions. We got Gustaf's brain." He shook the jar so that the brain moved. "The distribution of the exhibits started a lot of silly rumors. They said that Ernst Röhm's heart had been sent to the University Hospital in Leipzig and it had been contained in a test tube." He put the jar back on the shelf. "You must forgive me; physicians are inclined to develop a macabre sense of humor."

"What sort of success rate do you have, doctor?"

"They are all failures when they come here," said Wieczorek. "We only get patients for whom some other institution can do no more. For most of them we can merely keep the fires under control. It is like the job of your security service, isn't it? Are we drawn to such work, do you think?"

"Surely you are better equipped to answer that question," said Fiona.

"I cannot answer on your behalf, but for me and many of my colleagues I suspect that dealing in failure provides an excuse for a lack of success. And like you, perhaps, I enjoy the challenge of such fragile, complicated, and deceptive disciplines. Can you ever be sure that you are right?" He paused. "Right about anything at all?"

"Sometimes," said Fiona. "You still haven't told me about your methods."

"Carl Jung once said, 'Show me a sane man and I will cure him for you.' I think about that a lot. Methods? What can I tell you?" He looked at her with polite interest. "The treatment of seriously disturbed patients has changed radically over the years. First and foremost there remains the old-fashioned analytical session, in which patients are encouraged to delve into their own minds. As Freud discovered, it is a lengthy process. So along came the neurosurgeons, who drilled holes into the skull and destroyed brain cells and nerve fibers with surgical instruments.'' He waited while the horror of that became clear to her. ''Then came a time when it seemed as if electric shocks through the brain could provide lasting improvement, and that seemed to be the panacea everyone had awaited. It wasn't the answer we had hoped for. But the chemists were waiting their turn, and patients were given massive doses of Dexedrine, followed by Seconal and whatever new drug the West German chemical companies were anxious to sell. Now I suppose many specialists are beginning to think that, amid his claptrap, Freud may have had a few worthwhile ideas after all. But analysis on the couch is a very long process; we'll never have enough analysts to fight mental illness in that laborious way.''

''And where do you stand?''

''In the matter of treatment? I am a senior consultant here, but my staff doctors are permitted considerable freedom to choose what is best for their patients. We have mostly depressives and schizophrenics, some of them catatonics demanding a lot of skill and close attention. However, it is in the nature of our function, as a garbage can into which patients are discarded, that we treat a wide variety of illness. After many years of practice I have become reluctant to forbid any kind of treatment that a doctor, after proper study of a patient, thinks will be beneficial.''

''You forbid nothing?''

''That is my stated position.''

''Including lobotomy?''

''A seriously disturbed patient who becomes violent can sometimes be returned to something approaching normal life.'' He got up. ''Let me show you the wards.''

The clinic was hushed but not entirely silent. Most of

the patients were in bed, sleeping with that impassive calm that medicine provides. One small ward was in semidarkness. It held six sleepers who had been sedated for a week. It was, explained Dr. Wieczorek, the preliminary part of the treatment for most new arrivals. Underlying the smell of disinfectant there were all the disagreeable odors that warm bodies provide when crowded together in a closed room. He went to the window and raised the blind a fraction so that they could see the sleeping patients. Outside, she saw that the snow was falling much more heavily; the trees were rimmed with it, and passing cars left black lines in the road. Wieczorek adjusted the disarranged bedclothes. Sometimes, he joked, it took a week or two for their documentation to catch up with them.

The rooms were all lined with white tiles from floor to ceiling. There was something pitiless about the shiny hardness as it reflected the gray blankets. An ashen-faced patient stared at her but didn't register any emotion. Fiona had that guilty feeling of intrusion that afflicts all fit people in the presence of the sick. Wieczorek pulled down the blind and it was dark. As if in response to the darkness, one of the patients gave a muffled cry but then was quiet again.

Downstairs there was a large "association room" where half a dozen patients were sitting in metal chairs with blankets over their knees. Two of them, both middle-aged men, were wearing woolly hats. There was no sign of books or newspapers, and the patients were either asleep or staring into space. A TV set in the corner was showing an animated cartoon in which a hatchet-wielding mouse was chasing a cat, but the sound was switched off and no one was watching it.

"There is one patient you must meet," said Dr. Wieczorek. "Franz. He is our oldest inhabitant. When we got him, in 1978, his memory had completely gone, but we are proud to have made a little progress." He showed her into a bare room with a big square-shaped sink equipped for washing bedpans. There was a man sitting there in a wheelchair. His body had run to fat as a consequence of his confinement. His complexion was yellowish and his lips were pressed tightly together as if he were trying not to yell. "Come along, Franz. What about a cup of coffee?"

The man in the wheelchair said nothing and made no move, except that he rolled his eyes as if trying to see the doctor's face without moving his head. "I've brought a lady to see you, Franz. It's a long time since you had a visitor, isn't it?" To Fiona, Dr. Wieczorek said, "With patients of this sort the condition varies greatly from day to day."

"Hello, Franz," said Fiona, uncertain of what was expected of her.

"Say hello, Franz," said Dr. Wieczorek, and added, "He hears everything, but perhaps today he doesn't want to talk to us." He took the wheelchair and tipped it back to lift the front wheels clear over the step.

Wieczorek took Franz in his wheelchair along the corridor, continuing his small talk and seeming not to notice that Franz didn't answer. Fiona followed. When the chair was positioned in a small room with TREATMENT ROOM NO. 2 on its door, it was placed so that Fiona and the doctor could sit down and face the patient. Although he still hadn't moved his head, Franz had become agitated at coming into the room. He was looking at a small gray enamel cabinet in the corner. Its dial was calibrated in volts, and there was a mechanical timer and wires ending in what looked like headphones. Franz stared at the machine and then at Dr. Wieczorek and then back at the machine again.

"He doesn't like the electric shock treatment," said the doctor. "No one does." He put out a hand and touched Franz in a reassuring gesture. "It's all right, Franz. No treatment today, old friend. Coffee, just coffee."

As if by prearrangement a woman in a blue overall came in carrying a tray with cups, saucers, and a jug of coffee. The chinaware was thick and clumsy, the sort that didn't readily break if dropped. "I'll change my mind, if I may?" said Fiona as the doctor began pouring the coffee.

"Good. Changing people's minds is our specialty here. Isn't that right, Franz?" Dr. Wieczorek chuckled.

Franz moved his eyes and stared at Fiona. It seemed as if he could hear and understand everything that was said. Looking into his face, she wondered if there was something faintly familiar about him, but then she dismissed the thought.

"Poor Franz Blum was a hard-working young third secretary working in the attaché's office in London. Then one day he had a complete breakdown. I suppose it was the strain of being without his family in a strange country for the first time. Some people find it very difficult to adapt. The embassy shipped him back to Moscow as soon as it was realized that he was sick. Everything was tried, and although there were times when he seemed to get better, in the long term he just got worse and worse. It's a sad case. In a way he provides us with a constant reminder of the limitations of our science."

Fiona watched Blum as he reached for his coffee, extending two hands and picking it up with very great care.

"One confidential KGB report from London said that Franz was a spy for the British," said Dr. Wieczorek. "But apparently there is no hard evidence to support the allegation. There was never any question of his going on trial, but we were told the background in case it could help in diagnosis. There was an inquiry, but even your Stasi interrogators got nothing out of him."

She kept calm, very calm, but she turned her eyes away from Franz. "But you did?" This, then, was the man she had reported to Martin Pryce-Hughes, the one she had betrayed and consigned to this living death. Was Dr. Wieczorek in on that whole story, or was it all just need-to-know?

"We have that sort of patient sometimes. Franz wasn't easy to deal with. It's a long time ago now, but I remember it all clearly. When he didn't respond to the pills and injections, it became clear that electric shock would be the only way to help him. Not just the little sessions that are given to help depressed patients; we tried a new idea, really massive shocks."

Franz spilled a dribble of coffee down his chin. Wieczorek took a handkerchief and wiped it. Then he gently removed Franz's woolen hat and indicated for Fiona the shaved patches where the electrodes were applied.

"Shock," said Franz suddenly and loudly as the doctor fingered the bare skin.

"Good," said Dr. Wieczorek proudly. "Did you hear that? As clear as anything. Keep up the good work, Franz, and we'll soon be sending you home." He replaced the knitted hat on the man's head but it remained askew, giving Franz Blum an inappropriately jaunty air. As if the demonstration was over, Wieczorek stood up and grabbed the wheelchair. He pushed it back into the corridor, where a nurse was waiting to take it from him. "You didn't have your coffee," Wieczorek said to Fiona, as if suddenly remembering it.

"Is there much more of the clinic to see?" she asked.

"Nothing of consequence. Sit down and drink the coffee. I hope Franz didn't upset you."

"Of course not," said Fiona.

"He'll never go home, he'll never go anywhere," said Dr. Wieczorek. "He's institutionalized for life, I'm afraid. Poor Franz."

"Yes, poor Franz," said Fiona. "But if the KGB report was true, he was an enemy of the State, wasn't he?"

"An enemy of the people," Wieczorek corrected her sardonically. "That's far worse."

She looked at him. He was smiling. She knew then beyond any doubt that this was a charade, a charade acted out for her to guess the word. The word was "treachery," and the pathetic zombie they had made of Franz Blum was an example of what would be done to her if she should betray her KGB masters. Is that why he'd quoted Carl Jung, "Show me a sane man and I will cure him for you"?

"It's good coffee, isn't it?" said Dr. Wieczorek. "I have a special source."

"You're lucky," said Fiona. Perhaps this terrifying warning was a procedure that all senior Stasi staff were subjected to. There was no way to be sure; that was how the country was run. Carrot and stick; award in the morning and warning in the afternoon. This topsy-turvy clinic where the "sane" were cured was just how she saw this "workers' State" where the leaders lived in ostentatious grandeur in fenced compounds paced by armed guards.

"Yes, I am lucky," said Dr. Wieczorek, savoring his coffee. "You're lucky too; we all are."

18

London:

November 1983

BRET RENSSELAER WAS OVERPLAYING HIS HAND. IN TRYing to make Fiona Samson secure he'd even thrown suspicion onto Bernard Samson, suggesting that he might have been an accomplice to his wife's treachery. It was an effective device, for the Department was just as vulnerable to rumors and whispered half-truths as any other organized assembly of competitive humans. The trouble came because opinions were divided about Bernard Samson's integrity, and so a rumor started that another mole was at work within the Department. An unhealthy atmosphere of mistrust and suspicion was developing.

The discovery of the murdered Julian MacKenzie in a Department safe house in Bosham gave further impetus to the gossip. Thanks to what Miranda Keller had told him, Bret knew it was a case of mistaken identity; the KGB had been after Bernard Samson. But Bret took no action in the matter beyond getting Samson into the Number Three Conference Room and admonishing him in the presence of suitable witnesses. Samson shouted back, as Bret knew he would, and Bret ended up telling everyone who would listen that Bernard Samson was "beyond suspicion."

But spinning the web of deceit that he deemed necessary for Fiona's safety was taking its toll of Bret Rensselaer. He was by nature an administrator, brutal sometimes but sustained always by self-righteousness. Running the Economics Intelligence Section had been a task for which he was ideally fitted. But "Sinker" was different. His original plan to target the East German economy by draining away skilled workers and professional people was not as easy as it once seemed. Fiona was supplying him with regular information about the East German opposition and other reform groups, but they could not unite. His overall problem was that keeping "Sinker" such a close secret meant telling ever more complex lies to his friends and colleagues. It was vital that none of them should see the whole plan. This was demanding in a way he did not relish. It was like playing tennis against himself, crisscrossing the center line, leaping the net, wrong-footing himself, and delivering ever more strenuous volleys that would be impossible to return.

And this double life left him very little time for relaxation or pleasure. Now, at lunchtime on Saturday, a time when he might have snatched a few hours relaxing with friends at the sort of weekend house party he most enjoyed, he was sitting bickering with his wife about the divorce and her wretched alimony.

It was typical of Nicola that she should insist on having lunch at Roma Locuta Est, a cramped Italian restaurant in Knightsbridge. Even the name affronted him. "Rome has spoken" was a way of saying no complaints would be listened to, and that was exactly the way Pina ran her restaurant. Pina was a formidable Italian matron who welcomed the rich and famous while ruthlessly pruning from her clientele those of lesser appeal. It had become a meeting place for the noisy Belgravia jet set, a group Bret assiduously shunned. This being Saturday they were at their most insufferable, table-hopping and shouting loudly to one another, ordering their Anglicized food in execrable Italian. Bret's lunch was not made more enjoyable by discovering that just about everyone here seemed to be on first-name terms with his wife.

"You really believe it," she was saying. "Jesus Christ, Bret. You say you're poor, and you really believe it. If it wasn't so goddamned sneaky, it would make me laugh." Nicola had obviously taken a lot of trouble with her clothes and makeup, but she was out of his past and he felt no attraction to her.

"You don't have to tell everyone in the room, darling," said Bret softly. Knowing the sort of place it was, Bret had made appropriate sartorial concessions. He was wearing a suede jacket and tan-colored silk turtleneck. His normal attire, a good suit, would have looked out of place here on a Saturday lunchtime.

"I don't care if all the world knows. I'll shout it from the housetops."

"We went through all this before we were married. You saw the lawyers. You signed the forms of agreement."

"I didn't read what I was signing." She drank some of her Campari and soda.

"Why the hell didn't you?"

"Because I was in love with you, that's why I didn't."

"You thought separating would be like it was in old Hollywood movies. You thought I would go to stay in my club and you'd have the house and the furniture and the paintings and the Bentley and every other damn thing."

"I thought I might own half of my own home. I didn't know my home was owned by a corporation."

"Not a corporation, it's owned by a trust."

"I don't care if it's owned by the Boy Scouts of America. You let me think it was my home, and now I find it never was."

"Please don't tell me that you gave me the best years of your life," said Bret.

"I gave you everything." She stirred her drink so that the ice rattled.

"You gave me hell." He looked around the dining room. "I can't think why that woman Pina allows dogs in here. It's unhygienic." He took out a handkerchief and blew his nose. "And animal hair affects my sinus."

"It doesn't affect your sinus," said his wife. "You get your sinus and then you look around for something to blame it on."

Bret noticed that the demonstrative Pina was making her rounds. She liked to take her customers in a bear hug and scream endearments in their ear before discussing their food. "Yes, you gave me hell," said Bret.

"I told you the truth, and you found it hell." With quick, agitated movements Nicola opened her handbag to get her cigarettes. Under the handbag there was a copy of *Vogue* and a book called *Somebody Stole My Spy*. On the cover it said BETTER THAN LUDLUM in letters bigger than the author's name. Bret wondered whether she was really reading the book or had brought it here as some kind of provocation. She liked to make jokes about his "career as a spy."

When Brett leaned forward and lit the cigarette for her, he noticed she was trembling. He wondered why. He found it difficult to believe that he could cause anyone to become so distressed. "Jesus!" said Nicola and blew smoke high into the air, where it made little clouds in the plastic vines that hung from the ceiling.

Out of the corner of his eye he saw Pina coming. Bret detested her and decided to flee to the toilet, but he was too late. "And you know my husband," Nicola was already saying, her voice strangled as she was enveloped in Pina's beefy arms and drowned by a babble of Italian chatter.

Bret stood up and edged sideways to keep the table between them and nodded deferentially. Pina looked at him, rolled her eyes, and yelled in Italian. Bret smiled and gave a little bow to acknowledge what he thought was some flowery Roman compliment, but it turned out to be Pina shouting for more menus.

When they'd ordered lunch, or more accurately when they had agreed to the meal that Pina decreed they should have, Nicola went back to talking about the settlement.

"Your lawyer is a bastard," she said.

"Other people's lawyers are always bastards. That comes with the job."

Nikki shifted her attack. "They do what you tell them."

"I don't tell them anything. There's nothing to tell. The law is explicit."

"I'm going to California. I'm going to sue you."

"That won't get you anywhere," said Bret. "I don't live in California, and I don't own anything in California. You might as well go to Greenland."

"I'm going to take up residence there. They have communal property laws in California. My brother-in-law says I'd do better there."

"I wish you'd start using your brains, Nikki. The money my father left me is in a trust. We're not really a part of the Rensselaer family. My grandmother married into it late in life; she changed her children's name to Rensselaer. We never inherited the Rensselaer millions. I just have an allowance from a small trust fund. I told you all that before we were married."

She waggled a manicured finger at him. "You're not going to get away with this, Bret. I'll break that damned trust fund if it's the last thing I do. I want what I'm entitled to."

"Dammit, Nikki, you left *me.* You went off with Joppi."

"Leave Joppi out of this," she said.

"How can we leave him out of it? He's the third party."

"He's not."

"Nikki, dear. We both know he is."

"Well, you prove it. You just try and prove it, that's all."

"Don't drag this through the courts, Nikki. All you'll do is make lawyers rich."

"Who's having the *insalata frutti di mare?*" yelled the waiter into their ears as he bent over the table.

"I am," said Bret.

"You want the sole off the bone, madam?" the waiter asked Nicola.

"Yes, please," she said.

Bret looked down at the mangled lettuce, upon which sat four cold damp shrimp and some white rubber rings of ink-fish, and he looked at Nicola's delicious filleted sole. "Melted butter?" said the waiter, "and a little Parmesan cheese?" Nikki always knew what to order. Was it skill or was it luck? Or was it Pina?

Bret noticed that the bejeweled woman at the next table was feeding pieces of her veal escalope to a perfectly brushed and combed terrier at her feet. "It's like a damned zoo in here," he muttered, but his wife pretended not to hear him.

Nikki abandoned her sole and put down her knife and fork. "I gave you everything," she said again, having thought about it carefully. "I even came to live in this lousy country with you, didn't I? And what did I get for it?"

"What did you get? You lived high on the hog, in one of the most beautiful homes in England."

"It wasn't a home, Bret, it was just a beautiful house. But when did I ever see my husband? I'd go for days and days with no one to talk to but the servants."

"You should be able to cope with being alone," said Bret.

"Well, old buddy. Now *you'll* be able to find out what it means to be alone. Because I won't be there when you get home, and no other woman will put up with you. You'll soon discover that."

"I'm not afraid of being alone," said Bret smugly. He pushed the salad aside. His wife was always complaining of being alone, and today he had an answer ready, "Lots of people have been. Descartes, Kierkegaard, Locke, Newton, Nietzsche, Pascal, Spinoza, and Wittgenstein were alone for most of their lives."

She laughed. "I saw that in the letters column of the *Daily Telegraph* too. But those people are all geniuses. You're not a thinker . . . not a philosopher."

"My work is important," said Bret. He was put out. "It's not like working for a biscuit factory. A government job is a government job."

"Oh, sure, and we all know what governments do."

"What do you mean by that?" said Bret, with an uncertainty that was almost comic.

"They make the rules for you and break them themselves. They hike your taxes and give themselves a raise in pay. They take your money away and shower it onto all kinds of lousy foreign governments. They send your kids to Vietnam and get them killed. They fly in choppers while you're stuck in traffic jams. They let the banks and insurance companies shaft you in exchange for political campaign money."

"Is that what you really think, Nikki?" Bret was shocked. She'd never said anything like that before. He wondered if she had been drinking all morning.

"You're damn right it's what I think. It's what everybody thinks who hasn't got a hand in the till."

Alarm bells rang. "I didn't know you were a liberal." He wondered what the security vetting people had made of her. Thank goodness he was getting rid of her. But had any of this gone down on his file?

"I'm not a goddamned Democrat or a Liberal or a Red or

anything else. It's just that smug guys like you doing your 'important' work for the government make me puke.''

"There's nothing to be gained from a shouting match," said Bret. "I know you must be disappointed about the house, but that's outside my control."

"Damn you, Bret. I must have somewhere to live!"

He guessed Joppi was getting rid of her. Suddenly he felt sorry for her, but he didn't want her back. "That apartment in Monte Carlo is empty. You could lease it from the trustees for a nominal payment."

" 'Lease it from the trustees for a nominal payment,' '' she repeated sarcastically. "How nominal can you get? Like a dollar a year?"

"If it would end all this needless wrangling, a dollar a year would be fine. Shall we agree on that?" He waved his hand to attract a waiter, but it was no use. The waiters were all standing around a table in the corner smiling at a TV news reader who was being photographed cuddling a smooth-coated Chihuahua. "Do you want coffee?"

"Yes," she said. "Yes to both questions, but I want furniture—good furniture—in the first and cream and sugar in the second."

"You've got a deal," said Bret. He was relieved. Had Nikki resolutely pressed for the Thameside house it would have put him in a difficult position. He would have had to resign. There was no way that the Department would have tolerated his getting into a divorce action and the risk of its attendant publicity. And yet if he resigned, where would that leave Fiona Samson? He was the only person who knew the whole story, and he felt personally responsible for her mission. There were many times when he worried about her.

Bret looked up to see his chauffeur, Albert Bingham, easing his way through the crowded dining room. "What now?" said Bret. Nicola turned around to see what he was looking at.

"Good afternoon, Mrs. Rensselaer," said Albert politely. He reasoned that ex-wives sometimes resumed their authority as employers and should not be slighted. "I'm sorry to interrupt you, sir, but the hospital came through on the car phone."

"What did they say?" Bret was already on his feet. Albert wouldn't interrupt the lunch unless it was something very important.

"Could you be early?"

"Could I be early?" repeated Bret. He found his credit card in his wallet.

"They said you would know what it was," said Albert.

"I'll have to go," said Bret to his wife. "It's an old friend." He flicked the plastic card with his fingernail so that it made a snapping noise. She remembered it as one of his many irritating habits.

"That's all right," said Nicola, in the brisk voice that proclaimed her annoyance.

"Let's do it again," said Bret. He bent forward—the hand holding his credit card extended like a stage magician palming something from the air—and kissed his wife on the cheek. "Now that it's all settled, let's do it again." He heard the terrier growl as he trod too near its food.

She nodded. He didn't want to have lunch with her again, she could see that as clearly as anything. She saw how relieved he was at this opportunity to escape from her. She felt like crying. She was pleased to be separating from Bret Rensselaer, but she found it humiliating that he seemed pleased about it too. She got out her compact and flipped up the mirror to look at her eye makeup. She could see Bret reflected in it. She watched him while he paid the bill.

* * *

Bret's original appointment with the Director-General had been for drinks at six o'clock at his house in the country. Now the Director-General had phoned to suggest that they meet at Rensselaer's mews house in London. That was the call on the car phone that Albert had reported. The Department's calls were always described by Albert as being calls from an anonymous hospital, school, or club, according to Bret's company and the circumstances in which the message was delivered.

"Are you sure he said the mews house?" Bret asked his driver.

"Quite sure," said Albert.

"What a memory he has," said Bret with grudging admiration.

Back at the turn of the century, the mews house had been the stables and coach house for Cyrus Rensselaer's grand London home. The first time Bret saw the big house in the square it was an officers' club run by the American Red Cross. After the war it had been sold, but the uncomfortable little mews house had been retained. Just a couple of rooms with kitchen, bathroom, and garage, it was used by various members of the Rensselaer family and sometimes by lawyers and agents coming to London on the family's behalf. But because Bret lived in England, he had a key, and, by the generous consent of the other members of the family, he could use it when he wanted. In return Bret kept an eye on the place and had the leaky roof fixed from time to time. He hadn't slept there for years.

Bret was surprised that the D-G should remember he had access to the house and was annoyed that he should suggest it for their meeting. He had no consideration; the place was terribly neglected now there was no permanent tenant to maintain it. "Go to the mews right away," Bret told his driver. "We'll try and get it straightened out before Sir Henry arrives."

"We'll have half an hour or so," said Albert, "and Sir Henry might be late; he said that."

"It's just as well I remained in London," said Bret. "You never know where Sir Henry will turn up."

"No, sir," said Albert Bingham.

Bret settled back in the leather seat of his Bentley. He had been tempted to spend the weekend with some horsey friends near Newmarket and make a side trip to the D-G's house in Cambridgeshire. Then his wife had insisted they meet for Saturday lunch, and he'd stayed in town. It was just as well. A sudden dash back to London at short notice, just to satisfy the old man's whim, was the kind of thing that gave Bret indigestion.

"I'm sorry if this was an inconvenient meeting place," said Sir Henry Clevemore, when he arrived in the tiny upstairs room above the garage. He had knocked his head against the door frame but now, having fitted his huge bulk into a big, somewhat dilapidated armchair, he seemed quite content. "It was a matter of some urgency."

"I'm sorry it's not more comfortable here," said Bret. The room was dusty and damp. There were fingermarks on the mirror, unwashed milk bottles in the sink, and dead flowers on the bookcase. The only festive note was provided by the carpet, which was rolled up, stitched into canvas, and garnished with bright red plastic packets of moth repellent. Used by transients as a place to sleep, the house was sadly lacking in any sort of comfort. Even the electric kettle was not working. What a shame that Nikki was so difficult. This place would really benefit from a woman's touch.

Bret reached down to see if there was hot air coming from the convection heater. He'd put on the electric heating as soon as he arrived, but the air was musty. He resolved to do something drastic about refurbishing the place. He'd write to the lawyers about it. He opened a cupboard to reveal some bottles. "There *is* a bottle of whisky . . ."

"Stop fussing, Bret. We needed somewhere to talk in private. This is ideal. No, I don't want a drink. My news is that Erich Stinnes is flying here from Mexico City together with young Bernard Samson. I think we've done it."

"That's good news, sir." He looked down to see where the D-G's black Labrador was sprawled. Why had the old man brought that senile and smelly creature up into this little room?

"It's going to be your show, Bret. Let Samson do the talking, but keep a tight control on what's really happening. We must turn Stinnes round and get him back there."

"Yes, sir."

"But it occurred to me, Bret. . . ." He paused. "I don't want to interfere. . . . It's your show. . . . Entirely your show."

"Please go on, sir." Bret flicked the dust from a chintz-covered chair and sat down very carefully. He didn't want to get his clothes dirty.

The D-G was lolling back with his legs crossed, oblivious of the shabbiness of the room. The gloomy winter light coming through the dusty window was just enough to describe the old man's profile and make spots of light on the toes of his highly polished shoes. "Should we collar this damned fellow Martin Pryce-Hughes?"

"The communist? Ummm."

Bret's tone was too mild to satisfy the D-G. "That little tick who was the contact between Mrs. Samson and the KGB hoodlums," he said forcibly. "Shall we collar him? Don't say you haven't given it any thought."

"I've given it a lot of thought," said Bret, in the strangled voice that was his response to unjust criticism.

"You cautioned against pulling him in too soon after Mrs. Samson went over. But how long are we going to wait?"

Bret said, "You see, sir—"

The D-G interrupted him. "Now, with this fellow Stinnes arriving here, we have to consider to what extent we want Moscow to link Stinnes and Pryce-Hughes. If Stinnes is to go back there, we don't want them to think that he betrayed Pryce-Hughes to us, do we?"

"No, sir, we don't."

"Well, for the Lord's sake, man. Spit it out! What is on your mind? Shall we grab Pryce-Hughes and grill him or not? It's your decision. You know I don't want to interfere."

"You are always very considerate," said Bret, while really thinking how much he would like to kick the D-G down the narrow creaking stairs and watch to see which way he bounced off the greasy garage floor.

"I try to be," said the D-G, mollified by Bret's subservient tone.

"But another dimension has emerged. It is something I didn't want to bother you with."

"Bother me with it now," said Sir Henry.

"In the summer of 1978 . . ." Bret paused, deciding how much he should reveal and how he should say it. "Mrs. Samson . . . formed a relationship with a Dr. Henry Kennedy."

When Bret paused again, the D-G said, "Formed a relationship? What the devil does that mean? I'm not going to sue you for defamation, Bret. For God's sake, say what you mean. Say what you mean."

"I mean," said Bret, speaking slowly and deliberately, "that from about that time, until she went over there, she was having a love affair with this man."

"Oh, my God!" said the D-G with a gasp of surprise upon which he almost choked. "Mrs. Samson? Are you quite sure, Bret?" He waited until Bret nodded. "My God." The black Labrador, sensing its master's dismay, got to its feet and shook itself. Now the air was full of dust from the dog's coat; Bret could see motes of it buoyant on the draft coming from the heater.

Bret got his handkerchief to his nose just in time before sneezing. When he recovered he dabbed his face again and said, "I'm quite sure, Sir Henry, but that's not all. When I started digging into this fellow Kennedy's past, I discovered that he has been a party member since the time he was a medical student."

"Party member? Communist Party member? This fellow she was having it off with? Bret, why the hell didn't you tell me all this? Am I going mad?" He was straining forward in his chair as if trying to get up, and his dog was looking angrily at Bret.

"I appreciate your concern, sir," said Bret in the gravelly American accent that he could summon when he needed it. "Kennedy is a Canadian. His father was a Ukrainian with a name that couldn't be written on an English typewriter, so it became Kennedy."

"I don't like the smell of that one, Bret. Are we really dealing with a Russian national wielding a Canadian birth certificate? We've seen a lot of those, haven't we?"

"Ottawa RCMP has nothing on him. Served in the air force with an exemplary record. Medical school, postgraduate, and so on. The only thing they could turn up was an ex-wife chasing him for alimony. No political activity except for a few meetings of the party at college." Bret stopped. The fact that the fellow was being chased for alimony payments made Bret sympathize.

"Well, don't leave it like that, Bret. You're not trying to

break it to me that Mrs. Samson might have been . . ." The D-G's voice trailed away as he considered the terrifying complexities that would follow upon any doubts about Fiona Samson's loyalties.

"No, no worries on that account, Sir Henry. In fact they are both clear. I have no evidence that Dr. Kennedy has been active in any way—in any way at all—during the time he was seeing Mrs. Samson or afterward."

"How do you know?"

"I've been keeping an eye on him."

"You personally?"

"No, of course not, Sir Henry. I have had someone keeping an eye on him."

"Someone? What someone? A Department someone?"

"No, of course not, sir. I arranged it privately."

"Yes, but not paid for it privately, eh? It's gone on the dockets. Perhaps you didn't think of that. Oh, my God."

"It's not on any dockets, Sir Henry. I paid personally, and I paid in cash."

"Are you insane, Bret? You paid personally? Out of your own pocket? What are you up to?"

"It had to be kept secret," said Bret.

"Of course it did. You don't have to tell me that! My God. I've never heard of such a thing." The D-G slumped back in the chair as if in collapse. "What kind of whisky have you got?" he said finally.

Bret reached for a bottle of Bell's, poured a stiff one into a tumbler for the D-G, and gave it to him. After sipping it, the D-G said, "Confound you, Bret. Tell me the worst. Come along. I'm prepared now."

"There is no 'worst,' " said Bret. "It is as I told you. There is nothing to show any contact between Kennedy and the Soviets."

"You don't fool me, Bret. If it was as simple as that you

would have told me long ago, not waited until I faced you with collaring Pryce-Hughes.''

Bret was still standing near the bottles. He had never been a drinker, but he poured himself a tiny one to be sociable, took it to the window, and nursed it. He wanted to get as far away from the dog as he possibly could. The smell of the drink was repulsive, and he put it down. He pressed his fingers against the cold windowpane. How well he knew this little house. Glenn Rensselaer had brought him here while still wearing the uniform of a U.S. Army general. Glenn had been someone Bret had loved more than he could ever love the pathetic alcoholic who was his father.

"It's no more than a hunch," said Bret, after a long time of just looking down at the cobbled mews and the shiny cars parked there. "But I just know Kennedy is a part of it. I just know he is. I'm sure they put Kennedy in to run a check on Mrs. Samson. They met at a railway station; I'm sure it was contrived." He let a little whisky touch his lips. "She must have got through whatever test he gave her, because the signs are that Dr. Kennedy is in love with her and continues to be. But Kennedy is a bomb, ticking away, and I don't like it. I kept an eye on Pryce-Hughes because I hoped there would be some contact. But it's a long time ago; I guess I was wrong."

"Too much guessing, Bret."

"Yes, Sir Henry."

"Facts trump the ace of hunches, right?"

"Yes, of course, sir."

"You'll collar Pryce-Hughes?"

"I'd rather leave that a little longer, sir. I tried to provoke him into a response a few years back. I had someone produce an elaborate file that 'proved' Pryce-Hughes was working for London Central. It was a magnificent job—documents, photos, and all sorts of stuff—and it cost an arm and a leg. I went along when it was shown to him."

"And?"

"He just laughed in our faces, sir. Literally. I was there. He laughed."

"I'm glad we had this little chat, Bret," said the D-G. It was a rebuke.

"But the file I compiled to incriminate Pryce-Hughes could be very useful to us now, sir."

"I'm listening, Bret."

"I want to have that whole file revised so it will incriminate this KGB colonel, Pavel Moskvin."

"Isn't he the thug who murdered that lad in the Bosham safe house?"

"I believe he's a danger to Fiona Samson."

"Are you sure this is not just a way of using that damned file?"

"It will cost very little, sir. We can plant it into the KGB network very easily. That Miranda Keller woman would be perfect in the role of Moskvin's contact."

"It would be a bit rough on her, wouldn't it?" said the D-G.

"It's Fiona Samson we have to think of," said Bret.

"Very well, Bret. If you put it like that I can't stop you."

19

England:

Christmas 1983

G LORIA K ENT FELT MISERABLE . S HE HAD BROUGHT B ER-
nard Samson's two young children to spend Christmas with
her parents. She was tall and blond and very beautiful, and
she was wearing the low-cut green dress she had bought specially to impress Bernard.

"Why isn't he with his children?" Gloria's mother asked
for the umpteenth time. She was putting the Christmas lunch
dishes into the dishwasher as Gloria brought them from the
table.

"He was given Christmas duty at the last minute," said
Gloria. "And the nanny had already gone home."

"You are a fool, Gloria," said her mother.

"What do you mean?"

"You know what I mean," said her mother. "He'll go
back to his wife, they always do." She dropped a handful of
knives and forks into the plastic basket. "A man can't have
two wives."

Gloria handed over the dessert plates and then put plastic wrap over the remains of the Christmas pudding before
putting it into the refrigerator.

Ten-year-old Billy Samson came into the kitchen. He was

still wearing the paper hat and a plastic bangle that he'd got from a Christmas cracker. "Sally is going to be sick," he announced, without bothering to conceal his joy at the prospect.

"No, she's not, Billy. I just spoke to her. She's doing the jigsaw. Is the video finished?"

"I've seen it before."

"Has Grandad seen it before?" asked Gloria. It had been established that Gloria's father was Grandad.

"He's asleep," said Billy. "He snores."

"Why don't you help Sally with the jigsaw?" said Gloria.

"Can I have some more custard?"

"I think you've had enough, Billy," said Gloria firmly. "I've never seen anyone eat so much."

Billy looked at her for a moment before agreeing and wandering off to the drawing room. Mrs. Kent watched him go. The little boy was so like the photos of his father. She was sorry for the poor motherless mite but was convinced that her daughter would know only pain from her reckless affair with "a married man at the office."

"I know everything you want to say, Mummy," said Gloria, "but I love Bernard desperately."

"I know you do, my sweetheart." She was going to say more but she saw her daughter's eyes already brimming with tears. That was the heart-wrenching part of it. Gloria knew that only misery was in store for her.

"He didn't want to go," said Gloria. "This awful man at the office sent him. I had planned everything so carefully. I wanted to make him and the children really happy."

"What does he say about it all?" her mother asked, emboldened by the wine she'd had with lunch.

"He says the same things you say," said Gloria. "He keeps telling me he's twenty years older than I am. He keeps saying I should be with someone else, someone younger."

"Then he can't love you," declared her mother emphatically.

Gloria managed a little laugh. "Oh, Mummy. Whatever he does he's wrong in your eyes."

"When you first told us, your father couldn't talk about it for weeks."

"It's my life, Mummy."

"You're so young. You trust everyone and the world is so cruel." She packed the last dirty plate into the dishwasher, closed its door, and straightened up. "What is he doing today that's so important? Or should I not ask?"

"He's in Berlin, identifying a body."

"I'll be glad when you go to Cambridge."

"Yes," said Gloria without enthusiasm.

"Isn't his wife in Berlin?" said her mother suddenly.

"He won't be seeing her," said Gloria.

In the next room Billy pulled a chair up to the card table where Sally was working at the jigsaw, "A Devon Scene"; it was a present from Nanny. Sally had got two edges of it complete. Without saying anything, Billy began to help with the puzzle.

"I miss Mummy," said Sally. "I wonder why she didn't visit us for Christmas."

"Gloria is nice," said Billy, who had rather fallen for her. "What is separated?" He had heard that his parents were separated, but he was not sure exactly what this meant.

Sally said, "Nanny said Mummy and Daddy have to live in different countries so they can find themselves."

"Can't they find themselves?" said Billy. He chuckled, "It must be terrible if you can't find yourself."

Sally didn't think it was funny at all. "When she finds herself, Mummy will come back."

"Does it take long?"

"I'll ask Nanny," said Sally, who was clever at wheedling

things out of the quiet girl from Devon.

"Is Daddy finding himself too?" And then, before Sally could reply, he found a piece of sky and fitted it into the puzzle.

"I saw that bit first," said Sally.

"No, you didn't! No, you didn't!"

Sally said, "Perhaps Daddy could marry Mummy and marry Gloria too."

"No," said Billy authoritatively. "A man can't have two wives."

Sally looked at him with admiration. Billy always knew everything. But there was a look she recognized in his face. "Are you all right?" she said fearfully.

"I think I'm going to be sick," said Billy.

20

East Berlin:

February 1984

HUBERT RENN SELDOM VOICED HIS INNERMOST THOUGHTS, but had he done so in regard to working for Fiona Samson, he would have said that the relationship had proved far better than he'd dared hope. And when, in the first week of January 1984, he was offered a chance to change jobs and work at the Normannenstrasse Stasi headquarters, Renn declined and went to considerable trouble to provide reasons why not.

Hubert Renn preferred the atmosphere of the small KGB–Stasi command unit on Karl Liebknecht Strasse. And, like many of the administrative staff, he enjoyed the feeling of importance and the day-to-day urgency that operational work bestowed. Also, he'd adopted a paternal responsibility for Fiona Samson without its ever becoming evident from the stern and formal way in which he insisted that the office be run. Neither did Fiona Samson ever demand, or seemingly expect, anything other than Renn's total dedication to his work.

Renn did not find it difficult to understand Fiona Samson, or at least to come to terms with her. This mutual understanding was helped by the way in which Fiona had suppressed and reformed her femininity. The uncertainties and the misgivings that childbearing and marriage had left to her no longer influenced her thoughts. She was not masculine—men and their reasonings were no less puzzling now than they'd ever been—but she was simplistic and determined in the way that men are. Even at her most feminine, she had never fallen into the role of victim the way she'd watched her mother and her sister and countless other women readily play that part. Nowadays, whenever something came up that she was unable to deal with on her own terms, she asked herself what Bernard would do in the same situation. That often helped her to solve the problem, and solve it without delay.

Had she been perfectly fit, things would have been entirely endurable. But Berlin had got to her. For Bernard it was a second home and he loved it, but for Fiona it was a city of bad dreams. She had come to the conclusion that her bouts of depression and the nightmares from which she so often awoke sweating and trembling were not solely brought on by loneliness, or even by the guilt she felt at having abandoned her husband and children. Berlin was the villain. Berlin was eating her heart away so that she would never recover. It was nonsense, of course, but she was becoming unbalanced and she was aware of it.

In the privacy of her Frankfurter Allee apartment, when she was not slaving over work or trying to improve her German and her Russian, she did sometimes find time to reflect on the reasons why she found herself in this desperate situation. She dismissed the narrative analysis, the sort of reasoning beloved of psychologists and novelists, that would undoubtedly draw a straight cause-and-effect line through her authoritarian father, the boarding school, her secret government work, and its apotheosis in this assumption of another life. It hadn't happened like that. The ability to play out this role was something she'd worked hard to perfect; that part of her illness wasn't a manifestation of some flaw in her personality.

She'd liberated herself from being that little girl who'd gone to boarding school shivering with apprehension, not by marching or shouting slogans but by stealth. That was why the transformation was so complete. She had actually become another person! Although she would never admit it to a living soul, she had even given a name to this tough employee who went to work in the Karl Liebknecht Strasse every day and slaved hard for the German socialist state. The person was Stefan Mittelberg—a name she'd compiled when perusing a directory—a man's name of course, for in the office she had to be a man. "Come along, Stefan," she'd tell herself each morning, "it's time to get out of bed." And when she was brushing her hair in front of the mirror, as she always did at the start of each day, she would see hard-eyed Stefan looking back at her. Was "Stefan" a manifestation of emotional change? Of hardening? Of liberation? Or was "Stefan" the one who'd had the spontaneous love affair with Harry Kennedy? How else would one explain an act so totally out of character? Well, "Stefan" was a success story; the trouble was, she loathed "Stefan." No matter, perhaps in time she would learn to love this new tougher self.

In the office she concentrated upon becoming the perfect apparatchik, the sort of boss that a man such as Renn would want to work for. But she was a foreigner and she was a woman, and sometimes she needed help and advice when dealing with the devious intrigues of the office.

"How long will the new man be working here?" Fiona asked Renn one day when they were tidying away boxes of papers and celebrating a completely clear desk.

Renn looked at her, amazed that she could be so innocent and ill-informed. Especially since Fiona's Russian award had now come through. She'd been given it at a little ceremony in the hall at Normannenstrasse. Renn had enjoyed a share of the glory. "New man?" he said. He never rushed into such conversations.

"The young one . . . yellow wavy hair . . . ?" She paused. "What have I said?"

Renn found her ignorance both appalling and endearing. Everyone else in the building had learned how to recognize an officer of the political security service in Moscow. "Lieutenant Bakushin, do you mean?" he asked her.

"Yes. What is he here for?"

"He was one of the executive officers on the Moskvin inquiry."

"Moskvin inquiry? Pavel Moskvin?"

"But yes. It was held in Moscow last week."

"Inquiry into what?"

"Conduct."

"Conduct?"

"That is the usual style. Such inquiries are secret, of course."

"And is the verdict announced or is that secret too?"

"Lieutenant Bakushin is collecting further evidence. He will probably want to talk to you, Frau Direktor."

"But Moskvin has just been promoted to colonel," said Fiona. She still didn't understand what Renn was trying to tell her.

"That was simply to make it easier for him to give instructions to the embassy people while he is in London. Here rank does not count for as much as it does in the West. It is a man's appointment that decides his authority."

"And Lieutenant Bakushin's appointment is a high one?"

"Lieutenant Bakushin could arrest and imprison anyone in the building, without reference to Moscow," said Renn simply. It made Fiona's blood run cold.

"Have you any idea what Colonel Moskvin was accused of?"

"Serious crimes," said Renn.

"What sort of crimes are serious crimes?"

"The charges against Colonel Moskvin are something it is better we did not discuss."

"I heard that the colonel has many influential enemies in Moscow," said Fiona.

Renn stood still. For a moment Fiona thought he would murmur some excuse and leave the office—he'd done that before when she had persisted with questions he would not answer—but he didn't do that. Renn went around the desk and stood by her side. "Major Erich Stinnes is in London leading the English Secret Service by the nose and creating the sort of havoc I could not even guess at; Colonel Moskvin is also in England supporting the operation. Moscow was very unhappy at the death of an Englishman in a house in Bosham. Colonel Moskvin overstepped his authority. It is because he is unavailable that the inquiry has been staged at this time. The problem the colonel faces is that if the London operation goes well, Major Stinnes will get the credit for his courage, skill, and ingenuity. If anything goes wrong, Colonel Moskvin's support will be blamed." Renn looked at her and then hurried on. "And so meanwhile you are left the most powerful officer in the section." Renn looked at her; she still hadn't fully understood, so he went on. "Lieutenant Bakushin sees that. He will take evidence from you on the understanding that you see it too."

"You mean Bakushin will expect me to give evidence that will help to convict Colonel Moskvin of whatever it is he's accused of so that I take command?"

"Frau Direktor, wild rumors are going around. Some say Colonel Moskvin has been a long-term agent for the British. Mrs. Keller is also accused; perhaps you remember her from my birthday party? She fled to the West with her son, using what are believed to be forged United Kingdom passports." Renn smiled to relieve the tension he felt. "I am confident that the Moscow inquiry will find Colonel Moskvin innocent; he has friends and relatives highly placed in Moscow. I know how the system works. The lieutenant is simply collecting evidence for the inquiry. It will be expedient to show caution when you talk with him."

Fiona took a deep breath. "Have you ever read *Alice in Wonderland,* Herr Renn?"

"It's an English book? No, I think I have not read it." He dismissed discussion of the book politely but hurriedly. "But Frau Direktor, this means you must decide about the meeting in Holland. There is no one else who can sign the orders. With both Colonel Moskvin and Major Stinnes unavailable, we need someone senior with fluent English. I hope it won't mean getting someone from another unit."

"Not if we can avoid it," said Fiona. "But surely, Herr Renn, you understand my hesitation."

"You will go?" said Renn.

"I don't think so," said Fiona. She wanted to go; a trip to the West—just to breathe the air for twenty-four hours— would give her a new lease of life.

"If it's the risk of arrest, I can arrange for you to travel on diplomatic papers."

"No."

"Who else is there?"

She looked at him. She'd thought about it and been tempted, but now that Renn asked the direct question she had no answer ready. "I would have to clear it with Normannenstrasse. They would have to know."

Renn picked up a plastic box of floppy disks that was on Fiona's desk waiting for the messenger and toyed with it. "I really would advise against that, Frau Direktor," said Renn, his eyes averted and his face red with the embarrassment of such direct rebellion.

"Checking with them," explained Fiona. "Technically we all come under their orders."

"Frau Direktor, to seek instruction from Normannenstrasse, and on a matter which is entirely operational, would be creating a very important precedent. A dangerous precedent." He shook the box of floppy disks; it rattled. "Whatever happens in the careers of Colonel Moskvin and Major Stinnes, this department will I hope continue to function in the way it has done for twelve years or more. But if you ask Normannenstrasse to give you permission for something as normal as the trip to Holland, you'll be virtually putting us under their authority. What would happen in the future? No one here will enjoy anything like independence in any of the work we do. We might as well talk of closing the unit down and going to work in Normannenstrasse."

She took the box of disks from his fingers and put it back on her desk. Then she looked down at her notepad as if returning to her work. "I wouldn't want to do that, Herr Renn. You've already told me how much you hate that mad scramble for the Magdalenenstrasse U-Bahn."

Hubert Renn stiffened and his lips were compressed. By now Fiona should have learned that the sort of joshing that is a normal part of the conversational exchanges in British or American offices did not go down well in Germany. "But, Frau Direktor—"

"Just a joke, a silly joke," said Fiona. "I will of course do exactly as you advise, Herr Renn."

"I'll prepare your papers?"

"Yes, I'll go." She watched him as he collected together the work he'd done. Hubert Renn was, despite his protestations to the contrary, a complex personality. She'd not yet got over the way in which he was able to reconcile his anti-

Russian prejudices with his uncritical dedication to Marx and all his works.

Was Renn's advice—to assume authority beyond what was really hers and use it to make the journey abroad—the bait in some new and nasty trap that her enemies were setting for her? She thought not, but she couldn't be sure. Careful, Stefan! No one could be quite sure of anything over here. That was the most important thing she'd learned.

She stood up. "And there remains the matter of the doctor at the Charité Hospital?"

"Yes, Frau Direktor. These things always take a long time. There is a note on your desk."

"The note says only that it was all in order."

Renn came to her side. "Yes, good news, Frau Direktor. Herr Doktor Kennedy is completely clear. Even more than clear, a fellow traveler. We have used him for some minor tasks in London. He would probably have been used for more important work, except that he'd joined the party when he was a medical student."

Fiona felt ill. She sat down in her chair again. For a moment she couldn't get her breath. Then she was able to mutter, "The Communist Party?" Thank God she'd never confided in Kennedy; more than once she'd felt like doing so. He seemed such a dedicated capitalist with his airplane sales and deliveries, but that of course would be a good cover and, as she knew from her day-to-day work, the KGB financed thousands of such businesses to provide cover for agents.

"Yes. What a shame that no one saw his potential and warned him from doing that. Party members cannot, of course, be used for important tasks."

"Any dates?"

"Nothing since July 1978. Mind you, we have both seen recently how slack the clerks can be when filing the amendments."

Her head began to throb and she felt sick. "What did he do for us?"

"Details of that sort are not entered on our files. London Residency would have filed that directly to Moscow. I would guess it to have been surveillance or providing accommodation or arranging references; that's the sort of job such men are used for."

So that was it. July 1978, a month before the "accidental" meeting on Waterloo Station. She'd warned Martin off and so Moscow had simply found another way to monitor her. Yes, that would be time enough for Harry to be briefed and prepared. So Harry Kennedy had been assigned by Moscow to check up on her. Was that to be his role in Berlin too? "Nothing since 1978?"

"Shall I ask Moscow if he is still under instructions?"

"No, Herr Renn, I don't think that would be wise."

He looked at her and saw that she was not feeling well. "Whatever you say, Frau Direktor." He picked up some papers and tactfully left the room.

She swallowed three aspirin tablets; she had bottles of them everywhere but they seldom did more than reduce the intensity of the pain. She held her hands over her eyes. By concentrating her mind on old memories she could sometimes get over these attacks by willpower alone. Pictures of her husband and children flickered in the mind's eye, as blurred and jerky as old film clips. For a long time she sat very still, as someone might recompose herself after stepping out of a wrecked car unscratched.

21

Berlin:

March 1984

THE DIRECTOR-GENERAL, RESTLESS AND DEMANDING, was on one of his unofficial flying visits to Berlin. Frank Harrington, Berlin supremo, cursed at having his daily schedule turned upside down at short notice, but the old man was like that. He'd always been like that, and lately he was getting worse. Not only did he have sudden inconvenient inspirations that everyone was expected to adapt to without question, but Sir Henry was a terrible time-waster. Ensconced in the most comfortable armchair, with a glass of vintage Hine in his hand, Sir Henry Clevemore would talk and talk, periodically interjecting that he must depart as if he were being detained against his will.

That's how it had been that afternoon. The message from the D-G's office had requested "a German lunch." Tarrant, the old valet who had been with Frank longer than anyone could remember, arranged everything. They ate in the dining room of the lovely old Grunewald mansion that came with the job of Berlin Resident. Frank's cook did a Hasenpfeffer that had become renowned over the years, and the maid wore her best starched apron and even a lace hat. The old silver cutlery was polished and out came the antique Meissen china; the table had looked quite extraordinary. The D-G had remarked on it in Tarrant's hearing. Tarrant had permitted himself a smug little grin.

After lunch the two men had gone into the drawing room for coffee. That was hours ago, and still the D-G showed no signs of departing. Frank wished he'd asked about the return flight, but to do so now would seem impolite. So he nodded at the old man and listened and desperately wanted to light up his pipe. The old man hated pipe tobacco—particularly the brand Frank smoked—and Frank knew it was out of the question.

"Well, I must be going," said the D-G, as he'd said so many times that afternoon, but this time he actually showed signs of moving. Thank goodness! thought Frank. If he could get rid of the old man by seven he'd still be in time for an evening of bridge with his army chums. "Yes," said the D-G, looking at his watch, "I really must be getting along."

There was a chap Frank Harrington had known at Eton who went on to be a doctor with a practice serving a prosperous part of agricultural Yorkshire. He said that he'd grown used to the way in which a patient coming to him with a problem would spend half an hour chatting about everything under the sun, get up to go, and then, while actually standing at the door saying goodbye, tell him in a very casual aside what was really worrying him. So it was with the Director-General. He'd been sitting there exchanging pleasantries with Frank all the afternoon when he picked up his glass, swirled the last mouthful round to make a whirlpool, and finished it in a gulp. Then he put the glass down, got to his feet, and said once again that he would have to be going. Only then did he say, "Have you seen Bret Rensselaer lately?"

Frank nodded. "Last week. Bret asked my advice about the report on the shooting in Hampstead." Frank got to his feet and made a not very emphatic gesture with the brandy bottle, but the old man waved it away.

"May I ask what you advised?"

"I told him not to make a report, not in writing anyway. I told him to go through it with you and then file a memorandum to record that he'd done so."

"What did Bret say?"

Frank went across the room to put the bottle away. He remained slim and athletic in appearance. In his Bedford cord suit he could easily have been mistaken for an officer of the Berlin garrison in his mid-forties. It was difficult to believe that Frank and the D-G had trained together and that Frank was coming up to retirement. "I remember exactly. He said, 'You mean cover my ass?' "

"And is that what you meant?"

Frank stopped where he was, in the middle of the Persian rug, and chose his words carefully. "I knew you would file a written version of his verbal report to you."

"Did you?" A slight lift on the second word.

"If that was an appropriate action," said Frank.

The D-G nodded soberly. "Bret was nearly killed. Two Soviets were shot by Bernard Samson."

"So Bret told me. It was lucky our people were well away before the police arrived."

"We're not out of the woods yet, Frank," said the D-G.

Frank wondered whether he was expected to pursue it further but decided that the D-G would tell him in his own time. Frank said, "From what I hear in Berlin, a KGB heavy named Moskvin was behind it. The same ruffian who killed the young fellow in the Bosham safe house."

"Research and Briefing take the same line, so it looks that way." The D-G turned and came back to where he'd been sitting. Looking at Frank he said, "There will have to be an inquiry."

"Into Bret's future?"

"No, it hasn't quite come to that, but the Cabinet Office are going through one of those periods when they dread any sort of complaint from the Russians."

"Two dead KGB thugs? Armed thugs? Hardly likely that Moscow will declare an interest in such antics, Sir Henry."

"Is that a considered opinion based on your Berlin experience?"

"Yes, it is."

"It's my own opinion too, but the Cabinet Office do not respond to expert opinions; they are too concerned about the politicians they serve." The D-G said it without resentment or even displeasure. "I knew that of course when I took the job. Our department's strategy, like that of every other government department, must be influenced by the varying political climate."

"The last time you told me that," said Frank, "you added, 'But the tactics they leave to me.' "

"The tactics are left to me until tactical blunders are spread across the front pages of the tabloids. Did you see the photos of that launderette?"

"I did indeed, sir." Big front-page photos of the launderette, with the sprawled dead men and blood splashed everywhere, had made a memorable impression on the newspaper-reading public. But whatever was being said about the shooting in London's bars and editorial offices, the story printed was that it was another gangster killing, with speculation about drugs being offered for sale in all-night shops and launderettes.

" 'Five' are pressing for an inquiry, and the Cabinet Secretary is convinced that their added expertise would be valuable."

"A combined inquiry?"

"I can't defy the Cabinet Office, Frank. I will bring it up in committee and look to you for support."

"If you're sure that's the right way to do it," said Frank, with only the slightest intonation to suggest that he didn't think it was.

"It's a matter of retrenching before I get a direct order. In this way I will set up the committee and will be able to give Bret the chair," said the D-G.

"You think Bret will need that sort of help and protection?"

"Yes, I do. But what I want you to tell me is, will Bret have the stamina to see it through? Think before you answer, Frank. This is important to me."

"Stamina? I can't give a quick yes or no on that one, Sir Henry. You must have seen what has been happening to the Department since Fiona Samson defected."

"In terms of morale?"

"In terms of morale and a lot of other things. If you are thinking of the psychological pressure, you might look at young Samson. He's under tremendous strain, and to make it worse there are people in the Department saying he must have known what his wife was up to all along."

"Yes, I've even had members of the staff confiding their fears about it," said the D-G sadly.

"When a chap is having a difficult time with his wife he can get away to work; a chap having a hard time in the office can look forward to a break when he gets home to his family. Bernard Samson is under continual pressure."

"I understood that he has formed some kind of liaison with one of the junior female staff," said the D-G.

"Samson is a desperate man," said Frank with simple truth. He didn't want to talk about Samson's private life. Do unto all men as I would they should do unto me, was Frank's policy.

"I asked you about Rensselaer," said the D-G.

"Samson is a desperate man," said Frank, "but he can

withstand a great deal of criticism. He is a born rebel so he can fight back when called a traitor or a lecher or anything else. Bret is a quite different personality. He loves England as only the foreign-born romantic can. To such people the merest breath of suspicion comes like a gale and is likely to blow them away."

"Well done, Frank! Was it Literae Humaniores you read at Wadham?"

Frank smiled ruefully but didn't answer. He'd known the D-G ever since they were very young and shared a billet in the war. The D-G knew all about Frank Harrington's mastery of the Greek and Roman classics and, Frank suspected, was still somewhat envious of it.

The D-G said, "Will Bret crack up? If the committee turn upon him—as committees in our part of the world have a habit of turning upon a vulnerable chairman—will Bret stand firm?"

"Has this inquiry been given a name?" asked Frank.

The D-G smiled, "It's an inquiry into Erich Stinnes and the way he's been handled since coming over to us."

"Bret will take a battering," pronounced Frank.

"Is that what you think?"

"The Department is awash with rumors, Sir Henry. You must know that, or you wouldn't be here asking me these questions."

"What is the thrust of the rumors?"

"Well, it's commonly thought that Erich Stinnes has made a complete fool of Bret Rensselaer and of the Department."

"Bret was not experienced enough to handle a wily fellow like Stinnes. I thought Samson would keep Bret on the straight and narrow, but I was wrong. It now seems that Stinnes was sent to us on a disinformation mission."

"Is that official?" Frank asked.

"No, I'm still not sure what sort of game Stinnes is playing."

"A senior official like Stinnes sent on a disinformation mission can do whatever he likes and damn the consequences. He might well decide to come over to us."

"I share that view." The D-G took out his cigar case and for a moment was going to light a cigar. Then he decided against it. The doctor had told him to stop smoking altogether, but he always carried a couple of cigars with him so that he didn't become too desperate. Perhaps it was a silly idea to do that; sometimes it was torture. "You said that some of the staff were of the opinion that Bret had been made a fool of. What do the rest think?"

"Most of the staff know that Bret is reliable and resourceful."

"You know what I mean, Frank."

"Yes, I know what you mean. Well, there are some hotheads who think perhaps Bret was working with Fiona Samson."

"Working with her? They think Bret Rensselaer and Fiona Samson have both been under Moscow's orders for that long?"

"It's an extreme view, Sir Henry, but they spent a lot of time together. There are stories of them having a love affair—a couple of sightings in the wrong hotels, you know the sort of thing. Even young Samson is not entirely certain that it's not true."

"I didn't realize that such absurd stories were going around."

"People wonder what motivated Bret, after a lifetime behind a desk, to grab a gun, rush into that launderette, and try his hand at the sharp end. We have people trained to do that sort of thing."

"It wasn't quite like that," said the D-G.

" 'The gunfight at the OK Corral' was how one of the newspapers described it. I'm afraid that description has provided the basis for a lot of doubtful jokes."

The D-G sniffed audibly and then again. "Berlin smells of beer, have you ever noticed that, Frank? Of course it's not the only German town with that odor, but I notice it in Berlin more than anywhere else. Hops or malt or something," he added vaguely, as if wanting to declare his unfamiliarity with that plebeian beverage.

"You'll have to support him, Sir Henry. Visibly and unequivocally."

"I won't be able to do that, Frank. He must take his chances."

"What do you mean, sir?"

"There are good reasons why I can give him no support, no support whatsoever."

Frank was stunned. Despite the unwavering good manners for which he was famed, Frank was on the point of asking what the hell the Director-General was there to do, if it wasn't to support his staff when they were in trouble. "Are those reasons operational or political?"

It was as near as Frank had ever gone to open rebellion, but the D-G accepted the reproach. On the other hand, the decision not to confide the truth about Fiona Samson to Frank was a sound one. Stinnes had to go back to Moscow firmly believing that Fiona Samson was a traitor. To say there were operational reasons for not supporting Bret Rensselaer was only a step away from revealing the whole story of Fiona Samson's mission. "I can't go into that, Frank," said the D-G in a voice that drew the line across Frank's toes. If Bret Rensselaer was suspected of being Fiona's co-conspirator, so be it.

"One supplementary, Director," said Frank, his voice and form of address making it an official question. "Is Rensselaer to be left to die of exposure? Is he to wither on the vine?

Is that the purpose of the inquiry? I have to know in order
to formulate my own responses."

"My God, no! The last thing I want to see is Bret Rensselaer thrown to the sharks, especially the sharks of Whitehall.
I want Rensselaer to come out of this on top. But I can't go
in and rescue him."

"I'm glad you made that clear, Sir Henry."

The exchange of views had produced a stalemate, and
the D-G recognized it as such. "I still have a great deal of
work for Rensselaer to do, and he's the only one equipped to
do it."

Frank nodded and thought it was some sort of reference
to Bret's Washington contacts, which had always been important to the Department.

The story of the shooting in the Hampstead launderette that
had worried the D-G and which the newspapers and Frank
Harrington were pleased to call "The gunfight at the OK
Corral" started a week or so before the D-G's visit to Berlin.

Had Bret Rensselaer displayed his usual common sense
he would have kept well out of it. It was a job for the Department's field agents. But Bret was not himself.

Bret Rensselaer missed Fiona Samson, he missed her terribly. Over the time when they had been working together
they had met regularly and furtively, like lovers, and this had
added to the zest. Bret could not of course tell anyone of this
strange feeling he had, and his passion was not assuaged by
seeing Bernard Samson, deprived of that perfect woman,
going about his business in his usual carefree way. No matter
what some people said about Samson's anguish, Bret could
only see the Bernard it suited him to see. He was especially
outraged to discover that Bernard was now living with a gorgeous young girl from the office. Heaven knows how the

children were reacting. Bret was appalled by this but took great care to disguise his feelings in the matter. He could see no way to influence what happened to the Samson children. He hoped that Fiona wasn't going to accuse him of bad faith at some future time.

Bret's participation in the shooting in the launderette changed a lot of things. For him it was nothing less than traumatic: traumatic in the literal sense that the violent events of that night inflicted upon Bret a mental wound from which he never completely recovered.

For Bret, everything suggested that the contact with the KGB team in the launderette would be mere routine. There had been no warning that things would go as they did. One minute he was sitting next to Bernard in an all-night launderette in Hampstead, and the next minute he was in the middle of one of the most horrifying nightmares of his entire life.

They were watching Samson's shirts revolving in the suds. Samson had insisted that both of them bring laundry and had even produced a plastic bag of detergent; he said he didn't like the stuff they had in the shop. Bret wondered whether it was a mark of Samson's meticulous attention to detail or some sort of joke. Now Samson was intermittently reading a newspaper that was on his knee. He'd given Bret no indication at all that he had a damn great gun—with silencer attached—wrapped inside *The Times*. Samson had been chatting away about his father as if he hadn't a care in the world.

Bernard Samson could be an amusing companion when he was in a good mood. His caustic comments on his superiors, the government, and indeed the world around him were partly his defense against a system that had never given him a proper chance, but they sometimes contained more than a grain of truth. Bernard's reputation was of being lucky, but his luck came from a professional attitude and a lot of hard work. Bernard was a tough guy, and there can be no doubt that Bret's willingness to involve himself in this caper was largely owing to the fact that he felt safe with Bernard.

Bret was wearing an old coat and hat he'd bought at the Oxfam shop specially for this evening's excursion. In the bag, under Bret's soiled laundry, there was a heavy manila envelope containing forty one-hundred-dollar bills. It was funding. The money was to be given to a KGB courier when he used the code word "Bingo." Positioned in the street outside the launderette there were enough men to warn Bret about the courier's approach and—should Bret decide that he must be arrested—enough men to hold him. To Bret it seemed very straightforward, but it didn't turn out like that.

Things began with no warning from the men in the street. One KGB man had been hiding upstairs, in a room above the launderette, and when he came in suddenly he was brandishing a sawed-off shotgun. Then a second man entered; he too had a shotgun. One of the men said "Bingo," the code word. Bret remained completely calm, or that was how he remembered it afterward, and reached for the money to show them.

The sequence of the events that followed was disputed, although certainly everything happened in rapid succession. Samson said that this was when the car exploded in the street outside, but as Bret remembered it Samson took the initiative before that.

Samson did not stand up to fire his gun; he remained seated. He used Bret as a shield, and the rage that Bret felt when he realized that stayed with him for the rest of his life. Leaning forward far enough to see the intruders—there were now two of them—Samson calmly took aim and fired. He didn't even take the gun out of the newspaper that concealed it. The gun was silenced. Bret heard two thuds and was astounded to see one of the KGB men reel back, drop his gun, clutch at his belly, and fall over the washing machines spewing blood.

Samson was suddenly up and away. Bret remembered Samson pushing him roughly aside and seeing him stumble over the discarded gun on the floor, although in Samson's version he pushed Bret down to safety and then kicked the gun in Bret's direction. Samson even reproached him later for not picking up the gun and following him through the back door to chase the others.

Bret was suddenly left alone in the launderette watching the young KGB man die, vomiting and bleeding and mewling like a baby. Bret had never seen anything like this, it was brutal and loathsome. From upstairs somewhere there came more shots—Samson had killed another man—and then it was all over and Bret found himself pushed roughly into a car and was speeding away into the night, passing the police as they were arriving. To Bret's amazement Bernard Samson chose that moment to tell Bret he'd saved his life.

"Saved my life, you son of a bitch?" said Bret shrilly. "First you shoot, using me as a shield, and then you run out, leaving me to face the music."

Samson laughed. To some extent the laugh was a nervous reaction to the stress he had just been through, but it was a laugh that Bret would never forget. "That's the way it is, being a field agent, Bret," he said. "If you'd had experience or training, you would have hit the deck. Better still, you would have taken out that second bastard instead of leaving me to deal with all of them."

Bret had hardly listened; he couldn't forget the sight of the dying KGB man bent over, holding tight to one of the washing machines, while his frothy blood streamed out of him to mix with the soapy water on the floor.

"You could have winged him," croaked Bret.

Bernard scoffed at such naïve talk. "That's for the movies, Bret. That's for Wyatt Earp and Jesse James. In the real world, no one is shooting guns out of people's hands or giving them flesh wounds in the upper arm. In the real world you hit them or you miss them. It's difficult enough to hit a moving target without selecting tricky bits of anatomy. So don't give me all that crap."

It was no use arguing with him, but the bad feeling remained. Bret resented the way that Bernard Samson made quick decisions with such firm conviction and seemed to have no misgivings afterward. Women admired such traits, or seemed to, but Bret was finding every decision he had to make more and more difficult.

Bret was beginning to see that his own planning would have to entail ruthlessness at least the equal of Bernard's. But Bret's present state of mind didn't make things easy. Sometimes he sat staring at his desk for half an hour, unable to conclude even self-evident matters. Perhaps Bret should not have gone to the doctor and asked his advice. The Department's doctor was competent and helpful—everything one wanted from a physician, in fact—but he did dutifully report back to the Department.

Starting with no more than a slight loss of his usual power of concentration, and a tendency to wake up in the small hours of the morning unable to get back to sleep, things got worse and worse. Bret began to notice that he was being treated like an outsider. He was aware of being treated in a wary and distant manner even when he was chairing the committee. Substance was given to his suspicions when two subcommittees were formed and Bret was deliberately excluded from them. It meant that about three quarters of the people on his committee were able to have meetings to which he was denied access.

What Bret didn't know was the way in which his downfall was being masterminded by Moscow. Bret had not been targeted because Moscow suspected that Fiona Samson had been planted in Berlin, or for any reason except that he was suddenly vulnerable to the sort of sting operation they had proved so expert at many times in the past. Not only was Moscow able to blow on the embers and help the rumors, but as the operation proceeded there was false evidence planted. Some of it was crude enough to convince the real experts— like Ladbrook, the senior interrogator—that Moscow was try- ing to discredit Rensselaer, but that did not mean the experts could afford to ignore it.

The Director-General had a rough idea of what was hap- pening and thus decided to go to Berlin and talk to Frank Harrington. Frank was an old friend as well as a well-estab- lished member of the senior staff. That lunch and the subse- quent afternoon of chatting with Frank did not set the D-G's mind at rest. What Frank told him was little more than wash- room gossip, but it prepared the D-G for the phone call from Internal Security that said Ladbrook and Tiptree would like an appointment urgently. The caller boldly told Morgan, the D-G's assistant, that tomorrow would not be soon enough.

They were all waiting for the D-G in the Number Two Conference Room. There was Ladbrook, the senior interroga- tor, a decent quiet fifty-year-old who never got ruffled, and Harry Strang, a weatherbeaten veteran of Operations. With them was Henry Tiptree, the young fellow whom Internal Security rated as one of their brightest stars, and, sitting unobtrusively in the corner, the Deputy D-G, Sir Percy Bab- cock.

The table had been arranged with notepads and pencils, water jug and glasses. "Who else is expected?" asked the D-G, having counted them.

"We couldn't get hold of Cruyer," said Strang, "but I've left a message with his secretary."

"Are we expecting a long session, Percy?" the D-G asked his Deputy.

"No, very short, Director. Internal Security has something to put before you."

"Quite a crowd," remarked the D-G. He was well over six feet tall and broad-shouldered too. He towered over them.

"We'll need five signatures," said the Deputy gently.

"Um," said the D-G and his heart sank. They all knew what sort of form needed five signatures, one from Internal Security. "And no one taking notes?"

"That's correct, Director." Well, that was it then. The only way to save Bret from this humiliating investigation was to reveal the secret of Fiona Samson. And that was out of the question. Bret would have to take his chances.

They all sat down. The Deputy clicked his gold ballpoint while Harry Strang took out his cigarettes and then, remembering the presence of the D-G, put them away again. Tiptree, a tall thin fellow with well-brushed red hair and a ruddy complexion, poured himself a glass of water and drank it with elegant precision.

Ladbrook looked round the table. They were looking at him expectantly, except for Tiptree, who was now drawing circles on the notepad. "Would you like to start, Sir Percy?" asked Ladbrook diffidently.

"Tell the Director just what you told me," said the Deputy.

"I'm afraid it concerns senior staff," said Ladbrook. The D-G looked at him without a flicker of emotion showing on his face.

"Bret Rensselaer," supplied Tiptree, looking up from his pad. A lock of hair fell forward across his face, and he flicked it back with his hand.

"A leak?" said the D-G, but he knew what was coming.

"More serious than that," said Ladbrook.

"I have the file," said Tiptree, indicating a box file that he'd put on a side table.

"I don't want to look at files," said the D-G with a weary despair that came out like irritation. Everyone waited for the D-G to speak again, but he settled back in his seat and sighed.

Sir Percy clicked his ballpoint and said, "Since Bret often takes his orders directly from you, I thought you might want to interpose."

"Has anyone spoken with Bret?" the D-G asked.

"With your permission," said Ladbrook, "I propose a preliminary 'talk-through' as soon as it's made official."

"That's the usual way, is it?"

"Yes, Sir Henry, that's the usual way."

The Deputy said, "The interrogator wanted to be quite sure that Bret didn't cite you as a reason for not answering."

"On this sort of inquiry," added Ladbrook, "a loss of momentum like that can be difficult to make up afterward."

"I understand," said the D-G. He noticed Harry Strang get a pen from his waistcoat. So Harry knew how it had to end.

"He'll probably want to speak with you on the phone," said Ladbrook. "When I first tackle him, I mean. He'll probably want to put a call through to you."

"And you want me not to take the call?" said the D-G.

"Whatever you think best, Sir Henry," said Ladbrook.

"I'll bugger up your interrogation if I do take it, is that what you mean?"

Ladbrook smiled politely but didn't answer.

"Give me the form," said the D-G. "Let's get it over as quickly as possible." The Deputy handed his ballpoint to him and slid the papers across the polished table.

"I can do the rest of the paperwork," said the Deputy gently. "Morgan can countersign the chit on your behalf."

"It will be a nonsense," said the D-G as he put his signature on the form. "I can tell you that here and now. I've known Bret Rensselaer for years: salt of the earth, Bret Rensselaer."

Harry Strang smiled. He was old enough to remember someone using the almost identical words about Kim Philby.

22

England:

April 1984

HOW FAR CAN YOU RUN INTO A WOOD? ASKS THE ANCIENT
schoolboy joke. Halfway. After that you're running out. A
missile stops in the air and begins to fall back to the ground;
a sportsman's career reaches a physical peak at which begins
decline. A flower in full bloom falls; water at its most exuber-
ant disappears into vapor. For most things in nature there
comes a moment when triumph is doom in disguise. So it was
for Pavel Moskvin that lovely day in Berlin when, fittingly
enough, the first growths of spring marked the end of winter.

Erich Stinnes was also riding high. Everything had gone
as he'd predicted. The British seemed to have accepted him
at face value because they found it so difficult to believe that
anyone could resist their way of life. Stinnes had played his
role to perfection. *Tröpfelnweise,* drop by drop, he had worn
away the hard diamond face of Rensselaer's reputation until,
in front of the committee, he shattered it completely.

The culmination of all that Stinnes had worked for came
on what had promised to be a routine visit of the "Stinnes
committee" to Berwick House, where he was being held. An
eighteenth-century manor set in seven acres of attractive English countryside, its fifteen-foot-high stone wall and ancient

moat had made it easy to convert to a detention center. The Whitehall clerks, who had seized house and contents from its owners by means of some catch-all legislation, had done little to repair the damage caused by the Luftwaffe's bombs. There was a musty smell in the house, and if you looked closely enough at the rotting structure you'd find the woodworms were working harder than anyone.

The committee traveled together in a bus, except for Bret. He arrived in his chauffeur-driven Bentley, having used the lunch hour to squeeze in an appointment with the doctor. He looked drawn, and the skin under his eyes had blackened so that the eternally youthful Bret was suddenly aged.

There was such a crowd that they all sat around the big polished table in what at one time had been the dining room. On the paneled wall there was a huge oil painting. A family posed stiffly on a hill near the newly built Berwick House and stared at the painter as he extended to Gainsborough what is reputed to be the sincerest form of flattery.

The committee were all trying to show how knowledgeable and important they were. Bret Rensselaer sat at one end and thus established his authority as chairman. Stinnes faced him at the far end, an adversary's positioning that Bret afterward thought might have contributed to the subsequent fiasco. Bret looked at his watch frequently, but otherwise sat with that look of attention that people who sit on too many committees master, to conceal the fact that they are half asleep. He had heard it all before. Well, thought Stinnes, I'll see if I can wake you up, Mr. Rensselaer.

In a committee like that, there would always be a couple of know-alls. It was exactly the same in Moscow. Stinnes could have named their counterparts. The worst bore was Billy Slinger from MI5, a scrawny fellow with a thin, carefully trimmed mustache and a restrained Tyneside accent that Stinnes found challenging. He had been attached to the committee to advise on communications. Of course he felt he must prove to them all how clever he was.

Erich Stinnes had endured the ups and downs of his detention with little change, but there was not much to change. Stinnes was a tough middle-aged man with a sallow face and hair that he liked to keep as short as possible. When he took off his metal-rimmed glasses, which he did frequently, he blinked like an owl and looked around at the committee as if he preferred to see them slightly out of focus.

Stinnes fielded the questions artfully and let Slinger demonstrate his technical knowledge until he got on to signals procedures. This was something that Moscow had agreed he could disclose, so, quietly and conversationally, he went through the embassy routines. He started with the day-to-day domestics and went on to a few KGB encoding styles. These were technical developments that Slinger was unlikely to be familiar with, and thus unlikely to know that they had already been superseded or were used only for mundane traffic.

Out of the corner of his eye he watched Rensselaer uncoil like a serpent disturbed by the approach of heavy footsteps. "This is all new to me," said Slinger repeatedly, his accent more pronounced as he filled sheets of paper with notes scribbled so fast and so excitedly that his pencil broke and he had to grab another and ask Stinnes to slow down.

The other members of the committee became enthusiastic too. Between eager questions from Slinger, one of the committee asked him why he hadn't disclosed these gems earlier. Stinnes didn't answer immediately. He looked at Bret Rensselaer and then looked away and took a long time lighting up a cheroot.

"Well?" said Bret finally. "Let's hear it."

"I did," said Stinnes finally. "I told you during the first days, but I thought it must be stuff you knew already."

Bret jumped up as if he was going to start shouting. They

all looked at him. And then Bret realized that an argument with Stinnes in front of the committee was only going to make him look ridiculous. So he sat down again and said, "Carry on, Slinger. Let's get it down on paper."

Stinnes inhaled on his cheroot and looked from one to the other like a social worker in the presence of a combative family. Then he started to give them even more material: foreign country routings, embassy signals room times and procedures, and even embassy contact lists.

It took about an hour and included some long silences, while Stinnes racked his brains, and a few little Stinnes jokes, which—due to the tension in the room—everyone laughed at. By the end, the committee was intoxicated with success. Satisfaction flushed their faces and circulated through their veins like freshly sugared blood. And not the least of their triumph was the warm feeling they got from knowing that Bret Rensselaer, so cold and patrician, so efficient and patriotic, was going to get his rightful comeuppance.

As Stinnes left the room to be taken upstairs, he looked at Bret Rensselaer. Neither man registered any change of facial expression, and yet there was in that exchange of looks the recognition that a contest had been fought and won.

But Bret Rensselaer was not the sort of man who would lie down and play dead to oblige an enemy. Bret Rensselaer was an American: pragmatic, resourceful, and without that capacity for long-term rancor that the European is born with. When Bret faced the wall of opposition that Moskvin and Stinnes had between them constructed brick by brick, he did something neither of the Russians had provided for. Rensselaer went to Berlin and pleaded for the aid of Bernard Samson, a man he'd come to dislike, reasoning that Samson was even less conventional than he was and certainly far more savage.

"What do we do now?" Bret asked. Stampeded by Stinnes and faced with the prospect of arrest, Bret ran. He was a fugitive and looked like one, frightened and disheveled and lacking all that smooth Rensselaer confidence.

"What do we do?" echoed Samson. This was Bernard's town and both of them knew it. "We scare the shit out of them, that's what we do."

"How?"

"Suppose we tell them we are pulling out Stinnes's toenails one by one?"

Bret shivered. He wasn't in the mood for jokes. "Be sensible, Bernard. They're holding your friend Volkmann over there. Can't you see what that means?"

"They won't touch Werner."

"Why not?"

"Because they know that for anything they dream up to do to Werner I'll do it twice to Stinnes, and do it slower."

"Is that a risk worth taking?" asked Bret. "I thought Volkmann was your closest friend."

"What difference does that make?" asked Bernard.

Alarmed, Bret said, "Don't get this one wrong, Bernard. There is too much riding on it." Samson had always been a hard-nosed gambler, but was this escalating response the way to go? Or had Bernard gone mad?

"I know the way these people think, Bret. Moscow has an obsession about getting agents out of trouble. That is the Moscow law; KGB men ignore it at their peril."

"So we offer to trade Stinnes for Werner Volkmann?"

"But not before letting them know that Stinnes is going to go through the wringer."

"Jesus! I don't like it. Will Fiona be one of the people making the decision?" asked Bret.

Bernard looked at him, trying to see into his mind, but

Bret's mind was not so easy to see into. "I should think so," said Bernard.

"Frau Samson," said Moskvin, with exaggerated courtesy and an unctuous smile, "have you prepared charges against this West German national, Volkmann?"

"I am in the process of doing so." Fiona Samson fielded the question. She'd learned a lot about Moskvin in the time she'd been working here. Some people thought Moskvin was a fool, but they were wrong. Moskvin had a quick and cunning mind. He was pushy and gauche but he was not stupid. Neither was he clumsy, at least not in the physical sense. Every day he was in the basement, weight lifting in the gym, swimming in the pool, shooting on the range, or doing some other sort of physical exercise. He was no longer young, but he still had that overabundance of energy that is usually confined to childhood.

"Do you have another file on him, Comrade Colonel?" he asked sweetly.

Fiona was disconcerted by this question. She had created the Volkmann file that was open on her desk. "No more than what you've seen already."

"No more than this?" said Moskvin. He was able to make it into a very unfavorable pronouncement.

"I know—" She stopped.

"Yes? What do you know?"

"In the past he has worked for the SIS office in Berlin."

Moskvin looked at her. "Suppose Moscow wanted to see the file on Volkmann? Is this what we'd send?" He flipped the card cover of the file so that his fingernails made a click. It sounded empty.

"Yes," said Fiona.

Moskvin looked at her and made no secret of the extent

of his contempt. Intimidation was a part of his working method. By now she'd recognized him for what he really was. She'd known plenty of other men like Moskvin. She'd known them at Oxford: certain sorts of rowdy sportsmen, keenly aware of their physical strength and relishing the latent violence that was within them.

"I know Volkmann," she said. "I've known him for years. Of course he works for SIS Berlin. SIS London too."

"And yet you've done nothing about it?" Moskvin looked at her with contempt.

"Not yet," said Fiona.

"Not yet," he said. "Well, now we'll do something, shan't we?" He was patronizing her, smiling as tyrants do with small children. "We'll talk to Volkmann . . . perhaps scare him a little."

"How?"

"You might learn something, Frau Samson. He hasn't been told that he's being released in exchange for Major Stinnes. We must make him sweat."

"Volkmann gets his money from doing business in our Republic. Without that he would be penniless. He might be persuaded to work for us."

Moskvin eyed her. "Why would he do that?"

"He's back and forth all the time. That's why he was so easy to pick up. Why shouldn't he tell us what happens over there?"

"You could do that?"

"I could try. You say he's being held in Babelsberg?"

"You'll need a car."

"I'll drive myself."

"Bring him back here. I'll want to see him too," said Moskvin.

She smiled coldly at him. "Of course, Colonel Moskvin. But if we frighten him too much he won't come back."

It had happened before. That was the trouble with agents. You sent them to the West, and sometimes they simply stayed there and thumbed their noses at you. "He has no relatives here, does he?"

"He'll work for us, Colonel Moskvin. He is the sort of man who loves a good secret."

Now that she had equated Moskvin with those Oxford hearties, she found herself remembering her college days. How she'd hated it; the good times she'd had were now forgotten. She recalled the men she'd known and those long evenings in town, watching boorish undergraduates drinking too much and making fools of themselves. Keen always to make the women students feel like inferior beings. Boys with uncertain sexual preferences, truly happy only in male society, arms interlinked, singing together very loudly, and staggering away to piss against the wall.

She went to Babelsberg in the southwest of Berlin to get Werner Volkmann. It was not very far as the crow flies, but crows flew across the western sector of the city while good communists had to journey around its perimeter. It was just outside the city limits and thus not a part of Berlin; it was in Potsdam in the DDR, and so the British and American "protecting powers" did not have the legal right to come poking around here.

Volkmann was in the Ausland Block, some buildings that had started out as administration offices of the famous UFA film studios. Behind the empty film library building, and the workshops, there was an old back lot where the remains of an eighteenth-century village street built originally for the wartime film *Münchhausen* could be seen. "That was Marlene Dietrich's dressing room," said the elderly policeman who took her to the interview room. He indicated a storeroom with a padlock on the door.

"Yes," said Fiona. The same policeman had said the same thing to her the last time she was here. The interview room had a barred window through which she could see the cobbled yard where she'd parked her car.

"Shall I bring the prisoner?"

"Bring him."

Werner Volkmann looked bewildered when he was brought in. Hands cuffed behind his back, he was wearing a scuffed leather overcoat upon which there were streaks of white paint. His hair was uncombed, and he was unshaven.

"Do you recognize me, Werner?"

"Of course I recognize you, Frau Samson." He was angry and sullen.

"I'm taking you to my office in Karl Liebknecht Strasse. Do I need an armed police officer to keep you under observation?"

"I'm not going to run away, if that's what you mean."

"Have they told you what you are charged with?"

"I want a lawyer, a lawyer from the West."

"That's a silly thing to ask, Werner."

"Why is it?"

It was extraordinary that Werner, a German who came here regularly, still did not understand. Well, perhaps the best way to start was to make him realize what he was up against. "This is the DDR, Werner, and it is 1984. We have a socialist system. The people—"

"The government."

"The people," she repeated, "don't just control the politics and the economy, they control the courts, the lawyers, and the judges. They control the newspapers, the youth leagues, and the women's associations, the chess clubs and the anglers' societies. The privilege of writing books, collecting stamps, singing at the opera, or working at a lathe—in fact, the right to work anywhere—can be withdrawn at any time."

"So don't ask for a lawyer from the West."

"So don't ask for a lawyer from the West," agreed Fiona. "You'll have to sit in the back of the car. I can't remove the handcuffs. I can't even carry the key. It's a regulation."

"Can I wash and shave?"

"At the other end. Do you have any personal possessions here?"

Werner shrugged and didn't answer.

"Let's go."

"Why you?" asked Werner as they were walking across the cobbled courtyard to her Wartburg car.

"*Machtpolitik,*" said Fiona. It means negotiations under the threat of violence and is a uniquely German word.

None of the long-dead city officials who drew the outlandish shape of the old boundaries could have guessed that one day Berlin would be thus circumscribed and divided. Jutting southward, Lichtenrade—where the S-Bahn line is chopped off to become a terminal and where Mozart, Beethoven, and Brahms are streets that end at the Wall—provided an obstacle around which Fiona had to drive to get back to her office in central Berlin.

The normal route back was the main road through Mahlow, but Fiona went on back streets. That might have saved her a few minutes in traveling time, except that when she got beyond Mahlow she turned off to a sleepy little neighborhood beyond Ziethen. Here the prewar housing of a "*Gartenstadt*" had spilled over the Wall into the Democratic Republic. Bordered on three sides by the West, these wide tree-lined roads were empty, and the neighborhood quiet.

"Werner," said Fiona as she stopped the car under the trees of a small urban park and switched off the engine. She turned to look back at him. "You are just a card in a poker game. You know that, I'm sure."

"What happens to a card in a poker game?" asked Werner.

"At the end of the game you are shuffled and put away for another day."

"Does it hurt?"

"Within a few days you'll be back in the West. I guarantee it." A car came very slowly up the street. It passed them and, when it was about a hundred yards ahead, stopped. Werner said nothing and neither did Fiona. The car turned as if to do a U-turn but stopped halfway and then reversed. Finally it went past them again and turned to follow the sign that pointed to Selchow. "It was a car from a driving school," said Fiona.

"Why are you telling me this?" said Werner. The car had made him jumpy.

"I want you to take a message."

"A written message?"

Good old Werner. So he wasn't so simple. "No, Werner, a verbal message."

"To Bernard?"

"No. In fact, you'll have to promise that Bernard will know nothing of it."

"What sort of game is this?"

"You come through regularly, Werner. You could be the perfect go-between."

"Are you asking me to work for Moscow?"

"No, I'm not."

"I see." Werner sat back, uncomfortable with his hands cuffed behind him. Having thought about it, he smiled at her. "But how can I be sure?" It was a worried smile.

"I can't do anything about the handcuffs, Werner. It is not permitted to have keys together with prisoners in transit."

"How can I be sure of you?" he said again.

"I want you to go and talk with Sir Henry Clevemore. Would that satisfy your doubts?"

"I don't know him. I've never even seen him."

"At his home, not in the office. I'll give you a private phone number. You'll leave a message on the answering machine."

"I'm not sure."

"Jesus Christ, Werner! Pull yourself together and decide!" she yelled. She closed her eyes. She had lost control of herself. The driving school car had done it.

Werner looked at her with amazement and suddenly understood the panic she had shown. "Why me? Why now? What about your regular contact?"

"I have no regular contact. I have been finding my way around, using dumps. London would probably have sent someone in a month or so. But this is a perfect opportunity. I will enroll you as a Stasi agent. You'll report to me personally, and each time you do I will give you the material to take back."

"That would work," said Werner, thinking about it. "Would Sir Henry arrange material for me to bring?"

"All my reports must be committed to memory," said Fiona. She had done it now; she had put herself at Werner's mercy. It would be all right. Later she would get Werner to tell her about her husband and her children, but not now. One thing at a time.

Now he was beginning to believe. His face lit up and his eyes widened. He was to participate in something really tremendous. "What a coup!" he said softly and with ardent admiration. In that moment he became her devoted slave.

"But Bernard must not know," said Fiona, with enormous emphasis.

"Why?"

318 / Len Deighton

"For all kinds of reasons. He'll worry and give the game away. He's not good at concealing his emotions. You must know that."

He looked out of the window. Fiona had chosen her man well. Werner had always wanted to be a secret agent. He yearned for it as other people crave to be a film star or score goals for their country or host a talk show on TV. Werner knew about espionage. He read books about it, clipped newspapers, and memorized its ups and downs with a dedication that bordered on the obsessional. There was no need for him to say yes; they both knew he couldn't resist it. "I still can't believe it," he said.

The driving school car came into sight as it turned the corner. It slowed and stopped, the driver carefully indicating his intentions with unnecessary signals. "I think we should go," said Fiona.

"I'll do it," said Werner quietly.

"I knew you would," said Fiona gratefully as she started the engine.

She overtook the driving school car and turned as if heading back toward Mahlow. It was a silly precaution that meant nothing. "You're a brave woman, Fiona," said Werner suddenly.

"*No one,*" said Fiona. "Sir Henry and no one else, unless he authorizes it to you personally."

"How long will it go on?" said Werner.

"One year, perhaps two," said Fiona.

"I thought they might make me persona non grata," said Werner. "I was worried about my work."

"You'll be all right now," said Fiona. "It will be a perfect setup."

"Bernard must not know," said Werner. The idea of having a secret from his best friend appealed to him. One day he'd surprise Bernard. It would be worth waiting for.

"Let me tell you what to say when we get back to the office. You'll see a Russian KGB colonel named Moskvin. Don't let him bluff you or bully you. I'll make sure you are okay."

"Moskvin."

"He's not a long-term problem," said Fiona.

"Why not?"

"He's not a long-term problem," said Fiona. "He is being got rid of. Just believe me. Now let me tell you how we're going to handle this business of your reporting to me."

Two days later the exchange took place. Erich Stinnes went east to resume his work for the KGB while Werner Volkmann was freed and went west.

The KGB inquiry into the treason of Pavel Moskvin sentenced him to death. The court decreed that verdict, sentence, and execution must all remain secret; it was the KGB way of dealing with its own senior personnel. The local KGB commander, a general who had been a close friend of Moskvin's father, decided that "killed in action in the West" would be merciful and expedient, and so arranged matters. But Moskvin did not accept his fate readily. He tried to escape. The resulting exchange of fire took place on the abandoned Nollendorfplatz S-Bahn station in West Berlin, now converted to a flea market. Moskvin died. Bret Rensselaer, demonstrating his loyalty to the Crown, led the chase after Moskvin and was shot and hurt so seriously that he never resumed his duties in London.

The official British version of the events is very short. It was drafted by Silas Gaunt, who omitted any mention of the exchange of men because neither was a British national. It says that Pavel Moskvin, a KGB colonel on official duties in the West sector of Berlin, ran amok in the flea market. He fired his pistol indiscriminately until the Berlin municipal police were able to subdue him. Two passers-by were shot dead, four were injured, two seriously. Moskvin turned his own pistol on himself at the moment of arrest.

The secret file compiled by the West German government in Bonn had the advantage of detailed reports from both their intelligence service and the West Berlin police. It says that Moskvin was part of a KGB party who'd come West to arrange the exchange of a West German and a Soviet national held by the British SIS. This account says that Moskvin's death was an execution carried out by a KGB team which used two motorbikes to follow Moskvin's car. While it was halted on Tauentzienstrasse, near the KaDeWe department store, an accomplice threw a plastic bag filled with white paint over its windshield. Moskvin left the car and ran to the S-Bahn station, shooting at his pursuers. At this time civilians were injured by gunshots. When Moskvin jumped down from the platform to the train tracks, perhaps believing he could run along the railway and across the Wall, he was shot dead by a round fired from a Russian Army sniper's rifle. The perpetrator was never found but is believed to have been one of the KGB hit team who'd been seen coming through a checkpoint earlier that day. In support of this theory, it is pointed out that there was never a request for Moskvin's body to be returned to the East.

A few days after the shooting, an unofficial mention of the body by British contacts brought from the Soviets only puzzled denials that any Colonel Pavel Moskvin had ever existed. There was no post-mortem. The body was buried at the small cemetery in Berlin-Rudow, very near the Wall. It was at this time that the Russians spontaneously offered to return to the West the remains of Max Busby, an American shot while crossing the Wall in 1978. Some inferred that it was part of a secret deal. Both bodies were buried at night in adjoining plots. New drainage was being installed at the cemetery, and the burials were unattended except for workmen, a city official, and two unidentified representatives of the Protecting Powers. The graves were not marked.

There were other versions too, some less bizarre, some considerably more so. One report, neatly bound and complete with photos of Kleiststrasse, Nollendorfplatz, the S-Bahn station, the U-Bahn station, and a colored street plan showing Moskvin's path in a red broken line, had been assembled by the CIA office in Berlin, working in conjunction with its offices in Bonn and London. This revealed that Moskvin had been preparing material to incriminate falsely an unnamed U.S. citizen resident in London. It concluded that the KGB were determined that Moskvin should not be taken alive and questioned by the British.

Bernard Samson was seen firing at Moskvin, but his report, given verbally, said that his rounds all went wide. Some people pointed out that the great preponderance of rounds that Samson had been known to fire, prior to this, hit his targets. Frank Harrington might have thrown some light on the subject, for Frank had also been seen on the S-Bahn station brandishing a gun (something that stayed in the minds of those who saw him because Frank was never seen with a pistol before or since), but London Central never asked Frank for an account.

Bret Rensselaer was also there, but Bret was never questioned specifically. He was hit and severely injured, and by the time he'd recovered sufficiently to contribute his account, the reports were complete and the incident had passed into Berlin's crowded history. The doctors at the Steglitz Clinic saved Rensselaer's life. He was in the operating theater for three hours and went from there into an intensive-care ward. Next day his brother flew in on some specially assigned U.S. Air Force jet that came complete with doctors and nurses. He took Bret back to America with him.

23

England:
March 1987

BERNARD SAMSON WAS SPENDING THAT SATURDAY AT home with Gloria in their little house at 13 Balaklava Road, Raynes Park, in London's commuter belt. He was clearing all sorts of unwanted oddments from the garden shed. Most of them were still in the big cardboard boxes bearing the name of the moving company that had brought their furniture here.

Gloria was upstairs in the bedroom. The closet door was open to reveal a long mirror in which she was studying herself. In front of her she was holding a dress she had found in one of the cardboard boxes. It was an expensive dress with a Paris label, a dramatic, low-cut cocktail dress of gray and black, the barber-pole stripes sweeping diagonally with the bias cut. It belonged to Fiona Samson.

As she held it up she tried to imagine herself wearing it. She tried to imagine what Fiona was really like and what sort of a marriage she had enjoyed with Bernard and the children.

Bernard was wearing his carpet slippers and came noiselessly upstairs. Entering the room without knocking, he exclaimed, "Oh!" Then he recognized the dress she was holding and said, "Far too small! And gray is not your color, my love."

Embarrassed to be caught with it, Gloria put the dress on the rod in the closet and closed the door. "She has been away four years. She'll never come back, Bernard, will she?"

"I don't know."

"Don't be angry. Every time I try to talk about her you become bad-tempered. It's a way of blackmailing me into keeping quiet about her."

"Is that the way you see it?"

Still self-conscious, she touched her hair. "It's the way it is, Bernard. You want to have me here with you, and you also want to hang on to the increasingly unlikely chance that you will ever see her again."

Bernard went close and put his arms around her. At first her anger seemed assuaged, but as Bernard went to kiss her she showed a sudden anger. "Don't! You always try to wriggle out of it. You kiss me, you say you love me, and you shut me up."

"You keep asking me these questions, and I tell you the truth. The truth is that I don't know the answers."

"You make me feel so bloody insecure," said Gloria.

"I'm always here. I don't get drunk or run around with other women."

It was the sort of indignant answer he always gave, a typically male response. He really couldn't understand that it wasn't enough. She tried male logic. "How long will you wait before you assume she's gone forever?"

"I love you. We're happy together. Isn't that enough? Why do women want guarantees of permanence? Tomorrow I could fall under a train or go crazy. *There is no way that you can be happy ever after.* Can't you understand that?"

"Why are you looking at the clock?" she asked, and tried to move apart from him, but he held her.

"I'm sorry. The D-G is going down to Whitelands to see Silas Gaunt this afternoon. I think they're going to talk about Fiona. I'd give anything to know what they say."

"You think Fiona is still working for London, don't you?"

The question came like an accusation, and it shook him. He made no move whatsoever, and yet that stillness of his face revealed the way his mind was spinning. He had never told Gloria of that hidden belief.

"That's why you won't talk of marriage," she said.

"No."

"You're lying. I can always tell. You think your wife was sent there to spy."

"We'll never know the truth," said Bernard lamely, and hoped that would end the conversation.

"I must be mad not to have seen that right from the beginning." Her voice rose. "I was just the stand-in. I was just someone to take to bed, someone to look after your children and keep the house tidy and shop and cook. No wonder you discouraged all my plans to go to college. You bastard! You've made a fool of me."

"No, I haven't."

"Now I understand why you keep all her clothes."

"You know it's not like that, Gloria. Please don't cry."

"I'm not bloody crying. I hate you, you bastard."

"Will you listen?" He shook her roughly. "Fiona is a Soviet agent. She's gone forever. Now stop this imagining."

"Do you swear?"

He stepped back from her. There was a fierce look in her eyes and he was dismayed by it. "Yes, I swear," he said.

She didn't believe him. She could always tell when he was lying.

At that moment the meeting between the Director-General and Silas Gaunt was in full swing.

"How long has Mrs. Samson been in place now?" asked

Silas Gaunt. It was a rhetorical question, but he wanted the Director-General to share his pleasure.

"She went over there in eighty-three, so it must be about four years," said Sir Henry Clevemore. The two men had worked wonders and were rightly proud of what they had achieved. The East German economy was cracking at the seams, the government had become senile and could muster neither will nor resources to tackle the problems. Fiona's information had said that the Russian troops would be confined to barracks no matter what political changes came. The USSR had problems of its own. Bret Rensselaer's heady prediction about the Wall coming down by 1990, considered at the time no more than the natural hyperbole that all SIS projections were prone to, now looked like a real possibility.

They had got some fine material from Fiona Samson that had enabled the two of them to mastermind the campaign and facilitate contact with the most level-headed opposition groups. To protect her they had given her a few little victories and a few accolades. Now they were enjoying a feeling of great satisfaction.

These two were alike in many ways. Their family background, education, bearing, and deportment were comparable, but Silas Gaunt's service abroad had made him cosmopolitan, which could never be said of the aloof and formal Sir Henry Clevemore. Silas Gaunt was earthy, wily, adaptable, and unscrupulous, and despite their years together Sir Henry had always had reservations about his friend.

"Do you remember when young Volkmann came knocking at your door in the dead of night?" said Silas.

"The bloody fool had forgotten my phone number."

"You were in despair," said Silas.

"Certainly not."

"I'm sorry to contradict you, Henry, but when you arrived here you said that Fiona Samson had made a dire error of judgment."

"It did seem somewhat ominous." He gave a dry chuckle. "It was the only damn thing he had to commit to memory, and he'd forgotten it."

"Volkmann turned up trumps. I didn't know he had it in him."

"I'll get him something," said the D-G. "When it's over I'll get him some sort of award. I know he'd like a gong; he's that sort of chap."

"You know his banking business is being wound down?" said Silas, although he'd briefed the D-G on that already.

"He's taking over that flea-bitten hotel run by that dreadful old German woman. What's her name?"

"Lisl Hennig."

"That's the one, an absolute Medusa."

"All good things come to an end," said Silas.

"There were times," said the Director-General, "when I thought we would simply have to pull Mrs. Samson out and give up."

"Samson's a bull-headed young fool," said Silas Gaunt, voicing what was in the minds of both men. They were sitting in the little-used drawing room of Gaunt's house, while in the next room workmen were slowly rebuilding the fireplace of Gaunt's little study. This room had been virtually unchanged for a hundred years. Like all such farmhouse rooms with thick stone walls and small windows, it was gloomy all year round. A big sideboard held well-used willow-pattern plates and a vase filled with freshly cut daffodils.

Upon the lumpy sofa Silas sprawled, lit by the flickering flames of a log fire. Above him some steely-eyed ancestor squinted through the coach varnish of a big painting, and there was a small table upon which, for the time being, Silas Gaunt was eating his meals. Sir Henry Clevemore had made the journey to Whitelands after hearing that Silas was recuperating after falling from a horse. The old fool shouldn't have gone near a horse at his age, thought the D-G, and had resolved to say as much. But in the event he hadn't done so.

"Samson?" said the D-G. "You mustn't be hard on him. I blame myself really. Bret Rensselaer always said we should have told Samson the truth."

"I never thought I'd hear you say that, Henry. You were the one who—"

"Yes, I know. But Samson could have been told at the end of that first year."

"There's nothing to be gained from a post-mortem," said Silas. There was a plaid lap robe over him, and every now and again he pulled at it and rearranged it around his legs. "Or is this leading up to the suggestion that we tell him now?"

"No, no, no," said the D-G. "But when he started prying into the way the bank drafts came from Central Funding, I thought we'd be forced to tell him."

Silas grinned. "Trying to arrest him when he arrived in Berlin was not the best way to go about it, D-G, if you'll permit me to say so."

That fiasco was not something the D-G was willing to pursue. He got to his feet and went to the mullioned window. From here there was a view of the front drive and the hills beyond. "Your elms are looking rather sick, Silas." There were three of them, massive great fellows planted equidistant across the lawn like Greek columns. They were the first thing you saw from the gatehouse, even before the house came into view. "Very sick."

Suddenly Silas felt sick too. Every day he looked at the elms and prayed that the deformed, discolored leaves would become green and healthy again. "The gardener says it's due to the frost."

"Frost, fiddlesticks! You should get your local forestry

fellow to look at them. If it's Dutch elm disease they must be felled immediately."

"The frost did terrible damage this year," said Silas, hoping for a reprieve, or at least reassurance. Even unconvincing reassurance, of the sort the resourceful Mrs. Porter, his housekeeper, gave him, was better than this sort of brutal diagnosis. "You can see that, Henry, from the roses and the color of the lawn," Silas pleaded.

"Get the forestry expert in, Silas. Dutch elm disease has already run through most of the elms in this part of the world. Let it go, and you'll make yourself damned unpopular with your neighbors."

"Perhaps you're right, but I don't believe it's anything serious."

"There are still a lot of unanswered questions, Silas. If the time has come to pull her out, why don't we just do it without ceremony?"

Silas looked at him for a moment before being sure he was talking about Fiona Samson. "Because we have a mountain of material that we can't use without jeopardizing her. And when finally she comes back she'll bring more material out with her."

"We've had a good innings, Silas," said the D-G, returning to the chintz-covered armchair where he'd been sitting and giving a little grunt as he dropped into it.

"Let's not cut and run, Henry. In my memory and privileged knowledge, Fiona Samson has proved the best agent-in-place the Department has ever had. It wouldn't be fair to her to throw away what is still to come."

"I really don't understand this plan to keep her alive," said the D-G.

Silas sighed. The D-G could be rather dense at times. He'd still not understood. Silas would have to say it in simple language. "The plan is to convince the Soviets she is dead."

"While she is back here being debriefed?"

"Exactly. If they know she's alive and talking to us, they'll be able to limit the damage we'll do to them."

"Convince them?" asked the D-G.

"It's been done in the past with other agents."

"But convince them how? I really don't see."

"To give you an extreme example, she is seen going into a house. There is an earthquake and the whole street disappears. They think she's dead."

"Is that a joke, Silas? Earthquake?"

"No, Director, it is simply an example. But the substitution of a corpse is a trick as old as history."

"Our opponents are very sophisticated these days, Silas. They might tumble to it."

"Yes, they might. But if they did, it would not be the end of the world. It would be a setback but it wouldn't be the end of the world."

"Providing she was safe."

"Yes, that's what I mean," said Silas.

The D-G was silent for a moment or two. "The Americans are going to be dejected at the prospect of losing the source."

"You don't think they guess where it's coming from?"

"I don't think so. Washington gets it from Bret in California, and by that time anything that would identify her is removed."

"That business with Bret worked out well."

"He took a dashed long time before he understood that I couldn't have called off that arrest team without revealing the part he played in running Fiona Samson."

"I didn't mean that, so much as the way he went to convalesce in California."

"Yes, Bret has organized himself very well over there,

and using him as the conduit distances us from the Berlin material."

"I shouldn't think Fiona Samson submits anything that would identify her," said Silas. He never handled the material, and there were times when he resented that.

"I'm sure she doesn't," said the D-G, to indicate that he didn't directly handle the material either. "She is an extremely clever woman. Will you use Bernard Samson to pull her out?"

"I think he should be involved," said Silas slowly. "By now I think he guesses what is going on."

"Yes," said the D-G. "That's why you want to bring her home, isn't it?"

"Not entirely," said Silas. "But it is a part of it."

"The Soviets would leave someone like that in place for ever and ever," said the D-G.

"We are not the Soviets," said Silas. "Are you feeling all right, Henry?"

"Just a palpitation. I shouldn't have smoked that cigar. I promised my doctor I would give them up."

"Doctors are all the same," said Silas, who had abstained and sniffed enviously while the D-G went through a big Havana after lunch.

The D-G sat back and breathed slowly and deeply before speaking again. "This business . . . this business about switching the corpse. I don't see how we're going to handle that, Silas."

"I know of an American . . . a very competent fellow."

"American? Is that wise?"

"He's the perfect choice. Free-lance, expert, and independent. He's even done a couple of jobs for the opposition."

"Now wait a moment, Silas. I don't want some KGB thug in on this."

"Hear me out, Henry. We need someone who knows his

way around over there, someone who knows the Russian mind. And this chap is on the CIA's 'most wanted' list; so he'll not be telling the story to our friends in Grosvenor Square."

Sir Henry sniffed to indicate doubt. "When you put it like that . . ."

"Persona grata with the KGB, unconnected with the CIA, and arm's length from us. The perfect man for the job. He'll take on the whole show for a flat fee."

"The whole show? What does that mean?"

"There will be blood spilled, Henry. There's no avoiding that."

"I don't want any repercussions," said the D-G anxiously. "I'm still answering questions about the Moskvin fracas."

Silas Gaunt painfully lowered his feet to the floor and leaned across to the table to find some bone-handled knives in the cutlery drawer. He put three of them on the table and picked them up one by one. "Let me improvise a possible outcome. Body number one, slightly burned but easily identified. Body number two, badly burned but identified by plentiful forensic evidence." He looked at Sir Henry before picking up the third knife. "Body number three, burned to a cinder but dental evidence proves it to be Fiona Samson."

"Very convincing," said the D-G after a moment's reflection.

"It will work," said Silas, grabbing the knives and tossing them into the drawer with a loud crash.

"But isn't someone going to ask why?"

"Have you been following the reports about Erich Stinnes and his drug racket?"

"Drugs. It's true then?"

"Our KGB colleagues have wide-ranging powers. Security, intelligence, counterintelligence, border controls, politi-

cal crimes, fraud, corruption, and drugs have become a very
big worry for the Soviets.'' He didn't want to go into detail
about the drugs. It was a vital part of the operation. It en-
snared Stinnes as a trafficker and Tessa Kosinski as an addict,
but the D-G would get very jumpy if he knew everything
about the drugs.

"Stinnes," said the D-G. "Has he given us any decent
material since going back there?"

"He's playing both ends against the middle. He feels safe
from arrest by us, and safe from his KGB masters too. That's
what led him into this drug racket, I suppose. He must be
making a fortune."

"I think I see what you have in mind. Some drug-run-
ning gangsters engage in a shootout and Fiona Samson disappears."

"Precisely. That's why we have to time events to coin-
cide with a shipment of drugs. When Stinnes brings the consignment of heroin from the airport, we'll bring Mrs. Samson
to one of his contact points on the Autobahn—still in the
DDR, of course—and have Samson there waiting for her.
Stinnes will believe it's simply a rendezvous to transship the
drugs. We'll supply a vehicle. A diplomatic vehicle would be
best for this sort of show."

"And send Samson to get her?"

"Yes. But not Samson alone. Deserted husband and er-
rant wife reunited after all that time: a recipe for trouble. I'll
have someone else there, someone calm and dependable, to
make sure it all goes smoothly."

"And you say we have to bring in this American fellow?
Couldn't we do it with our own people?"

Silas looked at him. "No, Henry, we couldn't."

"May I ask why?"

"The American has had dealings with Stinnes already."

"Drug dealings, you mean?"

Silas hesitated and suppressed a sigh. He didn't want to go into detail. There would be problems getting everyone there. They would all have to be told a different story, and Silas hadn't yet worked it out. Like the rest of them in London Central, Sir Henry had only the barest idea of what went on in the field. Silas had been closer. "Let me give you an idea of what's involved, Henry. We will have to have a body there to substitute for Mrs. Samson, the body of a youngish woman. I don't propose we take a dead body through the checkpoints, especially not in a diplomatic vehicle, because if something happened the publicity would be horrendous. We'll also need to leave in place a skull with the right dentistry. We don't want the Russians to start asking why there is an extra skull, so the body will have to be decapitated. Decapitated on the spot."

"So how *will* you get the body there?" said the D-G, still puzzling over it.

"The body will walk there, go there, drive there . . . I'm not sure yet."

"You mean alive?" Sir Henry was deeply shocked. His body stiffened and he sat bolt upright. "What woman? How will he do this?"

"Better you don't ask, Henry," said Silas Gaunt gently. "But now you see why we can't use our own people." He waited for a moment to let the D-G regain his composure. "Bernard Samson will be there, of course, but we'll use young Samson simply to bring his wife out. He'll see nothing of the other business."

"Won't he . . . ?"

"The American subcontractor will stay behind and make sure the evidence is arranged to tell the story we want the Soviets to believe."

"And you'll deal with this American direct?"

"No, Henry. I think that would reveal the Department's

participation too obviously. I'll use a go-between. There's a fellow named Prettyman whom Bret uses for rough jobs. He's done a couple of things for us in the past. Very able, although not quite right for what I have in mind. I shall use him as a contact. No one will be told the full story, of course. Absolutely no one.''

"As long as you think you can manage this end.''

"Without Bret Rensselaer looking over my shoulder, you mean?'' Silas pulled a face. "We've managed this long.''

"I'll be glad when it's all done, Silas.''

"Of course you will, Henry. But we two old crocks have shown the youngsters a thing or two, haven't we?'' They exchanged satisfied smiles.

There was a knock at the door and Mrs. Porter brought tea for them. Tea was an elaborate affair at Whitelands, thanks to Mrs. Porter. She arranged it on Silas's little table, and the D-G pulled up a chair. There was buttered toast and honeycomb and caraway seed cake that only Mrs. Porter could make so perfectly. That seed cake took the D-G back to his schooldays; he loved it. She poured the tea and left them.

For a few minutes they drank their tea happily and ate their toast like two little boys at a picnic.

After a satisfied silence the D-G asked, "What was the truth about Samson's father? The real story, I mean. About the two Germans he was supposed to have shot?''

Silas poured more tea for them both. "Well, that's going back a bit. . . .''

"There's no harm now, Silas. Brian Samson is dead, God rest his soul, and so is Max Busby.''

Silas Gaunt hesitated. He'd kept silent so long that some of the details were forgotten. At first the D-G thought he was going to refuse to talk about it, but eventually he said, "You have to remember the atmosphere back in those days when

Hitler was newly beaten. Europe was in ruins and everyone was expecting Nazi 'werewolves' to suddenly emerge from the woodwork and start fighting all over again."

"I remember only too well," said the D-G. "I wish I could forget it. Or rather, I wish I were too young to have been there."

"The Americans had no real intelligence service then. Their OSS people were wasting their time looking for dead Nazis. Martin Bormann was at the top of the list."

"Berchtesgaden. It's coming back to me now," said the D-G. "There was some sort of trap?"

"They had captured a Nazi war criminal named Esser, Reichsminister Esser, in a mountain hut near Hitler's Berghof. There had been a lot of Reichsbank gold found in that neighborhood. Tons and tons of it was stolen by middle-rank U.S. officers and never recovered. After they took Esser away, the Counter-Intelligence Corps kept the hut—it was a house really, a rather grand chalet, in fact—and kept it under observation. Martin Bormann's house was between Hitler's Berghof and this place where they found Esser. The story was that there was penicillin and money and God knows what else hidden there for Bormann to collect and get away to South America. It was all nonsense, of course, but at the time it didn't seem so unlikely."

"What was Brian Samson doing, there in the American Zone?"

"He was responsible for a prisoner from London, a German civilian named Winter," said Silas. He offered the seed cake.

The D-G took a slice of cake. "Winter, yes, of course." He bit into it and savored it like old wine.

"Paul Winter was a Nazi lawyer who worked for the Gestapo and who seemed to have an unhealthy amount of influence in Washington . . . a congressman or someone.

There was a tug-of-war between the State Department, who wanted him released, the U.S. Army, who wanted him jailed, and the International Military Tribunal, who wanted him as a defense lawyer. Meanwhile we had the blighter locked up in London."

"He had an American mother, Veronica Winter. Her other son went to America and came strutting back in the uniform of a U.S. Army colonel. Reckless people, Americans, eh? He wasn't even naturalized."

"Very pragmatic," said Silas, unwilling to make such generalizations.

"I seem to remember that the mother came of a good American family. I heard she'd died of pneumonia in one of those dreadful postwar winters. She was a friend of 'Boy' Piper—Sir Alan Piper—who was the D-G at one time."

"Yes, Boy Piper was the one who sent me there to sort it out for the Department."

"Go on, Silas. I want to hear the story."

"There's not much to tell. The wife—Winter's wife, that is—sent her husband a message."

"Now this is the Nazi fellow?"

"Yes, Paul Winter, the Nazi lawyer."

"In prison?" asked the D-G, who wanted to get it quite clear.

"He wasn't in prison, he was in a billet. He'd been released in order to defend Esser. The Nazis accused at Nuremberg were permitted to choose anyone they wanted, even POWs from a prison cage, as their lawyers. The message said she was in this damned mountain hut, so off he dashed. He hadn't seen his wife since the war ended. His brother was a U.S. colonel, as I said. He got a military car or a jeep or something, and they both cleared off without waiting for permission."

"To Berchtesgaden?"

"And in particularly foul winter weather. I remember that winter very well. When this fellow Paul Winter got to the mountain house, his wife, Inge, was waiting for him. She'd had a child; she wanted money."

"Did he have money?"

"There was a metal chest buried up there. Esser had taken it and hidden it. During their sessions together he told Paul where it was. Then I suppose Esser must have told Inge Winter that her husband knew. They dug it up. It was gold, a mixed collection of stuff Esser had collected from the Berlin Reichsbank vaults, leaving a signed receipt for it."

"And her child was Esser's," supplied the D-G.

"How did you know?"

"It's the only part of the story that sticks in my mind."

"Yes. Paul Winter must have suspected it wasn't his. They'd been married for ages and had never been able to have a child. I can imagine how he felt."

"And the two Winter boys were killed. But how did they get shot?"

"That's the question, isn't it? If you want the truth, they were shot by a drunken U.S. sergeant who thought they were werewolves or deserters or gangsters or some other sort of toughs who might hurt him. That region was plagued with deserters from both sides who'd formed gangs. They stole army supplies on a massive scale, ambushed supply convoys, robbed banks, and weren't too fussy about who they hurt."

"The story I heard—"

"Yes, there were lots of stories. Some people said that the Winters were shot by mistake, by someone who was trying to kill Samson and the general who was with him. Some said they were shot by the sergeant acting on secret orders from Washington. Some said Max Busby shot them because he was in love with Paul Winter's wife or, in another version, involved in some black-market racket with her. It's impossible to prove any of those stories wrong, but believe me, I went into it thoroughly. It was as I told you."

"But the report said Brian Samson had shot them," said the D-G. "I remember distinctly. He was bitter about it right up to the day he died."

"Ah, yes. That was later. But at the time no one had any doubts. It was the drunken sergeant who was arrested and taken back to the cells. Only when the Americans asked for Samson to go and give evidence in their inquiry did things change. We couldn't let Samson face any sort of questioning, of course; that's been departmental policy since the beginning of time. When we refused to let Samson go down there, the Yanks suddenly saw a chance to get it all over quickly and quietly. By the time I arrived, all the depositions were scrapped and new ones written. Suddenly they could produce eyewitnesses prepared to swear that Samson accidentally shot the two men."

"That's despicable," said the D-G. "That verdict went on Samson's record."

"You're preaching to the converted, Henry. I protested about it. And when Boy Piper wouldn't support me I made a devil of a fuss. Sometimes I think I blotted my copybook then. I was forever marked as a troublemaker."

"I'm sure that's not true," protested the D-G, without putting much effort into it.

"I don't blame the Americans for trying it on, but I was furious that they could get away with it," said Silas mildly. "You couldn't entirely blame the men who perjured themselves. They were American soldiers, draftees who hadn't seen their families for ages. An inquiry might easily have kept them in Europe for another year."

"Was Busby a party to this?"

"Busby was the Duty Ops Officer at the Nuremberg CIC office that night. He was getting a lot of stick because he was in command of the party. He preferred an accident with some foreign officer as the guilty party."

"I can see why there was such bad feeling between him and Samson when he came to work in Berlin."

"That's why Busby went to work for Lange's people. Brian Samson wouldn't have him."

"And the wife?"

"She took the gold, probably changed her name, and disappeared from the story. There was no sign of her by the time Samson got to the house, and I never found her. She left Esser to face the hangman and took her daughter and went into hiding; perhaps that's what Esser wanted her to do. She was a very resolute and resourceful young woman. She worked in a nightclub in Garmisch, so she would have had no trouble contacting some people from whom she could buy permission to live in the French Zone, which is what she did. That removed her from British and U.S. jurisdiction. Eventually she got a French passport and took her gold and her baby . . ."

"And lived affluently ever after," supplied the D-G caustically.

"Crime does sometimes pay," said Silas. "We may not like to concede it, but it's true." He drank some tea.

"How much gold was there?" asked the D-G, helping himself to a second piece of seed cake.

"I saw the large metal box. It had been buried—the dirt was still on it. It was provost exhibit number one. About this big." Silas extended his hands to show the size of a small steamer trunk.

"Do you have any idea what that would weigh?" said the D-G.

"What are you getting at, Sir Henry?"

"No one could carry a box of gold of that dimension. It would weigh a ton."

"If she couldn't carry it, what would she do with it? Why would you dig it out in the first place, unless you were going to take it away?"

The D-G smiled knowingly. "Speaking personally, I might dig it up because too many people knew where it was."

"Her husband and Esser and so on?"

"And perhaps many other people," said the D-G.

"And then bury it again," said Silas, following the D-G's thought processes. "Ummm."

"Then there would be only three people who knew where it was."

"And two of them are dead a few minutes later."

"So now only Inge Winter knows where it is."

"Are you suggesting that she got this American sergeant to shoot her husband and her brother-in-law?"

"I've never met any of them," said the D-G. "I'm simply responding to the story you've told me."

Silas Gaunt said nothing. He tried to remember the evidence he'd examined so long ago and the soldiers he'd talked to. The sergeant was a flashy youngster with jewelry and a vintage Mercedes he was taking home to America. Was he really drunk that night, or was that a ruse to make the "accident" more convincing? And there was, of course, the sergeant's missing woman friend, who was a singer with a dance band. Silas never did find her. Were the woman friend and Inge Winter one and the same person? Well, it was too late now. He poured more tea, drank it, and put the mystery out of his mind.

Soon, reflected Silas, the D-G would retire, and that would sever his last remaining link with the Department. Silas found the prospect bleak.

The D-G got up, flicked some cake crumbs from his tie, and said, "I want you to promise me you'll have someone to look at those trees, Silas. It's a beetle, you know."

"I don't think I could bear to lose those elms, Henry. They must be about two hundred years old. My grandfather adored them. He had a photo taken of the house when they were half the size they are now. There were four of them in those days. They say one of them blew down the night Grandfather died."

"I've never heard such maudlin nonsense. Elms don't blow down, they're too deep-rooted."

"My mother told me it fell when Grandfather died," said Silas, as if the honor of his family rested upon the truth of it.

"Don't be such a fool, Silas. Sometimes you have to sacrifice the things you love. It has to be done. You know that."

"I suppose so."

"I'm going to send Mrs. Samson over to Bret when she comes out. California. What do you think?"

"Yes, capital," said Silas. "She'll be well away from any sort of interference. And Bernard Samson too?"

"No. Unless you . . . ?"

"Well, I do, Henry. Leave Samson here and he'll roar around trying to locate her and make himself a nuisance. Bundle him off and let Bret take care of them both."

"Very well." The grandfather clock, which Silas had moved to this room because he didn't trust the workmen not to damage it, struck 5:00 P.M. "Is that really the time? I must be going."

"Now, you're leaving all the arrangements to me, Henry?" Silas wanted to get it clear; he wanted no recriminations. "There's a great deal to be done. I'll have to have matching dentistry prepared, and that takes ages."

"I leave it to you, Silas. If you need money, call Bret."

"I suppose the special funding mechanism will be wound up once she's safe," said Silas.

"No. It will be a slush fund for future emergencies. It cost us so much to set up that it would be senseless to dismantle it."

"I thought Samson's probing into the money end might have made it too public."

"Samson will be in California," mused the D-G. "The more I think of that idea the better I like it. Volkmann says Mrs. Samson has aged a lot lately. We'll send her husband there to look after her."

24

Müggelsee, East Berlin:
May 1987

''How stunning to have the Müggelsee all to ourselves,'' said Harry Kennedy. He was at the tiller of a privately owned six-meter racing yacht; Fiona was crewing.

On hot summer days the lake was crowded with sailboats, but today was chilly and the lake was entirely theirs. It was late afternoon. The sun, sinking behind bits of cumulus—ragged and shrinking in the cooling air—provided fleeting golden halos and sudden shadows but little warmth.

The wind was growing stronger, pressing on the sail steadily like a craftsman's hand, so that the hull cut through the water with a loud hiss and left a wake of curly white trimmings.

Fiona was sitting well forward, huddled in her bright yellow hooded jacket complete with heavy Guernsey sweater and Harry's scarf, but still she shivered. She liked the broad expanse of the lake, for it enabled her to sit still and not have all the work of tacking and jibing and trimming that Harry liked doing so much—or, rather, liked to watch her doing. He never seemed to feel the cold when he was sailing. He became another man when dressed in casual clothes. The short red anorak and jeans made him look younger; this was the intrepid man who flew planes over the desert and the tundra, the man who fretted behind a desk.

She had seen a lot of him during that year he'd spent at the Charité. He'd taken her mind off the miseries of separation at a time she'd most needed someone to love and care for her. Now that he was working in London again, he saw her only when he could get a really long weekend, and that meant every six weeks or so. Sometimes he arranged to borrow this sailboat from a friend he'd made at the hospital, and she brought sandwiches and a vacuum flask of coffee so they could spend all the day on the lake. These trips must have involved him in a lot of trouble and expense, but he never complained. She couldn't help wondering if it was all part of his assigned duty of monitoring her, but she didn't think so.

Neither had he ever suggested the impossible, that she should come to London to see him. He knew about her, of course, or at least he knew as much as he needed to know. Once late at night in her apartment after too much wine he'd blurted out, "I was sent." But he'd immediately made it into some sort of metaphysical observation about their being meant for each other, and she'd let it go at that. There was nothing to be gained from hinting that she knew the real story behind that first meeting. It was better to have this arm's-length love affair, each of them examining the thoughts and emotions of the other, neither of them entirely truthful.

"Happy?" he called suddenly.

She nodded. It wasn't a lie; everything was relative. She was as happy as she could be in the circumstances. Harry sat lounging knee-bent at the stern, head turned, arm outstretched, elbow on knee, fingers extended to the tiller, looking like Adam painted on the Sistine ceiling. "Very happy," she said. He beckoned to her, and she moved to sit close beside him.

"Why can't it always be just like this?" he asked in that

forlorn way that her children had sometimes posed similarly silly questions. She would never understand him, just as she had never been able to understand Bernard. She would never understand men and the way their minds could be both mature and selfishly childlike at the same time.

"Ever been to the Danube delta? There's a vast nature reserve. Ships—like floating hotels—go right down the Danube to the Black Sea. It would be a wonderful vacation for us. Would you like that?"

"Let me think about it."

"I have all the details. One of the heart men at the Charité took his wife. They had a great time."

She wasn't listening to him. She was thinking all the time of the recent brief meeting she'd had with Bernard. They had met in a farmhouse in Czechoslovakia and Bernard had urged her to come back with him. It should have made her happy to see him again, but it had made her feel inadequate and sad. It had reawakened all her fears about the difficulties of being reunited with her family. Bernard had changed, she had changed, and there could be no doubt that the children would have changed immensely. How could she ever be one of them again?

"I'm sorry, Harry," she said.

"About what?"

"I'm not good company. I know I'm not."

"You're tired. You work too hard."

"Yes." In fact she'd become worried at her lapses of memory. Sometimes she couldn't remember what she had been doing the previous day. Curiously, the distant past was not so elusive; she remembered well those glorious days with Bernard when the children were small and they were all so happy together.

"Why won't you marry me?" he said without preamble.

"Harry, please."

"As a resident of the DDR you could get a divorce with the minimum of formalities."

"How do you know?"

"I explored it."

"I wish you hadn't." If he had talked to a lawyer, it might have drawn attention to her in a way that was undesirable.

"Fiona, darling. Your husband is living happily with another woman."

"How do you know?"

"I saw them together one evening. I almost stumbled into them in the crush at Waterloo Station. They were catching the Epsom train."

"You recognized them?"

"Of course. You showed me a photo of him once. The woman with him was blond and very tall."

"Yes, that's her." It hurt like a dagger in the heart. She'd known, of course, but it hurt even more when she heard it from Harry.

"You know her?" he said.

"I've met her," said Fiona. "She's pretty."

"I don't want to make you miserable, but we should talk about it. It's madness for us to go on like this."

"Let's see what happens."

"You've been saying that since the time we first met. Do you know how long ago that is?"

"Yes. No. . . . A long time."

"Living without you is hell for me, but being separated from me doesn't make you miserable," he admonished her, hoping for a contradiction, but she only shrugged. "We haven't got much time, Fiona."

She kissed his cheek. "Harry, we're happy enough this way. And we have lots of time." It was the same conversation they'd had many times before.

"Not if we were to start a family. Not much time."

"Is that what you want?"

"You know it is. Our children, Fiona. It's everything I want."

"You'd come and live here?" She was testing him now.

"I lived here before."

"That's not the same thing as living here permanently," she said.

"Do I hear a discordant note in the Marxist harmony?"

"I'm stating a fact."

"You don't have to be defensive, honey."

"You said you were a Marxist," she reminded him. It was unfair to remind him of something he'd said only once, and that in a heated argument.

"Yes. I said I *was* a Marxist. I *was* a Marxist a long time ago." The sail began drumming.

"But no longer?"

He pulled the mainsheet to adjust the sail before turning his head to answer. He was a good sailor, quick and expert in handling the boat and everything else he did. "I asked myself a question," he said.

"And?"

"That's all. Marxism is not a creed for those who question."

"No matter what the answer? Is that true?"

"Yes. Whatever the answer, one question gives birth to another. A thousand questions follow. Nothing can sustain a thousand questions."

"Nothing? Not even love?"

"Don't mock me." They were near the shore now: all forest, no sign of people anywhere. "Ready about!" said Harry in the flat voice he used when commanding the boat.

Stepping carefully she went forward, released the front sail, and watched him as he swung the tiller. The boom crashed across the boat as they passed through the wind, and instinctively he ducked his head to avoid it. She pulled in the jib and set the front sail before going back to sit down.

"Do you ever play let's pretend?" he asked as he settled back on the seat. It was another aspect of his childishness. Flying planes was childish too; perhaps he'd joined the Communist Party as some silly adventure.

"No," she said.

"I do. Sitting here, just the two of us in this boat, cruising across the Müggelsee, I pretend that you are an alluring Mata Hari and I am the heroic young fellow in your spell who has come to rescue you."

She said nothing. She didn't like the drift of this conversation, but it was better to see what came of it.

"Pursued by black-hearted villains. The other shore is safety, a place where we'll live happily ever after and raise our family."

"Sounds like *A Farewell to Arms*," said Fiona, without putting too much enthusiasm into the idea. "Did you ever read that?"

"The journey across the lake to Switzerland. Hemingway. Yes, I did it for my high school English. Perhaps that was where I got it."

"The woman dies," said Fiona. "They get to Switzerland, but the woman dies in hospital." She turned to look at him, and he seemed so utterly miserable that she almost laughed.

"Don't make jokes," he said. "Everything is perfect." She hugged him in reassurance.

Yes, everything was perfect for Harry. It was easy for him. But Fiona was coming to the end of her resources. She was desperately depressed, even out here on the lake with a man who loved her. Depression, she'd found, was no respecter of logical truth; it was some dark chemical cloud that descended on her at random and reduced her to jelly.

It was no good telling herself that it was nonsense. She'd given up her children and her marriage. Was she being paranoid to think that Bernard would have completely poisoned the children's minds against her by now? She had run away; why wouldn't they be hurt by such rejection? How could she hope to become wife and mother again?

The children were the most terrible sacrifice she had made, but there were other wounds too. She had lost friends and family, who now despised her as a traitor. And what was it all for? She had no way to judge the results, or the contribution she'd made. She'd begun to suspect that she was the lamb slaughtered at the altar of Bret Rensselaer's ambition. Bret's wounds were corporeal; his reputation was intact. Bret Rensselaer was the winner. So were Silas and the D-G. Three old men had sent her here, and those three would be the victors. What did they care about her? She was expendable, as useful and as readily discarded as a Kleenex tissue.

Fiona was the loser: Fiona, her husband, and her children. They would never recover from what she had done. Was any political—or, as Bret so liked to have it, economic—victory worth it? The answer was no.

Sometimes she felt like salvaging what little she had left. She felt like grabbing a chance of happiness with Harry, of severing her contact with London and just settling down in East Berlin as a hausfrau. But that would be no more than a temporary salve. The real loss was Bernard and the children; she wanted them to love her and need her.

"A penny for them?" said Harry.

"I was thinking about my hair," she said. "About having it cut shorter." Men were always ready to believe that women were thinking about their hair.

He smiled and nodded. She was looking much older

lately; they both were. A vacation in the Danube delta would be good for both of them.

That evening she had a meeting with Werner Volkmann. She waited there alone in her old-fashioned apartment looking out over the Frankfurter Allee, the wide main road that led eventually to Moscow and, perhaps for that reason, was once called Stalin Allee. It was a part of the procedure that agents running back and forth did not come up to the office. They met privately. She looked at her watch; Werner was late.

She tried to read but was too jittery to concentrate. She found herself trying not to look at *Pariser Platz,* which was hanging over her bed. It was in a neat black ebony frame. One evening she had taken it down and opened the frame in order to replace Kirchner's kitsch gaiety with an abstract print more to her taste. Behind the street scene she had been horrified to find a colored print of Lochner's *The Last Judgment.* As such medieval paintings go, it was a mild example of the violent horrors waiting for sinners in the next world, but Fiona, alone and tired and troubled, had been thunderstruck by the demented and distorted figures and terrifying demons. It was as if she were meant to find it lurking under the cosiness of the Berlin street scene. With trembling hands she'd replaced *The Last Judgment* back under the Kirchner and fixed it into its frame. But from that time onward she was never unaware of the presence of that tormented world lurking under the frolicsome *Pariser Platz.*

Werner apologized for being late. He was rainswept and weary. He said it was the strain of winding down his banking business and trying to run Lisl Hennig's hotel at the same time, but Fiona wondered if it was the stress of being a double agent. Werner was a West German national. If the security services became convinced that he was betraying them, he would simply disappear without trace or, worse still, become a patient in the Pankow clinic.

They chatted for ten minutes, the sort of unimportant talk they might have had if Werner were what he purported to be. Only then did Fiona disconnect the voice-activated microphone she had discovered on the first day she got here. Senior staff had their conversations recorded only by random checks, but it was better to be safe.

"Did you see the children?" Before answering he went and sat in the only comfortable chair with his overcoat still on. He wasn't feeling cold; Werner often kept his overcoat on. It was as if he wanted to be ready to leave at short notice. He'd even kept hold of his hat, and now he was fidgeting with it, holding it in both hands like the steering wheel of a heavy truck that he was negotiating along a busy road.

"I will see them next week," said Werner. He saw the disappointment in her face. "It's not easy to arrange it without Bernard asking awkward questions. But they are fit and well, I can assure you of that. Bernard is a good father."

"Yes, I know," said Fiona, and Werner realized that she had taken it as a reproach. He found it difficult to have a conversation with Fiona these days. She could be damned touchy. She was worn out. He'd told the D-G that over and over again. She said, "It might be easier if I were in Moscow or China, but it is impossible to forget that everything I love is so near at hand."

"Soon you'll be home. Here everything is changing," said Werner. "I see even diehard communists beginning to discover that man does not live by bread alone."

"Nothing will ever change," said Fiona. "You can't build a capitalist paradise upon a Leninist boneyard."

"Why so glum, Fiona?" She seldom revealed her personal views.

"Even if you waved a magic wand and declared Eastern

Europe totally free, it wouldn't stir. Bret's sanguine ideas about the economy don't take into account the human factor, or the immense difficulties of change evident to anyone who comes and looks for themselves. He talks about 'the market,' but all Eastern Bloc economies are going to remain dominated by the public sector for many many years to come. How will they fix market prices? Who is likely to buy decrepit steel works, ancient textile plants, or loss-making factories? Bret says the East will revive its private sector. How? Eastern Europeans have spent their whole working lives slacking off in overmanned jobs. No one here takes risks. Even in the KGB–Stasi office I find people are reluctant to take on new responsibility or make a decision. Forty years of socialism has produced a population incapable of decision-making. People here don't want to think for themselves. Capitalism won't appear just because there is no longer any law against it." She stopped. It was an unusual outburst. "I'm sorry, Werner. Sometimes I think I've been here too long."

"London thinks so too. The D-G is going to pull you out," said Werner.

She closed her eyes. "How soon?"

"Very soon. You should start to tidy things up." He waited for a stronger reaction and then said, "You'll be with Bernard and the children again."

She nodded and smiled bleakly.

"Are you frightened?" he asked, without really believing it was true.

"No."

"There is nothing to be frightened of, Fiona. They love you. They want you back."

For a moment she gave no sign of having heard him. Then she said, "Suppose I forget?"

"Forget what?"

She became flustered. "Things about them. I do forget

things, Werner. What will they think of me?'' She gave him no chance to answer and moved on to other things. ''How will it be done?''

''It might be changed, but at present the plan is to leave a car parked in the street outside. The keys will be under the seat. With the keys there will be an identity card. Use it only as far as the Autobahn, then throw it into a ditch somewhere where it won't be found. You'll drive down the Autobahn, dump the car at the roadside, and get into one with British plates. The driver will have a UK diplomatic passport for you.''

''You make it sound simple, Werner.'' London always made things sound simple. They believed it gave agents confidence.

He smiled and twirled the hat on the finger of one hand. ''London wants you to list your contacts here, Fiona.'' For years she'd thought of Werner as some soft woolly creature, henpecked by his awful wife. Since using him as her contact with London Central, she'd discovered that the real Werner was as hard as nails and far more ruthless than Bernard.

''I have none,'' she said.

''Contacts, good and bad. I'd give the bad ones careful consideration, Fiona. Office staff? Janitor? Has anyone said anything to you, even in jest?'' He pinched his nose between finger and thumb, looking up at her mournfully while he did it.

''What sort of anything?''

''Jokes about you working for the British . . . Jokes about you being a spy.''

''Nothing to be taken seriously.''

''This is not something to gamble with, Fiona,'' he said very firmly. ''You'd better tell me.'' He placed his hat on the floor so that he could wrap the skirt of his overcoat over his knees.

"Harry Kennedy. . . . He's a doctor who visits Berlin sometimes."

"I know."

"You know?"

"London has had him under surveillance since the day you first came here."

"My God, Werner! Why did you never tell me?"

"I had nothing to tell."

"I was with him today. Do you know that too?"

"Yes. London tells me of his movements. Working in the hospital means he has to make his plans well in advance."

"I'm sure he's not . . ."

"There to monitor you? But of course he is. He must be KGB and assigned to you. Kennedy arranged that first meeting with you in London; Bret is certain of it."

"Have you talked to Bret? I thought Bret was in California."

"California is served by scheduled flights, phones, and fax."

"Who else knows?" she asked anxiously.

He didn't answer that one. "Kennedy is a Party member from way back. Don't say you haven't checked him out, Fiona?"

She looked at Werner. "Yes, I have."

"Of course you have. I told Bret that you would be sure to. What woman could resist an opportunity like that?"

"That sounds very patronizing, Werner."

"Does it? I'm sorry. But why not tell me the truth right from the start?"

"Today he said how wonderful it would be if I were Mata Hari escaping to the West with him. Or some tosh of that kind."

Werner tugged at his nose, got up, and went to the window. It was night and, under floodlamps, workmen were decorating the Frankfurter Allee with the colorful banners and flags of some African state. All visiting dignitaries were paraded along this boulevard to see their colors thus displayed. It was a mandatory part of the Foreign Ministry's schedule.

In the other direction, the whole sky was pink with the neon and glitter of the West. How near it was, as near and as available as the moon. Werner turned back to her. Fiona was still as beautiful as she had ever been, but she had aged prematurely. Her face was pale and strained, as if she was trying to see into a bright light.

Werner said, "If Kennedy happened to be here at the time you were pulled out, he'd have to be neutralized, Fiona."

"Why would he be here at the time I am pulled out?"

"Why indeed?" said Werner. He picked up his hat, flicked at the brim of it, and put it on his head. Fiona climbed up on the chair to connect the microphone again.

25

Berlin:

June 1987

IT WAS HIS WAVY HAIR THAT MADE DEUCE THURKETTLE look younger than his true age. He was sixty-one years old, but regular exercise and careful attention to what he ate kept him in good physical condition. He put on his bifocals to read the menu, but he could manage most things without them, including shooting people, which was what he did for a living. "Steak and salad," he said. "Rare."

"The *Tafelspitz* is on today," said Werner.

"No, thanks, too fattening," said Thurkettle. He knew what it was, a local version of a New England dinner: boiled beef, boiled potatoes, and boiled root vegetables. He never wanted to see that concoction again. It was what he'd eaten in prison. Just the sight or smell of a plate of boiled beef and cabbage was enough to remind him of those years he'd spent cooped up on death row, waiting for the executioner in a high-security prison along with a lot of other men found guilty of multiple murders.

"Perhaps I shouldn't eat *Tafelspitz* either," said Werner regretfully. "Rare steak and salad, twice," he told the waiter.

It was Sunday morning. They were in West Berlin, Leuschner's, a popular barnlike café, with gilt-framed mirrors on the whole of one wall and a long counter behind which one of the Leuschner brothers served. Coming from the jukebox there was a Beatles tune played by the Band of the Irish Guards. The jukebox used to have hard rock records, but one of the Leuschners had decided to refill it with music to his own taste. Werner looked around at the familiar faces. On such Sunday mornings, this otherwise unfashionable place attracted a noisy crowd of off-duty gamblers, musicians, touts, cabbies, pimps, and hookers who gathered at the bar. It was not a group much depleted by churchgoing.

Thurkettle nodded his head to the music. With his bow tie, neatly trimmed beard, and suit of distinctly American style, he looked like a tourist. But Thurkettle was here to commit murder on the orders of London Central. He wondered how much Werner had been told.

Werner's task was to show him some identity photos and offer him any help and assistance he might require. After the job was done, Werner was to meet him on the Autobahn, in the small hours of the morning, and pay him his fee in cash. "You have transport arranged?" asked Werner.

"A motorbike. It's quick and nicely inconspicuous for this sort of caper."

Werner looked out of the window. People in the street were bent under shiny umbrellas. "You'll get wet," said Werner. "The forecast says storms."

"Don't worry about me," said Thurkettle. "This hit on the Autobahn is just a routine job for me. Rain is the least of my problems."

It had been a sudden last-minute decision, and a rush to get it all arranged. A message from Erich Stinnes had come announcing that a consignment of heroin had arrived at East Berlin's airport. He would bring it through tonight. Once he knew this, Thurkettle sent a signal to London that Fiona Samson could be brought out of East Berlin tonight. Werner had sent affirmation that Fiona was ready.

"These are the people you will see at the rendezvous."
Werner produced photos from his pocket and passed them
across the table. What exactly was going to happen, who was
to be murdered and why, Werner had not been told. His
presence at the rendezvous was not required. It was just as
well, for tonight he was committed to a big celebration at
Tante Lisl's, a fancy-dress party with all the trimmings. Just
about everyone he knew in West Berlin would be there. But
now the evening would be spoiled for him. He'd spend all
night worrying about Fiona Samson's escape.

Thurkettle pretended to study the passport-style pictures, but he had seen all these people before, at some time
or other. Thurkettle prepared carefully for each job; that's
why he was highly paid, and that's why he was so successful.
After a minute or two he passed the pictures back.

Werner tapped the photo of Stinnes. "This is your drug-
peddling contact. Right?"

Thurkettle grunted assent.

"Stinnes will arrive with this woman." Werner indicated
Fiona Samson's photo. "She will depart with this man." He
indicated the photo of Bernard Samson. "Probably this man
will also be there." He showed him a photo of Harry
Kennedy.

Thurkettle looked at Werner, at the photos, and then at
Werner again. "I'll take care of them."

Werner said, "Don't take care of the wrong people."

"I won't," said Thurkettle with a cold smile.

"Bernard Samson and Fiona Samson. Make sure they are
safe."

Thurkettle nodded. Now he felt sure that Werner Volkmann was not a party to the real secret: that Tessa was to die
and change identity with her sister.

"The Brandenburg exit," added Werner, who was anxious that there should be no misunderstanding.

"No sweat. I know the place. There's the half-completed highway-widening work. I went there yesterday and took a look-see. I'll have a shovel, coveralls, and a can of gas."

"Gas? Petrol?" Werner put a map on the table.

"To torch the car. The guy in London, who gave me my orders, wants the car burned."

"Afterward you'll meet me here." He showed the place to Thurkettle on the Autobahn map. "The cash will be in a leather case. If you don't want to carry a case, you'd better have something to put it in. When you are paid, come back up the Autobahn and through the Border Control Point at Drewitz into West Berlin. You'll go through without any trouble. In Berlin, phone the number I gave you and say the job is finished. From then on you are on your own. You have the airline ticket? Don't go back into East Berlin."

"I won't go back to the East."

"Have you arranged about a gun? I was told to make sure you had a gun if you needed it."

"The last time I found myself without a gun was in Memphis, Tennessee. I strangled two guys with my bare hands." He put a cardboard box on the table. "Here's one of them," he said, loosening the lid and holding it open an inch or two.

Werner looked into Thurkettle's cold eyes trying to decide whether it was a joke but, unable to tell, he looked down into the box. *"Gott im Himmel!"* said Werner as he caught sight of the contents. It was a human skull.

"So don't baby me," said Thurkettle, closing the box and putting it beside him on the chair. "Just have the dough ready."

"I will have the money ready."

"If you want to call it off, this is your final chance," said Thurkettle. "But once the job is done I'm like the Pied Piper of Hamelin; if I'm not paid I come back and do the job all over again. Get me?''

"I get you.''

"Used fifty-dollar bills,'' said Thurkettle grimly.

Werner sighed and printed circles upon the table with his wet beer glass. "I told you. I will have it ready, exactly as I said.''

"You do your thing the way you were told; I do my thing the way I was told; we get along just fine. But if you foul up, old buddy . . .'' He left the rest of it unsaid. He'd not yet encountered anyone so dumb as to default in payment to a hired killer. "Just one more time. I meet you on the Autobahn, direction west. I take the exit marked Ziesar and Görzke. You'll be waiting on the exit ramp. Going off the Autobahn is illegal for Westerners; just wait at the bottom of the ramp.''

They'd been all through it before. "I'll be there,'' said Werner. He wondered if the skull was real or one of those plastic ones they make for medical students. It certainly looked real, very real. He was still wondering about that when the steaks arrived. They were big entrecotes, seared and perfect, cooked and delivered to the table by Willi Leuschner himself. He put down a big pot of homemade horseradish sauce, knowing that Werner liked it. Willi had been at school with Werner, and the two men spent a moment exchanging the usual sort of pleasant remarks. The Leuschners were both coming to Werner's fancy-dress party that night. It seemed as if half of Berlin was planning to be there.

"More beer?'' asked Willi finally.

"No,'' said Werner, "we both have to keep clear heads.'' Willi scribbled the account on a beer mat and dropped it back on the table.

Deuce Thurkettle left Werner to pay the bill. His BMW bike was outside. It was a big machine with two panniers in which he stowed all his gear. The engine roared and he gave a flip to the accelerator before settling into the saddle. With a quick wave of the hand as he passed the restaurant window, he sped away.

He had a lot to do before getting to the rendezvous on the Autobahn, but seeing Werner was necessary. Thurkettle made a point of threatening his clients in that way. It was part of the fastidious attention to detail that made him so effective.

Another reason for his success was knowing when to keep his mouth shut. Whoever had briefed Werner Volkmann had obviously told him some fairy story. The briefing that Thurkettle had been given by Prettyman in a fancy suite in the London Hilton had been rather more complete and certainly more specific. Prettyman had told him that under no circumstances must anyone be left alive except Bernard and Fiona Samson. *No one left alive.* Prettyman had been very insistent about that.

The Brandenburg exit—the place arranged for Fiona Samson to change from one car to the other—was on East Germany's section of Hitler's Autobahn, built to connect Berlin to Holland and all points west. As well as being a major East German highway, this was one of the authorized routes along which Westerners were permitted to drive to West Berlin.

On this flat region immediately to the west of Berlin the rivers have spread to become lakes. It is a region of farmland and forest, and once outside the towns the traveler finds small, cobble-streeted villages where little has changed since the Kaiser's photo hung in the schoolrooms.

Even one of East Germany's two-stroke motorcars can get there from Berlin in well under an hour, and for Thurkettle's powerful motorcycle it was nothing. He arrived before dark.

The workers from the construction site had gone. Their earth-moving machines were neatly lined up, like tanks for an inspecting general.

Thurkettle broke the lock off the door of the portable hut used by the construction gangs and went inside. He used a flashlight to check his guns and ammunition and the stainless steel butcher's hacksaw he'd brought with him. Then he put on his coveralls and plastic medical gloves and looked at the skull and its neat dentistry. That done, he sat down, watched the pouring rain, and waited patiently for it to get dark.

Thurkettle had been told that someone of exactly the same build as Fiona Samson must be killed and left at the rendezvous. It was Thurkettle who thought of the idea of using Fiona Samson's sister. He was pleased with that. She was a drug addict, and such people are easy to control. His task was to put Fiona Samson into the car with her husband and let them depart alive. He then had to kill Stinnes and the sister, bury Stinnes in the excavated ditch the road workers had so conveniently provided close by, and burn the car with the sister's body inside it.

The Soviet investigators would never find Stinnes's body, because by the time they realized that Stinnes had not gone over the frontier with Samson, there would be a hundred tons of solid concrete and a section of Autobahn over the burial place. The burned body would be identified as Fiona Samson because the two women were very much alike except for the dentistry, and the skull he'd shown Werner had been prepared for exactly that deception. The trickiest task was decapitating the sister. Her head would have to go in the ditch with the Stinnes corpse. Otherwise the forensic team examining the car would find a burned body with two heads, and that would alert even the doziest laboratory assistant.

*   *   *

It all went amiss, right from the very start. Tessa, unreliable in the way that addicts usually are, did not arrive on time. Despite everything Thurkettle had arranged, she went off to Werner's fancy-dress party. Tessa should have arrived first. Thurkettle became so anxious that he went off on his motor-cycle, but came back when he recognized the car with Fiona and Stinnes in it. When finally Tessa did arrive, it was in the back of the Ford van with Bernard Samson.

Stinnes had arrived in a Wartburg, bringing Fiona Samson and Harry Kennedy too. And who could have guessed that Bernard Samson would arrive with some lunatic from London Central who thought it would be amusing to come directly from Werner's party wearing his fancy dress? A gorilla costume! Their Ford van arrived within five minutes of the Wartburg, and they parked in what Thurkettle approved as a good getaway position. The Wartburg was parked nose out, with its sidelights on. Thurkettle expected Stinnes to bring the heroin consignment out of the car, but no one emerged.

Everyone seemed to be waiting for something to happen. Thurkettle remained in the darkness and watched. He was standing behind one of the bulldozers when it all started.

A slim man dressed as a gorilla leaped from the Ford van and started jumping around, shouting and waving a gun. A gorilla! It looked so damned convincing that for a moment Thurkettle thought it was real. It took a lot to surprise Thurkettle, but the gorilla took him off guard. It must have taken Stinnes, or whoever was in the driver's seat of the Wartburg, off guard too, for someone switched on the car's full beams to see the gorilla more clearly.

The gorilla raised his pistol and was about to fire at the Wartburg. Thurkettle suddenly saw his reputation threatened and his fee in jeopardy. The Samson woman had to get away safely. Prettyman in London had been *most* specific about that. If Fiona did not arrive safely in the West, no fee would be paid beyond the small initial contract payment.

So Thurkettle fired at this crazy gorilla. His silenced gun made no more noise than a carefully opened bottle of wine. But by this time Thurkettle was rattled and his shot missed.

Then the gorilla fired. He must have heard Thurkettle's shot, for he was virtually in line with the barrel, where the silencer has least effect. The glass of the Wartburg's windshield smashed and Thurkettle thought Fiona Samson had been hurt. But then he saw her get out of the car. She shouted something, and then her doped-out sister came floating into view. Tessa came dancing, arms outstretched to display a long yellow diaphanous dress that was some sort of fancy costume.

There must be no mistakes this time. Thurkettle picked up the shotgun and aimed low. Tessa seemed to see him. She grinned as he pulled the trigger twice, hitting her with both shots. As she went down, the gorilla fired again, and this time his round put out one of the Wartburg's headlights. Thurkettle didn't like the way it was developing. Given the darkness, one or two of these people could get away. But he wasn't by any means certain how many people were there.

There were more shots, fired in rapid succession, a sign of nerves. Stinnes probably; he could be trigger-happy. One of them had to find a mark. The gorilla screamed, ran, stumbled, and crashed into the mud. Thurkettle stayed in the darkness. Somewhere in this muddy arena Bernard Samson lurked, and Samson was a pro. Then Stinnes stepped out of his car to make sure the gorilla was dead. What a reckless thing to do. Thurkettle remained very still in the darkness and kept silent.

"It's safe," called Stinnes. He beckoned to a second man, a tall fellow in a smart trenchcoat: Kennedy.

"How many did they send?" Kennedy asked. He looked around nervously, and the light from a single passing head- light caught his face. From his position, Thurkettle could see both men clearly and identified them beyond chance of mis- take: yes, Erich Stinnes and Harry Kennedy.

Then Fiona Samson walked forward. Some instinct or understandable trepidation made her walk so as to avoid the pool of light. London must have briefed her to go for the van, for she was heading toward it, past the men, when two shots were fired. They came from somewhere so close to Thurkettle that the sound made him jump half out of his skin. Fiona Samson disappeared. Damn!

Bang. Some damned great handgun. Kennedy jumped back, arms flailing like a rag doll as he was knocked over, and lay in the mud as still as a bundle of old clothes. He was unmistakably dead. Sometimes it goes like that, a lucky acci- dent and one shot is enough.

Bang. Again the cannon went off. Stinnes lurched round, firing his gun with one hand and clutching his neck with the other, the blood spraying through his fingers. It went every- where and spattered Fiona. That shot was enough to tell Thurkettle that these were not lucky accidents. There was someone, a too-damned-close-to-him someone, who'd si- lently clambered up onto a piece of heavy machinery to get a better vantage point, some cold-blooded someone who didn't say hands up, someone who hadn't perfected his shoot- ing on the range: Samson.

Thurkettle's mouth went dry. He always made it a rule not to tangle with professional hit men or pros like Samson. It was bad enough facing these KGB goons, but Samson was a number one no-no.

The remaining headlight of the Wartburg was switched off. It was dark now except when the lights of passing traffic swept across the mud and debris and the bodies. Thurkettle froze and hoped he hadn't been spotted. Neither Bernard Samson nor his wife had been told of Thurkettle's role in this drama. Only Tessa and Stinnes had expected him to be here, and they were both dead.

Thurkettle crouched lower behind the tracks of the bulldozer and looked at the eastern horizon. Soon it would be dawn. He didn't want to be here when it got light; any passing driver on the Autobahn might spot him. Cops might arrive. "Are we going to wait here all night, Samson?" he called finally. "You can take the woman and take the Ford and go. Take your gorilla too. I don't want any of you." When there was still no response he called, "Do you hear me? I'm working your side of the street. Get going. I've got work to do."

It was a breach of contract but only a minor breach; the two Samsons were on the side of the man who employed him. They'd just have to keep their mouths shut. Anyway, by the time they were debriefed, Thurkettle would have his money and be over the hills and far away.

Fiona Samson might still have been sitting there had she not used every last atom of willpower to get to her feet. Something inside her had snapped. Was this the breakdown of will that she had been dreading for so long? Inside her head there was a noise she couldn't recognize. It blotted out her thoughts and distorted her vision. She didn't know who she was and couldn't remember where she was supposed to be.

With the sluggish posture of a sleepwalker Fiona Samson emerged from the dark. Spattered with blood, and stumbling in the soft ground, she inched toward the Ford van. She was totally disabled by seeing Kennedy, dear sweet Harry whom she loved, so brutally shot dead, and not by an avenging husband but by a cold-blooded professional. Tessa too. The sister she cherished more than she could say was dead in a pool of blood.

This was that Last Judgment she'd discovered with such

a shock. Here were the monsters come to torment her for all eternity. Racked with sin, she had stepped out of the cozy world of the Pariser Platz into the bloody nightmare on the bedroom wall, and there would be no escape. Her mind numbed, and suffering an anguish from which she would never completely recover, she moved through her frenzied world like an automaton.

Bernard Samson watched Fiona get into the van. Then, suspicious to the last, he ran to get behind cover. When no shots were fired at him, he climbed into the Ford van beside his wife. The engine started and, slowly and carefully, bumping over the potholes, the van moved off. Only when the site was clear did Thurkettle decide it was safe enough to emerge from his hiding place.

Left alone, Deuce Thurkettle took off his trenchcoat so that only his coveralls would get soiled. He got his hacksaw and hastily but carefully started his grisly work. When the head was severed he dragged Tessa's body into the car and arranged it with the skull he'd brought with him. The other bodies—the man in the gorilla suit, Harry Kennedy, and Stinnes—ended up in the deep part of the excavations.

Thurkettle heaved a sigh of relief as he threw his blood-saturated coveralls into the muddy ditch with them. He tossed the guns after them and, using the shovel, covered everything there with mud and debris.

Setting fire to the car was easier. He watched the Wartburg burn and made sure that everything inside it was thoroughly consumed in the flames. Only then did he mount his motorcycle and ride away to collect his money.

Werner Volkmann was sitting in his Skoda car at the Ziesar exit ramp, as arranged with Thurkettle. Werner had spent the evening at the fancy-dress party of which he was the nominal host. He had drunk only mineral water, but now he was tired. Werner had always wanted to be a secret agent. He'd started doing little jobs for the British when he was still a teenager, and the whole business of espionage still intrigued him. But this was the finale. He knew that. The D-G had shaken hands with him and muttered something about an award: not money, some sort of medal or certificate. On his last visit to California, Bret Rensselaer had said what Werner had immediately recognized as a final goodbye. By tomorrow morning Werner would be back in his West Berlin hotel as a private citizen again. His career in espionage was over. He'd never tell anyone. Secrets shared were not his idea of what secrets should be.

He looked at the pistol that London Central had supplied to him that morning. He'd hoped they would give him something that would satisfy his romantic yearnings: a lovely Colt Model 1911, a stylish Walther P.38, or a classic Luger. Instead, London had sent him another of these cheap little "chamberless expendables." It looked like a gadget used to ignite the flame on a gas stove. Its surface was hatched to provide a grip but also to eliminate any surface upon which a fingerprint could remain. It used triangular-sectioned cartridges—"trounds"—in a "strip clip," and almost everything was made by a plastics corporation in America. It was new, unidentifiable, and in perfect working order, but it did not give Werner the satisfaction that he would have got from an old-fashioned weapon. Oh, well, one had to move with the times. He put the gun in his inside pocket where it would be easy to reach.

Dawn was breaking as Werner spotted Thurkettle arriving on his motorcycle. He waved airily to Werner and gave a little flip to the accelerator. Deuce enjoyed riding the big bike, but now the time had come for him to dispose of it. He'd parked a Volkswagen camper nearby. As soon as he'd collected his payment from this lugubrious schmo, he'd walk to where he'd left the camper. In it there were clean clothes, soap, towels, and food. Buried nearby he'd left a Swiss passport wrapped in plastic. The passport had a visa for a three-week camping tour of East Germany. He'd shave off his beard, change his appearance, and drift around seeing the sights like a tourist until the heat died down. Then he'd drive north and take the ferryboat to Sweden.

Thurkettle got off his bike and walked over to the car. The rain had soaked him to the skin and the exertions had left his muscles stiff. He remembered that the VW camper had a shower in it and wondered how long it would take for the water to get hot.

Werner lowered the car window. "Was there any difficulty?" he asked.

"Nothing I couldn't handle. But Fiona Samson is dead," said Thurkettle. It was what he'd been told to say. "One of the Russkie goons wasted her. Bernard Samson got away; so did some other woman. I don't know who she was; she was in a long yellow dress. She went with Bernard Samson."

Werner knew who the other woman was; it was Tessa. He'd seen her leave the party with Bernard. "Fiona Samson is dead? Are you sure?"

"It's not something I'd make a mistake about," said Thurkettle. He smiled; he liked secrets. The switch of identities he'd arranged for the two women was a secret Prettyman had told him to keep entirely to himself. "All the others are dead."

"Kennedy too?"

"Yeah, Kennedy too. And a guy dressed as a gorilla. There was a shoot-out. I was lucky to get away in one piece." He always embellished events when he came to collect his fee. Clients always wanted to feel they were getting value for their money. "Those Russkie sons of bitches came there all set to blow me away. If I hadn't been there, Bernard Samson would never have made it."

"My God! Poor Fiona," said Werner. He'd come to adore her over the months they'd worked together. She should never have taken on a task like that; the strain was too much for her. He'd seen her fading under the stress of it. At one meeting recently she had had a momentary blackout. She'd said it was too many late nights and made him promise to keep it a secret. Poor Fiona. He got out of the car and went back to the trunk. It was raining. He looked around him in the brightening dawn. There wasn't much time.

"Yeah, well, that's the way it goes," said Thurkettle philosophically. He smiled at Werner. He seemed like a genial fellow and Werner smiled too.

"I didn't realize it was still raining," said Werner.

"Is that right?" said Thurkettle, who was soaked to the skin.

"Do you want to sit in the car and count it?" Werner asked. "I don't want to stand here getting wet." He was going through his keys to find the one for the trunk.

"We'll just take a peek at it so I can see it's real."

"It's real," said Werner. "Used notes. Exactly as you specified. I got it from the Commerzbank on Friday."

He reached into the trunk of the car to get a leather document case. Carefully he put the case into Thurkettle's hands, saying, "Don't rest it on the car. The paintwork is brand new."

Thurkettle smiled pitifully. He was used to the sort of nervousness that Volkmann displayed. Clients were always timorous when dealing with a hit man. He held the case with both hands while Werner bent forward and fiddled with the lock. "It's a combination lock," explained Werner. He could smell the blood and filth on Thurkettle's clothes; it was the stink of the slaughterhouse. "You can make the combination

into anything you choose. I made it 1-2-3. You can't forget
1-2-3, can you?"

"No," said Thurkettle. Werner snapped the lock open
and pulled up the lid. There it was: fifty-dollar bills, line upon
line of them. "You can't forget 1-2-3."

It was while Thurkettle was standing there, holding the
new leather document case with both hands, that Werner,
gripping the curious-looking gun so it was hidden under the
case, pulled the trigger. A strip clip of eight rounds fired as
fast as a machine gun. They all went into Thurkettle's belly.

Eight rounds. It was only a little expendable, but at
point-blank range a weapon doesn't have to be a masterpiece
of the gunsmith's art for its effect to prove fatal.

The impact of these little medium-velocity rounds did
not knock Thurkettle down, he just staggered backward a
couple of paces, still holding the case in both hands and
staring at Werner in uncomprehending disbelief. Thurkettle's jerky movements caused the money to spill over, and a
gust of rainy wind started blowing it around. Thurkettle
watched his money floating away. He grabbed at some notes
but winced in pain. This couldn't be happening to him. He
was shot. Thurkettle was a professional killer and this jerk
was a nothing. . . .

As he staggered back, more and more money fluttered
away and he tasted the blood gushing up into his mouth and
knew he was done for. By now he was clutching the document case against his chest as if it might provide protection
against more shots, or comfort him in his final moments. He
embraced it tight like a lover, and the blood-soaked money
fell around his feet.

It was just before he fell down that Deuce Thurkettle
understood exactly how he'd been tricked. His eyes opened
wide in fury. Deuce Thurkettle was the only one who knew
for certain that Fiona Samson was still alive. Even this clown

who had shot him thought Samson had escaped with Tessa.

Well, he'd tell the world. He opened his mouth to tell the truth but only blood came out. Lots of it. Then he toppled to the ground.

Werner threw away his little expendable. That was the convenient thing about them. He watched Thurkettle die, for he knew that London would want a positive answer. Werner didn't feel compassion for him. He was a psychopath, and society is better off when such people are dead. Any last feeling he might have shown for Thurkettle had been removed when he heard that Fiona was dead. He'd told Thurkettle that getting Bernard and Fiona to safety was of paramount importance, and he'd failed to do it.

Werner prodded the body with the toe of his shoe, and kicked it to tip it into the ditch. He'd chosen this spot because of that deep ditch. He moved the motorcycle too. It would be found eventually—someone would spot the dollar bills beflagging the fields—but it was better to get the bike out of sight. He pushed the leather case into the grass, and the rest of the money fluttered aside. He didn't pick any of it up. The notes were probably marked or counterfeit. London Central had provided the money, and the British were very careful about money; it was one of the things he'd discovered soon after starting to work for them.

Bret Rensselaer was at La Buona Nova, a hillside estate in Ventura County, California. He was having an early breakfast by the pool when the coded message came telling him that Fiona and Bernard Samson were on the way to join him in California.

It was a truly beautiful morning. Bret drank his orange juice and poured himself the first cup of coffee of the day. He so enjoyed sitting outdoors inhaling the clear cool air that came off the ocean. Around the pool there were whitewashed walls where the jasmine, roses, and bougainvillea seemed to bloom almost all the year round. There were trees bearing oranges, trees bearing lemons, and trees bearing the maja fruit that his hostess called "Brets." It looked like a lemon but tasted like an orange, and calling it a Bret was perhaps her way of saying that Bret was sweet and sour. Or British, yet American too. Bret didn't know what was implied, but he went along with her joke; they had known each other a long long time.

People who had known Bret for a long time would say that he'd aged since being badly wounded at the Berlin shootout, but to the casual observer he was as trim and fit and agile as a senior citizen had any right to be. He was swimming and skiing and doing a routine of exercises. He wanted to look good when the visitors arrived.

He could not suppress a smile of satisfaction. They were coming. His plan to get an agent in the Kremlin, as Nikki had sardonically put it, had worked exactly as he'd predicted it would when he first took it to the D-G just after she ran out on him. Now there was only the long and interesting work of debriefing.

Bernard Samson would be here too. He had tried to get the old man to send Bernard elsewhere but it was good security to have him here where he could be supervised. Tessa's disappearance had to be accounted for; the idea that she had run away with Bernard was in every way believable.

This morning Bret would go through all his notes again so as to be prepared for Fiona's arrival. This would be the last job he would ever do for London Central, and he was determined that it should end perfectly. Werner Volkmann's last report said that Fiona was on the verge of a nervous breakdown, but Bret didn't give it much credence. He'd heard that too often about other working agents; it was usually the preamble to a demand for more money. Fiona would be all right. Good food, sleep, and the California air would soon bring her back to being her old self again.

Bernard Samson would go nowhere from here, of course. His career was at an end. It was strange to think how near Bernard had come to a senior position on the SIS staff. That evening so long ago, when Bret had gone to see the D-G, he had been all set to promote Bernard to German Stations Controller. From there he would have gone to the top floor and perhaps ended up as Director-General. Heaven knows, he wouldn't be facing any fierce opposition from the lineup of deadbeats that now occupied the top floor. Would Sir Henry and Silas and Frank Harrington, and the rest of that cabal who really ran things, have gone along with Bernard Samson in a top job? They were always saying what a splendid fellow Bernard was, and many of them thought the Department owed him something for the shabby way his father had been treated. But D-G? Any chance of Bernard as D-G had been eliminated that long-ago night when Sir Henry had revealed that Fiona was his choice to go over there.

Bret put down his coffee cup as a sudden thought came to him. The D-G must have known that choosing Fiona meant eliminating Bernard. There were others he could have chosen instead of Fiona, good people; he'd admitted that many times. So had the D-G's choice of Fiona been influenced by the fact that it would keep Bernard from getting the top job?

Bret drank his coffee and thought about it. There was always another layer of onion no matter how deep you went. Well, if it was true, the old man would never admit it, and he was the only one who knew the answer. Bret knew he could never really become English. They were very strange people, tribal in their complex allegiances. He finished his coffee and dismissed such thoughts from his mind. There was a lot of work to do.

Len Deighton was born in London in 1929. After service in the RAF he spent six years as an art student, finishing at the Royal College of Art. Upon graduating, Deighton became a successful free-lance illustrator, working in London and New York.

In 1960 Deighton went on vacation in France and started writing *The Ipcress File*, which was published to instant acclaim two years later. In the intervening years he has published almost a book a year—all bestsellers—both fiction and nonfiction, with ever-growing recognition from critics, historians, and the general public. His fans have included C. P. Snow, Ian Fleming, Richard Condon, as well as Julian Symons who called him "a poet of the spy story." Many of his books have been made into movies and, most recently, *Game, Set and Match* was a 13-part television series.

Deighton is married and has two children. He spends much of his time traveling for research. Apart from reading, his recreations are photography and cooking.